AMY'S HONEYMOON

For James

Acknowledgements

With huge thanks to everyone at Penguin, especially Mari Evans, Louise Moore, Claire Phillips, Claire Bord, Natalie Higgins and Clare Pollock. To Lizzy Kremer. To the charming staff of the Hotel de Russie, especially Evelina Conti, and to Sue Heady at Rocco Forte Hotels. To the wonderful Sarah Spankie. To Maryam Shahmanesh for the medical advice and friendship. To the incomparable Jana O'Brien. To Kate, Ruth, Victoria, Frances and Sarah again. And even more than usual, thanks to James Watkins for his support and possibly the idea.

CHAPTER
ONE

At eight in the morning, the tired-looking woman at the British Airways check-in desk barely glanced at Amy which was probably just as well because she would have thought her a complete divot for wearing sunglasses indoors.

"Flying to?" She yawned, scanning Amy's passport through the machine.

"Rome," Amy said.

A misty-eyed look came into the woman's eyes.

"Rome," she breathed, looking up. "Have you been there before?"

Amy removed her wraparounds. "No, never."

"You'll love it." She looked away, smiling at some distant memory. Then looked back at her computer. "Oh, there's a note here says it's your honeymoon! I can't think of a more romantic place to go."

"Really?" Amy said, trying to stop her voice from wobbling.

"Really. Before we were married, when I was working short haul, my husband and I used to snatch weekends there. Before the kids came . . ." She smiled again, more ruefully now. "Enjoy yourself while you can, that's what I say. Don't be in too much of a rush to start a family Mrs . . ." She peered at the name on the screen. "Oh, I'm sorry! *Doctor* Fraser." Then, suddenly snapping out of her reverie, she grew business-like. "Now. Then. So. Where is the lucky Mr Fraser?"

Amy had been rehearsing the line all the way to the airport. "He's on his way. Something . . . came up he had to deal with. He's going to catch me up."

"Oh dear," said the check-in woman. "You poor love. When was the wedding, then?"

"Yesterday. There was a problem with paying the caterers. He had to deal with it. So, like I said, he's going to catch me up." Amy's phone bleeped in her bag. Her heart leaped as she whipped it out, then plummeted like a diver from an Acapulco cliff as she saw the name *Gaby* on the text envelope.

How are you? she read. Immediately she deleted it.

"That was him," she told the woman, who was looking increasingly curious. "He'll be about half an hour."

"He'll be cutting it very fine," she said severely, then seeing Amy's tense face she softened, like butter in the sun. "Ah, bless. Don't worry. He'll make it." She tapped something into her computer, looked up and winked. "Bet he'll be chuffed when he finds out he's flying club class." The printer whirred and Amy's boarding pass chugged out. The woman grinned as she scribbled on a card. "And here's a pass to the lounge, so you can wait for him in style. Have a glass of champagne — though you probably had enough yesterday, judging from those circles under your eyes."

2

Just a week ago if you'd told Amy this would happen, she would have shrieked with delight. Gaby had told her exactly how to behave to get an upgrade and for years she'd followed those instructions to the letter: dressing smartly, hinting to the check-in staff she was a VIP, not demanding a low-calorie halal meal. But she had never had a result until now. And now they could have packed her in a crate in the hold with a gorilla on heat for all Amy cared.

"Thank you," she managed.

"It's my pleasure. Aah. Have a brilliant time. And don't worry. Even if he does miss the flight we can put him on the next one. Enjoy Rome. Don't forget to throw a coin in the Trevi fountain, then you'll be sure to return."

She asked a couple of questions about the contents of Amy's luggage and did she pack the bag herself, and for once Amy felt no compulsion to say, "No my Afghan cousin did and actually, yes, he asked me to carry a few parcels for him and now you mention it I *did* hear a strange ticking." So the lady waved Amy off with several more entreaties to enjoy.

All about her, squabbling families were gathered round overladen trolleys. Businessmen and women pushed through them, moving unnaturally fast as if their mechanisms had jammed on the wrong setting. Amy glanced at her watch. A whole hour and a half until take off. A week ago, she would have been beside herself at the prospect of all these duty-free shops to browse in and the free champagne and canapés waiting for her in the lounge. Now all she wanted was to find an empty toilet cubicle and hide.

"You're going to drink champagne," she told herself, "because it's your honeymoon."

Then she headed straight for the ladies, found an empty cubicle, sat down and cried.

"I can't go, I can't," she moaned softly.

Someone knocked on the door. "Are you all right in there?" Whoever it was sounded more outraged than sympathetic.

"Fine, thanks," Amy shouted, over-shrilly. "Just got . . . something in my eye."

She didn't have to go. She could go back to the Heathrow Express, get on a train and be home again in an hour and a half. She could hole up there, ordering in meals, growing her hair down to her ankles and spending the rest of her life like a Howard Hughes recluse. Except she couldn't, because in two weeks she'd have to return to work or she'd lose her job and then she wouldn't be able to pay the mortgage and she'd be homeless. And, anyway, Doug still lived there . . .

Her phone began ringing. Snuffling, she snatched it again from her bag. It would be him, it had to be. But, oh no, *Mum and Dad*. She'd better answer it, she supposed, they were having a tough enough time without her disappearing.

"Hello."

"Amy?" came two voices in stereo. "How are you, sweetie?" "Where are you?" "Are you with Doug?" "What's going on, sweetie?"

"I'm at the airport."

"The airport?" Dad exclaimed as Mum asked. "What on earth are you doing there?"

"I'm going on honeymoon."

"On honeymoon?" Mum gasped as Dad interrupted, "But Amy, you're not married."

"Well . . ."

"You and Doug made it up?" Her mother sounded so hopeful, Amy couldn't bear it.

"Um."

Her tone changed from anxious to suspicious. "You haven't gone and got married behind our backs, have you?" Her father chipped in, "Oh, Amy, you know how much I wanted to walk you up the aisle."

"No, don't worry. There hasn't been a wedding. I just need to get away for a bit."

"But, Amy, love," said Mum, sounding utterly bewildered, "I don't understand, aren't you going to tell us what happened? Granny's so upset. You know how much she loves a knees-up."

Amy couldn't stand this conversation. Her family had always wanted so much for her, she hated to let them down. "Not now, Mum, my flight's being called. I'll be in touch. Bye."

She sat for a minute on the loo seat, listening to the chatter of other travellers. "So I need to buy some deodorant." "Hurry up, we must get some euros before we board." "Hi, sorry, signal's terrible . . . Yeah, yeah, I'm on my way to Zurich. No, I'll be back tomorrow. Yeah, meeting. I know, boring as shit but it's got to be done."

It's got to be done.

Inhaling deeply, Amy stood up. Her legs felt as if they were full of San Pellegrino. She unlocked the door. Even though she hadn't peed, she went to the basin and washed her hands like the conscientious doctor she was. Puffy eyes stared back at her from the mirror, under perfectly plucked brows and navy-tinted lashes. She'd been so organized, getting them done a week in advance in case of any allergic reaction just like *Brides* magazine advised.

"It's got to be done," she said aloud this time, making the woman standing next to her in a head-to-toe hijab jump.

Then she walked out of the toilets, pushed her way through a gaggle of noisy Lithuanian pensioners on their way home after a cultural exchange and followed the signs to departures.

CHAPTER
TWO

The plane took off on time. As Amy sat in her padded Club World seat, gazing numbly out at the clouds, she thought back to where she'd been twenty-four hours earlier. She should have been in the registry office, exchanging rings and vows, instead she had been in a dressing gown, slumped on her friend Gaby's sofa in her living room in Balham, clutching a gin and tonic and weeping.

Gaby was Amy's best friend. They had met when they were living next door to each other in halls at Edinburgh University. At first, the two of them seemed very different: Amy was from a small town in Devon and had had a sheltered childhood; Gaby had been to a posh girls boarding school where the curriculum seemed to have consisted primarily of drinking bottles of cider at the end of the playing fields and snogging as many boys as possible from the school across the road. But Amy was chafing to escape her origins and, with her neighbour's encouragement, was soon downing pints in one at the union bar, dancing on tables at the freshers' disco and discovering the joys of marijuana and sex, separately and combined.

"Blimey," Gaby said, the morning after a particularly wild party. "You didn't hold back last night, did you? It's always the quietest ones who turn out to be the biggest goers."

Amy blushed. "I'm just having fun. That's what uni's meant to be about, isn't it?"

"Absolutely. I'm not disapproving. I'm impressed."

Amy calmed down a bit when she met Danny, another medical student, who became her boyfriend. On graduating, they moved to London to complete their medical studies. Gaby stayed in Edinburgh and got a PR job in travel. For nearly a decade she jetted journalists all over the world to inspect some new five-star spa or hotel. She was thirty-one by the time she went to live in London, where she set up her own travel company organizing holidays for what she called the "cash-rich, time-poor". One of these specimens happened to be a forty-something lawyer called PJ, who was newly divorced, extremely rich and also — in defiance of every cliché — very nice. Just before her thirty-third birthday, Gaby and PJ had married on a lawn in Wiltshire, in front of two hundred of their closest friends. A month later she gave birth to a son, Archie.

It wasn't quite a fairy-tale ending — PJ's ex-wife Annabel was always giving him grief, as were his two teenage daughters. Still, Gaby was happy, although she'd been pretty poleaxed when just nine months after Archie was born she found out she was pregnant again.

At times, Amy was a bit intimidated by Gaby's organizational powers. She was the kind of person who defrosted the freezer twice a year, turned her mattress once a month, stuck photos of her shoes on the boxes and bought and *actually used* those gizmos that clean the dishwasher. At other times, Amy tired of Gaby's obsession with the *Harper's Bazaar* "What's Hot and What's Not" list and her position on the new Balenciaga bag waiting list.

But underneath the superficiality there lay a heart more golden than a Labrador's. There had been so many times when Amy couldn't have done without Gaby, especially not the previous day. She'd arrived at her house, which smelt of paint from on-going redecorations and had a bubble-wrapped double buggy in the hall, at 7 a.m. As soon as she heard the wedding was off Gaby immediately set to work contacting everyone on the guest list, followed by calls to the registry office and the reception venue.

Then she set to work making Amy a huge gin and tonic and answering Amy's phone, which rang approximately every twenty seconds.

"Hello? . . . No, it's her friend Gaby . . . Oh, hi, John. I remember you. How are you? . . . Oh, I'm sorry to hear that. No, Amy's not here, I'm afraid . . . Yes, it was a bit of a surprise . . . I know flights *are* expensive . . . Really, that much? . . . I don't know where she is . . . She'll call you . . . Yes . . . Bye."

"Your old friend John," she said, putting the phone down. "Very pissed off. He's flown in from France and he's staying at the Landmark. Says he's spent nearly a grand on a non-existent wedding."

Amy clutched her head. "Oh God, this is awful."

"Oh, for Christ's sake. Stop worrying about him! Think about yourself. You're the one who's been jilted at the altar."

Amy winced. Gaby never phrased anything delicately, if a brutal version was available.

The phone rang again. "Hello? Oh, hi, Mrs Gubbins, it's Gaby. No, I'm afraid Amy's not here. I don't know where she is. Yes, she forgot her mobile. She's a bit distraught right now . . . Oh, well I'm sure she'll call you back soon . . . Yes, it's terrible. All those relatives . . . well, since you're all in London maybe you should go out for dinner anyway. See a show. There might be tickets for *Mamma Mia* . . . Well, think about it . . . If I do hear from her I'll get her to call you . . . No, no, unfortunately I don't think she's with Doug. No, I don't know what happened . . . Of course I'll tell her you called. Bye."

She hung up. "Your mum again. You really are going to have to call her, Amy."

"I know. I will." Amy started crying again. "Oh, Gaby, this is a nightmare. My poor parents. This has cost them a fortune."

"Hardly a fortune. You were complaining they only gave you three grand for the wedding."

"That was horrible of me. Three grand is a lot to them." It was. Amy's dad worked for the council and her mum was a housewife. "We should have taken out wedding insurance."

"It wouldn't have made any difference. Insurance doesn't cover change of heart."

"Oh, bloody hell, how am I ever going to make it up to them?"

"Three grand is nothing compared to what a divorce could have cost you. You know what bloody Annabel and the girls cost PJ? One hundred and fifty grand a year."

This didn't make Amy feel much better. "There's all the money I spent. And more than a hundred guests' time wasted. How could I have done that?"

Gaby stamped her foot. "How many times do I have to tell you? You didn't do anything. This is Doug's fault for being a fool." Her eyes narrowed. "Are you sure Pinny's got nothing to do with it?"

Before Amy could reply, PJ walked into the room, in an orange rugby shirt and pink cords, carrying Archie fresh from his Gina Ford noon to 2p.m. nap. PJ looked as if he'd stumbled, channel surfing, across an ad for tampons. Girlie weeping wasn't really his thing.

"So then, Amy. How's it going?" He glanced at his wife, hoping she would prompt him further, then seeing no help added, "What are you going to do about the honeymoon?"

"The honeymoon?"

"Oh, shit," said Gaby, her hand flying to her mouth. "I can't believe I didn't think of it. I hate to say it but . . . if you cancel now you won't get a refund. Far too last minute."

"You *are* joking."

"I'm not, I'm afraid. I can make some phone calls for you, see what I can do. But at best you're still going to

11

have to pay at least seventy-five per cent of it. Hotels are bastards when it comes to cancellations."

"Oh, bloody hell."

"Look, I'll try to sort it out," she promised, though from her tone Amy knew the chances of success were minimal. "I'll get on the blower right now."

"I never thought about the honeymoon."

Gaby was scrolling down names on her phone. "Ah. OK. Not sure they'll be in today but it's got to be worth a try. I'll just go into the study." PJ and Amy were left smiling awkwardly at each other.

"Lovely weather," said PJ, peering through the half-open shutters at the gentrified street. "Would have been a great day for the wedding. It's too bad." He saw Amy's face and hastily said, "How about another g & t?"

They talked determinedly about cricket, while Archie pushed round the room the wagon Amy, his godmother, had given him for his christening. Occasionally he wrapped his arms around her legs. The sight of his chubby face, the smell of his baby curls, the sound of his high baby voice gabbling nonsensically made Amy feel a little cheered as did the alcohol PJ continued to ply her with. By the time Gaby came back in, she was quite woozy.

"Not good," she said. "They just won't give you a refund. They say even last week it would have been OK, but twenty-four hours is way, way too short notice."

Amy knocked back the rest of her drink in one.

"So, in addition to wasting everyone's time and money and making myself a laughing stock, I have also spent nearly ten thousand pounds on a holiday I can't go on."

"And you were meant to be leaving tomorrow morning?" PJ asked.

"Yup."

"There's just one thing for it," he said. "You still go on honeymoon. On your own."

Both women looked at him incredulously. "Don't be silly," Amy said. "I can't do that."

"Why not?"

"Well . . . because it's a honeymoon. You go with your husband."

"Except you don't have a husband," PJ pointed out. "But you can't let all that money go to waste."

Amy thought about it. She'd booked the time off work. The idea of being somewhere far away from people she knew was very tempting. Plus where else was she going to spend the next couple of weeks? She could hardly go home because, as far as she knew, it was still Doug's home too, and much as she loved Gaby, the prospect of a fortnight in a spare room in Balham with a happily married couple and a toddler in the other rooms, was equally unbearable. She could go to her parents — but their disappointment was even more painful than hers.

"Two weeks in Italy on my own . . ."

"You don't have to be on your own," Gaby said slowly. "I could come with you."

"Really?"

"Well, yeah. I'm owed a few days' holiday. I couldn't go tomorrow because on Tuesday I've got my twenty-week scan. But I could come out on Wednesday. Faviola will be here." Faviola was their "amazing" Filipina nanny. "It would only be for a few days, I don't think I could do the whole of the Capri stay without guilt kicking in." She gave Archie a quick squeeze. "But I haven't been away on my own since he was born. And it would better than nothing, wouldn't it?"

"It would be fantastic," Amy breathed. "Are you sure?"

"Of course I'm sure. A break would do me good. PJ can pick up the rest of the slack, can't you, darling?"

"Absolutely," he agreed good-naturedly.

"By the way, I was meaning to ask you. I haven't felt the baby kick yet. Is that normal? Or should I be worried?"

"It's normal," Amy said, who was used to these kinds of questions from friends. She turned to PJ. "Are you sure you don't mind?"

"Not in the slightest. Love a few days to myself, with the next Test match about to start. Oi!" he yelled as Gaby thumped him.

Amy turned to Gaby. "We can lie in the sun. Go to museums." All the things she'd dreamed of doing with Doug. Her throat tightened.

"Eat pasta and pizza." Gaby smiled. "Ice cream — or, God, actually, no, maybe not ice cream because it might not be pasteurized. Lie by the pool. Go out on the town. Meet some Romeos. Because if you can't pull a new guy in Italy you need to check your birth certificate to make sure you really are a girl."

"Oi!" PJ repeated and for the first time in twenty-four hours Amy almost smiled.

"I don't want to pull. I'll never love again."

"That's what you *say*. But wait until lecherous Luigi's whispering sweet nothings to you in the moonlight."

The phone rang again. "Hello?" Gaby's face changed. "Oh, hi, Mrs Fraser. Um, unfortunately she's not here at the moment. I don't know where she is. Yes, I know. I know it's very upsetting . . . No, I don't know where Doug is, I'm afraid . . . do you?"

Amy winced. The thought of Doug's mum on the warpath was more than she could stand. At least she'd never see her, or any of the Fraser clan again. Perhaps there were some advantages to the break up.

"OK, sorry," Gaby said. "Yes. Yes. I'm sure he is upset, but Amy is too." She gritted her teeth. "Yes, I'll get her to call you. But I don't know when that will be. Nobody knows where she is right now, you see." She hung up. "You know who that was."

Amy thought of days and days more of such conversations. She couldn't take any more of this.

"You're right. I've got to get out of here."

"Yay!" Gaby held out her palm for a high-five. "You go, girl. You're going on honeymooooon! And don't worry about the few days alone. It'll be good for you. You'll be empowered. I promise."

CHAPTER
THREE

In the living room of the Picasso Suite of the Hotel de Russie, Rome, Hal Blackstock was munching his way through the fruit piled high in a giant bowl while idly flicking through the channels on his giant plasma screen, which apparently had been left behind by George Clooney after an extended stay. Soap opera, rerun of *Friends* in Italian, rerun of *ER*, soap opera. Oh good. Football. For a minute he paused, but it was two obscure Turkish teams that even he had only vaguely heard of, so he carried on until he came across two harsh-faced blonde girls with very obvious boob jobs writhing around on a sheepskin rug.

"Wicked," he said. "Russian porn. This'll do very nicely."

"Oh, Hal," sighed Vanessa, his assistant, who was sitting at the tiny desk in the corner, going through his itinerary.

Hal grinned at her as he turned up the volume. "God, I love to hear them moan in their Slav accents. It's so sexy."

"You're dreadful," Vanessa said calmly, as usual refusing to rise to the bait.

The blondes started simulating simultaneous orgasm. Hal yawned and flicked on. "Hey, *Scooby Doo* in Italian!" He watched for five minutes, but then got bored and continued flicking. For a while he settled on motorbike racing. Perhaps he'd have a kip. But the maid was still in the bedroom unpacking his Vuitton case. She was small and busty, quite foxy, but Hal had steered clear of hotel staff ever since that girl who'd brought him room service in the Isle of Man sold her story to the *Sunday Mirror*.

He felt a tingling under his T-shirt. Oh God, that spot again. He'd had it for a few days now, on the left-hand side, second rib down, south-south-west of his nipple. When he'd first noticed it, he thought it was a bog-standard whitehead. But it was swollen, very tender, more so than most whiteheads, and it had lingered for a while now without showing the slightest interest in shrinking. He frowned, then searched for something to distract him.

"So what's on the agenda today, Nessie? Nessie?" But for once she wasn't listening, outraged by the contents of her laptop screen.

"I thought as much," she exclaimed. "This is *not* the best suite in the hotel. You should be in the Nijinsky or the Popolo. Both are much better."

Hal glanced over to his terrace that looked out over the immaculate, formal gardens climbing the hill behind the hotel.

"The view's pretty good from where I'm sitting."

"Not good enough," Vanessa said, the pink spot on the end of her slightly upturned nose growing darker.

17

"Here we only have a view of the garden. From the other suites you see the Roman rooftops."

Hal yawned and wondered about having a go on the PlayStation. "I'm sure I'll live. I've seen rooftops before."

"But that's not the point," Vanessa said, her eyes narrowing. She picked up the phone beside her and jabbed zero with the end of her pencil.

Vanessa had been working for Hal for three years now and was by a long shot the best PA he had ever had. His own Miss Moneypenny, with a voice that made the queen sound common, she had a brain like an iBook and the ruthlessness of Attila the Hun. No detail was too small to escape her eagle eye, no person too important to dodge her bawling outs when everything was less than perfect for her boss.

Of course, the fact that she — like most women — was in love with Hal helped. There had never been anything between them. Not that Nessie wasn't a bit of a looker with her immaculate blonde hair and long legs. Once or twice, bored and horny and stuck in some vile suite in Moscow on yet another junket, he had considered it — even got as far as picking up the phone to call her room. But he'd always hung up in time.

Far, far more entertaining in the long run to watch the devotion behind her Sloaney, despotic eyes; the fleeting pain, instantly concealed, on entering his suite in the morning to discover yet another nineteen-year-old he had found in a nightclub, yawning and wearing his Thomas Pink pyjama top. More recently there had been the disdain every time she put through a call from

18

Flora or was asked to order her flowers. Hal wasn't stupid. He knew sex would spoil everything, that he would break Vanessa's heart and have to fire her and that no replacement could be a zillionth as efficient or as tigerish in protecting his interests.

Just listen to her now. "*Si*, yes, Signor Ducelli, please." Signor Ducelli was the hotel manager; he had greeted Hal with much charm and a promise to do "anything, but any . . . theeng to make your stay more comfortable".

Hal listened in amusement as Vanessa set to work.

"Yes, hello, Signor Ducelli. How are you? . . . Well, I'm sorry to say things are *not good*. The suite is adequate, but I can't understand why Mr Blackstock isn't in the Nijinsky or the Popolo suite. Those *are* your best ones, aren't they? Could you see us moved straight away?" Vanessa's mouth pursed. "I see . . . Well, no, of course Justina must stay where she is. But can't the honeymooners be persuaded to swap? I mean, this is Hal Blackstock we are talking about here. They'd probably be happy to do it . . . Can't you ask? . . . Why not? . . . I'm sorry, Signor Ducelli, but this really isn't good enough. I shall be seeing to it that the studio makes sure its stars avoid the de Russie in future . . . No, there may be two Picasso lithographs in this suite but Mr Blackstock owns his own Picasso oil painting, so . . . I quite understand the suite is already taken, but I don't understand why you can't ask them to move . . . No, *I'm* sorry, Signor Ducelli. Goodbye."

"Good try, Nessie," Hal said, stretching back in the sofa, "but no cigar. Never mind."

"Trying to fob us off by saying this suite has two Picasso lithographs," she brooded.

"I don't have a Picasso oil."

"*I* know that. But Ducelli doesn't." She frowned. "The Nijinsky's out because Justina's staying there."

Justina Maguire was Hal's co-star in *The Apple Tree*, the dog of a film he was in Rome to promote. She was a twenty-one-year-old airhead bulimic from Laguna Beach, with a body like a toothpick. Hal loathed her.

"Jesus, I didn't realize they'd put her in the same hotel as me. Well, just so long as there is absolutely zero chance of hooking up with her."

"But the Popolo's occupied by honeymooners," Vanessa mused. "Of course they'll swap. If Signor Ducelli won't do it I may just have to tackle the problem myself."

"No, don't do that," Hal said wearily, scratching his groin. Mostly he found Vanessa's Rottweiler tendencies amusing, but sometimes it was embarrassing hearing her badger restaurant managers for the best table, airline stewards for the best seats, fashion PRs for free clothes. Still, Hal couldn't pretend he didn't like all that. And he knew how it was in the film world — tantrums about who had the biggest Winnebago, the flashest limo to drive you to the set each morning, the best table at the Ivy, the private jet as opposed to mere seats in first class.

"Leave the honeymooners alone," he said now. "Let them have some fun before he starts cheating on her and she lets herself go."

20

"So cynical," Vanessa said brusquely. "But I *shall* ask. In my experience, they'll be honoured to swap with Hal Blackstock. If they argue I'll chuck in a couple of free tickets to the premiere."

The phone rang.

"Ah, that's probably Signor Ducelli now, telling me he's persuaded them."

She picked up. "Hello?" Her tone switched from aggressive to ingratiating. "Ah. Yes, hello, Flora. Yes, I'll just see if he's available."

"Of course I'm available to Flora," Hal yelled. God, Nessie could be ridiculous. He picked up the extension on the side table. "Hello, darling."

"Is that Mr Jarse?" came Flora's languid upper-east-side tones.

He couldn't help giggling. "Speaking."

"Mr Hugh Jarse?" Flora sighed. "Don't you ever get bored checking in under these stupid names?"

"Never."

Hal imagined her in her suite in Jamaica, rolling her eyes in exasperation. Flora didn't exactly approve of his schoolboy sense of humour.

"So how are you, darling? It must be . . ." he glanced at his Rolex. "Horribly early there."

"It's just before seven. I've been up since five, though, meditating, then I had a swim. And in half an hour we're off to visit the women's refuge. So how's it going with you?"

"Oh, same old, same old. Only been here an hour. Hotel's OK, I suppose, though Nessie couldn't get me the best suite." He said the last bit loudly, sticking out his tongue, knowing it would piss Nessie off no end. Why was she hanging around? "Hang on a sec, darling." He gave his best imperious look. "Vanessa, could I have a bit of privacy, please?"

To his amusement, the tips of her ears flushed. "Of course, Hal," she said smoothly. "I shall go and resolve this suite nonsense." And she tapped out of the room on her Patrick Cox wedges.

"Honestly, I think that woman would wipe my bum if I asked her to," he said as the door shut.

"Hal! Don't be so disgusting! You'd be lost without Vanessa."

"I'd be lost without you." He said it in the silly, cheesy romantic-hero voice he always put on with Flora. By pretending he was in a movie, he didn't have to question whether he actually meant what he said.

"Oh, Hal, that's so sweet." Flora too sounded as though she was reading from a script.

"So how are the girls?" Flora had two small daughters by her ex-husband, the French conductor Pierre de Belleville Crécy. Hal didn't really do children, but he was surprisingly fond of them in small doses. Often, they could be more of a laugh than their mother.

"They're wonderful. Been enjoying the beach. Learning about marine eco-systems. So what's your day's schedule?"

"Interviews all day tomorrow, and we know what that'll be like. 'Hal, when are you going to marry Flora?' 'Hal, are you still in love with Marina?' Blah, blah, blah, blah-di-di-blah."

22

He shouldn't have said that. The two subjects most guaranteed to push Flora's angry buttons. Sure enough: "Tell them you don't talk about your personal life," she snapped.

"I will, but it's still so fucking tedious." To change the subject, he added, "And I've still got that spot."

"What spot? Oh, that one on your chest?"

"Yeah. It really hurts," he added, only mildly exaggerating. "If I put pressure on it, I can feel pain spreading out in a wave."

"Then don't put pressure on it," she said, as if addressing a cretin.

"All right, I won't." He sighed. "You don't think it's anything serious, do you?"

"No. But if you're worried, you should see a doctor."

"Oh, no. There's no need for a doctor." Hal hated that idea. Either he'd be told what he had was terminal, which he couldn't deal with, or — which had until now been the case with his various ailments — he'd be told there was absolutely nothing to worry about and he'd feel like a time-wasting fool. Time to change the subject. "Couldn't you come a bit earlier? Leave those silly Jamaicans alone? After all, it's their fault they were stupid enough to try to smuggle drugs."

"Hal! You know it's not like that. Do you have any idea what desperate poverty these women live in?"

"Sorry! I was only joking. It's just . . . it would be so much more fun if you were here."

"I'll be with you soon enough," she said. Flora was arriving on Tuesday to accompany him to the premiere on Wednesday night, after which they had a week booked at the Quisisana in Capri. "And in the meantime you can have plenty of fun on your own. Rome's an incredible place."

"Yeah, but I've seen it all before. I wanted to show it to you. Impress you with my Italian. Relive my past." Hal had read Italian and French at Cambridge and as part of his degree he'd spent a year in Rome. His Italian was pretty rusty now but he'd been looking forward to practising again. It would remind Flora that he wasn't just a handsome face spouting inane lines. Sometimes Flora could be a little patronizing about her status as a serious actress, compared to his as a romantic-comedy lead.

"I'll be with you in a couple of days. Hal, my car's just arrived. Look, I'll call you when I get back, shall I?"

"Sure," he said.

"OK. Talk to you later."

"Bye, darling."

He hung up and fell back on his bed, annoyed. Why had he mentioned Marina? He knew Flora couldn't stand any mention of his ex. And why the getting married question? Flora must know people asked him all the time. Nonetheless, he always managed to dodge the subject as if it was an alien trying to zap him in one of his PlayStation games.

He got up and padded into the bedroom. He opened his wardrobe door and pressed 1102, his birthday, into the keypad of his safe. The door swung open. Hal removed a blue velvet padded box and opened it. Inside, shone a huge diamond surrounded by tiny grass-green emeralds. Flora had a lot of amazing

24

jewellery, but she would never have seen anything like this ring before. He grinned as he imagined presenting it to her. Of course he hadn't 100 per cent made up his mind this was what he wanted to do, but this hotel could definitely be the right setting. He'd propose over dinner, on the terrace. Though now he thought about it, it *was* a shame they only had a view of the gardens. The rooftops of Rome would be far better. Plus they were a little bit overlooked here, people in other rooms could see them as could anyone out on the terrace if they looked up. Nessie was right. As usual.

Nervily, he grabbed the remote and began channel hopping again. Eventually he found one of his own movies, which appeared to have been dubbed into Bulgarian. God, only five years ago but he'd been so much better-looking then. He glanced at his watch. Just gone one. When Nessie got back he'd get her to order some lunch, then maybe he'd have a kip, then a workout. Hal didn't know why he felt so listless at the moment. It must be nerves. After all, he was on the verge of making a life-changing gesture and even someone as laid back as himself was bound to feel a little on edge.

CHAPTER
FOUR

Rome airport was disappointingly just an airport like any other, all unflattering strip-lighting, endless walkways and adverts for mobile networks. Amy made her way through passport control on autopilot, collected her Snoopy suitcase from the carousel and walked through customs. On the other side of the barrier, a burly uniformed man with a sign reading "Mr and Mrs Fraser" was standing, yawning. She tapped him on the arm.

"Hello, I'm Mrs Fraser."

"Good afternoon. I am Vincenzo." He looked around. "And . . . Mr Fraser?"

Amy swallowed. She was going to have to get used to this. "He's coming later. Some problems he had to sort out. He'll be on a later flight."

"A later flight? But this is your honeymoon."

"Yes. I know. It's a pity, but there you go!" She let out a little strangled laugh. "I'll just have to wait for him."

Vincenzo picked up her Snoopy case, which she'd thought such a witty buy when she spotted it in a vintage shop near Brick Lane. Now it just made her feel retarded. She followed him out through the terminal doors. The heat slapped her in the face like an angry lover.

"Oh, it's hot!" she said originally.

Vincenzo gave her the look that remark deserved. "It's August. Too hot to stay in Rome. Everyone is on holiday." His English was perfect, Amy noted, with just the faintest trace of a Birmingham accent.

"Except you," she replied, following him into the multistorey car park.

"No, me, I prefer to be here." Amy expected him to expand, but he had stopped beside a big black Mercedes. Gaby *had* asked her if she was really sure she fancied Rome in the height of summer. "It'll be scorching and the place'll be half empty," she'd said. "But I will be able to get you a much better deal on the suite."

"The hotel has air-conditioning, hasn't it?" Amy had retorted. "And Rome *is* Doug's favourite place in the world which he's always wanted to show me." And when Gaby assented, Amy had cried, "Let's do it!"

She climbed in the back of the car. Minutes later Vincenzo was driving her along a stretch of motorway lined by scorched wasteland and the occasional multiplex. They could have been on the outskirts of Milton Keynes. Even the crazy driving she'd expected was non-existent, the road was almost completely empty and the speedometer stuck stubbornly on 130 kph. Worst of all, the sun, which Amy had been yearning for, was absent. Instead the day was damp and grey, like a forgotten T-shirt at the bottom of the laundry basket.

"It is your first time in Rome, signora?"

"Yes. First time in Italy." She hadn't imagined it like this. Amy had envisaged blue skies, crazy guys zipping in and out of the traffic on Vespas, accordions playing "That's Amore" and little old ladies beside the road making their own pasta. But then again, she'd imagined she'd be here with her husband.

She remembered her phone. She'd turned it off for the flight; she scrabbled for it and turned it on. Maybe Doug had called while she'd been at twenty-five thousand feet? Sure enough, when she dialled voicemail she learned she had seven new messages. But, as she listened to each one, the tiny bud of hope wilted and died. It was friend, after friend, after colleague, after distant relation, after vague mate of Doug's she'd met once for ten minutes in the pub, calling to find out if she was OK in voices that dripped sympathy underscored with prurient glee at the prospect of finding out what had gone wrong. There were six texts to that effect as well.

Sod them. Amy wasn't going to tell anyone anything.

"Where are you from in England?"

"London."

"You know Nuneaton? I spent two years there, working in a bar."

"I don't. But that explains your excellent English."

Vincenzo nodded, satisfied, as he turned off the motorway and onto what looked like a narrow country lane with trees on either side. Then it widened again and they were in what must have been the suburbs. The road was lined with modern apartment blocks, painted peach, their shutters closed. Occasionally Amy saw signs reading Pizzeria, Trattoria, Gelateria. Barely a soul was on the streets. The roads got wider and a bit busier, as Vincenzo drove on. They passed a huge brick pyramid.

"The tomb of Caius Cestius," said Vincenzo. "He visited the pyramids in Egypt and decided to build one for himself."

"Oh, right," Amy said, wondering if she should know who Caius Cestius was. Rising up in front of her was the first real sign she was in Rome, the Colosseum, just as she remembered it from *Gladiator*.

"*Colosseo*," Vincenzo confirmed. "Where the Christians were fed to the lions."

"Of course." Amy knew just how they must have felt.

"And on your left you can see the Forum." Amy peered through the smoky windows at what looked like a demolition site. Then came a much more modern, vast, Colgate-white edifice, with steps at the front and pillars, topped with statues of chariots driven by what looked like angels.

"The monument to King Vittorio Emmanuele. We call it the wedding cake." As Amy flinched at the reference, he continued. "Is the only ugly building in Rome."

He drove on up a long, narrow street lined with shops. There was a wide square with a carved column on the left, which Vincenzo said was the Piazza del Parlamento, then he turned right and they went through a huge square with a small fountain in the middle and people everywhere.

"La Piazza di Spagna." To her right, Amy saw steps, again absolutely covered in people, climbing up to an elegant church. "This is where the Roman boys come to *rimorchiare*. Pick up the girls. But this does not interest you. You are on honeymoon." They carried on down a long, narrow street. "And this is Via del Babuino. And *ecco*! Your hotel."

The Hotel de Russie was a high, stone building right on the road. A bellboy in a chic grey uniform and top hat opened the car door for her, then removed her suitcase from the boot. There was an awkward moment when she thanked Vincenzo but realized she couldn't tip him as she'd forgotten to buy euros at the airport.

"I'm so sorry."

"Don't worry," Vincenzo said. He held out his hand. With a start, Amy noticed his nails were perfectly manicured and painted a dainty shell pink. "Enjoy your stay, signora."

Amy followed the bellboy through the doors and left into the lobby. It was minimalist with a stone floor and high ceilings. At the front desk, a bald young man smiled at her. "Welcome, Mrs Fraser. So excellent to have you at the Hotel de Russie."

"Actually," Amy said. "It's Doctor Fraser." She thanked the Lord that her medical qualifications meant she could dispense with the Mrs tag she had no right to. She thought she'd hold on to Fraser for a bit, though. After a lifetime of Dr Gubbins it was the least she deserved. She'd been looking forward so much to a decent surname, she'd already changed her name on her bank cards, her passport, her Tesco Club Card.

Well, she was just going to have to change them all back again. Another thing to add to her to-do list, along with posting that inevitable ad on eBay. "One Vera Wang knock-off wedding dress. Size 10. Never worn."

"Oh, I'm sorry," the receptionist said, "a doctor. *Mamma Mia!*" So Italians really did say that. "How clever. Wonderful. And . . . Mr Fraser?"

This was a nightmare. "He's coming on a later flight."

"Ah, I see," said the receptionist smoothly. "*Allora*, no problem. Could you just fill out this form for me and let me have your passport?"

She filled it out giving her fraudulent name. She fiddled in her bag for her passport and a tampon fell onto the stone floor. While she scrabbled to pick it up, a man with a Yorkshire accent shouted, "Hey, excuse me."

"Yes, Mr Doubleday," said the receptionist, the same friendly smile on his face.

"I'm not happy with my room. I'd like to be upgraded to a suite immediately."

"Oh, I am so sorry, Mr Doubleday, all our suites are booked."

Amy turned to look at the man. Fifties, short, with stubby, greying hair, a scowling mouth and a forehead so shiny he looked as if he'd just polished it. He wore slacks and a golfing jumper. Over his neck hung a selection of cameras.

"There's nothing you can do about this?" He was snarling. "I'm a very important guest, you know."

"I'm so sorry, sir. It is a very busy time of year. There is a film premiere on Wednesday and many people are staying with us."

"I know there's a film premiere, mate. I'm here to take pictures of it." And the man stormed off.

"What an idiot," said another English voice, this time female and rather posh. Amy turned again. A middle-aged woman in a sensible navy sundress smiled at her. Behind her, stood a quiet-looking man in a T-shirt and shorts.

"Don't you think? Complete numbskull."

"He was a bit rude," Amy agreed.

"A bit rude!" The woman snorted. "He's a dick!"

"Marian!" the man said gently.

"Well, he was, Roger. You know I call a spade a spade." She smiled again at Amy, showing a row of strong, horsey teeth. "Have you just arrived? It's lovely here. You'll enjoy it."

"I'm sure I will." Amy turned back to the desk.

"Are you on honeymoon?"

Catching the eye of the receptionist, Amy said, "Yes."

"Us too," said Marian.

"Oh, I . . ."

"Second honeymoon," she explained. "First came here forty years ago, can you believe. Now the brats are all grown, we thought we'd come back and relive our youth. We're skiers, you see."

"Oh? Is it cold enough at this time of year?"

Marian honked with laughter. "Very good, very good. No, SKIERS. Spending the kids' inheritance. We've only just kicked our eldest out. He's thirty-four."

"My age."

"Yes, but you are obviously a sensible married lady. He was a dope-smoking drifter. So where is your husband, dear?"

"Marian . . ." said Roger, weakly.

"He's just gone up to the room," Amy said softly, hoping the receptionist wouldn't hear.

"I hope we meet him. We must all get together for a drink some evening. Anyway, mustn't keep you. Doing the Villa Borghese this afternoon. *Ciao*, as they say."

With a merry wave she marched off, Roger in her wake. Amy turned back to the desk. The receptionist smiled and gestured to a bellboy with a kind, creased face. "Have a lovely honeymoon, Doctor Fraser. Tommaso will show you to your suite."

CHAPTER
FIVE

Amy followed Tommaso through a high-ceilinged lobby furnished with tasteful modern sculptures. At the back, glass doors led to a courtyard filled with tables under huge white parasols. They turned left and Tommaso pressed the button for a lift. They took it to the sixth floor, where they emerged into a beige carpeted corridor. They walked towards the end, where Tommaso inserted a key card into the wall and pushed open a pale green door.

"After you, signora."

She stepped into a living room.

"Wow."

It wasn't huge, but it was beautiful with yellow walls decorated with black and white photos of flowers, a sofa and a desk. She'd be frightened to sit down in case she messed anything up.

"Here is the bedroom, signora."

Amy followed Tommaso into a bedroom filled with balloons. Everywhere. In the shape of pink hearts. Each one bore the message "Amy & Doug" in silver, squiggly writing. It couldn't have been more kitsch. Gaby must have arranged it, then forgotten to cancel.

"Happy honeymoon," Tommaso said.

"I . . . Thank you." Amy felt that familiar tickling in her nose and burning in her eyes. Tommaso gave her a panicked look.

"Signora, look here," he cried, like a mother trying to distract a toddler from a tantrum.

He opened the doors to a terrace. There was a lemon tree, pots of geraniums and two white-cushioned day beds lying side by side. Under a white parasol, a table had been laid for two with a white cloth, sparkling silver cutlery, gleaming porcelain, candles and flowers. The perfect setting for a romantic sunset dinner à deux. Amy couldn't bear it.

"It's beautiful," she managed to say.

"But come here, signora," Tommaso said, gesturing her towards the parapet. Beneath them, a wide square fanned out with a pointy obelisk in the middle, a huge gateway at one end and at the other — so close to Amy she could almost touch it — the huge dome of a church.

"Look, signora, la Piazza del Popolo. Here we are, right in the heart of Rome."

"Yes."

He gave her a worried look. "Come, signora," he said, gesturing her back inside. "This is the bathroom."

"Mmm." She nodded numbly at the mosaic on the wall.

"You want me to show you how to work the television? The stereo? The shower?"

"No, thank you. I'll work it all out by myself."

"Richard Gere always stays here. And Madonna. Sting. Leonardo DiCaprio." As an afterthought, he added, "And Victoria Beckham was here recently."

"Wonderful."

"And don't forget, signora, we have a beautiful leisure centre with sauna, steam room, hydrotherapy pool. Is in the basement."

"Oh, right." Amy was desperate for him to go, but still he hovered. Of course. He wanted a tip.

"I'm so sorry, I haven't got any euros yet. Can I tip you later?"

"No problem, signora." He smiled sympathetically. "If there is anything you want, you just ask for me. Please remember, we are entirely at your service. Nothing too great. Too small."

Can you turn the clock back a week? Tell me this is all a bad dream? "Thank you," she said, trying to smile. "I'll remember that."

On his way down in the lift, Tommaso was puzzled. He genuinely didn't mind the lack of a tip; he was concerned for this woman with the black hair tied in a knot on her head and long, spindly legs. She didn't look anything like the women who normally stayed in the Popolo suite, who were either businesswomen in crisp suits who immediately started bombarding him with questions about power points and Broadband access or wives (and often mistresses) with expensively rearranged features, although no amount of money could disguise the dissatisfaction in their eyes. Not that this woman looked happy. Where was her husband? Tommaso had been married coming up to thirty years and had never spent a night apart from his wife. Chance would be a fine thing, he joked to his friends, though he didn't actually mean a word of it.

36

Upstairs, in the Popolo suite, Amy sat on the bed and cried and cried and cried. She couldn't believe it: here she was in this luxurious setting with a perfect view and all she wanted to do was climb in the bath, put her head under the water, and never emerge again.

"This can't be happening to me," she howled aloud, then stopped as she heard a doorbell ring. She strained her ears, sure she had imagined it but there it was again. Him! He'd come! She dashed to the door and opened it. A woman stood there. Tall, almost as tall as Amy, in a fitted suit and with glossy blonde hair pulled back in a tight ponytail.

"Hello. I mean, *buon giorno.*"

"Hello," said the woman in a crisp English accent. "So sorry to trouble you. Vanessa Trimingham. Congratulations. I hear you've just got married."

"I —"

"Lovely. Now. Sorry to have to break it to you, but there's been a bit of a mix up. I'm the personal assistant to Hal Blackstock who is also staying in this hotel . . ." She paused for a moment to let the momentousness of this sink in. "Normally this is his suite. But those silly billies at reception appear to have messed things up and booked you in here. So, Mr Blackstock was hoping you would swap suites. He's bang opposite in the Picasso, so there's virtually no difference."

"Excuse me?"

"Yes, if you could swap suites Mr Blackstock would really appreciate it."

Amy couldn't believe it. "No thank you," she said. "I want to stay where I am."

A note of steel entered Vanessa's voice and her eyes went hard, like Charles Bronson's in *Death Wish* when his entire family had been massacred and he was out for revenge.

"Um, I'm terribly sorry but I don't think you quite understand me. We're talking about *Hal Blackstock* here. You *do* know who he is, don't you?"

"Of course I do," Amy snapped. Everyone bloody knew Hal Blackstock. A British film star. Early forties at a guess. Astonishingly good-looking in that good-teeth, wispy-fringed, upper-class genes kind of way. A bit too clean cut for Amy, but Gaby had always had a thing for him and he was Amy's mother's ideal man. He'd been in lots of costume dramas in the early nineties, playing the dashing hero, then done a couple of Hollywood blockbusters. He was almost as well known for his relationship with Marina Dawson, a game-show hostess who'd accompanied him to Hollywood, where she became the face of Magic Cosmetics and bitchy judge of *Catwalk*, a TV modelling competition that had been going for years now. On the nights Doug was playing with the band, it was Amy's idea of heaven to snuggle up in front of it.

Marina and Hal had split up a couple of years ago and now she was dating some billionaire. Since then Hal had faded a bit from view — he hadn't done a movie for ages that Amy could recall, though in the past few months he had been all over the magazines that littered the waiting room at the surgery for his relationship with Flora de Belleville Crécy, who was a very beautiful actress (was there any other sort?) who did a lot of charity work.

"So we shouldn't have any problem?" Vanessa persisted.

"I didn't say that," Amy retorted. "This is my honeymoon. I don't want to swap."

"The Picasso suite is perfectly lovely."

"Well, in that case Hal shouldn't have a problem."

"But he *always* stays in this suite."

"Do him good to have a change then." Amy couldn't quite believe she was having this conversation. "Now, goodbye."

Amy shut the door. "Bloody cheeky cow," she breathed. She sat down on the bed and gazed at the splendour around her. It was certainly quite something to think Hal Blackstock would like to change places with her. Gaby would spontaneously combust when she told her.

Ring, ring, ring.

The phone! Amy looked round, unable to decide which handset to pick up. Eventually, she grabbed the one on the desk. "Hello?" She was less hopeful this time, but a spark still remained. Vanessa's voice doused it.

"I'm not sure you've understood me. Mr Blackstock *always* stays in the Popolo suite. And he has very kindly offered you and your husband tickets to Wednesday night's premiere of his film *The Apple Tree*."

"Sorry," Amy said. "But I . . . I mean *we* . . . booked this suite three months ago. For my . . . I mean our . . . honeymoon and I'm *not* swapping."

Hanging up, she giggled for the first time since her hen party.

"Come on, Amy Gubbins," she said aloud. "You're going to see Rome."

CHAPTER
SIX

Amy's first outing in Rome was a disaster. It didn't help that the heat was stifling, that walking down the street felt as if she was wading through thick soup, that the lovely linen shift dress she'd changed into was soon soaked in sweat and crumpled around her like a wet rag.

When she and Doug had gone on weekend breaks — to Stockholm, to Lyons, to Barcelona, to New York (wonderful weekends, or almost wonderful were it not for the fact Amy always had to organize them, pay for them, sort out foreign currency and arrange transport to and from each airport), she would spend hours after booking in front of her computer, reading old travel articles, finding out about important details like the words for "please" and "thank you" and the country's tipping policy (nothing in egalitarian Sweden, at least 15 per cent in New York if you didn't want to be chased down the street by a waiter wielding a meat cleaver). She'd make neat lists on Post-its of things to see and do, restaurants to eat in and shops to browse.

But she'd been so busy with the wedding, she hadn't had time to think of the honeymoon. And now she didn't have the heart to open the *Time Out* guide she'd bought a week ago in Daunt Books on Marylebone High Street after a last-minute visit to the caterers to inspect the wedding cake she'd agonized so long over choosing. A week ago when everything seemed still on track.

So Amy wandered, hoping to stumble across some must-see place like the Forum or the Piazza Navona. At first things had been promising: the Via del Babuino was full of gorgeous antique shops and hip boutiques, but as it was Sunday nearly all of them were shut. Then she took a wrong turn and ended up in a gloomy backstreet near the station, full of tatty shops selling plastic figurines of the Pope. The only other people around were either tired-looking transvestites or Africans trying to flog her fake Valentino handbags. Eventually, she found a cashpoint. Glancing round for muggers, she slid in her card, instructed the machine to speak English to her, and jabbed in her pin. She'd get out the maximum — five-hundred euros — and that should do her for most of the stay.

You have insufficient funds for this transaction, she read on the screen. *Please check your balance.*

Heart in her mouth, Amy pressed a few more keys. Her balance came up on screen. Nine hundred and ninety-five pounds overdrawn. Bugger. Usually Amy set herself a strict limit of five hundred. It must have been those bloody Emma Hope shoes that had tipped her over. She calculated furiously. Her salary would reach her account by the middle of the week, until then she could only take out the equivalent of forty-five pounds. Of course she could live on her credit card but then what would she pay that off with? Christ! She'd always laughed at people who were bankrupted by their weddings and now she'd gone and done exactly that.

"Calm down," she told herself, as the euros slid out into her palm. "You'll just have to live cheaply for a few days."

Hungry and thirsty, she sat down outside a café and ordered an espresso because she was pretty sure that was Italian for espresso. After twenty minutes, the sour-faced waiter brought her a mouthful of liquid tar which was nothing like as good as you got in Starbucks round the corner from work. She drank it in five seconds, decided against ordering a sandwich, and asked for the bill.

"Ten euros," he said.

Amy calculated frantically. That was about seven quid.

"*Scusi?*"

"Ten euros."

"But that's ridiculous," she said. "It's a total rip off."

"You sit at a table you pay more," he explained unsmilingly. "If you want an espresso for one euro, you stand at the bar."

Shaking from rage and caffeine, she paid up. The bastard. Amy had always thought Italians were a race of jovial souls who believed in *la dolce vita*. She was so upset she couldn't face the idea of lunch. What might they charge her for that? Anyway, she hated the idea of sitting alone in a restaurant, broadcasting the fact she was a jilted bride. Why had she listened to Gaby? She'd been totally wrong: going away on your own wasn't empowering, it was vile.

A wave of terror hit her. What on earth was going to become of her? She'd lost the love of her life, the man she'd planned to grow old with. She needed to call him. But pride plus a fear he might be with Pinny held her back.

By six o'clock after more aimless wandering through hot, dingy backstreets she was starving. Why had she rejected the cardboard croissant they'd offered her on the plane? Not only that, she had a blister on both toes from walking for hours in flip flops over cobbles and her shoulders were sunburned because she'd ignored the advice she gave patients about how, whatever the weather, you must always wear sunscreen because rays could penetrate the thickest clouds.

At the Hotel de Russie, the doorman (a different one from when she arrived) regarded her dubiously.

"Excuse me, signorina," he asked, "but are you a guest here?"

"Yes, I am," Amy said haughtily. "I'm staying in the Popolo suite."

He looked sceptical. "Can I see your key card?"

She pulled it out of her bag. He looked deeply embarrassed.

"I am so sorry, signorina. I do this for the guests' protection, you understand."

"It's OK," Amy muttered.

Back in the suite, she lay on the bed and stared at the ceiling for a long time.

"You'll feel better when you've eaten," she told herself. She seized the room-service menu from the desk and began scanning it. She didn't want seabass or loin of veal, she'd be quite happy with a bowl of pasta. Spaghetti with fresh tomato and basil, that would do. Then she noticed the price. Seventeen euros fifty, plus a four-euro room-service charge.

Amy frowned. She'd never been able to do exchange rates. Thirty-five pounds. No, no, the other way, more like fifteen. But still. She just couldn't do it, she'd spent all her money on this damn wedding and honeymoon. She looked down the menu for a cheaper option. Nope, the pasta was as good as it got. And then there was the question of drink. A tiny bottle of water from the mini bar cost five euros and she was wary of drinking tap water. But it was either that or back onto the now darkening streets for that humiliating — and probably equally expensive — meal alone. Unless . . .

There was a third way.

Half an hour later, she was back in the room sitting on her bed, with a double cheeseburger, extra-large fries and a Diet Coke from the McDonald's she'd seen on the corner of Piazza di Spagna. She'd smuggled the food in, in her handbag, past the doorman. Ooh, the fries were good, hot and salty, though she wished she'd remembered to pick up some ketchup. She imagined her and Doug, tucked up, feeding each other. He was probably sharing his chips with Pinny now.

She thought of all the patients she'd lectured on the importance of cutting junk food from their diets. But obviously such rules didn't apply when your heart was broken; it didn't matter if the pounds she'd lost for the wedding piled back on again, if her heart buckled under all the saturated fat and her immune system shut down from vitamin deprivation because no one was ever going to love her now. She was going to grow into an old spinster, with warts on her chin. She would smile broodily at babies in the supermarket and they would scream with terror.

Amy picked up the remote and flicked through various game shows featuring hordes of scantily clad women then settled on the news in Italian. The presenter was speaking so quickly you'd have thought he was running from a rabid Rottweiler. Amy couldn't understand a word, although she got a vague idea from the graphics. Each story was punctuated by an appropriate gesture: when the newsreader reported some more bad news from the Middle East he raised his hands to heaven; when he described what must be a train crash in India he tapped his heart in sympathy; when he announced that starlet Justina Maguire was in town for the premiere of her film, *The Apple Cart*, co-starring Hal Blackstock, he kissed his fingers in appreciation of her beauty.

She looked at her bedside clock. Just after eight. She could run a bath and lie in it for hours and then go to bed. Catch up on sleep. God knows, she needed to do that. She lay in the foamy water until her toes wrinkled, but when she got into bed she couldn't sleep, not surprisingly as it was only just after nine — or eight British time. She tossed and turned. She tried three different pillows from the ones in her wardrobe, but

46

none worked. She tried to count sheep but her mind kept flicking to Mum and Dad and their hurt. Come on, she told herself, Madonna's slept in this bed. And Richard Gere. And Victoria Beckham.

That made her feel a bit queasy.

Out of nowhere, Tommaso's voice floated into her head. "We have a beautiful leisure centre with sauna, steam room, hydrotherapy pool. Is in the basement."

OK, she'd follow the advice she always gave patients when they came to her moaning they couldn't sleep. Do some hard exercise. Physically exhaust yourself. Sex, of course, was ideal, but Amy was never going to have sex again. She grabbed the red and black bikini Gaby had persuaded her to buy as part of her trousseau, pulled the hotel robe around her and set off for the basement.

CHAPTER
SEVEN

Hal was still edgy. He'd spent the whole afternoon watching golf on Eurosport and flicking through the pile of magazines on the table. He was in the middle of the thirteenth when Vanessa arrived to talk him through the schedule for the next few days.

"Oh dear," he said, laughing with a lightness he didn't feel. "I've lost my touch."

"I'm sorry?"

"I'm bloody number forty-seven. Outrageous!"

"What are you talking about?"

He held up a copy of *People* magazine.

"The world's fifty sexiest men issue," he declaimed in a mock-American accent. "I'm sure I did better than this last year."

"You were number eleven last year," Vanessa confirmed, as if Hal didn't know.

"Bloody Hugh Grant. Ralph Fiennes. Jude — sodding — Law! They're all higher up than me." He kept his tone mocking. Because it was all a joke this fame malarkey, anyway. Everyone knew that. Lists and awards and whatever didn't matter one iota. Though it was annoying that the women's list, which had come out a month ago, had placed Marina at nine (a giant

48

leap from last year's twenty-seven) and Flora at fifteen (no change).

"The others have had a much higher profile than you this year," Vanessa reassured him. "Hugh had a movie out and so did Ralph."

"So did I," he reminded her.

"Yes, but . . ." Ha! Now she was at a loss for words. Even Vanessa couldn't argue that *The Apple Cart* actually counted as a movie; it was just something he'd done as a favour for his old Cambridge mate Ben Balanton who desperately needed to raise a few grand to pay his third wife's alimony (though Ben hadn't bloody returned the favour, refusing to show up to the Italian gig, saying he had to take his fourth wife on holiday), not to mention placating Hal's parents who had made a few gentle comments about the fact that since he didn't seem to be working much at the moment perhaps he should start helping Flora with a few of her charity projects.

Hal's parents liked Flora. Well, maybe "liked" was too strong a word. Flora wasn't exactly the cosy, daughter-in-law type, but she'd been very polite about Mum's seafood risotto, even though two-thirds of the evil carbs ended up in Hal's pocket. But these days Hal suspected his parents wouldn't mind if he came home with a one-eyed Hungarian shot-putting champion, so long as she was fertile. For the Blackstocks couldn't have cared less about his film career so desperate were they for grandchildren. Grandchildren, which, annoyingly, were his sole responsibility to produce since his brother Jeremy, a lecturer in particle physics, lived with his hairdresser boyfriend, Stan, in Minneapolis.

"It's time for your workout, Hal," Nessie said, smoothly avoiding the question of *The Apple Cart*. "Signor Ducelli's going to escort you to the leisure complex."

"Oh God. I don't know if I'm in the mood for a workout now."

Vanessa's expression didn't even flicker. "Shall I tell them you've changed your mind?"

"No, no," he said sulkily. "It's fine. I'll go." Though Hal wasn't entirely sure this was a great idea. He could feel that spot again, pressing against his T-shirt. Maybe it wasn't a good idea to expose it to chlorinated water or to the world at large for that matter. It was the kind of thing a paparazzo hiding in the drainage system would snap with his long lens and then *Heat* would be full of close-ups saying "Hal has a pimple". Then some medic would spot it in his daughter's copy and exclaim, "Hang on, this is no pimple, it's a life-threatening tumour . . ." He would contact Hal via Callum, his agent, and . . .

"Anything else you need for this evening?" Nessie was asking. "Shall I order you some dinner in the room? Or do you want to go out? The concierge has made provisional reservations at a few restaurants."

Go out. Once that was automatically what he would have done. Got the concierge and Nessie and the local film PR to put together a crowd of the foxiest babes in town and hit a restaurant, followed by a club. Take one, or maybe two of them back to the hotel. But now Flora was in his life this option was closed, the paps would snap him leaving with some bird and the next day he'd be all over the gossip mags and there would be hell to pay.

"No, I won't go out. Order me a meal. Pizza or something. And find out if there's any football or cricket on."

"No problem, Hal," she said. Behind her the suite's doorbell ding-donged. "Ah. That'll be Ducelli."

So after Hal had changed into his tracksuit, Ducelli, who was as smooth as one of his hotel's body lotions, escorted him to the leisure centre in the basement.

"I 'ope you are enjoying your stay in Rome, Mr Blackstock. Just remember, if there is anything we can do to make your stay more enjoyable you need only ask. We can arrange a tour of some of the monuments, perhaps. You can go by night, if you are worried about the attention from the public. Or we can provide you with a Vespa, if you wish to tour on your own. The helmet provides good anonymity. Mr Pitt tried this option last time he stayed here and he very much enjoyed it."

"Oh yes. And which suite did Mr Pitt stay in?" Hal didn't really care but he wanted to tease the man.

Ducelli looked embarrassed. "Ah. He was in the Popolo suite. But unfortunately for you, this time, it was already reserved."

"I know. By honeymooners. Very sweet. Surely you could find a way to move them on. This is Italy, after all." He put on his best Al Pacino voice. "Mak a dem an offer dey can't refuse. A horse's head in da bed. That'll sort 'em out."

Ducelli laughed weakly. "I'm so sorry, sir. It is completely impossible. I hope you understand." He unlocked the door to the spa complex and led Hal through the reception area to the gym, where he gestured around the empty room. "It's officially closed now. No one to disturb you during your workout. And afterwards if you wish you may have a dip in the hydrotherapy pool. I will lock the door behind you, so no one else can come in. Here is a key. Spend as long as you like here. Enjoy it."

Once Ducelli had gone, Hal pulled up his sweatshirt and examined his chest. The spot was still throbbing; he could swear its pus-filled eye was winking at him. It was just a bloody pimple; he should have got Nessie to run out for some Clearasil or its Italian equivalent. He'd call her when he got back up to the room and get her on the case. He climbed on the treadmill. Five miles, he decided. That would be plenty of exercise for one day. Hal's life was a constant battle between laziness and vanity. Usually vanity won, but he hated the idea of anyone knowing that he actually had to work to keep his pecs in shape. Ever since boarding school, when he'd spent prep time horsing around and annoying the monitors, making up for it with secret study sessions with a torch after lights out, Hal had been obsessed with coming top without breaking the slightest sweat.

As he jogged, his mind drifted to Flora, in her hotel room in Jamaica, reading the girls a story, then nibbling on a salad, before settling down for the night with a volume of Proust. Unlike him, Flora didn't see what was embarrassing about self-improvement. It was hardly that she came across as a bimbo, despite her looks. She had an impeccable, upper-east-side, first-off-the-Mayflower, background; her dad (now dead) had been a distinguished theatre director and her mother (still alive and a pain in the behind) had been a very successful stage actress until she gave it all up to sit on the boards of various charities.

Flora had been to the smartest boarding school in America and would have gone to Harvard, were it not for a friend of the family offering her the role of Ophelia in a new film of *Hamlet*. She'd got an Oscar nomination for that and had been acting ever since, with the odd break to marry Pierre, pop out her pretty children, and do good works in the developing (not "third", you weren't allowed to call it that any more) world.

She and Hal met at a dinner party held by Mitch Weldon, a pop star, who'd been around for ever and knew everyone and had no idea how to spend his billions except on entertaining other superstars. Hal was a year out of his relationship with Marina. In fact, she'd just that week taken up with that tosser Fabrizio de Michelis, while Flora had recently divorced, amid rumours of Pierre's womanizing (annoyingly, she'd never told Hal *exactly* what had gone wrong). She was only thirty, with her first Oscar just under her belt for her part as a speech-impaired aid worker, and was the most eligible divorcee imaginable. The world was agog to see who she would hook up with next.

From the moment Hal heard she was on the guest list, he decided it would be him.

He was delighted when Mitch sat them next to each other at dinner and only slightly taken aback when instead of wanting to bitch about Madonna's latest album she engaged him straight away in an argument about third- (sorry, *developing*-) world debt, an argument which Hal had been ill-equipped to engage in. A week after the dinner he'd got Nessie to phone Flora's assistant and ask her out for dinner. She'd said no, she was en-route to a tour of Siberia, to publicize the threat of global warming on the permafrost.

For a while, the whole thing was forgotten; he was having excellent sex with a very pretty Slovakian lapdancer. Then one day out of the blue Nessie announced Flora's assistant had called inviting him to a fundraising ball for one of the charities she devoted so much of her time to. He'd gone, he'd sat next to her, he'd read up on developing-world debt and managed to impress her and two months later they slept together.

It was the longest anyone had ever kept Hal waiting, ever since Marianne Powers from the girls' school had refused to let him get to third base for fear of being thought a slut. It made a refreshing change from the starfuckers who normally mobbed him. Although, if he was completely honest, the wait hadn't been entirely worth it. Sex had been surprisingly jerky and awkward. But sex wasn't really the point of him and Flora. Sure, it was important, but everyone knew that in order to enjoy a long-term serious relationship you had to look at the bigger picture.

54

Hal thought about the ring waiting in the safe. He imagined Flora's delighted face when he slipped it on her slender finger. But when it came to imagining when that might be, his vision grew more hazy. He'd sent Vanessa out to buy it from Asprey's a couple of months ago, after a rather upsetting encounter with Marina at an awards ceremony. But next time he'd seen Flora, he'd been coming down with one of his migraines and the time for proposing just wasn't right. And then he'd thought, where was the rush? They'd only been together a year, she was still pretty raw from her divorce. It couldn't be good for her daughters to have their mum hurrying into something new, and her schedule was so busy for the next year he couldn't see how they would fit a wedding in. Plus, he simply couldn't face all the press hoo-ha that would surround an engagement.

But, he thought, as he slowed for a second to draw breath, maybe he was being silly. Maybe he should just get on with it. He was never going to find someone more beautiful, not to mention richer or better connected. And though Hal hated to admit it to himself, it did turn him on that Flora came from this high-class background, that she was on first-name terms with the Kennedys and the Gettys, that she had never had to learn that with cutlery you worked from the outside in, she just *knew*, that she'd grown up in an apartment the size of a small village.

He couldn't help comparing it to Marina's tiny family home in the cul-de-sac in Swindon, where they'd had to sleep on a mattress on the floor of her little sister's room and go downstairs to use the bog, and the family had been agog to know if they'd ever met Jordan and had eaten their dinners in front of the telly with their jaws gaping open. Perhaps Hal was a snob for thinking so, but so be it.

A proposal in Rome, after all, would be pretty fabulous — something to tell the grandchildren. He quickened his pace. Mmm. Having thought about it, maybe it would be better to have the suite with the view of the rooftops. Much better than some garden which you could find anywhere and with everyone on the restaurant terrace gawping up at them. In the morning, he'd get Nessie to put renewed pressure on the honeymooners.

"Agh!"

He'd been so deep in thought, he'd not noticed the StairMaster, which had been slowing, had come to a complete halt, causing him to fall off.

"Damn!" he said from the floor. But nothing was broken or even bruised.

OK. That was a sign he'd done enough exercise for one day. Heaving himself off the floor and pulling off his shorts and T-shirt so he was wearing only his pink flowered boxers, he headed across the corridor to the spa area. He opened the door of the steam room and stepped into a hot, dense cloud that made everything invisible. His nostrils filled with the smell of eucalyptus. He groped his way to the wooden bench, lay down and exhaled deeply.

"Waagh."

Rivulets of sweat ran down his skin.

"Ooof."

In his stomach, a bubbling tube of gas began to writhe downwards through his intestines and towards his bowel. Must be the cannellini beans he'd had for lunch. Hal always found the sensation strangely pleasurable. He lifted his left buttock and let rip noisily.

"Woorgh. Better out than in."

It was what he and Jeremy had always said to each other, tucked up in their twin beds in the converted attic of their semi in Didcot. The memory made him laugh. Oh, another one was coming.

Paaaarp. Even Hal was a bit taken aback by its loudness. But as the decibels died away, he heard another sound. A giggle. Soft. But a definite giggle.

"Hello?" he said, sitting bolt upright, his hand automatically flying over his spot. "Who's that?"

A woman's voice spoke through the steam. English. Youngish.

"Sorry. I didn't mean to give you a fright."

"Bloody hell," Hal said. "I thought I was alone."

"Sorry," she said again. "I came down for a swim, but the pool turned out to be a giant jacuzzi, so I've been in here for ages. Think I fell asleep. I feel like a prune."

Through the mist he could vaguely see her now, sitting up. Dark hair piled on her head. A flushed, red face. A red and black bikini concealing rather fabulous breasts.

He lay back on the wooden slats, but he could hear her breathing. It unnerved him. This was a real-life woman, rather than a movie star or a model. Apart from make-up girls and stylists, Hal hadn't been in contact with an ordinary member of the public for more than a decade. It was a bit like sharing a steam room with a Martian, probably not dangerous, but nonetheless unnerving.

"So," he said awkwardly, "are you having a nice time in Rome?"

"Yes, thank you," she said. "Are you?"

"No, not really." She must know who he was, but he guessed he'd better play the false modesty card. "I'm an actor, you see, here to promote one of my films and it's terribly dull."

"I know who you are," she said. "You tried to swap suites with me. Or rather your assistant did."

A light went on in Hal's head. "So *you're* the honeymooner?"

"Yes," she said after the tiniest pause.

"The one who turned Vanessa down?"

"That's right."

Hal peered at her through the steam. Clearly this was a once-in-a-lifetime experience for her. It had to be worth a shot. He lowered his voice and fluttered his eyelashes at her, his classic cute British fop pose. It never failed.

"Listen. Are you sure you wouldn't be willing to swap? You see, it would really mean a lot to me. My girlfriend's coming out in a couple of days and she always stays in your suite. It would be so fearfully, fearfully kind of you. And I'd make it up to you. How about VIP tickets for you and your husband to the premiere of my movie on Wednesday? And to the after-show party too. It'll be frightfully glamorous. You'd really enjoy it."

"No, thank you."

Hal was shocked. People very rarely said no to him.

"Are you sure? I think you'd find it terribly exciting. And my suite really is jolly nice. It's got two Picasso lithographs."

The woman stood up. "Well if your suite's jolly nice, then I'm sure your girlfriend will be perfectly happy in it. Just as I am perfectly happy in my suite. So, please, don't ask me again, OK?"

She pushed open the door. A whole load of steam whooshed out. Her face was all red and flushed, her mascara had smudged under her eyes. Nonetheless, Hal noted, she had fantastic legs.

"Enjoy the rest of your stay," she said.

"Um, you won't be able to leave," Hal said. "The door's locked and I have the key."

"Well, hand it over."

For a silly second, he thought about teasing her, but then he relented. He handed her the key he'd been clutching in his sweaty palm.

"Leave it in the door," he said.

"I will," she said, and left the steam room, leaving him alone and steaming on the bench.

CHAPTER
EIGHT

Back in the suite, Amy still found sleep elusive. The pool, though beautiful, hadn't been for swimming, which was a big disappointment. Amy loved swimming; she too rarely had the time for it, but when she did she found the rhythm of the strokes and her breathing could take her to a meditative state where any problem — from Doug's latest behaviour to whether she had just misdiagnosed a breech baby — could be calmly gauged and sorted. After a swim she could have returned to bed, her mind flushed of debris. But now she was agitated, not only by the events of the past week but by her encounter with Hal Blackstock himself, who had turned out not only to be flatulent but also — and Amy guessed this was no surprise — a patronizing prick.

She wished she could tell Doug about it. She picked up her phone, pressed D on her contacts list and was rewarded by her favourite picture of him asleep on her Heal's sofa, one hand resting on his chest the other flung behind his head in a gesture of abandonment. The temptation to call was overwhelming. Somehow she resisted. Where would it get her? They'd agreed on a cooling-off period; begging him to reconsider would

60

only aggravate things. Anyway, Amy didn't think Doug would change his mind.

Doug, Doug, Doug. She thought about how they'd met three years ago on a wet March night. Amy was thirty-one. Having finally finished her medical training, she'd found a job as a GP at an inner-city practice in Islington. Partly she loved it — the variety of patients in the catchment area was extraordinary, from City bankers with stress hernias to Bangladeshi teenagers with not a word of English but two children and another on the way. But part of her found it gruelling. Amy had read about urban poverty and deprivation, but had no idea how it would actually feel to visit a family of six living in a two-bedroom flat on the sixteenth floor with damp walls and a crack den next door and how infuriated she'd feel when, after suggesting to the parents they should stop smoking to save money and their health, they told her to mind her own business.

Still, job stress apart, Amy had the perfect life she'd dreamed of as a little girl growing up in a small seaside town. Having paid off her student loan, she immediately got herself on the property ladder. Her one-bedroom flat in Clissold Park was her pride and joy even though she had no spare cash or energy to turn it into the dream pad she'd promised herself. What money she did have she liked to spend on exotic holidays, nice clothes and going out virtually every night of the week.

Not only was her career on track, on paper her love life was perfect as well. She'd been with Danny since her final year at Edinburgh, they'd moved to London together and he was now a senior house officer doing general surgical training at a teaching hospital. Danny was everything a girl could wish for: successful, reliable, kind. Not bad-looking, although a little uninspiring in bed. He played rugby every weekend and mended Amy's guttering. Amy's parents adored him. They had been together for eight years and everyone wondered when they were going to get married — it seemed weird enough that they weren't living together. In fact, Danny had been suggesting it ever since they moved to London, but Amy had always said where was the rush, living apart made their time together more special and anyway, he worked in south London, while she was north. When the day came, they'd find somewhere in the middle.

She never said, even to herself, that when she contemplated that day she felt like she'd heard a nail going into her coffin.

Over the past — what, three, four, five years? — Amy had fallen out of love with Danny. She found his habit of blowing his nose in his underpants revolting and the way he always fussed over who got the biggest portion at dinner pathetic. She was bored by his rugby crowd with their simpering wives and girlfriends who seemed to think there was no greater way to spend a Saturday than shivering on a freezing touchline. She was relieved that at least twice a week, he did a night shift and she was therefore free to do exactly what she liked with her friends, without worrying that he'd show her up by coming out in his jeans jacket with Led Zep embroidered across the back.

In fact, she'd begun despising him to the point where she deliberately wore nasty knickers when she knew she was seeing him — who cared what Danny thought? — and made no effort to do exciting things together, instead using him as a human pillow to snooze on while watching reality television. He was a comfort blanket, but one she had outgrown. She'd even started hoping he'd let her off the hook by getting an unturndownable job in New Zealand or meeting someone else. At the back of her mind, Amy knew she was behaving badly in not knocking their relationship on the head. But she just didn't have the nerve. He would be devastated and she also secretly feared that she'd never find anyone else who would adore her as much.

But on that March night, things were finally coming to a head. Danny and Amy had just returned from a holiday in California. Amy had been looking forward to it, hoping it might revive their romance. But pretty much from day one it had been a disaster. They'd had a few fun days in LA, staying with an old friend, but Danny had had such bad jet lag that he kept insisting they leave cool spots like the Skybar and the Viper Lounge at 10p.m., which infuriated her. He'd made her even madder in Las Vegas, where he insisted they only stayed one night because he wanted to press on to San Francisco, where he'd spent his gap year between school and uni.

When they drove through the empty desert, he enraged her by insisting on sticking to the speed limit of 40 mph. Then she annoyed him by taking the wheel, going straight up to 90 mph and immediately getting flagged down by a police car that had picked them up on the radar. Then he wanted to pass through Death Valley as rapidly as possible when Amy wanted to stay at least a night. The worst had come fifty miles from Yosemite when they had a seemingly innocuous discussion about what they fancied for dinner.

"I'm in the mood for Chinese, what do you think?" Amy said.

Danny's mouth set like Charlie Brown's. "I don't want Chinese. I fancy a big dessert. Chinese places don't do dessert."

This inoffensive remark made Amy burst into hysterical tears. She cried all the way to the next motel where a worried Danny had to hustle her through the lobby and run her a bath where she cried more and more and more as the impossibility of their future crystallized before her. By the time she'd finished crying the restaurant was closed and no Chinese or dessert was available at all. Somehow they limped through the rest of the fortnight, but the last vestiges of hope had died. They had sex once. It was over in three minutes. Amy knew she had to end things soon, but she still couldn't quite find the courage.

Anyway, on that Friday night, she and Gaby had gone to see a new band called Ambrosial in a church hall in Southgate. They were there because Pinny, Amy's flatmate when she first moved to London, was the lead singer. Pinny and Amy had hooked up via an

Internet ad and from day one had hit it off when they discovered a mutual fondness for partying.

Pinny was very different to Gaby. Gaby was blonde and bosomy with hangups about her weight and a fondness for Estée Lauder and wrap dresses. Pinny was effortlessly skinny (well, not effortlessly, the fact that she hardly ate helped, but she genuinely didn't see the point of eating when she could be smoking Marlboro). She wore faded little T-shirts, no bra and jeans that accentuated her ice-cream scoop of a stomach with its diamanté belly ring. Although she didn't look girly, her behaviour could be shamelessly so — she was for ever running her fingers through strange men's hair in order to get them to give her cigarettes and answering the door to the TV licence man in a flimsy camisole, leaving him so taken aback, he let her off the thousand-pound fine.

Pinny's approach to life was utterly carefree. She'd fluffed her A levels, since when she'd had a variety of jobs from barmaid to anthropologist's assistant. As soon as she got bored, she moved on. It helped that her dad was the chairman of a bank and she had a substantial trust fund to fall back on, so work would always be a hobby rather than a dreary necessity. She had the same attitude to love. While Gaby fretted about finding Mr Right, Pinny simply enjoyed a procession of much older and much younger men. There'd been a lord and a sailor from HMS *Beaver* (he gave Pinny a pair of knickers with the ship's name embroidered on them), an Ethiopian minicab driver and a Chinese-American graduate student called David Moo, who had an alarm clock shaped like a cow, which cried, "Moo, moo, get up!"

Amy and Pinny had a lot of fun together, even though Pinny did have a rather disconcerting habit of wandering about their flat in knickers and a vest whenever Danny was around, not to mention a tendency to denigrate Amy's work with remarks like, "Do you really think you should be prescribing so many antibiotics? Why don't you tell your patients to try crystals?" But she had a good heart and a confidence Amy admired. Pinny believed that somehow she'd get by — and she always did. For all her outwardly hedonistic attitude, Amy could never have been so laid back. Whenever they found themselves at a party in some godforsaken spot like Ongar, it was always Amy who fretted about how they'd find a taxi home, while Pinny would laugh and say something would turn up, and it always did (usually in the form of some guy whose knee she'd sat on offering them a lift in his BMW). Pinny would never have stuck with Danny out of inertia and fear; she'd have long moved on to the next adventure.

Gaby wasn't a fan of Pinny's, considering her a flake and a flirt, but since she had no better offer that night she'd consented to come and see the band. So there they were, sipping flat beer from plastic cups and waiting for Ambrosial to come on stage. Amy was sceptical. Pinny had a good voice and she certainly looked rock 'n' roll with her shock of bleached blonde hair and springy frame, but could she really be any good? Surely this was just another of Pinny's hobbies which would last about a week before she decided she was better suited to professional skydiving.

Having agreed to this, Amy told Gaby about the holiday.

"It was just awful, Gaby. I don't know what to do. I'm thinking of maybe finding a job with an aid organization in Africa because we can't go on like this."

"Oh dear," Gaby said, but before she could give any concrete advice, the band ran out, forty-five minutes late.

"About time." Gaby tutted. "Why is it only gigs that never start on time? I mean, when you go to a play they don't keep you waiting for hours while the actors have another spliff backstage."

Her rant was interrupted by four loud chords from a bass guitar. And then Pinny started to sing.

Amy was transfixed. Pinny was a sex vixen, writhing and gyrating while crooning tunefully into the microphone. The audience was going mad, leaping up and down, holding out their hands so she could touch them. The songs were fantastic: catchy, sharp, punky but with an undercurrent of pop. But Amy's first concern wasn't the music. Most of her attention was on the lead guitarist who was tall, with a bullish neck, cropped brown hair and a perfect set of teeth. Amy found him extremely attractive. Nor was she alone, judging by the coterie of teenage girls clustered around his corner of the stage, who screamed every time he moved his rather chunky body.

"They're fantastic," she bellowed in Gaby's ear.

"They're not bad," Gaby acknowledged, grudgingly.

They were on for forty minutes, then did two encores. Afterwards, a sweaty, triumphant Pinny made her way to the bar, followed by the other band members. Amy's eyes followed the guitarist and his fan club, who, with much giggling, crowded round him.

"You were amazing," she could hear them saying. "You're gorgeous." "We love you."

"Wow," she said with genuine enthusiasm to Pinny. "You must feel like a goddess."

"It was fun," Pinny agreed. "God, get me a pint someone. I'm gasping."

"A diva already," Gaby said under her breath, before saying aloud. "You must be so pleased to have found something you really enjoy. At last."

"Yeah," said Pinny, either not getting or ignoring the sarcasm. "I am. Though this is only a hobby for now. All the boys have day jobs, except Hank, our manager. None of us can make a living from doing it full time. Hey, let me introduce you."

"Oh, whenever," Amy said, blushing. She was oddly unwilling to meet the guitarist, knowing she would be too shy to utter more than a few platitudes. But Pinny insisted, and so she found herself shaking hands with Gregor the bassist, Baz the drummer and finally, Doug the lead guitarist and songwriter.

"You were great," she managed, ignoring the leggy sixteen-year-old who was flamboyantly flicking her long blonde curls just behind her.

"You think?" Doug seemed genuinely pleased. He had a faint, rather sexy Scottish accent. "I messed up a bit on 'My Mum's an Alien'. Did you notice?"

"Not at all," said Amy truthfully, wondering what it would be like to kiss him.

He asked Amy how she knew Pinny and what she did. "I'm a GP," she said, a little embarrassed. "What about you? When you're not playing the guitar."

"Oh, I'm a dull professional." He smiled. "A solicitor. Very, very boring. But a GP! That means you must be seriously clever."

"Oh no, no, no," muttered Amy, who heard this all the time. "Just need a strong stomach for blood and guts and the details of people's toilet habits."

"And was that what you always wanted to do?"

"I always wanted to help people, yes." Actually this wasn't strictly true. Amy hadn't known what she wanted to do, but she'd been unfashionably good at science at school, and her mother and father had almost expired with joy when her careers advisor suggested medicine, so here she was.

"That's great," Doug said. "I've been writing songs since I was a little boy. Always wanted to be in a band, but my dad wouldn't let me. Said I had to go to uni first, get a sensible degree. And I thought I could always get a degree *and* be in a band and when I graduated I had massive debts so I decided I might as well become a lawyer. Pay the bills. Do the music on the side. But now Ambrosial's starting to get a following, I'm beginning to wonder if I shouldn't devote myself full time to it. Follow my dream."

"We should all follow our dreams," said Amy, though she wasn't actually talking about Doug, but about her urgent need to brush away the lock of hair that had fallen over his left eye.

"You're so right," Doug said, as a middle-aged, grey-haired man, who Amy took for the church hall's vicar, approached. "Amy, this is Hank, our manager. Hank, Pinny's friend, Amy." Hank and Amy smiled and shook hands.

"So was there anyone in the audience tonight?" Doug asked, a little strangely since he could have hardly failed to notice the hundred or so enraptured fans.

Hank pulled a face as he nodded at a short man in a yellow sweatshirt talking to one of the prettier girls. "Matt Rees from Convex. But we all know he's a twat. Just comes to pull birds. Only acts he's interested in are James Blunt clones he can make a quick buck on." He turned to Amy. "Anything a little bit different, a bit edgy, you can forget. None of the record companies will take a punt on anything original. It's so unfair."

"So unfair," Doug agreed. Amy could never have predicted how many times she'd hear that phrase in the years to come.

"The people with genuine talent just get passed over," Hank said.

"So unfair," Amy said and the men turned and nodded at her in approval.

"*She* gets it." Hank smiled.

Doug smiled too. "Can I buy you a drink?" he said and Amy's stomach turned over with a mixture of delight and guilt as she caught Gaby eyeing her suspiciously. She prayed Pinny would have the sense not to ask her what Danny was doing that night.

70

CHAPTER
NINE

Amy woke disoriented, her bleeping phone interrupting a vivid dream about losing her bride's garter in a swimming pool. On instant red alert, like some crack SAS team member, she crawled across the Gobi Desert of her bed and snatched the handset from the table. He'd cracked. He was calling to say he couldn't live without her and he wanted ten children and a guinea pig.

Danny
Heard your news. Bad luck. Let me know if I can help in any way. Thinking of you. x

Why did he always have to be such a gentleman? His nobility made her feel so much, much worse. She rolled back on the bed, those ever-present tears welling up again.

"Stop crying, you wussy," she barked, in her scary Sergeant Foley voice from *An Officer and a Gentleman*. "Pull yourself together."

She opened her curtains to see the Piazza del Popolo bathed in sunshine. At least the weather had improved. She'd shower and then go down to breakfast, which was included in the room rate. Thank goodness, because Amy was starving and she'd already checked out the room-service option: sixteen euros for coffee and a croissant. In the shower, she spent a couple of minutes trying to work out the controls, still managing to spray boiling lava straight into her eyes. Then, having not pulled the curtain properly, she ended up drenching the floor. Eventually she dressed in shorts and a T-shirt, wincing as the cotton brushed against her already peeling shoulders. Finally, she took the lift downstairs.

Breakfast was on the dining terrace; a uniformed woman greeted her.

"Signora," she said pleasantly, "your room number?"

"I'm in the Popolo suite."

The woman's eyebrows circumflexed. It must have been the first time in the history of the hotel that the occupant of a suite had come down to mingle with the proles.

"Ah. So a table for two?"

"No. No. Just . . . one of me. My husband isn't hungry."

"Of course." She gestured to a waiter and gabbled something. Probably along the lines of, "This woman is a loser, who's trying to delude us all she's married."

"Signora," he said, with a follow-me gesture and — in Amy's paranoid mind — a vaguely pitying look. Amy followed him across the terrace, past glamorous couple, glamorous couple and glamorous couple, to the very far corner. She was sure everyone was looking at her, wondering what someone so obviously not a member of the international jet set was doing there.

"Tea, coffee?" he asked as Amy sat down.

"Oh, coffee please. And maybe some toast?"

He gestured indoors. "There is the buffet. It has everything you need."

"Oh. OK."

So Amy had to make the walk of shame back across the terrace, convinced that every eye was upon her. Her eyes swivelled gently from side to side, checking out her fellow guests. As well as glamorous couples, there were perfect families, with blonde mummies, handsome daddies and perfectly behaved children in Junior Dior T-shirts. She felt like a leper.

She cheered up a bit when she saw the buffet. Every possible kind of food was laid out: cheeses, cold meat, fruit, yoghurt, smoked salmon, cereals, loads of yummy-looking cakes, various breads. Her stomach let out a little grumble. She wasn't doing the walk again, so she needed to work out how much she could pile on one plate. She started with some strawberries and grapes, added a chunk of bread, then a couple of slices of ham. Oh, and how about a Danish? And here under a silver dome were scrambled eggs and bacon and mushrooms. Amy loved a cooked breakfast. After months of dieting, it was time to let rip. She began loading her already full plate.

"Someone must be hungry," said a cool voice behind her. She turned round. There in cream slacks and a blue cashmere T-shirt was Vanessa. Her plate bore three grapes.

"I didn't eat much yesterday," Amy said hastily.

"Of course not," Vanessa said. "Any more thoughts about the swap?"

So she didn't know about the steam-room encounter. "Yes. I'm going to stay where I am."

"Fine. Shame you won't go to the premiere party. But then I guess you and your *husband* will have other things to do." Her long neck craned around the room. "Where is he?"

"He's not feeling very well this morning," Amy said vaguely. She nodded at Vanessa. "Bye, then."

"Goodbye. Enjoy the rest of your *honeymoon*."

Shaken by the encounter, Amy was only mildly cheered by breakfast. The ham was delicious, the pastry exquisite, the eggs slightly runny, just the way she liked them. She wasn't sure she had room for the rest of the food on her plate. But she didn't have to eat it all now. Perhaps she could take some away with her for later, solving the problem of having to buy expensive meals? Bugger, if only she'd brought a handbag down with her. But there was always her huge, white linen napkin. Glancing around to make sure no one was looking, she put a couple of slices of smoked salmon, some rye bread, some slices of kiwi, a pot of yoghurt and a large ball of buffalo mozzarella into it and folded it up. Now she could make sandwiches in the room and she'd no longer have to suffer the ordeal of being ripped off in dodgy cafés.

She finished her coffee and looked around again. The terrace was emptying now, just a few couples left. Sure she was unscrutinized, Amy rapidly tied a knot in the napkin, then shoved it under her top. She got up slowly and, one hand on her belly, headed towards the stairs.

"Hello!"

It was Marian from yesterday, nodding and waving from her corner table. Beside her, Roger sat staring gloomily into a pot of yoghurt.

"How are you?" Marian cried eagerly, beckoning her over.

Hand still placed firmly on her stomach, Amy moved slowly towards them. "Hi!" she said brightly.

"How's the honeymoon?" Marian asked. "Sorry, did you tell us your name?"

"Amy," she said as Marian threw up her hands in delight and pointed at the bump in her stomach.

"Oh, hello! I didn't notice yesterday. Congratulations."

"Shotgun wedding, was it, huh?" Roger chortled, suddenly looking much happier.

"Er. Yes. Ha. Ha. Well, you know . . ."

"I did wonder when I spotted you pigging out at the buffet," Marian said. "So when's it due?"

"Christmas?" Amy tried.

"Really?" Marian's long forehead crinkled as she did the maths. "You look further gone than that. I used to be a midwife, so I know a thing or two about all this."

"Maybe it's twins." Roger smirked.

"Rog!" Marian smacked his hand hard. "So where's your husband, Amy?"

"Oh, he's . . . gone back up to the room. Had to make a work call."

"Men! They're always so busy." She smiled at Amy, woman to woman. "It's all I can do to keep Roger away from that blessed mobile of his. And the computer! Always checking the cricket scores or what have you."

"Yes, well . . ." Amy looked around, urgently trying to extricate herself. "See you later. Have a lovely day."

She continued her pregnant walk across the terrace, down the steps, through the lobby to the lift. She pressed the button and the doors slid open. She stepped in and watched them close.

"Wait! Wait!" yelled a very loud male voice. It was nasty Mr Doubleday from yesterday approaching. Amy searched for the button to hold the doors open but couldn't find it.

"Wait, I said!"

He stuck out his arm and the doors stopped in their tracks, then opened again.

"Well, thanks for your help," he snapped, stepping in. He was followed by a woman, much younger, with a round, pretty face, long hair that was perhaps a couple of shades too blonde for her skin tone, velour tracksuit pants that showed off a pert bottom, a strip of brown tummy and a top that Amy had seen in Chloé during the epic hunt for wedding shoes. She smiled at Amy apologetically.

"Sorry!" Amy said, as the doors slid shut again like curtains at the end of a first act. "I did try."

"Three, press three," he said impatiently, leaning over her to reach the controls. His elbow nudged Amy and, with a crash, her stash rolled out from under her T-shirt and fell on the lift floor.

"Bloody hell, have you got some kind of eating disorder?" he asked, as the lift pinged open at the third floor.

"Just taking some food up to my husband," Amy said, kneeling down to grab a squashed Danish and various pieces of ham. The woman bent over too and passed her a dirty-looking bread roll.

"Come on, Lisa, this is our floor," he said, virtually pulling her through the doors. They shut, and before Amy could stop them, the lift started zooming down. She was still on her knees as the doors reopened and Vanessa stepped in.

"Oh, hello, you again," she said with a smirk. She looked at the food in Amy's arms. "Still hungry are we?"

"Just taking some food up to my husband," Amy repeated.

"There is such a thing as room service," Vanessa said crisply, as the doors opened at the fourth floor. "Enjoy your little picnic," she added, leaving Amy fuming.

CHAPTER
TEN

Like Amy, Hal was woken by his bedside phone ringing.

"Oh, fucking hell, fuck off. Who the fuck is it?" He grabbed the handset. "Yes?"

"Morning, Hal." Vanessa's voice was as smooth as alabaster. "How are you doing?"

"Fine until you woke me up."

"Sorry about that," she said insincerely. "But the first round-table interview starts in an hour. And breakfast's on the way up. It'll be with you in five. I'll be along in half an hour to brief you."

He hung up, then lay back on the pillow thinking through the events of last night. Oh, bloody hell. Who was that girl he'd farted in front of? She claimed to be a honeymooner but she was probably an undercover reporter on the phone to the *News of the Screws* right now, exposing his wind problem. Not that it was a laughing matter. Maybe he had something serious. Like bowel cancer. Then he remembered his other problem. He felt his chest. Yes, the spot was still there, even bigger this morning, a volcano of pus emerging from the jungle of his chest hairs. Shit. It should have gone by now. Something was desperately wrong; he knew it.

He could send out for zit cream or he could call in a dermatologist, but Hal wanted to deal with it quicker than that.

The doorbell rang.

"Yeah. Come in." He hauled himself out of bed and pulled on his towelling robe.

A waiter wheeled in a trolley.

"Good morning, Meester Blackstock. 'Ow are you today?"

"Never felt worse," he snapped, but the waiter's blank, uncomprehending expression immediately filled him with remorse.

"I pour your coffee? Or I leave it for you?"

"Oh, pour it for me." Hal always felt faintly ridiculous having minions doing everything for him, like Prince Charles getting someone to squeeze toothpaste onto his brush and holding out a cup for him to wee into. But then again, why not? Fame was a bugger, so he might as well enjoy some of the perks. Talking of which . . .

"You couldn't bring me a bowl of boiling water, could you?" he asked. "And a needle? And some antiseptic cream? And some plasters? And a box of matches?"

The waiter reacted as if he'd asked what the weather was like today. "Needle, antiseptic, plasters, matches," he repeated very carefully. "Why certainly, Mr Blackstock. Just give me ten minutes."

After he left, Hal looked at his breakfast. A mixed platter of tropical fruits, a steaming espresso and a huge freshly squeezed orange juice. Not the most exciting start to the day, but necessary if he was going to keep in good nick. Number forty-seven. How depressing to have slipped so quickly. Of course all this "world's sexiest" stuff was ridiculous but — in a reversal of his and Jeremy's farting gag — it was better to be in than out.

Hal looked around, taking in the stylish furnishings, the plasma screen, the doors leading to the beautiful terrace. He thought back to a time, fifteen years ago, when he would have whooped with delight to have been shown to such a suite. He remembered checking in to the Ritz in Madrid, how he had bounced on the big bed, gone through the channels on the TV, been impressed by the umbrella in the closet. Marina, meanwhile, had been stuffing her bag with mini shampoos and conditioners, then ringing housekeeping and demanding more.

"You'd take anything that wasn't nailed down," he'd teased her.

She nodded in happy agreement. "They're going to think we've won a competition."

Marina. She'd enjoyed the journey so much more than he had. In the States, everyone saw them as this glamorous, upper-crust couple but in fact both of them had come from pretty much nowhere. Hal's background was only marginally smarter than Marina's; he had grown up in Didcot, an armpit of a town in Oxfordshire. His mum was a secretary, while his dad owned a bed shop which had grown to a small chain, allowing him to send his sons to a minor public school.

There the other boys had teased him — "Henry's dad sells beds! Henry's dad sells beds!" — and Henry, as he was known then, had been obscurely ashamed and vowed he would never do such menial work. That aside, however, he'd loved school. He was one of the brightest pupils and undeniably the best-looking. All the birds from the local girl's school had crushes on him and in A-level year he had shagged all the prettiest ones. Even the elusive Marianne Powers had given in to him in the end.

He'd got a place at Cambridge — one of only five the school had managed in the past twenty years. And it was at Cambridge he'd begun to reinvent himself.

He'd seen on day one that the university had two distinct types of students. In the majority were the goody-goody swots from mediocre schools like his who had always done their homework and passed their exams and now intended to pass more exams (though to make their CVs look better they usually embraced some extra-curricular activity like rowing) and get good jobs.

And then there were the beautiful people, the ones who'd been to major public schools, for whom Cambridge was a birthright, not only because their superior genes had endowed them with high IQs but also because their families had had links with their colleges for more than three hundred years. Now they had arrived, they intended to do no work at all. Worrying about something as bourgeois as a career was the height of vulgarity. No, they were here to have parties, host champagne breakfasts, push each other off punts into the river and have as much sex as possible.

These people studied things like English and history of art, they wore cords and open-necked shirts and carried round teddy bears. Henry wanted to be part of that crowd so badly it hurt. There were a few things standing in his way: he was at Girton, which must have been the uncoolest college in the whole university, while the in-crowd all seemed to be at Trinity; and he was reading French and Italian, which wasn't as nerdy as maths or engineering, but was still a bit too serious. Then there was the obstacle that the beautiful people had all been at school together, while Henry's only former schoolmate was Nigel Wilson, who wore an anorak and was big in the real-ale society. But Henry did have one thing in his favour — his looks. Thick, blond hair; huge blue eyes fringed with dark lashes; long, straight nose; full lips and a strong chin, a package that hinted quite falsely at aristocratic stock.

With such an appearance, it wasn't hard to infiltrate the gilded circle — the girls, with their cut-glass accents and perfect skin that spoke of a life of nutritious meals, all wanted to sleep with him, and the guys accepted him as one of them. Henry quietly dropped Nigel and spent so much time at Trinity or in the café near the art-history faculty that soon everyone assumed he belonged there. Quickly, Henry worked on his image. Out went the jeans and sneakers he'd packed, in came a pair of brogues and a tweed jacket from Oxfam. He held traditional tea parties on the Backs — the lawns that led down to the river — serving egg and cress and cucumber sandwiches and Earl Grey. He joined the Claustrophobes, an elite drinking society, with only twelve new members admitted each year, who had an annual dinner where titbits like fried grasshoppers were served and each member was expected to drink until he vomited. He started referring to Mum and Dad as Mummy and Daddy.

Some time in his second year he started acting in university plays — mainly because Jemima Arthur-Hills whom he was going out with at the time was playing Juliet in *Romeo and Juliet* and persuaded him to audition. He didn't get Romeo, that would have been a bit much given his lack of experience, but he did get Mercutio, which was arguably a more interesting part, and the review in the university paper, *Varsity*, raved about him. Hal was struck with the acting bug. He'd never been quite sure who he wanted to be, so it was great to be handed a skin and told to inhabit it. He got parts in several more plays, received more rave reviews and shagged a whole load more cute babes.

Still, acting was never something he took particularly seriously. He assumed that after graduation he'd get a job in banking or management consultancy or one of the other professions his mates mentioned if they absolutely had to discuss anything as vulgar as the world of work.

But then came the third year which language students had to spend abroad. Hal, entranced by visions gleaned from Merchant Ivory films, chose Italy and was offered a place as a language assistant at a state school in Rome. Looking back, it had probably been the best year of his life. He found a tiny attic apartment in Trastevere, the former working-class quarter which was gradually being colonized by wannabe bohemians. In the mornings he taught the kids (all the girls fancied him and gave him little presents and cried at the end of the year when he left). In the afternoons, he taught at Intra-English, a private school which had just won a contract with the military to teach English to all the boys at the local naval station.

That was a hoot. The school was run by a laid-back Scottish woman called Sandra, who had absolutely no interest whatsoever in what the clients learned so long as they paid their bills on time. Each teacher had a textbook, which they went through with the students for about fifteen minutes before both sides got bored and started chatting about football in Italian. Consequently Hal's Italian improved exponentially — and he was paid for it. When they'd exhausted the debate of Lazio versus Roma they'd play cards — hearts or racing demon. Hal insisted they spoke English, so at least all his pupils could say "hearts, spades, joker and jack".

Occasionally he'd feel guilty and would get them to do some reading — usually from an English-language magazine or comic. They were especially fond of *Viz* and soon they could all say "Finnbar Saunders and his double entendres" and "Fat Slags". Hal did worry a bit when years later Italy was among the countries to send troops to Afghanistan — he could just see his boys trying to negotiate with Taliban forces with a vocabulary consisting of Johnny Fartpants and Sid the Sexist.

In the long school holidays, he found work as a tour guide, showing groups of American teenagers round the Holy City. It was a fantastic gig. Every shop or bar you took them into gave you commission and Hal even bought a printing press to mock-up fake admission tickets so he could charge for sights that were actually free. Plus, some of the girls were very cute. Even now, years later, he'd occasionally open the *National Enquirer* to discover some blowsy housewife from Des Moines, Iowa, claiming she'd taken Hal Blackstock's virginity on a hot Italian night.

When he returned to Cambridge after that golden year, everything was a bit different. Most of his mates had graduated and quietly found jobs as trainees in banks. At weekends Hal went to visit them in their shared houses in Clapham and Battersea and didn't like the glimpses he got into their lives at all. Waking at seven every morning, putting on a suit, going into an office on a packed tube, doing whatever it was office people did all day and coming home again. All right, they were earning decent money, but still they were living in boxes. Trapped.

He decided to wait until after finals (in which he got a 2:1 — something he occasionally mentioned in interviews when they went on a bit too much about his talent for "light comedy") before making any decisions. But shortly before the first exam his mate Ben Balanton, who was an aspiring director, said he was taking a play up to Edinburgh for the festival and offered Hal the leading role. Hal accepted; the play was a huge hit and ended up doing a nationwide tour before transferring to a London theatre. Hal found himself an agent and was put up for a number of jobs in TV, theatre and film. Before he knew it, he was an actor with enough work trickling in to make a comfortable and interesting living.

Crucially, he had never really had to struggle. Hal knew himself well enough to know that even a couple of rejections in a row would have made the whole thing seem like way too much hard work and knocked him off course. He was always amazed when he met other actors who wanted work so much they would have knitted a jumper out of their own intestines to get a part. Trying too hard — no, trying at all — was humiliating. But Hal never had more than a month or two unemployed, and if he did get turned down for a part, another one always came up within the next week or so. Anyway, if things didn't always go 100 per cent right it didn't really matter because everyone knew acting wasn't a proper job: it was just dressing up and being paid over the odds for it. Much more attractive than his friends' lives.

Or so he had thought then, Hal reflected ruefully, pouring himself another cup of strong, black coffee. If he'd known what it would be like when he was a household name — the red carpets, the film festivals in obscure towns, the days like today with the back-to-back interviews — he would have applied for every office job going.

Dring went the door and here was the waiter again with his gear, which he no doubt took for drug equipment. Hal tipped him — not quite as generously as he would have liked, but he only had five euros in his pocket — and took the stuff into the bathroom. The spot was now approximately half a centimetre in diameter. For a moment Hal was transported back to the two-up, two-down in Didcot, locked in the bathroom upstairs (amazing to think there'd been only one to serve the whole family), setting to work on the zits that were the only blight of his adolescent years.

He remembered the drill: dip the needle in the boiling water, lay the hot flannel on the pustule for five minutes to soften it up. He took the needle out of the water (he had forgotten rubber gloves and had to wrap his hand in a towel to extract it), lit a match and placed it in the centre of the flame. With a sudden stabbing movement, he jabbed at his chest. There was a brief explosion of pain; gunk gushed out onto the flannel. He washed the wound, dabbed it with Savlon and covered it with a plaster. That should do the trick.

There was another ring at the door.

"Hal," called Vanessa, "they're waiting for you downstairs."

"Yeah, yeah, I know. I'm just getting dressed."

"May I come in, Hal? I'll brief you while you're getting ready."

CHAPTER
ELEVEN

Vanessa was carrying a clipboard.

"Right. This morning we've got a round table with six journalists — four European, one Kiwi, one Japanese, so that shouldn't be too taxing. Then a one-on-one with Italian *Marie Claire*. Then another one-on-one with Christine Miller from the *Daily Post*, plus a photo session afterwards."

"Oh, Christ. Can't I perform open-heart surgery on myself with a rusty instrument instead?"

"No, Hal, you cannot. It'll be fine."

"Have you told them no questions about Flora?"

"I have. But you know they'll ask anyway."

"If they do, I'll walk out."

"No, you won't, Hal. You'll say: 'no comment'."

"Why?" he asked belligerently, pulling on his socks.

"Because if you walk out it'll be headlines all over the world tomorrow. The tabloids'll do a number about how ungracious you are, how you have no sense of humour."

"I don't."

"I'd recommend you behave, Hal. That's all I'm saying. Are you ready now?"

"As ready as I'll ever be."

They left the suite, stepped into the lift and headed four floors down. "It's only going to be twenty minutes," Nessie reassured him.

Hal sighed. In the early days, he'd quite enjoyed the publicity side of the job — the chance to flirt with pretty girl interviewers and say outrageous things. But in recent years, it had become so burdensome. The slightest throwaway remark was seized on and taken out of context, so when he'd joked with some pretty boy from *Attitude* that he fancied Jude Law, it had gone all round the world: "I'm gay!" says Hal. With one homosexual son on her hands already, Mummy had not been amused. But then everything about his job appealed to him less and less these days, not least the fact that, at forty-three, he was growing too old for the boyish comedy heroes he had made his speciality, while the meaty, dramatic parts never came his way, clogging up the letterboxes of Sean Penn and Philip Seymour Hoffman.

Then there was the question of *The Apple Cart*. He'd known from the first page of the script that it was unmitigated horseshit. But he owed Ben for getting his career started. More importantly, it gave him a chance to star next to Justina Maguire, currently Hollywood's hottest property and whom he knew Marina loathed. He took the decision alone, his agent, Callum, was unenthusiastic, even though he was going to pick up 10 per cent. Flora had urged him not to do it. "You have to stay true to your artistic centre," she'd said. But Hal didn't have an artistic centre. Wasn't sure he had any centre, come to that. So he signed on the dotted line.

OK, so the movie might get a pasting, but who cared? He would follow the line of his hero, Michael Caine, who once said of some dud, "I have not seen the film, but I hear it is terrible. However, I have seen the house that it paid for, and it is superb."

But it was one thing to joke about such things with your mates and another to open the papers, as he'd done the day *The Apple Cart* was released in the US, and read the first universally dire reviews of his career. "Blackstock breezes through yet another role as if bored and unconcerned with the film happening around him," was about the best anyone had to say about it. "Unmitigated disaster, Balanton and Blackstock should be ashamed of themselves," was typical. Hal laughed the whole thing off, telling everyone the reviewers were quite right, but inside he'd felt shaky and cold. Why hadn't he listened to Flora? Now he looked a fool. And the worst thing of all was that everyone said there was more sexual chemistry between breakfast TV presenters than between him and Justina. Marina must have read that and laughed.

And now he would have to endure yet another press grilling on why he'd agreed to participate in such a fiasco. *Grit your teeth and bear it, Hal,* he told himself, adding Marina's favourite line, *It's better than wiping bums in an old folks' home.*

Or was it? "I'm going to give up acting soon," he told himself under his breath, as he walked down the corridor to the conference room. "It bores me. Holds no new challenges. Going to get on with my novel. Retrain as something meaningful." He toyed with announcing this to the journalists, but decided against it. Those kind of statements could backfire. Better to present the world with a fait accompli.

They were waiting for him round a table.

"Gosh, gosh. How terribly nice of all of you to come out for boring old me. I can't think why you bothered."

There was a communal titter. Hal relaxed. The old self-deprecation number got 'em every time. He held out his hands in a gesture of humility.

"So? What can I do for you good people?"

An earnest man with thick glasses and a polo neck, who clearly yearned to be writing essays on political deconstructionism for obscure art magazines, rather than asking stars what perfume they wore, leaned forward.

"Thomas Schlieffer. German *Glamour*. Mr Blackstock, in your view, is Ben Balanton's approach to movie-making best described as post-modern or is it more of the *nouvelle vague* variety?"

He pushed his tape recorder under Hal's nose and nodded eagerly.

"Ben?" Hal said, sitting back in his chair and looking at the assembled gathering. "His approach to movie-making? I'd say it was more of 'The studio's written me an enormous cheque let's just get this piece of crap made' approach." He bared his teeth and smiled at the assembled company. Half of them chuckled sycophantically, the other half looked utterly baffled.

"Is he really so cynical?" said the German, looking as if he'd just heard his home had been flattened by a hurricane.

Hal glanced at Nessie sitting in the corner. Imperceptibly she shook her head. OK. Time to stop arsing around and play it safe. "Sorry, guys, I was only joking. That was off the record. Ben is a wonderful artist. Working with him was a marvellous experience. And not just with him. I mean, the whole cast and crew were so great, so professional and funny. We really had a lot of laughs. And I think this is the best thing Ben has done in quite a few years."

"You don't think it's a bit of a comedown from work like *Analyse Love* to making a film about a farmer and his Alsatian?" a toothy middle-aged woman asked. She was ugly and completely right. Hal hated her.

"And you are?" he snapped.

"Helena de Moretti. Italian *Vogue*."

"Italian? Don't you want to ask me about my time in Italy as a student?"

"No, thank you."

Hal ignored her. "It's great to be back here. I lived in Rome for a year when I was twenty. One of the happiest times of my life. I drove a Vespa, lived in an attic in Trastevere, taught English, learned to cook —"

"Did you have a girlfriend?" asked a young, dark woman with a husky voice.

"Um. Gosh. I had a few! I mean, Italian women, come on."

The room rippled with laughter and Hal smiled, satisfied he'd deflected the dodgy questions. But the ugly Italian persisted.

"I was asking, Mr Blackstock, do you think *The Apple Tree* is a comedown?"

OK, deep breath, deep breath, be patient. "Hey. No. It's not a comedown. I mean, it's true *Analyse Love* was a masterpiece but there's a place for everything in this business. *The Apple Tree* is a lovely little story; it's meant to make people laugh, brighten their day and there's room for that in this miserable world, I think we'll all agree. Next question?"

A suited Japanese man stuck his tape recorder forward.

"Mr Blackstock, Junichiro Kanai, *Tokyo Lights*. Have you ever been to Tokyo in the spring?"

Yes! Top question! "I have and it's a beautiful city. The cherry blossom is — er — lovely and . . ." If he kept on in this vein he would infuriate all the other journalists and leave no time for them to prod deeper into his disintegrating career. As he bumbled to a close, the only babe in the room, a smooth-looking blonde with dirty eyes, cleared her throat.

"Mr Blackstock. Marion Demazière. *Jeunesse Fran-çaise*. Is it true you 'ave a French cousin?"

Ca-ching. Another winner. Hal liked this journalist. Perhaps he could get her number and . . . but no. "No, it's not true. Wish it was, though. Because French women are gorgeous. I adore them. They are truly the sexiest women on the planet. Yes, I'd love to have an excuse to visit France more often."

"But what would Flora say about that?" said the Italian woman slyly.

Bugger. He'd walked straight into that one. "Flora loves France too," he said frostily. Everyone began frantically scribbling in their notepads. Across the room, Nessie rolled her eyes.

"OK, time for one more question," she said firmly.

A tall, lanky man. "Hi. Jim Pallett. *New Zealand Age*. Do you know Russell Crowe?"

"Yes, though . . . what relevance has this to *The Apple Cart*?"

"Nothing. But he's a Kiwi."

"Isn't he Australian?" At the man's hurt expression, Hal changed tack. "Yes. Of course. Well. Yes, I've met Russell and he's a really, really lovely guy. A lot of fun. Of course, I don't know him well, but . . ."

"OK!" Nessie snapped. "Time's up."

"Ah, please, just one more question," purred the French babe.

"Just one more," said Nessie magnanimously, as she'd given her the Sultan of Brunei's cash card and pin number. Hal braced himself for the "How are things going with Flora?" Under his shirt he could feel a throbbing. He put his hand to his heart. Oh, my God. The spot had grown, swollen, so now it felt like a hard-boiled egg beneath his breastbone. Shit. This was very nasty. He itched to get on the Internet and check it out.

"Have you spoken to Marina yet about her engagement? Congratulated her?" As the woman spoke, she flashed a tabloid under his nose with a laughing Marina all over the front page.

"Is Marina engaged?" Hal said. He felt his heart swelling like dough, yet he kept his voice perfectly steady, his smile unwobbling. He looked at the newspaper more closely. There she was, the love of his life for ten years, in the arms of that permatanned bozo, Fabrizio.

"You didn't know?" Everyone in the room sat up. Pens scribbled violently on note pads. Three tape recorders were thrust under his nose.

"Guys," Nessie said, "this is just tabloid gossip for now."

"No, it's not," said the Italian. "Reuters confirmed it an hour ago."

"And Mr Blackstock is going to be speaking to Miss Dawson in due course and offering her his heartfelt congratulations."

"Yes," said Hal as they all gazed at him expectantly. There was a buzzing in his ears. He felt as if he were very high up in the sky, looking down on himself. "Yes, I am. I'm delighted for Marina and Fabrizio, I wish them all the very best."

Nessie stood up. "All right, I think you've got enough now. Mr Blackstock is very busy. Thank you all for coming."

"Thank you," echoed Hal, as they got up, mumbling. "Thank you. I do appreciate you taking the time." He glanced at his Rolex. He could make it back to the suite to check out the news before the next interview. As he walked out of the room, he heard the Japanese reporter say to the French girl, "A pity. We would much rather have done the interview with Justina Maguire, she is so hot right now."

"Sure," agreed the French girl. "We wanted her too, but she's only doing a one-on-one with US *Vogue*. We had to settle for Blackstock."

CHAPTER
TWELVE

Amy had hoped her first proper full day in Rome was going to be an improvement, but in the end it was even hotter, more lonely and frustrating than the day before. In the morning she decided to go to the Vatican. She took the metro, which seemed a pretty pathetic affair, compared to London's tube, because she thought it would be a lot less stressful than walking and the idea of a bus frightened her in case she didn't know how to pay the driver or when to get off. She found herself trapped in a carriage with three gypsy children, pestering her for money. She gave them a couple of coins but after that they only harassed her more and in the end she had to get out at the next stop and wait for another train in order to shake them off.

She had planned to go to the Vatican museums and the Sistine Chapel but they were closed because it was some Catholic feast day. So she headed for St Peter's Basilica, but just as she was walking through the lofty portals a nun grabbed her by the shoulder and berated her for even thinking of entering the holiest place in Christendom wearing shorts.

"But . . ." protested Amy, pointing at the man in front of her, who was wearing a T-shirt saying

97

Windsurfers Do It Standing Up. The nun, however, was unmoved.

"Shame on you," she spat, crossing herself.

Defeated, Amy bought a slice of pizza from a takeaway shop for lunch and ate it standing in the dappled shade of a plane tree. Having studied the guide book more closely and discovered virtually all the sights were closed on Mondays, she decided to go window shopping even though she'd wanted to reserve that activity for Gaby. But it was lunchtime and it turned out nearly all the shops were closed until four, so instead she wandered aimlessly about the cobbled and undeniably pretty streets of what was called the "historic centre" constantly glancing at her mobile to see if she'd missed a call and feeling more and more despondent. She brooded endlessly on her situation. She'd lost her future with the only man she'd ever truly loved. Perhaps she'd been too fussy? Perhaps she should have compromised? After all, nobody had it perfect.

Meanwhile, the bloody shorts were causing her even more problems. At the sight of her, drivers honked their horns like huntsmen sighting prey. Shopkeepers, shading themselves in doorways, hissed like snakes. Men on scooters, even those with girls on the back, slowed down and muttered what she was sure were vile obscenities.

Her phone started ringing. The usual dart of hope shot through her, but the caller ID acted as a swift antidote.

"Hello, Mum," she said, trying to sound cheery.

"Sweetheart! Where are you? Are you with Doug?"

"No, Mum. I'm in Rome. On my honeymoon. Alone."

"Oh, darling! And you haven't heard from him?"

Amy screwed up her eyes as if she was about to be punched. "Not a word," she confessed.

"Oh, Amy." Disappointment squelched down the line. Her parents had always wanted so much for her, it scared her. She was an only child, born to them late after years of false hopes, and they'd sacrificed so much (in vain, as Gaby always pointed out) to give her ballet lessons, judo lessons and violin lessons, to make sure she went to a good school and to university. The day she'd qualified as a doctor had been the happiest of their lives, the day she'd got engaged to Doug had been a close second. Actually the day she'd brought Danny home had been second; they'd never really warmed to Doug, though they had pretended to.

It was wonderful to be loved so much, but often it was a burden. There were times when all Amy wanted to do was be held in her mother's arms. Instead, she ended up having to do the comforting, pretending her lacerated heart was merely grazed.

"Mum, please don't worry. I'll be OK."

"I just can't understand it. I'm so upset with Douglas. How could he do this to my little girl?"

"Mum . . ."

"Do you want me to call him?"

"No!"

"And, listen, sweetie. Everyone's phoning about wedding presents. I mean, not that they begrudge the money, but they want to know. Do you keep the gifts as a . . . kind of consolation prize? Or do you send them back? I mean, it's really up to you. Apparently Auntie Joan bought you a toaster and Joan Millikins got you a croquet set."

"I think you should send them back. But don't worry. I'll deal with it when I get home. And in the meantime, you'll never guess who's staying in my hotel. Hal Blackstock!"

"Hal Blackstock?" This perked her up. Amy's mother had always had the hots for Hal Blackstock, even more than Harrison Ford, and on the nights one of his films was being shown, dinner was eaten in front of the telly on a tray with no disturbances allowed.

Amy told her mother how handsome he was, omitting the flatulence, and by the time she hung up her mother was much cheerier, obviously convinced Hal Blackstock was her future son-in-law. Amy, on the other hand, was more depressed than ever. She longed to call Doug, but instead she speed-dialled Gaby.

"How's it all going?"

"It's great," Amy said, watching a policewoman in unfeasibly high heels and a tight uniform checking her make-up in a parked Fiat's wing mirror. "The hotel's incredible and guess what? Hal Blackstock's staying here too and he wanted to swap suites with me."

"No!"

Amy related the steam-room incident to some very satisfying gasps and I don't believe its.

"Will he still be there on Wednesday? I'm planning to get a flight in the morning. My scan's at ten tomorrow."

"So you reckon you'll be here by Wednesday evening?"

"Definitely. We'll go out for a delicious pasta supper. I can't wait. By the way, I'm assuming you've heard nothing."

"Nothing. But I didn't expect to."

"All the same" — Gaby inhaled crossly — "he should have called you. Oh shit, I've got to go. Client on the other line. Be in touch tomorrow with my flight details. Love you."

Love you. It was what your boyfriend was supposed to say at the end of a phone call, not your best friend. But when was the last time Doug had said it to her? Not often in the past few months during all the arguments about place settings, flower arrangements and steps for the first dance. And when, for that matter, had she said it to him?

As Amy wandered back to the hotel, she thought about those early idyllic days with Doug. After an appropriate number of drinks had been consumed that March night and Gaby and even Pinny (who kept her mouth shut though she did seem to be giving her the evil eye) had left, Amy had gone back to Doug's grotty shared flat in Pimlico "to listen to music". She'd pretended to be interested in the obscure bands he played her and both gabbled inanely until 4a.m., when finally there was a pause in which both silently acknowledged there was nothing left to say and this was where it was going and they could wait no longer.

So Doug jumped on her.

Despite their drunkenness, the sex was spectacular. Amy had never known anything like it. After years of in-out missionary coupling with Danny she felt transformed into a porn star, her body tingling, her muscles aching as they came alive after a long sleep.

In the morning Doug got up and went to the shops. While he was gone Amy had a quick snoop for evidence of other girlfriends, but found nothing except a half-eaten packet of Hob Nobs seven months past their sell-by date under his bed, which momentarily turned her stomach but was so un-Danny she had to laugh. Then Doug returned with the papers and croissants and Amy's terror that this would be a one-night stand and any minute he would send her packing with her bus fare evaporated.

Of course, Doug should have been *her* one-night stand. She omitted to tell him she already had a boyfriend who had been saving lives while she'd been making passionate love. She left about noon, having made love twice more. Her mouth was very dry as she said goodbye, but then Doug said, "Hey, I'll get your number from Pinny."

"Oh, I wouldn't do that," she said hastily, terrified at what Pinny might reveal. "I don't think she should know about us — I mean about what happened."

Doug shrugged. "Fair enough. Pin's always had a bit of a thing for me. Well, give me your number now."

All the way home, her skin felt taut and rosy, as if it was one size too small for her. There was a message from Danny on the machine saying he'd see her that night and did she fancy maybe an Indian and a DVD?

For the first time she felt guilty. Danny wasn't the man for her, but he was a decent man and she was behaving disgustingly. She was just wondering what to do, should she dump him that night, or should she hedge her bets and hold on just to check Doug really was into her when her mobile rang. *Pinny*. She regarded the phone fearfully, like a lump of plutonium. She'd leave it. No, she'd answer it. Because even though she didn't want to talk to her, it would bring her closer to Doug.

"Hi!" she gushed. "You were amazing last night."

"So what happened to you?" Pinny didn't sound quite as chilled as usual.

"What do you mean?"

"Baz said you left with Doug."

Amy's heart was in her mouth. "Yes, we shared a taxi home."

"But you live nowhere near each other."

"I know. I dropped him at King's Cross."

"Right. If you're sure."

"Of course I'm sure," Amy fibbed huffily.

"Doug can be trouble, Amy. Just so you know."

"Nothing happened, Pins."

She told the same lie to Gaby, who sounded less narked but more worried. And then she had a miserable day, too strung out to sleep, too tired to do anything useful, gnawing at her cuticles and checking her phone. That night, Danny came over. Amy decided she was too exhausted to embark on a break up so they shared an Indian and watched a DVD, then brushed their teeth side by side and went chastely to bed — like any other Saturday night. The next day Danny had to go to work at noon. Amy went back to bed, teeth chattering in misery as she resigned herself to the fact she would never see Doug again. But around six, as it was growing dark outside, her phone bleeped.

Can't stop thinking about last night. Can we do it again soon? x

Before she could stop herself she'd texted back.

How about now?

And so began the most exhausting and exciting three weeks of Amy's life, three weeks where she spent all night in Doug's arms, all day trying to stay awake on adrenalin and caffeine pills and the rest of the time composing texts to Danny telling him she had to work late and she'd see him at the weekend. She should have felt very, very bad but her obsession with Doug was an anaesthetic on her conscience.

Finally, after her nerves could take no more and Amy was as convinced as she'd ever be that Doug wanted to be her boyfriend, she summoned up the courage and told Danny there was someone else. He took it as badly as she'd expected: crying a lot, begging her to change her mind, describing how he'd imagined babies and growing old together. Amy felt horrible, but the more he pleaded the more she knew she was doing the right thing. Having done the deed, she went straight round to Doug's, got into bed with him and put Danny right out of her mind.

After that Danny called her, sobbing, a few times in the middle of the night. He wrote her impassioned letters which she put away without reading. She had frequent nightmares about him and how she'd lazily strung him along for so many years. But at the same time, she felt gloriously lucky to have escaped from what seemed like a long, lethargic sleep and to have found true passion. True love.

CHAPTER
THIRTEEN

Those first few months with Doug were bliss. After what she now thought of as her Sleeping Beauty years, Amy was transformed into one half of the ultimate party couple, enjoying its youth and money to the utmost. They drove round London on his Vespa. One night they ate in a smart restaurant, the next travelled miles to the suburbs to hunt out some Korean dive they'd read about. They went on expensive mini-breaks to hip hotels and had cheap weekends away in grimy B&Bs. They took a lot of drugs (as a doctor, Amy knew this wasn't a good idea, but as a thirty-one-year-old hedonist it was fine). They had tender, passionate, adventurous, explosive sex.

On the rare occasions they stayed in and didn't get naked, Doug would sit on the floor strumming his guitar and singing his compositions to her in his falsetto voice. Sometimes when he sounded a bit castrated she had to suppress a giggle, but mostly she felt moved and honoured. Just think, if she'd been with Danny, they'd have been inert in front of *Celebrity Big Brother*. On other occasions, they watched subtitled black and white movies snuggled on the sofa. Doug's favourite film of all time was *La Dolce Vita* and the night he slipped it in the DVD machine was obviously a test.

"What do you think?" he asked at the end, in a tone reminiscent of Amy's junior-school teacher asking her to recite the eight times table and inspiring exactly the same desire to please in her breast.

"Incredible," she said, nodding earnestly.

Actually, she'd found it a bit rambling and dull, but Marcello Mastroianni was gorgeous and Anita Ekberg standing in the Trevi fountain was sex personified. Doug nodded, pleased.

"I love Rome," he said. "Love Italy. The Italians lead the perfect life, or would do if they had any decent bands. All their musical energy got used up doing opera."

"I've never been."

"Really?" He stroked her hair and smiled. "Then one day I'll take you there."

Most of all, however, she went to watch Ambrosial. The band had a gig pretty much every week, in some obscure corner of London, and every week they attracted a bigger crowd. Watching them, from a privileged backstage position, Amy couldn't help feeling extraordinarily proud — and a little shocked — that she, Amy Gubbins from Salcombe, had bagged this beautiful, sexy, cool man. She'd always felt a bit drab in comparison to Pinny and a bit clueless in comparison to Gaby, but with Doug at her side, she was finally good enough.

Gaby had been great about them getting together, saying she'd liked Danny but this was about Amy's happiness and she'd support her whatever she did. Pinny had been far less gracious.

"Like it wasn't bloody obvious," she said darkly, when Amy finally confessed. "Well, good luck. I just hope you know what you're getting into."

From that day, her friendship with Pinny cooled. Amy detected a definite snideness in Pinny's behaviour to her, and, for her part, she found it hard to relax around someone prettier than her, who had designs on her man — not that Pinny was the only one. Amy quickly got used to groupies shoving her out of the way at gigs, and having women look straight through her as they focussed on Doug.

But miraculously, Doug seemed happy enough with her. After six months Amy asked tentatively if he'd like to meet her parents and Doug yawned and said why not? So they went to Salcombe and the house she grew up in. Mum and Dad, who had been gutted at the loss of nice Danny, were nonetheless very welcoming to Doug and he was perfectly polite back. Amy's granny, whom she adored, came over from her bungalow down the hill and laughed at all his jokes.

"So what do you think?" Amy asked conspiratorially when they were alone together, while her mother and father gave him a tour of the vegetable patch.

"He's very nice, sweetie. And so handsome. Ooh, just like that chappie on the telly."

"What chap on the telly?" Amy was pleased.

"You know. The one who judges the singers. Very rude, but very good-looking."

"Not Simon Cowell?" Amy asked, knowing as she spoke that Granny had it spot on.

"Yes, that's the one. Gorgeous."

Amy decided not to share this with Doug. Apart from that, the trip was a roaring success. On the way back to London, she told him she loved him and after only a tiny pause Doug told her he loved her back.

So when did it peak? When was the best day and how soon after that did Amy realize she was no longer walking on air, that somehow, without noticing, her feet had fallen a little closer towards earth? Try as she might, she couldn't remember the first night they'd gone to bed and, rather than jumping each other's bones, just slept. Although she remembered the emotion — slight anxiety that Doug had gone off her combined with smugness that they had moved on to the next level of coupledom, when things were about more than sex, they were about cosy companionship.

Nor could she pinpoint when it had moved from that to the occasional definite reluctance to put out — because she was tired, because she had a big day at work tomorrow, because she was really enjoying her book and wanted to finish the chapter before sleep overtook her, because she was upset about the old man she'd seen today whose daughter was trying to kick him out when he had nowhere else to go. But the reluctance was only occasional and Doug always won her round. She could sleep when she was dead. She was a little less philosophical about being dragged to a gig in some obscure corner of the Home Counties and not getting back until two in the morning, but she always went.

The threat of Pinny and the groupies loomed far too high for there to be any option.

After nine months, Doug moved in with her. There was no great discussion; his landlord had given him notice on the place in Pimlico and the next day he turned up at Amy's in Pinny's estate car and began unpacking black bin liner upon black bin liner.

"All right, Doug?" Amy heard Pinny say as she helped carry the last bag up the stairs. "Remember there's always my spare room if things don't work out."

Despite the weeks it took to recover from this, Amy was ecstatic. She had a fantasy which, she now realized shamefully, had been gleaned from TV adverts about them getting up late on a Sunday morning and ambling down to a restaurant to meet their friends for brunch, about him chopping vegetables and her doing fancy things with a wok.

The reality, of course, was somewhat different. Amy hadn't taken into account the practical difficulties of fitting all Doug's possessions into her bijou space. There were his hundreds of CDs, not to mention hundreds more bloody LPs from the days when man hunted woolly mammoths, which he never played because he had no turntable but point blank refused to get rid of. Though the music clobber was nothing compared to some of Doug's other stuff. Take his giant Swatch watch, for example, which covered a whole wall. It was a garish yellow and blue with a kangaroo in the middle whose arms pointed to the time.

"Isn't it cool?" Doug said smiling. "We could put it here." He pointed at the wall on the far side of the

110

bedroom, which, in an unprecedented attempt at Martha Stewartdom, Amy had covered in Osborne and Little wallpaper costing £190 a roll. "Get rid of that granny pattern. Surprised you didn't rip it out when you moved in."

Amy swallowed this insult. "Doug, we are not putting the watch up anywhere. It's hideous!"

"Do you think so?" He looked devastated.

Amy used her gentlest voice, the one normally reserved for telling patients they had a fatal disease. "It's the ugliest thing I've ever seen. It's going to Oxfam."

"No, you can't do that! Look, suppose we move to a bigger place. I'd have it in my studio. Let's just put it away for now."

Of course, the moving to a bigger place argument with its promise of permanence swung it. So the Swatch joined the framed film posters for *Betty Blue* and *From Russia With Love*, the batik tablecloths he'd picked up in his year off in India, the ugly African figures he'd bought on holiday in the Gambia, the revolting flowery mugs his aunt had given him for his twenty-first, in an overflowing kitchen cupboard.

"If a year passes and you don't miss them, they're going to Oxfam," Amy warned and he'd said, "Yeah, yeah." Sixteen months had passed and she could never quite summon the energy to carry out her threat. Though she did, with some chivvying from Doug, find time to buy the biggest plasma screen then on the market and subscribe to Sky.

The clutter wasn't the only problem. Like most men, Doug was a slob, who genuinely didn't care if there was a ring around the bath and would never dream of washing vegetables before putting them away in the fridge (Amy had treated too many patients with gastric nasties not to err on the side of caution). It was very tricky, not least because if she ever complained Doug would snarl in a most adolescent way that he thought he was living with his girlfriend, not his mum.

Terrified of upsetting him, Amy tended to complain (mildly) to her friends.

"I think you're being a bit hard on Doug," said Madhura, one of the doctors at the practice, who had a perfect, doting boyfriend who ran her hot baths without asking and did the weekly shop and whom Amy secretly considered a total wimp. "I mean, which would you prefer: a house out of an interiors magazine or a messy man who gives you good loving? I think you need to relax more, Amy."

"Maybe you should buy a place together," Gaby suggested when Amy took her woes to her. "If it belongs to both of you, you can design it together and then you won't feel so territorial and he'll be more house proud. I mean, he's earning enough money for you to be able to get something OK. And you really ought to be thinking about moving up the ladder."

She was right. The next evening, over supper, Amy put the idea to Doug. She thought he'd be enthusiastic. After all, he was always moaning about how far her flat was from the tube, but instead he shook his head.

"I don't think so."

"Why not?" Amy felt an actual physical pain. What was he saying? Didn't he want to be with her?

"Because buying a new place would cost a fortune and it's not how I want to spend my money right now."

"Right," she said, as nausea rose in her throat. How could she have got it so wrong? She really thought they were happy. Why hadn't she hung up that bloody Swatch? Been more of a vixen in bed last night?

He got up, walked round the table and put his arm round her shoulder.

"Ames, I've been putting off telling you this, but . . ."

Her surroundings advanced and receded on her, just like that time she'd fainted in a queue for the cinema. *OK. You're definitely leaving me.*

"I don't think I can stay in my job. I'm going to have to quit."

Relief made her even giddier. It was a second before she asked, "But why? What's wrong?"

He sighed. "You know why. I hate it. It's just not me. Sitting at a desk in front of a pile of documents. Looking up obscure points in dusty books. It's boring, Amy. It's soul destroying. There has to be more to life."

"Of course, there's more," Amy said, shaken. She knew Doug moaned about work occasionally but she'd never heard an outburst like this. "You don't live to work, you work to live. It's what we do with our spare time that's important. Our jobs fund our lifestyles."

"It's different for you," Doug protested. "Your job's worthwhile. There's nothing worthwhile about rich bastards working out ways to screw money out of other rich bastards."

"There's not that much worthwhile about referring people to see an ingrowing-toenail specialist," Amy retorted, although she didn't completely mean it. "Come on, Doug. Life's not perfect. We've got it far better than most."

Amy considered the subject closed. But Doug wouldn't let it rest. He spent more and more time working on new songs and hassling Hank to find Ambrosial gigs further afield. The day came when the head of his firm told him off for writing tunes when he should have been drawing up a will. Then he overslept after getting back from a gig in Luton at five in the morning and was given a verbal warning. Then he called in sick when he was actually stuck in Glasgow having missed the dawn flight. They found him out and he got a final, written warning.

"Doug!" Amy said, appalled.

"Doug what? It's for the best, Amy. I can't spend the rest of my life as a wage slave. It's just not me."

"But without your wages, how can we pay the mortgage?" Amy fretted.

"You paid the mortgage before I came along," he pointed out quite reasonably.

"I guess, but . . . rates keep going up." What she really meant was how can we buy a bigger place, with a child's room and a garden? All the things Danny had been pushing for which had repelled her then but which, over the past few months, had somehow become her dream, a secret dream, however, since Doug had no truck with fantasies of suburban domesticity.

"Can't we compromise?" she tried. "You keep plugging away at the band but keep the day job? If the band makes it, of course you can pack it in."

Doug agreed and an uneasy calm reigned. But then just a month later came a crisis when Doug's boss asked him to work late on the same night Ambrosial had a big gig. Doug said no. The gig was a storming success, but the next morning he was unemployed.

"Babe, it'll be OK," he promised her, seeing her horrified expression. "Why don't we have another compromise? I'll give the band a go for a year and if it doesn't work out I'll find a proper job."

Reluctantly, Amy agreed. She had a bad feeling about it all. But she needed Doug, like she needed to breathe. Plus, she'd dumped Danny because his staidness and reliability had driven her to distraction, so it would be absurd of her to complain that his replacement was artistic and flighty. Amy had made her choice and now she was going to have to make it work.

CHAPTER
FOURTEEN

Before his one-on-one with Italian *Marie Claire*, Hal demanded a twenty-minute break. He returned to his suite, opened his laptop and googled Marina Dawson and Fabrizio de Michelis: 3,552 results. He clicked on the first.

Today the engagement was announced between *Catwalk* presenter and model, Marina Dawson, and her tycoon boyfriend of a year. "It's been a bit of a whirlwind but we couldn't be happier," said Marina, 34. "We're thinking of getting married at the Cipriani in Venice before Christmas."

"Thirty-four! The cheeky mare!" Marina was six years younger than him, which made her thirty-seven this December. Hal couldn't believe the press let her get away with it. He clicked on a few more links. A picture came up of Marina at some awards ceremony, dazzling in dark green. She certainly was a beautiful woman, his ex. Although with that wide mouth and big bust her looks were rather obvious. Rake-thin Flora was far more of a thoroughbred, with generations of good breeding behind her. With her bone structure she

116

wouldn't need plastic surgery to preserve her looks — well, possibly the odd jab of Botox — she would age gloriously, whereas he could imagine Marina getting a bit blowsy.

He'd better call her and congratulate her, he supposed. But not today, maybe tomorrow. He couldn't say exactly why the news of the engagement had shaken him so. After all, it was he who'd ended it with Marina — despite the mountains of newsprint in which "friends" of hers had hinted at the contrary. Well, all right, actually she'd ended it, but only because he'd given her no choice.

But still . . . it was weird to think of someone who had been such a major part of his life for so long moving on to a chapter of her life in which he wouldn't feature at all. After all, this was someone he'd allowed to squeeze his blackheads, who'd chased him round the room naked, brandishing a wax strip and threatening to depilate his butt crack, until they'd both collapsed in hysterical exhaustion. How could all that ultimately mean nothing? There was no way she and Fabrizio could have achieved the same level of intimacy. They'd only been together a year and, knowing their schedules, they'd probably spent a week of it together. Of course he'd been thinking about getting engaged to Flora, but that was different — Flora quite clearly had a brain while Fabrizio was a lobotomized chunk of mahogany. Actually, that wasn't strictly true — on the handful of occasions Hal had met him, he'd seemed like a surprisingly nice guy for the heir to a shipping fortune. Funny and laid back. But still, he had a face like the cake in Macarthur Park and he was certainly no candidate for the Nobel Prize for science. Could Marina really be in love with him?

He thought about announcing his engagement to Flora. But if they got engaged right now, everyone would say he had asked her out of spite which would obviously be totally untrue.

Hal's mind buzzed round these thoughts like wasps round a jam pot all the way through the next interview, during lunch and through a shattering hour with Christine Miller from the *Daily Post*. She was an annoyingly pretty blonde with a reputation for character assassinations. She tried every conceivable way of getting him to open his heart about Marina and Flora and with every possible means, Hal stonewalled her. At the end, both were bad tempered and they shook hands with barely concealed dislike. After that, he had to endure another hour with Simon, the middle-aged *Post* photographer, who — unusually for a snapper who normally trowelled it on — had all the charm of a maximum-security prison warder. Hal was exhausted.

In the evening he worked out with the exercise equipment he'd had brought up to the suite (no way was he going down to the public space again). He ate dinner alone in front of an Eddie Murphy film from a selection of DVDs sent up by the concierge. When that ended it occurred to him he really ought to call Flora.

"Hello? Hal?" For some reason her drawly tones had him immediately on edge.

"Hello, darling. How's it all going?"

"*Really* well. The opening of the refuge was a huge success. Hopefully we'll have loads of coverage in tomorrow's papers."

"Mmm," Hal said, thinking that the coverage might well be eclipsed by the Marina engagement story. "That's wonderful, darling, well done."

"Thank you. I'm so excited. I'm glad you rang, though, because there's just one thing."

"What thing?" he said, feeling a sudden shard of unease beneath his breastbone.

"Well, darling, I hope I will be with you on Wednesday, but there are some things going on with the foundation which might take longer than I thought to wind up. So I could be a day or so late."

"What?"

"I don't know for sure. But Friday or Saturday might be easier for me. I've got Henrietta looking into flights right now. Don't worry, sweetie. I'll be with you before you know it."

"Oh, fucking hell," he said. "I don't want to be alone here any longer than I have to be."

"Hal, it'll only be a day or two. Don't be so selfish. The foundation is terribly important you know."

"But it's the premiere on Wednesday night," he whined.

"Sweetie, I am so sorry, truly I am. But I don't think I have a choice."

Hal knew the reason he most wanted her there was so he'd have her on his arm at the premiere. If she wasn't, the papers would have a field day, "Hal all on

119

his own while Marina plans wedding of the century." But he knew better than to tell Flora this.

"Look," he said sulkily, "do whatever's good for you. I'm not bothered either way. I've got to go."

"Hal, don't be like that! You're more of a child than the girls."

"I'll talk to you soon," he said coolly. "*Ciao*, darling, as they say in Rome."

He hung up. Dammit. Why did he get the feeling everything was spiralling out of his control? His ex, who just two years ago had been desperate to marry him, was now engaged to a man who was richer than him. And his girlfriend, who was undeniably the perfect woman and far more suitable than Marina in every way, was passing over the pleasure of his company because she preferred hanging out with jailbird drug smugglers.

He felt a pulsating beneath his shirt. Gingerly, he stuck his hand underneath it and stroked the spot. Oh God, it had expanded even more. And the pain was definitely worse. Right. He was going to check it out. He grabbed his laptop and googled: "Spot pustule itchy stubborn."

Bling. His search revealed 18,702 results. Randomly, he clicked on the fourth one: "Interim guidelines for smallpox response and management."

His blood ran cold. Oh Christ, he knew it. He had smallpox, probably infected by some insane fan who'd jabbed him with the tip of an umbrella.

No, come on, Hal, don't be ridiculous. He tried the first result, which would tell him it was only a spot, inflamed because he had pricked it: "Skin cancer warning signs."

Fuck! Hal slammed the lid of the laptop shut. Skin cancer. He'd known all those sunbeds the studio had persuaded him to use before the BAFTAs a couple of years ago had been a bad idea. Shit. He was dying. And what would he have to show for it all? A handful of cheesy romantic comedies, a mourning girlfriend with an Oscar. No children. Nothing meaningful.

Yes, he definitely would propose to Flora on the night she arrived. They'd marry quickly — nothing flashy, a small ceremony maybe at George's villa on Lake Como and then he'd get her pregnant as soon as possible. At least then there would be something left of him, something to console his parents whose son had been taken from them before his time . . . but he was getting carried away. No point planning his own funeral (cremation definitely, Hal had had a phobia about being buried alive ever since seeing *The Vanishing*) until he'd seen a doctor. He'd get Nessie to call one in the morning. But maybe by then it would be too late. The cancer might have spread and there would be no time for chemo and radiotherapy.

Calm down. It was just a spot which had gone a bit septic. Perhaps he'd given himself blood poisoning. Septicaemia. His arm would have to be amputated, or his leg. Maybe both? Would that be the end of the world? After all, look at Heather Mills McCartney whom he'd met at one of Flora's benefits; she still seemed to cope OK, though he remembered stuff during the divorce about how she'd had to pee in a bedpan. Oh, Christ. That was going to be him. He'd been a fool to have left it so long. He had to get it seen to right away. He looked at his watch, nearly midnight. Well, too bad. This was an emergency.

He picked up the phone and called reception.

CHAPTER
FIFTEEN

The phone woke Amy with a start. She cleared her throat before answering, "Hello?"

"Doctor Fraser?" said a voice with an Italian accent.

"Yes?"

"So very sorry to disturb you. This is Signor Ducelli, the manager."

"Yes?"

"We have a little bit of a problem and we were wondering if there was any way you could help us. If you want to that is . . . You are under no obligation."

Amy knew it. Mariah Carey had just arrived and she needed to make way for her.

"It depends . . ."

"Of course! It is just . . . you are a medical doctor, Doctor Fraser?"

"Yes."

"With wide experience?"

"Well, fairly wide."

"Forgive me for asking. It is just you look so young." Ah, the charmer. "Now, you see the problem is a guest in this hotel has been taken ill. He requires urgent medical attention. But the doctor we normally use is nowhere to be found. We think he must be on holiday."

"Well then, the guest should go to hospital." Rule number one of doctoring — never get out of bed if there was absolutely anyone else you could pass the buck to. She glanced at her bedside clock — 23.36 — Christ.

"No, Doctor Fraser. It is a little bit more delicate than that. This is a *famous* guest. We cannot just call in any old doctor. Discretion is of the utmost importance. So we think, and we decide, who is better to treat Mr . . . I mean, this VIP guest . . . than another VIP guest?"

"But it's nearly midnight. I was asleep."

"Doctor Fraser, I know. And as recompense for your kindness, we will be more than happy to make your entire stay at the Hotel de Russie complimentary. And your husband's. When he arrives."

Amy's brain switched straight from neutral into fifth. "Right! OK! I'll just be a moment. Just need to get dressed."

"You are too kind, too kind. Now, when you are ready, you go to the Picasso suite down the corridor from you. And I tell you in strictest confidence, the name of the patient you have to treat is . . ." He lowered his voice theatrically, although of course she already knew.

"Mr Hal Blackstock."

Half an hour had passed before Hal heard his bell ring.

"Thank God for that."

When Hal first spoke to Ducelli, he had said no problem, they'd have a doctor with him within the hour. But then Ducelli had called back sounding less confident, saying they'd had an unforeseen problem and then called again, sounding very chipper, saying everything was under control.

"Coming!" he yelled and opened the door. Standing there was Ducelli and a tall dark woman in shorts and a faded T-shirt. She looked oddly familiar.

"Meester Blackstock, so sorry to have kept you waiting. A little problem with our usual doctor. But don't worry. We have for you instead Doctor Fraser who is staying with us."

He remembered.

"The honeymooner?"

"That's right," she said. "I'm on my honeymoon. But I'm also a graduate of Edinburgh medical school, a qualified general practitioner and a fully paid-up slave of the NHS."

"Are you, indeed?" He eyed her respectfully. This could be the woman who pronounced his death sentence.

"So what can I do for you, Mr Blackstock?"

"Um. It's private," he said witheringly with a look at Ducelli, who immediately took the hint.

"So, Meester Blackstock, I will leave you here with this bee-yoo-ti-ful young lady, I mean this . . . distinguished doctor, who will attend to your every need."

"Is there an all-night pharmacy nearby?" the doctor asked. "Just in case we need it?"

"Si, si, dottoressa. A member of staff is on standby should you need anything."

"Great. I'll let you know."

125

"Many thanks for your help, dottoressa."

"It's no problem."

After more fawning, Ducelli finally left. "Right," she said, as soon as the door was shut, "so what's wrong?"

"Well, it's a bit embarrassing . . ."

"Don't worry. They all say that."

"No, it really is."

"I'm sure it isn't. Just tell me." Her voice was unexpectedly gentle.

"Well, the problem is . . . I think I've got septicaemia. My arm and leg are going to have to be amputated."

"Septicaemia?" She raised an eyebrow.

"But it could be skin cancer. I did get badly burnt when I was a teenager, on holiday in Spain. And I've used sunbeds," he added like someone confessing to a priest they'd had sex with a donkey.

"Skin cancer? So what are your symptoms?"

"I've got this spot on my chest and I burst it with a needle. Sterilized, but now it won't heal and I read . . ."

"Mr Blackstock, I'm sure you don't have septicaemia. Or skin cancer. But even if you do, it's very curable." She looked around the room. "Hmm. Nice suite. To be honest, I can't tell the difference between this and the Popolo."

Despite himself, he giggled. "You have a city view. I only get garden."

"Oh, you poor thing." She smiled. It was a surprisingly wide one, revealing a very cute gap between her two front teeth. "Now, Mr Blackstock, I never thought I'd be saying this to you, but could you remove your shirt, please, so I can inspect this spot?"

He pulled his T-shirt over his head, feeling very benevolent. It must be quite thrilling for her to see a movie star strip off at close quarters. Yes, she'd probably go and blab to all her friends about it, but really, so what? It wasn't like she was going to diagnose him with herpes or anything. Though, fuck, what if it was skin cancer and she told a friend, who told a friend and it was all over the papers before he had a chance to call Mummy and warn her? He'd better do that first thing in the morning. She'd be upset, but he'd reassure her that amazing treatment was available these days and fortunately he was in a position to pay for the very best. And so what if he did lose all his hair? He had a thick enough thatch — unlike that Fabrizio de Michelis who he swore was thinning on top — to be confident most of it would grow back.

She was standing close to him now.

"I think it's a boil," she said.

"A what?"

"A boil. Nothing to worry about. It'll clear up in a couple of days. Put some cream on it, and don't go poking at it with any more needles. Sterilized or not. Yuk."

Hal felt euphoria, like all the Ecstasy hits he'd ever had rolled into one (not that he'd had that many). It was like being reborn. *Thank you, God, for my second chance*, he thought. *Thank you. I promise now I'll try to be a better person. I'll give more of my money to charity and I'll visit Mum and Dad more and I will marry Flora and have four bouncing babies with her.* Though he wasn't actually sure if Flora would appreciate the effect four would have on her figure. Maybe three, then. Or two.

"You're sure I'm all right?"

"Positive."

"Sure I don't have skin cancer?"

"I can't be a hundred per cent sure unless I check every mole on your body. Which I'd rather not at this time of night. There are plenty of clinics in London I could recommend if you want to be thoroughly vetted. I take it you're able to go private?"

Hal began to feel embarrassed. "No, no, look, it's OK. I'm so sorry to have got you out of bed. Your poor husband. Not much fun on your honeymoon."

"It's not a problem," she said quickly. Then she gave a little yawn. "Sorry. May I just wash my hands?"

"Oh, of course." He nodded at the bathroom. "Yours is probably bigger."

"Probably."

She emerged a moment later, looking confused.

"So your girlfriend has already arrived?"

"My girlfriend? Uh. No. She's not getting here for a couple more days."

"But all those cosmetics. The Clarins and Lancôme stuff . . ." She slowed down as she saw his face. "Oh. Is that yours?"

"You need a bit of help if you don't know when your picture might be taken," he said defensively.

"Of course," she said, failing to keep a smile from her lips. Hal forgave her because it was such a sweet one.

"Thank you. It was jolly kind."

"Oh, don't worry about that. The hotel's making it up to me."

"You're not going to tell your friends what a prat I am?"

"Of course not. Bound by the Hippocratic oath never to reveal anything about my patients. Now, good night, Mr Blackstock. Get some sleep."

"Thank you," he repeated, suddenly, oddly, wishing she'd stay.

"You're welcome," she replied and shut the door, leaving him with nothing to do but get into bed and finally go to sleep.

CHAPTER
SIXTEEN

Back in bed, once more Amy found sleep impossible. She threw off her sheet, then pulled it back on again, opened the window, then shut it. Turned the air-conditioning up and turned it down. She inspected her phone to check if any middle of the night messages had arrived while she had been in the other suite, but of course there was nothing.

Instead, she found herself masochistically trawling back through her old texts, texts from just a week ago when everything had been on course. Down, down, she scrolled. To keep her phone's memory free, she usually deleted old ones when she was bored on the bus, but some she'd kept for sentimental reasons, or because she'd just never got round to it. That first text from Doug that made her heart almost stop with joy. Doug saying he'd be back late and not to wait up. Doug saying there'd been an A&R man at the gig and things were definitely looking hopeful. Doug saying he was at the supermarket and sorry, what was it Amy had specifically asked him to buy again? Doug texting her that the band was sacking Hank as manager.

130

"We think he's ripping us off, stealing from us," Doug explained when he got home from what had clearly been a very impassioned session in the pub.

"How can he be ripping you off when you don't make any money in the first place?" Amy demanded. She'd come to admire Hank, who certainly earned whatever tiny amount he got for the amount of energy he put in to organizing minibuses to ferry the band to gigs in obscure towns, sourcing Gregor's drugs in the same small towns and then driving them back to London from those small towns, in the middle of the night, because everyone else was too wasted to take the wheel.

"Babe, it's a done deal," Doug said. "Anyway, it's cool. We've decided I'll be manager. Which means an extra twenty per cent of the profits go straight to you and *moi*."

Useless to point out that 20 per cent of the profits added up to about 900 quid a year. Basically it meant Doug — who since he'd left the solicitors had been working in a dull but flexible job in telesales — was penniless. The meals out, the cinema trips all continued but somehow they became tainted because Amy was having to fund them all. It wasn't that she minded paying exactly, but it was symbolic of what was happening to their relationship where more and more she felt she was doing all the work.

On a typical day, she would get up at seven. Doug would still be asleep and would continue to sleep when she left for the surgery at eight and would still be sleeping when she phoned home at ten to remind him to buy more food for the pet fish. She'd get home around six, exhausted emotionally from the day's sob stories, to find a stash of new DVDs scattered around the telly, the TV listings well thumbed and the bed still warm, while the washing machine she had loaded that morning was still full of damp clothes and the Post-its, which Amy considered the key to life, crammed with instructions like "Renew parking permit", "Buy washing tablets" were ignored.

Amy yearned for someone to pour her a gin and tonic, but usually found herself going through the recycling bin, removing the plastic bottles that Doug put there without fail, even though Amy explained without fail that this council didn't recycle them. She longed for someone to talk to about her day and snuggle up with in front of the telly but, like a vampire, Doug seemed only to come alive at night and used the evenings to disappear into the bedroom with his laptop, arranging gigs and sending schmoozy emails to A&R men.

Or worse, Doug would be out at a gig — not just Ambrosial's — he said it was important to keep his eye on the competition. Of course, he always invited Amy to come too, but despite the groupie threat, she refused increasingly often, because she was so exhausted after work and was beginning to resent the band culture for the way it had overturned her life.

She understood where Doug was coming from. His dad was a high-flying lawyer who'd pressured him to follow in his footsteps, a decision he always regretted. His older brother, Alan, who, from Amy's few encounters with him, seemed a bit of a prick, had always mocked his musical ambitions. Doug had spent years arguing with his family, deriding their bourgeois values, saying there was more to life than making money. If the band failed, the loss of face would be devastating. Amy felt guilty about her own, secret, bourgeois values. She clung to the fact that just the smell of Doug on a pillow was enough to make her knees buckle. And life with Doug was still infinitely preferable to life with Danny. Doug made her laugh (most of the time), Doug talked about more interesting things than who was going to the rugby ball. Doug had made Amy understand the meaning of carnal knowledge. Most importantly, Doug was a challenge. Amy had been bored with Danny, but Doug kept her on her toes. However much he annoyed her, he still had the upper hand. She hated to admit it, but even when she was crying over his carelessness, at least she was feeling something, rather than the numbness Danny induced.

But still, Amy was starting to find the vagueness of her future a bit embarrassing. People were asking questions about where she and Doug were going. Mum, Dad, Granny, Madhura, Andrea and Rosa who worked on reception at the surgery. All mentioned in passing that it had been — what — a year and a bit now, and did she and Doug have any long-term plans?

"We're happy just the way we are," Amy lied, head held high. It offended her feminist principles to be hankering for marriage like some heroine in a Barbara Cartland novel. But at the same time, Amy wanted an

133

answer more than anyone. This wasn't just about wanting to wear a white dress and throw a party. It was about a burgeoning sense that the cycle of work, dinners out, foreign holidays and trips to the cinema, which, in her twenties, had been so satisfactory was no longer enough, that she needed to feel her life was progressing.

Things came to a head one evening when she had done a late surgery. Her penultimate patient had been a twenty-one-year-old man with an array of frightening tattoos. He complained of pains in his head. He said his best friend had made him take some pills.

"How did he make you?" Amy asked. "Did he force feed you?" She wasn't being sarcastic; in this area things like that happened all the time.

"No, he said they were Viagra, so I swallowed a handful."

Looking at his notes, Amy could see he'd actually taken a huge overdose of E and was lucky to still be alive. She prescribed him something for the headaches though just to make him happy, not because she thought he needed it.

"And you won't go taking drugs again?" she said, as the paper chugged out of the computer.

"That depends."

"On what?"

"On if I need some Viagra."

The next patient was Sophia Franklin, a stressed lawyer. While she wittered on about how she couldn't sleep, Amy's mind was elsewhere reflecting on the fact that if she had a pound for every person she saw whose life had been messed up by drugs she'd be living in the Bahamas by now. But she and Doug still spent most weekends smoking dope and doing the occasional line or pill. Danny had loathed drugs and Amy had thought him square and boring, but now she conceded he had a point. Why was it all right for them to indulge because they were middle class, but not the unemployed and the poor? As Sophia continued complaining, Amy made a decision. There were going to be no more drugs. It was hypocritical.

"So what do you think I should do?"

"Huh?"

"I feel so empty, so depressed. My job is, like, so stressful. I can't sleep for all the adrenalin pumping through my body. I'd like you to prescribe me some sleeping pills."

This, traditionally, was where Amy blathered on about sleeping pills being the last resort and how she'd prefer her to have a glass of hot milk and do some breathing exercises and put lavender drops on her pillow. But her mind was elsewhere.

"Fine," she said. "I'll write you a prescription."

Sophia looked amazed. "Oh, gosh. Are you sure? I mean, do you think sleeping pills really are the answer? Maybe I should just try a glass of hot milk. Or what do you think of yoga?"

"These'll sort you out," Amy said, tapping at the computer. "One a night."

"Wait," Sophia said, "there's one more thing. I'm trying to get pregnant. Do you really think pills are a good idea?"

Oh, for Christ's sake. "No. If you're trying to get pregnant, taking sleeping pills is probably a bad idea," Amy said. "I wish you'd told me." She ripped up the prescription. "I'm sorry, but it'll have to be the hot milk."

"I've been trying for a few months now," she said, as Amy was about to motion her out of the door. "Do you think anything's wrong with me?"

Amy smiled, while trying to conceal her impatience. "Sophia, that is a whole new appointment." She glanced at the notes on her screen. Sophia was thirty-nine. "At your age, getting pregnant can take some time."

"I know. But six months? Do you think I've left it too late? Do you think I should have IVF?"

"I think we need to make another appointment to discuss the options," Amy said robotically.

"But I'm here now!"

So in the end, she had given Sophia another twenty minutes. Amy was so used to seeing women like her, she knew the drill off pat. Attractive, successful, in their late thirties, who, for whatever reason, had put off having children until the last possible second and were now discovering that actually it was a second too late.

Having finally ushered Sophia out, Amy wearily packed her bag and put on her coat. In the lobby she bumped into Madhura.

"Hiya, Amy. How was your day?"

"Pretty shocking. Yours?"

"Oh same, same. God, you'll never guess who I bumped into last night, though."

"Who?" said Amy, uneasily.

"Danny."

"Oh. Right." Amy was still having nightmares about Danny. She couldn't forgive herself for the way she'd wasted his time and her cowardice in not ending it years ago.

"He was with a girl. Holding hands. They seemed very happy." Madhura looked at Amy anxiously. "You don't mind me telling you that, do you?"

"No, no, of course not," Amy croaked. "That's great for him. Anyway, I'd better run. See you tomorrow."

Going home on the bus, Amy tried to work out how this news made her feel. Relieved, mainly, that she was off the hook. Curious whether this girl was prettier than her. And unreasonably miffed that Danny, who had proclaimed himself heartbroken and devastated, had already recovered. Obviously, she wasn't as irresistible as all that. Her thoughts moved on to Sophia and her ilk. Only a year ago, having a baby had seemed about as relevant to Amy as ice-hockey tactics or Greek folk dancing. But in the past few months that had begun to change: a few friends from uni were pregnant; and Amy was seeing more and more women with problems conceiving. The realization was dawning that if she wanted children, and she did — ideally a boy and a girl — she would have to do something about it, and sooner rather than later, if she wasn't to end up another IVF casualty. She needed to have a talk with Doug. But Doug wasn't really into talks, he liked things easy and fun and no pressure. If Amy asked him what he'd like for supper he was apt to fly off the handle, shouting he didn't know and why was she hassling him? So forget the talk. Far better to take the softly-softly approach than risk Doug running screaming for the hills.

She unlocked the front door and walked into the kitchen. The washing-up from last night's dinner still sat in the sink. Doug, Gregor, Baz and Pinny were lying on the sofa. Pinny had her head in Baz's lap and her feet on Doug's knees, Amy noticed uncomfortably. They were half watching a football match while indulging in their favourite pastime of bitching about A&R men. An enormous spliff was being passed around.

"They're all such tossers," said Gregor. "Wouldn't know real talent if it sat on their laps and took all its clothes off."

"Danny from Upstairs was there last night, wasn't he?" said Pinny, rolling another spliff on her ironing-board stomach. "What did he say?"

Doug shrugged. "He said it was OK, but the songs weren't quite together yet. He'll come again in a few months."

"He wasn't even listening to the songs. He was on his phone for the first three, I saw him." Watching unnoticed in the hallway, Amy waited for the inevitable: "What gets me."

"What gets me is none of them have any guts. They're all looking for the next Coldplay. They're so frightened of their bosses they don't actually know what they like any more. They just stick to the bland and predictable. Oh, hi, Amy."

"Hi," she said frostily.

"Hey." Doug waved. "I was saying that a breakthrough can't be far off."

"Right," Amy said.

"I just don't know how much longer we can carry on," moaned Gregor. "I mean if these guys are so thick they can't see how great we are, I'm not sure I want to give them the satisfaction of signing us."

"Doug, can I have a word in the bedroom?" Amy said. Reluctantly, he hauled himself up.

"Could you send your friends home, please?" Amy said when he'd shut the door.

"What? *Why?*"

"I'm knackered. And I'm not in the mood for company." She couldn't quite bring herself to say "they're taking drugs and I've decided no more drugs in the house." Doug would think she'd gone mad. She'd save that revelation for another time.

"Ames! I can't do that. It'd be rude."

"It was rude of you not to warn me they'd all be here."

He looked at her, confused. "But Amy, you don't mind the guys being here. I mean, they're your friends too. Especially Pinny. What's wrong with you? You used to love the place being full of people."

"I'm tired," she said, flopping on the bed.

"You're always tired. I'm sure you didn't use to be this way; you used to be more fun."

Amy was wounded. "I *am* still fun when I get a chance."

"What? A chance like this?" Suddenly his hand was up the front of her shirt. Despite her crossness, Amy felt a flicker in her groin.

"Doug, what are you doing? All the others are next door!"

"So? A chance like . . . this?"

Now he was unbuttoning her trousers. She giggled and her hands slipped under his T-shirt.

"A chance like this is good."

They emerged from the bedroom fifteen minutes later, slightly dishevelled and — in Amy's case — in a much, much better mood. Doug was right. She needed to lighten up. And stop worrying about babies, for Christ's sake. There was still oodles of time for that discussion and knowing Doug, one day he'd simply surprise her and say children were his heart's desire, so for now why risk the grief?

Remembering that night, she buried her head in her hands and groaned.

Why hadn't she asked him then? Why was she such a coward, always dodging potential confrontation? Crying was meant to send you to sleep, but it was at least an hour before Amy finally drifted off.

CHAPTER
SEVENTEEN

Amy woke to the sound of her doorbell ringing and the door opening.

"Hello?" she croaked like a teenage boy.

A pretty maid bustled in. "Excuse me, signora! I did not know the room was occupied."

"Shit!" She rubbed her sticky eyes and looked at the clock on the television, 10.03. "Can you give me ten minutes?"

"*Si*, signora."

Quick! Breakfast stopped at 10.30. She'd shower when she got back, she thought, pulling a sundress over her head. As she opened her door, she saw an envelope had been pushed under it. Once again, her heart tiddly-winked. It had to be a message from Doug. She waited until she was in the lift, before ripping it open. Two tickets fell out and a handwritten note.

Dear Doctor (I don't know your name),
So sorry to have troubled you last night. Please accept an invitation to the premiere and party afterwards for you and your husband. And no, I'm

not going to ask for anything (even a suite swap)
in return.
  Yours spottily,
  Hal Blackstock

She smiled as she surveyed the embossed invitation to attend a film premiere in the Piazza di Spagna followed by a reception on the Hotel de Russie's terrace. The lift doors pinged open and she hurried across the courtyard to the almost deserted dining area. Waiters were clearing away the tables for lunch.

"Hey, Amy!"

She looked round. It was Marian and Roger sitting at a corner table, with a very glamorous woman. It took Amy a second to register it was the blonde she'd seen in the lift with the vile Mr Doubleday.

"Hi!"

"How are you, Amy? Where's hubby this morning?"

"He's got a migraine," Amy explained smoothly.

"Oh poor thing," Marian said. "I've been dying to meet him. He could have joined us. We're having a champagne breakfast to mark our thirtieth wedding anniversary. Do sit down, love, and meet Lisa. She's another Brit, you know."

Amy and Lisa nodded at each other in a very British way and mumbled hello.

"Amy's here on her honeymoon."

"Oh, lovely," said Lisa. She had a Cockney accent. Amy noticed a huge diamond nestling in her cleavage and another on her ring finger.

"Want to join us?" Roger asked, nodding at the champagne bottle.

"I . . ."

"Ah, come on, Amy," Roger bellowed. "Can't have you sitting on yer ownsome lonesome."

Marian raised a warning finger. "Roger, she can't drink champagne." As Lisa looked confused, she stage whispered, "There's a little one on the way."

"Oh, right!" A smile spread over Lisa's pretty face. "Congratulations. I hope you managed a couple of drinks at your wedding. I can't think of anything worse than not being able to get bladdered on the big day."

Amy suppressed a smirk, then turned to the young waiter who was hovering behind them.

"Now be careful," Marian warned her. "No soft-boiled eggs for you, dear. Remember, I was a midwife. So any advice, feel free to ask."

"Tea or coffee?" the waiter asked.

"Coffee, please."

"Oh no," Marian interjected. "You can't have that. So bad for the baby."

Amy debated revealing that she was, in fact, a doctor, well versed in explaining to fifteen-year-olds why smoking in pregnancy wasn't a good idea, but she didn't have the energy. Besides everyone knew that midwives hated doctors only marginally less than they hated women who chose epidurals and to bottle feed.

"Oh, I'm sure a little cup won't hurt," she tried.

"Oh no, no, even one can be perilous. Better safe than sorry, eh?"

"OK, tea then," Amy said grumpily. She hated tea in the morning.

"Oh, tea's just as bad. All that caffeine. She'll have a herbal," Marian told the waiter. "Peppermint. Far the best for you, dear. Apart from anything else it'll stop that ghastly heartburn. I had it in all my pregnancies. Now, you are doing your pelvic floors, aren't you? They're terribly important. That is unless you want to end up doing a widdle every time you sneeze."

"Excuse me," Amy said, getting up. At the buffet, she piled her plate high.

"Mmm, eating for two," Marian observed as she returned.

"I put on four stone when I was pregnant with my daughter," Lisa said. "Was a right bloody heifer. Took for ever to shift it. So be careful, love, go easy on the chocolate digestives."

"You've got a daughter?" Marian asked, excited.

"Emily. From my first marriage. She's nine." A flicker of sadness passed over her face.

"Where is she now?"

"With my sister and her children in Sevenoaks. I speak to her every day. She's having a lovely time."

The conversation moved on. Roger talked about the history of some of the churches they had visited yesterday. Amy noticed he and Marian were holding hands under the table. Her eyes filled with tears. She would never find someone who felt that way about her.

Marian stood up. "Well, we'd better get going, Rog. So much to do today. I thought we'd have a tour of the

144

catacombs where the early Christians were buried. But we must all get together for a drink at some point."

"That would be lovely," Amy said over her shoulder, just as Marian raised a finger and cried, "Now take it easy in the heat, dear! And remember, no pâtés or unpasteurized cheeses which includes Gorgonzola, I'm afraid."

Alone together, Amy and Lisa grinned a little warily.

"What are you going to do today?" Amy asked.

"I don't know, really. Simon's working all day, so I'm at a bit of a loose end. Thought maybe I'd go shopping. Though I did that yesterday. What about you?"

"Well, I'm not sure. My husband's migraine's so bad I can't do anything with him." They eyed each other for a second, then Amy blurted, "Would you mind if I came with you?"

CHAPTER
EIGHTEEN

The first thing Hal did on waking was touch his chest. Damn! The spot was still there. That doctor had been wrong. He definitely had blood poisoning and was going to need an amputation. He rolled out of bed and staggered into the bathroom, squealing as he ripped off the plaster and stared at the mirror.

OK. The spot was a *bit* smaller, he had to concede, though he was going to keep a very close eye on it. He grabbed the antiseptic cream and shoved on a good dollop. Better make sure Nessie got hold of some more.

What time was it? he wondered, ambling back into the bedroom. Help, only ten past eight. A whole day yawned ahead of him. This was the day he'd insisted be kept free for him to "enjoy Rome" but how the hell was he going to do that on his own? He'd have been better off getting his time filled with interviews and shoots. At least that way the hours would have passed quicker.

But then the phone rang.

"Hello?" he said, half expecting it to be Marina.

"Hal?" said a strong Belfast accent.

"Ahem, who's calling?" he said teasingly.

"Fuck off, you bastard. You know it's me. Callum."

"Callum? Oh yeah, I do vaguely recall meeting someone called Callum." He decided to stop messing. "How are you, mate? Are you in Rome?"

"I am and I'm very well. Arrived late last night. Had to show some loyalty to my favourite client. How's it going?"

"Fucking awful. I'm having to whore myself around promoting this shitty movie."

Callum laughed. "It's a hard life, isn't it? So listen, what are you up to today? Are you able to hang out?"

"Absolutely," Hal said, feeling stupidly relieved at his reprieve from a day's solitude. "Where are you staying? Do you want to have breakfast?"

"I'm at the Hotel Baglioni very near you. I'd love breakfast but I have a ton of calls to make, so how about lunch? I could come over."

"OK," Hal said without thinking and then, "Actually, no. Let's go out. Rediscover some of my old haunts. Remember, I used to live here."

"Did you? When was that?"

"When I was a student." Hal was piqued Callum had forgotten. It was one of his USPs being able to speak Italian and French. An agent should remember that kind of stuff.

"Oh, yeah. I keep forgetting you're not a complete airhead," Callum said. "OK, sounds fun. Where do you suggest?"

For a second, Hal's mind went blank, then he said, "There's a place in the Ghetto called Da Emilia. I'll get Nessie to book us a table. Can't remember the exact address."

"Don't worry, the concierge'll tell me. Sounds fun. Can't wait to hear you speak Italian. *Ciao*, then."

"*Ci vediamo*," Hal said, hanging up smiling. Callum had been his agent for — bloody hell — more than twenty years now. Sure he could be a pain in the arse sometimes, hassling Hal into looking at scripts that read like they'd been written by mentally challenged yaks and going for meetings with obscure East European art-house directors, but he was also a good laugh. Hal had spent a lot of excellent weekends at his cottage in Wales, singing karaoke late into the night in the kitchen. Marina had always loved going there, he thought with a pang. He'd taken Flora once. She had been a bit tense because the girls were staying with Pierre. She'd wanted to go to bed at nine, which was precisely when Callum's girlfriend Robyn (one of a long succession, though she had been around for a few years now) started dishing up dinner, and the low ceilings had made it impossible for her to do her yoga stretches.

Oh well. Hal picked up the phone again and asked Nessie to ask his driver to pick him up at half past twelve to take him to the restaurant. But pacing up and down the suite not knowing how to fill the next couple of hours, Hal remembered something. He picked up the phone again.

"Nessie, hi. Listen. Could you get Ducelli off his arse and have him sort me out a Vespa?"

"A Vespa? Do you know how to drive one?"

"Of course. I bloody lived here for a year, didn't I?"

148

"Do you think you'll be safe on it?" Nessie asked. "Won't the paps follow you?"

"Ducelli suggested it. No one will be able to recognize me," Hal said. "I'll be wearing a helmet. I can zip around Rome anonymously. It's genius. Apparently Brad did it."

"Well, so long as you're careful, Hal."

"I'm always careful," Hal lied.

Within the hour, Ducelli was accompanying Hal to the hotel's underground garage where a brand new, shiny light blue Vespa stood waiting for him.

"Perfect," said Hal. "It's perfect."

"Is beautiful, no?" Ducelli said, smiling. "I think you will enjoy."

"Oh, I most certainly will." Hal pulled the helmet over his head and climbed on. He twisted the key in the ignition and felt the bike throb beneath him.

"You know where to go?" Ducelli asked anxiously. "You don't need a bodyguard?"

"No bodyguard," Hal yelled over his shoulder as the bike bumped off. "I'm just going to have fun!"

He drove up a ramp, pulled up at the entrance to the street and turned right into the Via del Babuino. Straight along the road, then round the Piazza del Popolo, dodging in and out between white vans and Fiats. A Porsche honked at him and he honked back. This was bliss. Hal was free, no one was looking at him and if anyone was — well, so what? He turned into the Via di Ripetta and sped along.

A nun stepped out into the middle of the road. Hal remembered a piece of Roman lore, how the only safe way to cross a street was to follow a nun or monk — even the widest boys in their Ferraris stopped for them. Giggling, he put his foot on the accelerator and headed straight at her. With a scream, she jumped back. Hal looked over his shoulder and saw her shaking her fist at him.

Snorting with mirth, he carried on. There was time for a quick detour, so he found his way to Via Arenula and over the bridge that crossed the torpid trickle that was the River Tevere in high summer and into Trastevere, his old stamping ground with its mishmash of houses painted pumpkin, apricot and ox blood.

He passed the bakery where he used to go every morning for cornetti — nasty Italian croissants that tasted of dust, but which were part of the essential Roman experience. There was the hardware store where he bought the little stove-top coffee machine, after his Italian friends had freaked at him trying to serve them Nescafé. Over there was the bar where he liked to have his evening *birra*. Hal felt an odd tightening at the back of his throat. What a bugger that no one could tell you in advance when was going to be the happiest time of your life, so you could relish it, rather than waste it worrying about how to pay the next bill.

He couldn't drive onto Piazza Santa Maria with the fountain in the middle, so he pushed the bike a bit to have a look. They'd cleaned up the front of the church in the corner so the mosaics at the top, which had always been a grimy yellow, now sparkled gold and vivid in the sunshine. On his right was the narrow alleyway that led to the Pasquino cinema — naturally,

150

shut for August — where they showed movies in their original English and in summer they pulled the roof back and you sat watching the screen under the stars.

He drove on, amazed at how his memory of those intricate streets had stayed intact when he couldn't have told you what he'd eaten for lunch yesterday. He headed towards the bridge that took him to the Via Giulia with its rows of dusty antique shops. In one, an old man was carefully repairing a chandelier. A dog snoozed under a parked Vespa, a line of washing hung across the street, causing him to duck.

From there all the traffic restrictions meant he had to park again before taking a quick walk to peek at his favourite square: the tatty, vibrant Campo di Fiori where a gang of cleaners were sweeping up old flowers, rotting grapes, wasp-chewed figs and pistachio shells from the morning market. Then he got back on his bike and headed for the old Jewish ghetto where he detoured briefly in Piazza Mattei to admire the dinky fountain with four marble tortoises drinking the water.

Then back, round a corner into what looked like a cul-de-sac. A man lying under his motorbike, using one hand to mend it and the other to smoke a spliff, stuck his face out and greeted a passing nun by her first name. Hal parked the bike and, climbing off, spotted Callum, sweaty in wraparounds, in front of an ancient building draped with vines with the name Da Emilia above the wooden door.

CHAPTER
NINETEEN

"Hey!" Hal shouted.

"Hey!" Callum exclaimed, whipping the shades off his ski-slope nose. "Good Lord, Hal Blackstock. You're slumming it, aren't you? Where's the limo with the blacked-out windows?"

"I got rid of it," Hal said. "I've been reliving my past. Good to see you, man." He held out his hand and Callum pumped it.

"So where's this you've brought me?" he said, nodding at the faded door behind him. "It looked so ethnic, I didn't dare go in on my own."

"It's the best restaurant in town. Or rather, it was twenty-three years ago." *Bloody hell, twenty-three years.* "I know it's not fancy, but it's the real deal."

"It'll make a refreshing change," said Callum, pushing open the door. "Well, come on."

Hal followed him rather nervously. It was just as he remembered from all those years ago, the cool stone floor, the dark green tablecloths. Ceiling fans whirred softly over the room, which was deserted apart from a couple of businessmen negotiating quietly in the corner.

"Just as well we booked." Callum smirked.

"It's August," Hal said defensively. "No one's in town." He remembered the restaurant as heaving, the food as sublime and visits there a rare treat when one of the Americans he guided round the city had tipped him extra generously. He missed that Hal, the unjaded Hal who got excited about going out to eat.

An old lady in a black dress, who Hal recognized as Emilia, bustled out of the back room. Inevitably she'd aged. All those years ago, she'd made a tremendous fuss over him, slipping him free puddings and calling him her English son. But now her eyes were misted over with cataracts, her walk slow and, despite his global fame, she showed absolutely no sign of recognition. Hal, who'd been planning an emotional reunion, sure she'd been following his career with pride, felt paralysed with shyness and decided to say nothing.

"*Si?*" she said.

"*Er. Abbiamo riservato un tavolo. Il nome è Signor Jarse.*"

"*Che?*"

Hal swallowed. He repeated himself more loudly and slowly.

"*Che?*"

Callum stifled a giggle. "We have a reservation," he said. "Mister Jarse."

"*Ah, si, si!* Signor Jarse." She pointed at a table in the corner. "Here, please."

They sat down, Callum grinning broadly.

"So much for the fluent Italian."

Cheeky so-and-so. Sometimes Hal wondered why he didn't fire him. Marina's agent, Nora, had always been: "Oh yes, Marina. No, Marina," which was why they nicknamed her "three bags". But secretly Hal liked the fact Callum took the piss out of him. Almost no one else did any more. "My accent must have got a bit rusty," he said huffily, "or she's a bit deaf."

"Don't worry, you can translate the menu," said Callum, screwing up his eyes as she presented them with two pieces of paper. "I can't understand a bloody word of this. Oh no, I lie. *Pesce alla spada*. That's swordfish, isn't it? I'll have that."

"Yes do, it's Tuesday."

"What's that got to do with anything?"

"You only eat fish on Tuesdays or Thursdays — those are market days." Hal smiled, remembering. "Italy's full of mad rules, especially relating to food."

"Yeah, like what?"

"Never put cheese on a fish dish, so no Parmesan on your seafood linguine."

"Which I would only order on a Tuesday!" Callum cried.

"Fast learner, aren't you?" Hal delved into his memory. "OK, so no side salads, they come after the meal. Never drink fruit juice with anything except a pastry."

"God, your co-star would have difficulties sticking to that one."

"She would, wouldn't she?" said Hal. Justina had driven everyone nuts on the set of *The Apple Tree* with

154

her rigid adherence to a juice diet. "What else? No cappuccinos after ten a.m."

"No cappuccinos? But it's how I love to finish a meal."

"Ah, no!" Hal cried, waving his hands in mock disapproval. "All that milk and sugar sloshing around in your stomach spoiling your digestion. Are you a complete philistine?"

"Bloody hell, I thought Italians were all free-wheeling anarchists. I didn't realize there were all these regulations."

"Oh, yeah. It surprised me too when I arrived. I thought they were an anything goes bunch but there's rules for everything — rules banning petrol stations from selling food, rules for deciding when department stores can hold sales, rules for restricting how far in advance a taxi can be ordered, rules for how many locks a front door must have. Even in Naples where it looks like complete bedlam, you realize everyone's stopping at green traffic lights to make way for the cars going through the red ones."

"You are a mine of information, Hal."

"And the worst thing," said Hal, now on a roll, "is that much as I love Italian food you can get sick of pasta and pizza. But when you fancy a curry your Italian mates all look like you've suggested a plate of roast dog. If mamma didn't make it when they were bambini then they simply don't want to know. I used to yearn for a vindaloo." He smiled, recalling his disastrous attempt to broaden his Italian friends' horizons by making them a Pad Thai. "But, hey, it's

155

been a while. And for the moment I quite fancy a plate of something really Roman. So shall we go for it?"

Half an hour later, he and Callum were leaning back in their chairs, groaning at the empty plates in front of them. They'd started with antipasti of cured meats, gone on to *carciofi alla giudia* — fried artichokes — and then Callum had his swordfish, while Hal had eaten a huge plate of lamb sweetbreads in a lemony sauce with fried potatoes and broccoli on the side. He would have to do double time in the gym tonight, but it was worth it.

"Christ, Hal, I know you're on a mission to destroy my youthful beauty, but this is really a step too far." Callum laughed, patting a distinctly rounded belly under his burnt-orange T-shirt. "You're going to make me fat!"

"That was the intention." Hal grinned. "Head off the competition."

"What's your hotel like?" Callum asked, mopping up some juices with the bread. "I hope they've put you in a better suite than Justina."

"Hers is better than mine," Hal admitted. "Much, much bigger and with its own steam room." He'd checked it out on the hotel website. "I've got my eye on the one across the hall from me, it's got a view of Rome and all I can see are some gardens. You could be anywhere. But some honeymooners nabbed that. Weird. I met the wife last night and she's only a doctor. Don't know how she can afford it."

"Doctors earn shedloads these days. Robyn's dermatologist made about three times what I do."

Hal vaguely wondered why Callum was using the past tense but he wanted to stick to his topic of conversation. "Yeah, but this is the National Health."

"Her husband must be some loaded banker wanker."

"I guess." But thinking about Amy, Hal thought this very unlikely. He'd met plenty of bankers' wives and they all looked the same, expensively streaked honey-blonde hair, lots of beiges and taupes, crisply ironed linen and silk. They didn't wear faded, baggy T-shirts and have frizzy hair piled on top of their head in a purple bulldog clip. Come to think of it, none of them were doctors — nearly all were full-time mothers albeit with equally full-time nannies. The few who worked had interior-design businesses or boutiques selling maternity clothes "because I found it so hard to get anything stylish when I was pregnant".

Still, bankers weren't the only people with money, he supposed, though he couldn't think who else made any, apart from movie stars, of course.

"A doctor," he said reflectively. "You know, I really admire people like that. Doing something proper with their lives, rather than dressing up in silly costumes and fannying around reciting words that other people have written for them. Meeting her really made me think. Perhaps I should retrain. Do something meaningful with my life."

Callum smiled politely. He'd heard it all before, not just from Hal but from all his clients. "You could do that," he said. "After all, Daniel Day-Lewis jacked it all in to become a cobbler. But before you make any dramatic decisions, have a think about what I'm going to tell you."

"Oh yeah?" Hal said, finishing the last drops of their carafe of red.

"I've got an Andreas Bazotti script here with a fantastic part in it for you. Not comedy, proper drama. We're talking little gold statues all round for this, Hal. It would completely change your profile. Could you turn off the telly for ten minutes tonight and read it?"

Hal felt a little tussle inside him. He was on the verge of giving up acting, but Andreas Bazotti was a very hot director, young, funky and edgy. Everyone was clamouring to work with him. Flora, he knew, would put on four stone and grow out her highlights just for the chance of a cameo in one of his movies.

"Think of John Travolta in *Pulp Fiction*," Callum continued, cleverly reading his thoughts. "This part could do the same for you, Hal."

For the first time in about five years, Hal felt a tingle of excitement that wasn't related to sex or winning at PlayStation. Acting a proper part rather than some comedy fop; getting nominated for an Oscar; winning an Oscar and thereby proving to the world he was more than Flora's arm candy, that he was a contender, not just some pretty boy who could deliver a funny line. Yet at the same time, the Hal that never liked to be seen making an effort held him back.

"I could take a look, I guess," he hazarded.

"You do that, mate." Callum took a sip of water. "If you like it, we need to get you on a plane to LA sharpish. You should see Andreas by the end of the week."

"By the end of the week?" Hal pulled a face. "I don't think I can do that. Flora's coming out, remember? We're going to have a little holiday in Capri."

"Uh huh," Callum said. "You've had quite a few holidays this year, haven't you Hal?"

"Cal! You don't believe all that shit you read in the papers, do you?"

"Of course not." Callum smiled.

"There haven't been that many. OK, so we went to Kenya for new year."

"Oh yeah."

"In February we went to Mauritius. Then in March and April we were at Flora's place in Barbados. But that wasn't a holiday!" he added triumphantly. "She was working."

"*She* was?"

"Well, yeah, I was too! I read some scripts. Thought a bit about my novel. I'm getting a plot together."

"So, then what?"

"Then in June we went to Prague — but I did have meetings there. We only had a weekend off. And then last month I was doing press for the bloody movie in LA, so that was work too."

"Although you did take a week off at that lodge in Big Sur."

"Whatever. So that's it." Hal counted. "Only two proper holidays and the odd weekend here and there. That's not excessive."

"No, no, not at all. You work very hard. But look at this script. You may decide it's worth missing a few days' holiday for." He paused. "My phone was ringing off the hook yesterday. Marina's engagement."

"Oh yes," said Hal lightly, feeling his heart plummet like a broken elevator. "I heard about that. I must congratulate her."

"Yeah, that would be in order. I sent her flowers."

"How long do you give it? A year? Nine months?"

Callum shook his head. "Christ, you cynic. You know, Hal, you may not believe this, but when I bumped into her and Fabrizio at Cannes they seemed really happy."

Hal swallowed. "That's great."

"How do you feel about it?" Callum said. "God, that wine was good. I'm going to have another glass. Shall we order some more?"

"I feel fine," Hal said, looking down at his plate. "Marina's free to marry whoever she likes."

"But it must be a bit weird after all that time together."

"Yeah, but we didn't work out. Our relationship died years ago. For the past three years at least we were just chugging along. If it hadn't been for our jobs keeping us apart for such long chunks of time we'd have split years earlier."

"Maybe. Maybe if you'd spent more time together you'd have had something more solid to build on."

"Maybe," Hal said politely. What was this, a Relate session? "But Marina wasn't right in the end. She was too loud, too ambitious, too in your face for me."

She was a lot of fun. A sudden picture flashed in his brain of the two of them playing strip tennis on Callum's court when he and Robyn were stocking up at the supermarket. Marina in her bra and nothing else, he in his socks. He'd tried to persuade Flora to do the same but she'd looked at him as if he were talking of something unmentionable, like anal fissures.

Callum shrugged. "I'm sure you're right. I mean, of course you're right."

"Flora is a lot better for me. She's less . . . grabby. Doesn't care about the parties and the red carpet and posing for the paparazzi. She's beautiful and intelligent and . . . well bred. I'd say she was my ideal woman."

"That's great, Hal. I'm very happy for you. And she's coming out tomorrow then?"

"Actually, she's not. Some problem with the foundation. She's not going to make it until the weekend. So you'll have to be my date tomorrow night."

"Oh! I'll have to remember to wear my prettiest frock." There was a pause. "Would you like to read this script today, Hal?"

Hal paused. "I don't know. I was planning on just taking it easy."

"It's an easy read. I think you'd enjoy it."

But suddenly the prospect of the script was too much for Hal. Once he'd read it, he'd have to make a decision about whether to go for the part and decisions frightened him.

"Not today, mate. I'm not in a reading mood. Tomorrow."

"OK," Callum said blandly. "But don't sit on it too long. It's very hot. If we want to stake a claim to it we need to move fast. Why not read it tonight? I'll have it biked over."

"We'll see." We'll see had always been a favourite Hal expression, delaying the moment of commitment. It used to drive Marina nuts. "I was thinking about a workout and an early night."

"You'll enjoy it. Please, for your Uncle Callum."

"We'll see."

CHAPTER
TWENTY

Lisa knew where to go. "Got to be the Via Condotti," she said as they walked down the hotel steps. "It's the Bond Street of Rome, the concierge told me. I did the Via del Corso yesterday, but it was a bit downmarket. Tomorrow I think I'm gonna go to the designer outlet. It's just outside Rome and it's got ninety-five shops. Come with me if you like."

"Mmm," said Amy. Normally she loved to shop but she'd done more than enough in the run up to the wedding. And tomorrow Gaby would be here. "Perhaps. If my husband's still ill. Though I shouldn't be shopping really. I'm completely broke after the . . . the wedding."

"I bet you are. Think Simon's gonna be bankrupted after ours. I've got it all planned; we're hiring Jordan's wedding coach and I'm getting a dress just like hers with Swarwhatsit crystals and everything and a mini version for Emily. Not too big a bash, maybe just fifty people, because Simon doesn't have that many friends, but then our honeymoon's gonna be in the Seychelles." She hugged herself with excitement. "I cannot wait. I've just gotta persuade Simon that Emily can come too and everything'll be perfect." She stopped to look left as they crossed the road. "What about you, what was your wedding like?"

"Lovely," Amy said vaguely. She looked at Lisa more closely. It was a shame she wore so much make-up, because underneath there was a very pretty face: a straight nose, a big mouth and huge brown eyes that were almost obscured by layers of mascara. Her blonde hair was gleaming, her skin burnished. "Watch out for that scooter! So where's the wedding going to be?"

"I've found a gorgeous country house near Guildford. It's where the singer from Rockdoodle married that footballer. Where was yours?"

"In a registry office. And the reception was at a place called the Cinnamon Club in Westminster." Amy recalled all the stress and arguments surrounding the choice of venue, Mum's tears when she'd broken it to her that she wouldn't be marrying in a church because neither she nor Doug was remotely religious, nor in Salcombe because it was too far to expect all Doug's Scottish relatives to come.

"So you're from London? Whereabouts?"

"Hackney." Amy smiled proudly. As a girl who couldn't wait to get out of the country, it never failed to give her a thrill telling people she lived in a district with a street known as "murder mile", where it was easier to buy drugs than fresh vegetables.

Lisa frowned. "Bloody hell, you poor love. I'm from Walthamstow, myself. Don't you want to get out?"

"No, not really," Amy said, thinking how Danny always used to talk about moving to Surrey or Kent. "I mean, sometimes I get a bit sick of kids in hoodies hanging around at the end of my street and having to walk over needles on my doorstep, but I love the buzz of it all. I can't imagine ever getting bored with it."

Lisa rolled her eyes. "You'll get bored quickly enough once you have a kid. All those bloody junkies hanging round the buggy. I was out of the city fast as I could. Mind you, it didn't help that Emily's dad had buggered off. Left me with a toddler and a bundle of debts. Had to go and live with my mum for five years until I paid them off. Worked in the lingerie department in Debenhams in Croydon. Which isn't the worst job, not by a long shot, but still."

"You poor thing," said Amy. She heard stories like this every day at the surgery but they never failed to make her shudder.

Lisa brightened. "Yeah, well, it's OK now because I've found Simon. Don't need to work any more. Emily can have everything she's ever wanted. He's rich, you see. Massive house, huge garden, room for a swimming pool if we wanted and a hot tub." She smiled at Amy and changed the subject. "Have you got a nice room? Ours is lovely, but Simon was pissed off we couldn't get a suite. All booked up, they told him, even the junior ones. Are you in one?"

"I am actually," Amy was embarrassed.

"You lucky cow," Lisa said without rancour, as they passed a priest bellowing into a mobile phone. "One of the big ones?"

"The Popolo suite."

"Wow! That's like one of the three best." She lowered her voice. "You do know who's in the other ones?"

"Yes, Hal Blackstock and Justina Maguire." Amy smiled at the memory of the pimple. Of course she could never reveal that but there was nothing to stop her boasting about the other story. "Actually, Hal Blackstock wanted to swap suites with me. I mean us. He's got a garden view but he wanted a Rome view. But I turned him down."

"You never!" Lisa hooted. "That's hilarious. You should tell Christine. She'd probably pay you something for that." She pulled a mobile out of her bag. "Here, I'll call her now."

"Who's Christine?"

"Christine Miller?" Lisa searched Amy's face for a glimmer of recognition, then gave up. "She's like the chief interviewer on the *Daily Post*. That's who Simon works for. He's a photographer for the *Post*. Their longest serving. Thirty years. That's why they're in Rome — to do an interview with Hal Blackstock. Did it yesterday, actually. Si said Hal was a tosser but he says that about everyone. Christine said he was hard work. Today, they're trying to get pictures of Justina looking anorexic."

"Oh, right."

"Honestly, you should tell Christine about Hal trying to swap. She'd find that hilarious."

"Do you mind, only I'd rather not," Amy said. "It's just . . . I don't want people knowing I'm here."

"Oh, yeah?"

"Yeah. I've got this . . . very jealous ex, you see, and he's upset about me getting married, so . . ."

"Oh right!" Lisa was clearly the kind of woman who thrived on intrigue. "Bloody hell. I had one of those, he was a nightmare. Sneaked into my garden and stole my knickers off the line. OK, enough said. Forget it." She nodded at the Prada shop on her right. "We could go in there, but the concierge said the one round the corner's better."

They crossed the Piazza di Spagna, with its hordes of tourists and horse-drawn carriages waiting for a fare. To the left, the Spanish Steps were covered in teenagers singing along to guitars, exhausted-looking Scandinavian girls slumped against their backpacks ignoring the attentions of some determined-looking Italian boys. Dozens of artists painted very bad watercolours. Lisa took a sharp right into the Via Condotti packed with Russians and Americans perspiring in the morning heat.

Amy was thinking it was lucky she hadn't told Lisa the farting story. Let alone the saga of the spot. But Lisa's attention had moved on from Hal to the far more immediate concern of the Prada window display.

"Oh, wow! Aren't those boots adorable?"

Before Amy could answer, Lisa had opened the door. Amy followed her in, inhaling a soapy cologne smell mingling with the conditioned air. The carpet was thick and mauve like a 1970s bathroom suite, the assistants gorgeous.

"C'mon," said Lisa marching up the stairs.

The first floor consisted of a warren of rooms, one for shoes, one for bags, one for wispy underwear that was being minutely examined by a loud group of

Chinese women and a couple for clothes. Almost without thinking, Amy drifted towards a chiffon top and stroked it lovingly, like she would a kitten.

"You'd look great in one of those," Lisa said.

Amy smiled, taking it as just a bit of girl banter.

"No, you would," Lisa insisted. "Try it on. Oh. No. I guess there's no point if you're up the duff. All stretchy A-line smocks from now on. Elasticated waistbands. Big knickers."

"Actually," Amy confessed, "that was a bit of a misunderstanding. I'm not pregnant. I think I was just looking fat the other morning."

Lisa laughed. "Oh shit! I'm so sorry. You must be mortified. I didn't think you looked very pregnant, but then it was early days." She grinned. "Well, excellent. In that case, nothing to stop you treating yourself to a new, Italian wardrobe."

"Except I can't afford it," Amy said, but Lisa ignored her.

"What size are you. Twelve?"

"Ten," Amy said defensively. She had made a huge effort to lose some pounds for the wedding.

"Mmm." Lisa was politely sceptical. "But English sizes are larger than European. Maybe try a forty-two. Like I said, I used to work in Debenhams," she carried on as she rifled through the racks, "so I know a bit about all this." She pulled out a pair of black trousers, selected a couple of tops and then ushered Amy into the changing room. "See what you think."

Shutting the curtain behind her, Amy pulled her dress over her head and regarded herself in her M&S

bra and knickers. She pulled the chiffon top over her head, unconvinced. It looked like the kind of thing a granny would wear. But she was transfixed by her reflection in the mirror. This was astonishing. She looked . . .

"Gorgeous," Lisa breathed, poking her head around the curtain.

"Yeah, but it's five hundred euros," Amy said gloomily, looking at the price tag. She'd wasted so much money on a seed-pearl headdress and Smythson invitations, she knew it couldn't be justified. "Listen, doesn't Rome have anywhere like River Island?"

"Just try the trousers on."

She didn't need much encouragement. Suddenly her huge bottom seemed whittled away to a size six. Just as she was about to put her own clothes back on, Lisa reappeared with a dress. Not just any dress, but a pale pink silky one with thin straps and a billowy skirt and a slightly nipped-in waist. The perfect dress. The dress you dream about finding as you rummage around Primark but never do find because it's in Prada.

Even before Amy had done up the zip, she'd never seen herself look so incredible. She didn't know her waist could be this small, her cleavage so enticing. She marvelled at herself in the mirror. This was not the Amy that usually stared back at her every morning. *Maybe if I'd spent my money more wisely and invested in some pieces* — she knew that was the right word — *from Prada he'd have felt differently. Was that what I did wrong?* But she knew that was crap. Doug liked girls who wore skinny jeans and vintage T-shirts, not designer-clad dollies.

When she came out of the changing room, both Lisa and the assistant gasped.

"Incredible," Lisa breathed.

And it was. Pale-faced and scruffy-haired, Amy still looked the most dazzling she ever had in her life. Sort of how she'd hoped to look on her wedding day.

"You have to have it."

"I can't," Amy said, not daring to look at the price tag. "When would I wear it?"

"Oh, bloody hell, Amy. You're on honeymoon! Aren't there going to be a few romantic dinners in posh restaurants?"

The irony made Amy smile. Lisa wasn't to know that the future highlight of her year was going to be the surgery Christmas dinner at PizzaExpress. But then she remembered.

"Actually," she confided, "I have been invited to the premiere of *The Apple Tree*. And the party afterwards."

"Have you? How did you manage that then?"

"Hal heard I . . . we . . . were on honeymoon and sent us some tickets."

"No! Really? Shit. Christine's been dying to get tickets for that, but the publicity people are being right sods. You should tell her. It'd make a lovely story. Show Hal up in a really good light."

"Oh, no, no . . . I'd rather not."

"Maybe you could tell Christine some of the party details. No names or nothing. She'd pay you."

"I'm not even sure I'm going to go," Amy said.

Lisa looked incredulous. "What, in case your husband's not well enough? Sod him. You should go anyway. It'll be a bloody excellent laugh."

Amy thought about it. She hadn't really planned to go to the party, but why not? After all, Gaby would have arrived by tomorrow evening and she'd absolutely love it. So what if nasty Vanessa asked more questions about where her husband was? For a second, she wondered how Gaby's scan was going and if she would find out the baby's sex, then Lisa's unmelodious voice called her back to the present. "If you're worried about money, I'll buy it for you."

"You can't do that!"

Lisa shrugged. "I don't see why not. I've got Simon's American Express card. I was going to get my mum a leather jacket, and my sister a dress, and of course loads of things for Emily."

"Yes, Lisa, but you really can't buy stuff for me. It wouldn't be right."

"It's not me buying, it's Simon. He doesn't care. So long as there's a bar he can help himself to."

"That makes it even worse. Thank you, but no." Amy shook her head, but at the same time couldn't stop staring at her reflection. She did have to have it. A dress that made you look so incredible was an investment. And when — if — no *when* she saw Doug again, she could wear it and his heart would melt. Thanks to the hypochondriacal Hal Blackstock, she *had* got the hotel stay for free, so she wasn't quite as poor as she thought.

"You're going to a film premiere," Lisa said. "Forgive me if this comes out the wrong way, but I think you're going to need something a bit smarter than what you've got on now."

She was right. "OK, I'll take it."

Lisa clapped her hands. "You go!"

"Can I take your card, madam?" said the hovering assistant.

He disappeared downstairs, leaving Amy sitting on a chair, breathing heavily. A couple of minutes later, he returned with his little machine. Amy didn't even look at the total. She was so broke already what was a Prada dress on top of it all? Instead, she jabbed in her pin number. Lisa applauded.

"You did the right thing."

Amy smiled broadly. "I did, didn't I? But no more shopping now, please. I'll be bankrupt."

"OK. No more shopping. For you. But I'm only just beginning. We've got Gucci, Dolce and Gabbana, Versace, Miss Sixty, Diesel — did you know Diesel was Italian? Ferragamo, Fendi. Oh bloody hell, it goes on and on." She glanced at her watch. "But first let's just have a pit stop."

CHAPTER
TWENTY-ONE

After a quick consultation with the guide book, Amy suggested the Caffe Greco, next door. "It's where Stendhal and Goethe and Keats all used to hang out."

"Cool. Who do they play for, Lazio?"

But the Caffe was so heaving with tourists that after a peek through the doors they decided against it.

"OK, how about . . ." Amy frowned as she flicked through the pages. "How about the Bar della Pace? 'Ideal for celebrity spotting', it says here."

"Really?" Lisa licked her lips in anticipation. "Then that's where it's got to be."

With Amy map reading, they made their way through backstreets, across the tiny square dominated by the huge Pantheon and into the long, rectangular Piazza Navona with its fountains, bars full of chattering tourists, cartoonists squatting on stools and Africans selling jewellery. Bar della Pace was just off it, in a picturesque square dominated by a church. The tables outside were all full of chattering, beautiful people. Seeing a couple getting up to leave, Lisa dived for their table. Amy sat down beside her, her Prada carrier bag at her feet. It was ridiculous, but the sight of it made her feel the best she had in days.

"Thanks for making me buy the dress. I needed to be cheered up."

She wanted Lisa to ask her why, to probe a little so she could have permission to come out with the whole, horrible story. But Lisa's mind was elsewhere.

"Did you go to boarding school?"

Amy was surprised. "No. Though my boyf — I mean my husband did. Why?"

"Did he like it?"

"No, he absolutely hated it. Said it was miserable being stuck in an institution all day, with disgusting food and compulsory runs before breakfast." Amy's heart twisted, as she thought of Doug describing his school days. Despite his vehemence, he had been so funny about them, she'd laughed until tears came.

"That's what I thought." Lisa sighed. "You see, Simon thinks Emily should go to boarding school. Says it's the best environment for children. He wants her to start next term."

"But she's nine!"

"He says plenty of kids go away to school at nine. He did."

Amy was appalled. "You can't let him do that."

Lisa frowned. "Well, maybe it's for the best. She'd get an excellent education. One of the reasons I'm marrying Simon is to give her all the advantages I never had. Oh, *ciao*," she said, smiling at a waiter, who smiled back, smitten. "*Dos Proseccos, por favor. Gracias.*" She turned back to Amy. "You wouldn't have thought you could make so much money just being a photographer, but he's been with the *Post* for so many years and he

174

knows all these expenses fiddles. And until he met me he never had anyone to spend it on." She smiled happily. "What does your husband do?"

"He plays guitar in a band," Amy said reluctantly, counting down for the inevitable question. Five, four . . .

"*Really?* Do I know them?" Lisa was looking at Amy with new interest. It was a look Amy had got very used to over the past few years.

"No. They're called Ambrosial, been doing the rounds for years now with absolutely no sign of a record deal."

"Your husband's a rock star?" Lisa said, ignoring everything Amy had just said.

Amy felt a weary sense of déjà vu. "Yes. And I'm a doctor."

"Wow, what an amazing job."

"Thank you."

"You should tell Christine. She could get him some great publicity." Two glasses of fizzy stuff were placed in front of them. "Oh, thank you. Cheers." They clinked glasses and Amy took a sip of the Prosecco. The bubbles tickled her nose. "Is he very good-looking? I hope I get to meet him."

"He's all right," Amy said wearily. "But he's not a god." Time to change the subject. "So where did you meet Simon?"

Lisa smiled. "On the Internet, if you must know. He was a lonely divorcee. I was a lonely widow. At least that's what I told him. I mean, Emily's dad might as well be dead for all the contact we have." Seeing Amy's shocked expression, she laughed. "Don't worry. I'm not going to commit bigamy. We were never married in the first place. For our first date, Si took me into town, to the Ritz, and I thought: thank you very much, I could get used to this. I mean, I like him too," she added, before Amy could make some obvious inferences. "He's a bit, well, a lot older than me, but he's ever so kind. And he has a lovely big house."

"Yes, so you said."

"He's fifty-five. Been married once, but it didn't work out. Said it's been hard to meet anyone because he's always travelling: following Princess Diana to Africa and the Beckhams on their skiing holidays. I think it sounds amazing, but he says it's a lonely life. Different hotel every night. That's why he was dead chuffed I could come with him to Rome. Says it makes all the difference, having someone to drink the mini bar with. And that's why he wants Emily to go to boarding school so I can travel more with him. Which is lovely for me, but I don't see why Em can't come at least some of the time." She took another sip of her drink, then continued, "He's a bit funny around Emily, but he'll get used to her. Like I said, he's refused point blank to let her come on the honeymoon, but I think that's when they could get to know each other. He never had children, you see, said he never wanted them. So sometimes he finds her a bit noisy, but that'll change it, won't it?"

"I'm sure it will," Amy said in the tone she used with her patients when she realized arguments were pointless.

"I hope so." Lisa looked at the menu. "What are you going to have? A salad for me, I think." She patted her stomach complacently. "Got to watch my figure with the wedding coming up."

"I'll have a sandwich," Amy said, just as two youngish men in shades, chinos and stripy shirts with the collars turned up, hovered over them.

"*Buon giorno, signorine*," said the more handsome one.

Lisa eyed them appraisingly. "Hiya."

"You are English?" The man smiled. "We are sorry to disturb you. But we are wondering if we can share your table."

The tiny terrace was packed. Lisa nodded amenably. "Why not?"

They sat down and introduced themselves. The handsome one was Massimo, the less handsome Luigi. Twenty-five, studying at business school, in Rome for a few days before they headed off to their families' holiday homes in, respectively, Sardinia and Sicily. Both spoke excellent English, the result of annual visits to language schools in Brighton. They ordered four more Proseccos and everyone toasted each other with "chin, chin", which, Luigi informed them, was the Italian for "cheers".

"And you, ladies?" Massimo asked solicitously. "What do you do in Rome?"

Amy was about to open her mouth and tell the usual lie, when Lisa kicked her sharply under the table.

"Ow!" she yelped, but it was drowned by Lisa saying, "Oh, we're just here for a few days, R&R. Girls' break. You know: shopping, spa."

"And you like Rome?" asked Massimo, leaning forward.

"Yeah, we love it, don't we, Amy? At least what we've seen of it so far which has mainly been the shops." She giggled and the two men giggled back, entranced. Something about Lisa reminded Amy of Pinny. Pinny who, notably, had not been in touch. With a stab, Amy thought about how she might be comforting Doug.

"And the Forum? The Colosseo? San Pietro? Have you seen these?" asked Luigi, who appeared the more serious of the two.

"What? Oh, no. Not yet. Well, it's so bloody hot, innit? And the shops are air-conditioned."

The two men laughed uproariously, then gabbled quickly to each other in Italian. Massimo cleared his throat.

"Are you free tonight, perhaps, ladies? We can show you some of the sights of our beautiful city."

Amy opened her mouth to say she was as free as a bird, but again Lisa kicked her.

"Ah, afraid not, guys. Some do at the hotel tonight. But we're free tomorrow, aren't we, Amy?"

"Um, yes. Well, I think so . . ."

The men smiled. "Then tomorrow," Massimo said, "we give you a personalized tour. Do you have the *telefonino*? We'll call you."

Lisa gave him her mobile number and the men leaned over and kissed both women politely. They smelt of pressed linen and Eau Sauvage.

"*A domani*," they cried and headed off into the steamy Roman afternoon.

"Sorry about that," Lisa said, watching Massimo's retreating bottom. "But I didn't think it helped for them to know we were spoken for." She smiled at Amy. "And of course, if your hubby's better you don't have to meet them tomorrow. But I might. Be more fun hanging out with two Romeos than going to a mall, I reckon." She looked round for the waiter and made a pay the bill sign with her hand.

"Ah, no signorina," the waiter said. "The two gentlemen, they take care of things."

"I like them more and more," said Lisa, with a huge guffaw.

CHAPTER
TWENTY-TWO

Hal had had his most enjoyable day in ages. At about four, Callum glanced at his watch and exclaimed that he'd better be off; they would be waking up in LA soon and he needed to make some calls.

"We could meet for dinner later?" Hal said hopefully.

But Callum shook his head. "I don't know, Hal. I'll be on the phone until late in the night. Maybe you should read that script."

"Maybe," Hal said reluctantly.

"Just a few pages. Come on. Do it for your Uncle Callum."

"We'll see." His phone rang. "Oh, it's Flora. I'd better take it. Hello, gorgeous."

"Have you been drinking, Hal?"

Hal's good mood evaporated like snowflakes on a bonfire. "No," he lied. "Well, just a glass. I'm having lunch with Callum."

"Oh, say hello," she said distractedly. "Well, things are *not good* here. The girls have got chickenpox."

"Chickenpox?"

"Yah. So I'm afraid I'm going to be delayed even more. The earliest I'm going to be able to join you is the weekend. That's if they're looking better. At the moment they're both really sick. Cosima's throwing up everywhere, it's ghastly, and Milly's got the most vile spots."

"Poor things," Hal said. "But I mean, the nanny's there, isn't she? Do you have to stay?"

"Hal! My daughters are very ill. What kind of mother would I be leaving them to come and swan around with you?"

"I guess you can't," Hal agreed resignedly. "But you'll be here on the weekend?"

"I hope so. We'll just have to see how they're doing. It's a shame but there'll be other holidays, won't there? I mean, I am talking to Holiday Hal."

Hal flinched at the use of this nickname. "I guess," he said. "But I was particularly looking forward to this one."

"I know, but what can I do? Listen, I've got to go."

He hung up feeling hollow. So much for his bloody proposal in Rome. Of course, Flora might make it out in time for Capri, but it didn't look like he could count on it. Was the chickenpox an excuse? Was she going off him? But that was impossible, he was Hal Blackstock and he'd ended every relationship of his life, if you counted Marina, which he did.

He felt Callum's eyes upon him.

"Sorry, mate, sorry. Just been blown out by Flora. Her kids are sick."

"Oh, Christ!" Callum looked concerned. "What's wrong with them?"

"Chickenpox."

"Send her my sympathies. I remember having it when I was a kid. So itchy."

Hal was peeved. Never mind the kids, surely he was the one who should be receiving sympathy? "She won't be here for the premiere tomorrow night." Which of course meant Hal would have to go to it all on his own. The world would go nuts comparing his single status to blissfully coupled-up Marina and Fabrizio.

"You'll just have to go with Justina. I've heard she has no date."

"Isn't she going with that muppethead from the boy band?"

"No, apparently they've split so you can do each other a favour."

"We'll see." Hal would rather escort a member of the Nazi party than Justina, but he wouldn't go into that now.

"Mate, I've got to be going," Callum said. "I'll call you in the morning; let me know what you think of the script." He took his credit card back from the signora and deposited some euros on the table. "I take it you're going to Vespa back?"

"That's right," said Hal.

"See you. Thanks for choosing this place. It was fun."

"Sure. *Ciao.*"

For a moment, Hal sat there bereft. Of course Flora wanted to be with the girls, but he couldn't help feeling rejected. Marina loved someone else. Flora preferred her children. Callum would rather spend the afternoon bellowing into a speakerphone than hanging out. The signora had forgotten him. He was no one's number one.

"Oh, get over yourself," he said to the empty room.

"*Che?*" said Signora Emilia, sticking her head out of the kitchen.

"*Niente! Grazie.*"

"*Prego,*" she said, disappearing again.

The rest of the afternoon lay ahead as empty as a prairie. He had his Vespa, he could go anywhere. He flicked through a mental Rolodex of the Roman sights. But he'd seen them. What was the point in going again? He went outside and climbed back on the bike and a sudden memory of him and Marina riding a scooter along the Corniche in Cannes assailed him. Bugger. Much as he hated the thought, he really should call her as soon as he got back to the hotel. He still couldn't believe she had recovered so quickly from their decade together and found love again.

As the bike chugged up the Via del Corso, he thought back to the night it had finally all imploded, when — unusually for them since they spent so little time in any one place — they were at his house in Marylebone. They'd just got back from a fashion-week party where she had got a bit drunk and been all over Andre Agassi.

"That was fucking embarrassing," he'd snapped at her in the car on the way back. "You do know he's the happily married father of two?"

"So? Does it ever stop anyone in our world?" she'd retorted, kicking the driver's seat with her stiletto. "Anyway," she'd added, "I don't know why you're bothered. It's not as if I'm your *wife*. I can flirt with who I like."

"*Whom* I like," Hal corrected her bitchily. He always liked to rub in the fact that she had left school at sixteen, while he had a Cambridge degree. Thinking about it now, he realized he was always putting Marina down in their final days together. Deep down, Hal knew why. It was because she was getting more and more famous with every series of *Catwalk* achieving record viewing figures, while he seemed incapable of making a film that wasn't garbage.

It shamed him even to think it, but Hal was jealous of Marina — of her increasingly bigger name, of her bigger wage packet and of the fact she genuinely didn't care the show she hosted was trash, while every bad review cut Hal's soul to the quick. Funny how he wasn't nearly as jealous of Flora even though she was more successful than he was and in the same field. He guessed it was because Flora had been born at the top of the mountain, so there was no point in trying to compete whereas he and Marina had started at base camp — and for years he had been several hundred feet higher up than her. She would have never got anywhere if she hadn't been his girlfriend, hanging off his arm at premieres in skimpy dresses, so the fashion world — who'd rejected her as too brassy in the past — were suddenly all over her.

For a moment, Hal was distracted by this thought, then he returned to his and Marina's homecoming. Marina had stormed straight to the living room and grabbed the whisky bottle from the art-deco drinks cabinet.

"I think you've drunk enough," Hal said.

"Oh, don't be such a pompous twat! I've already told you, you have no say over me, you're not my husband."

"Look, Marina, why the sudden stressing about marriage? You know we're not getting married. It's not what you and I are all about."

"Oh, yeah? So what *are* you and I all about?" Her face was contorted into a snarl, but oddly enough Hal felt more desire for her than he had in months. "Walking up red carpets together. Being a power couple. Giving the public two for the price of one?"

"Hey! It's you that loves all that. Not me. You know I never wanted it."

"So you say. But you've done very well off the back of it, haven't you?" She pulled a cigarette from her purse and lit it with her pearl lighter. "Whereas I . . . have to put up with the constant humiliation of 'Why isn't Marina married? Why won't Hal tie the knot?' "

"You never give the impression you mind," Hal protested, thinking of all those interviews where she'd said marriage just wasn't very sexy, that she'd so much rather be someone's girlfriend than their wife.

"Yes, because that would be even more bloody humiliating. But of course I want to get married, Hal. I'm almost thirty-five. I want to have a baby before it's too late."

"A baby?" This was news to Hal. Marina had always struck him as about as maternal as a black widow spider. When she was with friends' kids, her expression was like someone holding their breath in a lift where someone had farted.

"Yes, a baby! I'm a woman. Women want babies. It's what we were put on the planet for."

Hal stared at her, suddenly seeing it. Him, Marina and a squodgy little mini-me in a blue romper suit, bleating "Dada". Yes, a baby might be rather fun. But then again, no . . . he didn't know. If he and Marina had a baby, they would be tied together for ever and ever whether he liked it or not. They'd have to get married at the very least to keep the parents happy, and if they got married then Hal would never be able to marry anyone else and . . . he didn't know, but it was a big world and there were a lot of women out there and he hated the idea he would be officially unavailable to them.

And although Marina was great fun she was never the woman Hal had dreamed of marrying. That woman's parents lived in a big rectory in the country, rather than a semi in Swindon. She had been to boarding school and Oxbridge, just like him. Read books instead of gossip magazines and spoke the Queen's English rather than with Marina's faint West Country burr, which could make her sound a bit simple (though the longer she spent in the States the posher she became, knowing the Yanks went crazy for an upper-class English accent).

She brought him back to the present. "So, Henry Blackstock. What do you have to say to that?"

"Um. We'll see," he said.

186

"We'll bloody see. You've been saying that for ten sodding years. How long does someone need to make up their mind?"

Marina always looked irresistible when she was pissed off, her eyes flashed bright blue and her cheeks went all pink. He went over to her and put his hands on her shoulders.

"Let me think about it. We'll talk in the morning." His hands moved firmly on her bum, the sign he wanted sex.

"What are you doing? Get that hand off me! You disgust me. We're about to break up and all you can think of is fitting in a quick shag."

"We're not about to break up," he said, keeping his hands where they were. "Hey, I've told you: I'll think about it."

She removed his hands and slapped them. "Stop that immediately. And listen to me. We are not having sex again until I am wearing an engagement ring. Have you got that? And now I am going to bed. In the spare room. Good night, Hal!"

"Marina, wait!" he called lackadaisically, but she was already halfway up the stairs and when he banged on the door of the guest suite she shouted at him to fuck off. The next morning she left before he got up and in the evening when she returned after a day lunching with some of her gay pals she calmly told him she was setting an ultimatum: a month in which to propose or she was off. Hal didn't take this entirely seriously. Marina adored him and surely she *must* know he adored her and didn't seriously want to be with anyone else. He just didn't like this pressure.

The month passed before he knew it — she was in the States for most of it filming *Catwalk*, which turned out to be the most successful series yet. He went skiing and then did some voiceovers for *My Sister's Cat*, a cartoon, which, despite OK reviews, was a flop — his fourth in a row as bloggers kept reminding him during his daily Google of himself.

Before he knew it, decision day was upon them; she was back and telling him sweetly over the phone from her flat in Little Venice that she would cook him dinner that night.

He arrived at her place, a knot in his stomach. She was looking lovely in a fifties-style wide skirt and low-cut top that displayed her bust to best advantage. She'd cooked him his favourite fillet steak and fried potatoes. Tiramisu to follow. She ate it all with gusto and Hal was touched — she'd be living on cabbage soup for the following month to make up for it, but she knew how much he liked girls with an appetite; it was one of the many things that had bonded them during their LA years, laughing at the women nibbling on carrot batons and sushi.

"So?" she said, after dinner as they sat on the sofa nursing glasses of brandy.

"So."

"You know why you're here," she said.

"Do I?"

In retrospect, that was the most annoying thing he could have possibly said, but she failed to rise to it.

188

"I think you do. It's deadline day. Have you made up your mind?"

He said nothing.

"Hal!" she said a little more sharply. "Have you made up your mind?"

"You know I don't like being pressured," he said uneasily.

"Well, *you* know I don't like being taken for a fool for more than ten years," she said equably. "So I think after all this time it's only fair for you to tell me what you want us to do."

"Did Suzanne put you up to this?" he asked. Suzanne was Marina's older sister and she'd always been a bit sniffy with him, suspecting (rightly) that he found her three-bedroom house in a modern estate in Penge a bit of a comedown after the Hotel Copacabana in Rio or wherever they'd just been.

"No one put me up to this. It's my decision. So what do you say?"

"Marina." He reached for her long, slender hand. Her nails were a bright pink he found rather gaudy. "You just have to give me a little more time."

She stood up. "Sorry, Hal, but you'll have to go now. You've had plenty of time. I don't see how you can possibly need any more."

"Mazzer!"

"I'd like you to go now, please." She bent down and kissed him on the cheek. "I love you, Hal, but you and I are over now. I need to be getting on with my life. I'll get Marco to take you home, shall I?"

"What?"

"I'd drive you home myself, but I've probably had a bit much to drink. But Marco can drive you." Marco and Antonella were Marina's live-in couple.

"Mazzer?" His tone was less indignant, more pleading now.

"What?"

"This is stupid. You can't just end it like this."

"It's not just like this. There've been ten years leading up to it and a final month's warning. Now it's over." She picked up the phone and dialled through to her housekeeper's room. "Hi, Antonella. Could you get Marco to drive Mr Blackstock home, please? Thank you. Yes. Straight away." She hung up and smiled at him. "Marco'll be ready for you in five minutes."

"Marina. We have to talk."

"No, Hal. We've talked. I know all I need to know. Have a nice life. Goodbye."

All the way home, he bristled with indignation. Marina was mad. This was just another one of her showbizzy tricks. Of course it wasn't over. She'd call him as soon as he walked through the door and laugh at him, saying she'd taught him a lesson. Mind you, Hal wasn't sure how forgiving he'd be. If he'd been unsure about wanting to get married before, he definitely was now. You didn't play silly games with Hal Blackstock; it was childish and insulting.

But the phone didn't ring when he got home and in the morning it didn't ring either. After a couple of days he was beginning to get rather worried in case a heartbroken Marina had taken an overdose and he called her. She picked up on the fifth ring.

190

"Hello, Hal." She sounded very chirpy. In the background was clamour and laughter.

"Hi. Um. Where are you?"

"In the South of France, staying with Mitch. We're sitting on the terrace, eating langoustines. It's heaven."

"So, um. You've been all right?"

"Of course! Why wouldn't I? And you?"

"Oh, I'm fine."

"Hal, you know I think it's rude to take phone calls in company so we'll speak later. Nice to hear your voice. Bye."

She didn't call back. A year later she'd hooked up with that twat de Michelis. He never heard from her again, though once or twice he bumped into her at functions and they exchanged pleasantries like distant acquaintances. He thought every day about texting or emailing her, asking to meet. But, as ever, the thought of being seen to make an effort left him paralysed. Suppose she said no? He'd be even more humiliated than he was already. It was bad enough with the whole world remarking on how one day he and Marina had seemed happy together, the next she was on the arm of a tycoon.

"Friends" of the couple told various newspapers that she'd been carrying on for months behind Hal's back, that she'd dumped him a year ago but they'd kept it a secret for the sake of his faltering career. Hal resolutely stuck to a shrug and a "that's just how these things go". Even when Mummy asked him, even Jeremy, he replied vaguely that it had fizzled out and then changed the subject. A few weeks after she met Fabrizio, Vanessa had alerted him to an interview in *Hello!*

"On a trip to Argentina, Marina Dawson talks about her split with Hal and her new life with boyfriend Fabrizio." His heart was hammering so hard he thought it might jump through his ribcage. There was Marina, busty and dark, watching polo through binoculars, riding a horse on the pampas and saying, "What Hal and I had was very special. But in the end we both realized we were more like brother and sister than boyfriend and girlfriend. Moving on was hard but it was necessary. We wish each other the very best."

"Well, there we are then," he said, shutting the magazine. "*Finito*." He'd always hated the way Marina yabbered to the press, and doing it without his permission was the pits. He was better off without her; he should have seen it years ago. And for the next few months, he had a blast; he slept with dozens of gorgeous women, some of whom he'd fancied for years and then, just when people were starting to raise eyebrows and comment on his playboy lifestyle, he met Flora.

SO THEY ALL LIVED HAPPILY EVER AFTER had been one newspaper headline juxtaposing a picture of Hal and Flora with one of Marina and Fabrizio. Hal had spent a long time studying that shot. Hah! They looked like a couple of smiley carrots, dressed in matching white jeans and pastel polo shirts. He looked at the picture of him and Flora leaving the Ivy, her holding up a hand to block the paparazzi shot, him following, eyes to the ground. She wore a grey wool coat, her blonde hair was in a chignon. They were so much more elegant a pair.

Hal had arrived at the back gate to the hotel. Immediately, a porter opened it. He drove down into the garage where another porter was at hand to help him remove his helmet and usher him through the back corridors, towards the lift.

"Mr Blackstock," cried Ducelli, "did you enjoy your tour?"

"Very much," said Hal. Over his shoulder, he saw the doctor from last night walking into the lobby with a horribly over-made-up footballer's wife type. For a second he was intrigued, but as he entered the lift other thoughts took over. In his suite, he picked up his phone and, after a deep breath, pressed the number he had been considering deleting for months. What was he going to say? Shit, maybe he should hang up. But . . .

"Hi. Marina here. Leave a message. Thanks."

"Marina? Uh. Marina. It's Hal. Long time, no speak, huh? So, congratulations. All the best. Anyway. Yeah, that's all I wanted to say. Good. Uh. Goodbye then."

Mouth dry, he pressed the red button and then flung the phone across the room. A vein was throbbing in his temple. Oh no. One of his migraines coming on. Hal was going to turn all his phones off now and go to bed. Perhaps he'd take the Bazotti script. But he really wasn't sure he wanted to read it. Suppose the part was amazing and he went for it and didn't get it? Or suppose he did get it and ballsed it up and everyone laughed at him for thinking he could change his career's direction?

In the end, he decided it couldn't hurt to take a look. Hal had a feeling he might need something to distract him from other, darker thoughts.

CHAPTER
TWENTY-THREE

Just as Amy and Lisa were leaving the café for more shopping Lisa's mobile rang. Simon had spent a day trying to get pictures of Justina Maguire looking skinny and was eager for his fiancée to return to the hotel.

"Shit, he's probably going to want sex," said Lisa, slipping her Motorola back in her Fendi bag. "Bollocks. Still, what can you do, eh? That's my job now. Better than sorting bras into the right sizes and putting knickers back on hangers."

"I guess so," said Amy, giggling. The two Proseccos had gone to her head. It was a long time since she'd felt drunk and carefree, she realized. Well, carefree wasn't exactly the word — she was still eaten up over Doug, of course, but it had been a long time since she'd sat with a girlfriend in the sun and giggled and even longer since she'd flirted, however ineptly, with two strange men.

Companionably they wandered back, down cobbled alleyways and under arches. They stopped for a bit to watch a mime artist and to check out a jewellery stall manned by a grey-haired hippy. Glancing down at a drain cover, Amy saw the initials SPQR. Wasn't that what the Roman centurions had on their shields in

Asterix? The Senate and the Roman People, the phrase drifted back to her from a school lesson. For the first time Amy began to see the point of the city, to feel its charms work upon her.

"Shame we couldn't have gone out with the boys tonight," Lisa mused, as they approached the hotel. "But Simon wouldn't exactly have been chuffed if I'd disappeared for the night and I doubt your poor, ill rocker would have been either."

"No."

"Fancy a drink with me and Si?" Lisa asked, as they entered the lobby. "Or are you dying to get back upstairs to the invalid?"

Amy was eager to prolong any human contact as long as possible. She was also very curious about Simon. "No, no, Doug's probably asleep. I'd love to have a drink." Out of the corner of her eye, she noted Hal Blackstock walking towards the lift. For some reason, her face flushed scarlet. Hastily, she turned her back.

Simon was waiting under a parasol on the lower terrace, in front of a very large glass of beer and some bowls of exotic-looking nibbles.

"All right, darling?" Lisa chirped, pecking him on the cheek as she plonked down beside him. "Simon, this is Amy. We've just been shopping. Amy, this is Simon."

"Hiya." Morosely, he held out his hand.

"So how was your day?"

"Crap. We had to bribe some bloke to get on his roof terrace, so we could take pictures of Justina on her roof terrace. Which is about the size of the *Titanic*. Bloody nightmare."

"But you got what you wanted?"

"In the end," he admitted. "I got her in her bikini."

"Looking too skinny."

"Looking like a famine victim."

Lisa smiled up at a pretty waitress. "Oh, *ciao*! Martini, please. You have one too, Amy. They're the house speciality."

"OK," said Amy, even though she didn't really like Martinis. But when it came, it was impressive with an accompanying glass full of ice and a spoon laid across it laden with caviar.

"So what's Hal Blackstock like?" she asked, emboldened by alcohol.

"He's a twat."

"Ah, no," Lisa exclaimed. "I told you, Amy, he says that about everyone — Justin Timberlake. Bill Clinton —"

"Now *he* was a mega-twat."

"Madonna. The Queen of Jordan. Have you ever photographed anyone you actually liked?"

Simon thought. "Tiger Woods was all right. He autographed my baseball cup."

"I think Si's been doing his job too long," Lisa exclaimed. "It's all foreign travel, going to India with Prince Charles or flying to Hollywood to do Tom Cruise, but Si acts like he's working down a coal mine."

"Celebrities are just people," Si said. "People who happen to be far more screwed-up, vain and neurotic than you and me. Why get excited about meeting one?

They don't give a toss about you. You're not going to become best mates and end up playing golf together. And travel's travel. A plane's a plane. A hotel room's a hotel room. I mean, it was all right in the old days when we flew business, but management's so fucking mean now, we're lucky to get a seat in the hold."

"Oh, it's not that bad," said Lisa, raising her glass in Amy's direction. "Si's always moaning about the good old days, before management got nasty. Though, personally, I think getting to stay for free in a hotel like this and calling it work is pretty bloody fantastic."

"We're only here because it's where Hal and Justina are staying and Christine wangled some discount. And the old days *were* bloody better. You banked all your salary and lived off your expenses. Bills in for this, bills in for that. You'd grab a sandwich for lunch, then produce a blank bill for the Ritz. Now no one has any fun any more. And someone like me, who's been in the business thirty years, is being asked to stand around hotel steps and restaurants to take pictures of Justina Maguire looking skinny or with a hole in her tights. As if I were a bloody *pap*."

"Si hates paps because they earn more money than him," Lisa explained breezily. She shrugged. "What's wrong with pictures of Justina Maguire? She *is* too thin. Definitely got an eating disorder. Sets a bad example to young girls like Emily. What do you think, Amy? Amy's a doctor."

"I . . ." Amy began as Simon said, "They're too fat or too thin. Either way, I can't believe that's how I'm

198

reduced to making a bloody living, doing close ups of women's arses."

"Most men wouldn't have any problem with that." Lisa chortled, nudging him gamely. Amy had to admire her perseverance. "So tell us more about Hal. Why exactly was he such a tosser?"

"Oh, just all lah-di-dah. Going through the motions. Looking bored. Clearly thought I was beneath him. I have to say, his ex, Marina, *is* a lady. Always remembers your name. Poses just how you ask her. Never looks bored." For a moment Simon was lost in reverie and what was clearly a rather large crush on Marina Dawson. Amy eyed him curiously. He was so unattractive with his unimpressed eyes and red bulbous nose, the legacy of too much drinking in foreign bars. Was a swimming pool really adequate compensation for marrying someone like him?

She was torn from her thoughts by her phone ringing. As usual, her first thought was Doug, but it was Gaby.

"And about time too," she said, as she pressed the green button. "I thought you'd forgotten all about me."

"Oh no, I hadn't. I was just . . . held up." Gaby sounded odd. Shaky. Not like herself at all. Amy felt a horrible sense of foreboding.

"Just a second, Gaby. Excuse me," she said to Lisa and Simon, "I have to take this call in private."

"No worries." Lisa took a pen from her bag and scribbled on a napkin. "Here's my number. Call me if you want to hang out another time."

"Great, thanks," Amy said, shoving it in her bag. "See you later." She got up and walked up the steps that led from the bar to the terraced garden.

"How are you? How did it go?"

"Well, we're having a girl," Gaby said.

"A girl! Oh, how lovely." Amy was genuinely delighted, though she couldn't help feeling a pang at the thought of the future she'd surely lost.

"Yes. It's great news. We're thrilled. But Amy . . . there's a problem. They say my cervix is dodgy and the baby might be born far too early. This afternoon they stitched it up to try and keep the baby in. And now I've got to go straight to bed and rest, to try and prevent a premature labour."

"You've got an incompetent cervix?" Amy couldn't help switching into professional mode.

"That's the one. Oh, Amy. I'm so worried."

"Don't be," Amy said, even though she was terrified. "If you rest as much as possible you'll be fine. Just don't lift a finger. Get PJ and Faviola to wait on you hand and foot. And remember there's so much we can do to help premature babies these days."

"I know, that's what they told me. But it's so scary. And I feel so bad about not being able to run around with Archie. And then there's you. Are you going to be all right out there on your own?"

"I'll be fine," Amy said, despising herself for not meaning it. "Shall I come home? I could look after you."

"Oh no, you don't have to do that. Mum's getting the next train to London. And PJ's being amazing. But

200

listen, I'm at the end of the phone for you. Nothing else to do now, except sit on my already fat arse. So call me whenever you want."

"And you call me. Any time," said Amy and hung up, shocked and dazed.

CHAPTER
TWENTY-FOUR

After the phone call, Amy went straight back up to her suite. There, she lay on a lounger on the terrace, feeling faint with worry. It was one of those frequent times when she considered her medical knowledge more of a curse than a blessing. An incompetent cervix wasn't just a horrible term, it was a very serious condition. Yes, there was a good chance Gaby could hold off giving birth for several weeks, but it would still be miserable for her being bed bound with a toddler and so much else to do. And even stitches and bed rest might not hold the baby in and, although she'd told the truth when she said there was a great deal that could be done now for premature babies, a great number still died, or — worse, in Amy's opinion — were born with mental or physical disabilities. Modern medicine had improved the world so much, people tended to assume they and their children were immortal, but Amy knew that pregnancy and childbirth were still fraught with pitfalls.

She tried to think of her and Gaby in happier times. She remembered an evening in June a couple of years ago. It was a Friday and they were in Gaby's Audi Quattro, driving down the M4 towards Somerset. They were singing along to their guilty secret: *Headlines and*

Deadlines — the Hits of A-Ha, while sharing a giant packet of Skittles.

"God, that was good," Amy breathed, after their tuneless conclusion to "Take on Me". "It's been ages since I've been able to indulge."

"Now's your last chance." Gaby grinned. "You ain't gonna hear any music as brilliant for a while."

They were heading to Glastonbury where Doug and the band had already been for a couple of days. Not performing, as infuriatingly the organizers had passed them over, but hanging out, getting stoned, enjoying the vibe. Amy didn't quite know how they were managing to do that, given it had been pouring with rain every day for a week. She kept thinking about Doug's packing. He'd thrown four T-shirts, four pairs of boxers, four pairs of socks and two pairs of jeans into his rucksack. She'd suggested he took a kagoul and wellies, but Doug had looked pained and said kagouls and wellies weren't cool. She'd called him that morning and said that from the pictures she'd seen in the news, she thought Doug might be uncomfortable walking around all weekend in his Adidas and she was more than happy to go to a camping shop and pick up some boots and rainwear for him. But Doug disagreed.

"Amy, since when did you turn into your granny? I can't wear nylon gear. I'll look like I'm on a camping weekend."

"But you *are* on a camping weekend." Doug had made quite a few granny jibes ever since Amy announced she was giving up drugs. They hurt her, but

203

they also made her more determined to stick to her guns.

"No, I'm not. This isn't a bloody school trip to the Lake District. This is the most special event of the year, and I have to look the part."

"Doug says Glastonbury's better when it rains," Amy said now to Gaby. "He says it's when the true spirit shines through."

"Hmm. Let's bloody hope so." Gaby chewed her lip as a lightning bolt cracked over Swindon. "PJ already thinks I'm insane to want to be part of this. But everyone *has* to do Glastonbury once. It's like bungee jumping or visiting the Taj Mahal. Tick it off the list before you die."

"I guess," said Amy, who had done neither. She decided to change the subject. "How are the wedding plans going?"

Gaby and PJ had got engaged a couple of months ago, since when Gaby had already found a venue, chosen a dress and arranged thank you presents for the ushers. There was still a year to go and Amy wasn't sure how she'd fill the rest of the time.

"Don't ask!" Gaby cried, clearly delighted she had. "At the moment we've got the guest list down to four hundred and fifty and I just don't see how we can lose anyone. But we're going to have to."

Amy smiled sympathetically. Her phone rang. It was Doug. "Hey, how's it going?"

"It's great," said Doug, not entirely convincingly. In the background, Amy heard clashes of thunder and torrential rain. "Except I've had to climb to the top of the highest hill to call you because it's the only place in the Vale of Glastonbury you can get mobile reception. So you're going to have to listen very carefully to the instructions I give you for finding us because you won't be able to call me when you get here."

"It's not too muddy?"

"It's a bit muddy. But that's all right. We're having a laugh."

"I could stop in Bristol and get you some rain gear."

"Amy, you know what I think about rain gear. Forget it. If you want to look like a primary school teacher, then that's your lookout. No, I was calling to say that the field we were in has been flooded, so we've moved to higher ground."

Amy took careful notes of their new position and assured him she and Gaby should be there by about 10 p.m.

"So how are things with Doug?" Gaby asked, as they passed Bristol. "Any sign of a you know?"

"A what?" Amy said blandly, as if she didn't know exactly what her friend was talking about.

"You *know*. Do you think he's getting serious?"

Amy sighed. "Oh for God's sake, Gaby. You know Doug and I don't care about that kind of thing." Amy had decided a while ago that this would be her official response to the interminable question.

Gaby bit her lip, then said, "Have you talked about having a baby?" She knew that was what Amy wanted, though even she had no idea how much.

"No. I'm frightened it'll scare him off."

"Why should he be scared? He's what? Thirty-two? You've told me there are grandfathers at your practice not much older than that. And he'd be bloody great to have a baby with. I mean, he doesn't have a proper job. He could stay at home and be a house husband."

"Oh, I don't think Doug would like that."

"Well, there have to be some advantages to going out with someone who isn't a wage slave. I mean, it's great PJ earns so much money, but I barely bloody see him. He's late for everything and then he spends the whole night looking at his mobile."

"Doug's exactly the same, but he earns no money," Amy said sadly. "It's just . . . the business he's in, it's so tricky." She wished she didn't always have to apologize for Doug.

"Is anything happening with the band?" Gaby asked.

"Not really. I mean, they're doing plenty of gigs, but there's no hint of a record deal."

Gaby moved into the outside lane. "I saw Danny the other day," she said casually, "on Oxford Street, as you do."

Something lodged in Amy's throat. "Oh yeah? How was he?"

"Do you want to know this?"

"Yes."

"He's engaged."

"Well, good for him," Amy said, delighted at how normal her voice sounded. "That's what he always wanted." Silence fell. Amy analysed what she really thought: relief Danny was off her back; fresh indignation he'd got over her so quickly; but most of all frustration. She felt she was being left behind in the race of life, that when she was eighty she'd still be going to Glastonbury and worrying if Doug was warm enough.

It was just past nine when they pulled up in the Glastonbury car park, which was about the size of Bangladesh. It had briefly stopped raining and was still light, but the sky was the colour of cannabis smoke. A steady apocalyptic thumping rent the air. They unloaded Gaby's Cath Kidston tent from the boot, put on their wellies and set off towards a high perimeter fence.

"It looks like something from *The Great Escape*," Gaby said.

"It's meant to keep out gatecrashers."

"Or to stop us from running away."

Amy laughed, but she was beginning to feel uneasy. It didn't help that as they approached the site, more and more people passed them heading in the opposite direction. They looked like an uprising of medieval peasants, caked head to toe in mud, filth crusted in their hair, their eyes wild as if they had seen a sight too terrible ever to share. Some of them were crying.

"Oh, shit," Amy said, as the rain began to fall again.

Having passed through the gate, they were met by a scene of near total devastation: brightly coloured tents slipped down a hill in a mudslide; shivering people waded knee-deep in tea-coloured water full of empty bottles of cider and crushed cigarette packets.

"It's like a Hieronymous Bosch painting brought to life," Gaby gulped.

Hoods pulled up, they began sliding down the hill, desperately grabbing at fences, tents and other people in order to stop themselves being swallowed up by bubbling pools of manure.

"Doug said they'd be in the real-ale tent," Amy shouted, over the sobs of a teenage girl who'd had everything stolen. "And then at eleven they were going to see Babyshambles."

The look on Gaby's face was that of a soldier in World War One who'd just been asked to go over the top. "Maybe we should cut our losses and go back to the car? Drive to Bath. There are some lovely hotels there."

It was so tempting. "I can't," Amy said. "I can't just blow Doug out. There's no way of calling him and, anyway, he'd think I was pathetic."

Gaby nodded understandingly. "PJ's going to wet himself when I tell him about this. Well, I'll give it one night. Just so I can tell the grandchildren."

It took them a miserable hour wading across a quagmire to get to the real-ale tent, which was full of people getting as drunk as possible to blot out their misery. Doug, Baz and Pinny were standing in one corner clasping pints.

"Where's Gregor?" Amy asked, as she hugged them gingerly.

"In the medical tent," Pinny said. "They think he's got trench foot."

Amy surveyed the three of them. Pinny was wearing wellies dotted with pink stars, her blonde hair was plastered to her face and her mascara was running.

Infuriatingly, the overall effect was one of waif-like cuteness. Doug and Baz, however, looked like survivors of a terrible natural disaster. Their faces were wan, their feet covered in enormous clumps of mud, which carried on up their shins and well past their knees.

"That's horrible," she cried. "Your feet must be freezing. God, Doug, I saw a stall selling wellies back there. Please let me go and get you some."

Pinny smirked. Doug's face was grimly determined.

"Ames, just drop the welly talk. You sound like my mum."

Baz who had been studying the programme, exclaimed, "I don't fricking *believe* it. Those wankers Unsuitable are playing tomorrow. How come they got a slot and we didn't?"

"Fucking unfair," Doug cried.

It was the most uncomfortable night of Amy's life. She quickly discovered it was impossible to sit down as every flat surface was filthy. And trying to walk across what had become a slippery cesspit was exhausting. After standing about a mile away from Babyshambles, watching them on giant screens, they went to their tent. It was still upright but Doug had pitched it just in front of a row of stinking portaloos. Amy couldn't sleep a wink so worried was she they'd be flooded by raw sewage. In any case, it was hard to relax what with the din of pounding rain, feet falling over the tent ropes and drunken shouts of "What arsehole pitched his tent *here*?" Three times the front of the tent was unzipped and a face appeared shouting, "'Aving it laaaaarge. Oh sorry, mate, wrong tent," then disappeared again. In the morning, to go to the loo, Amy had to stand knee-deep in mud in a latrine and then queue for fifteen minutes just to wash her hands under a standpipe.

"Don't bother," Doug said.

"Doug, I have to wash my hands. If I don't I'll probably get e-coli. And that's no joke. People die of it."

"Yadda, yadda." He looked truly terrible.

"Are you sure you want to stay another night?"

There was a moment's pause.

"Well . . ." he said, but before he could continue, they heard a loud "Cooee" as a bedraggled, but somehow enticing Pinny came sliding towards them, wrapped in a parka and clutching a bottle of vodka. Amy felt a pang for their former closeness, mixed with jealousy that Pinny could look so genuinely happy.

"Isn't this wicked?" she breathed. "I'm looooving it."

Doug instantly revived. "Course we're going to stay," he announced. "I'm having fun! Anyway, my ticket cost a hundred and fifty pounds. I need to get my money's worth."

Gaby joined them, hugging herself in the drizzle. "OK, I've done my token night. I'm officially bailing out back to London where they have pavements and no cow pats and I can watch this fiasco on BBC2. Anyone who wants to come with me is welcome." She looked challengingly at Amy. Amy looked at Doug, just as Pinny slipped, squealed and grabbed him for support.

"Suit yourself." He shrugged. "If you don't get Glastonbury, there's not a lot I can do to persuade you otherwise."

"It's OK," Amy said. "I'll stay."

CHAPTER
TWENTY-FIVE

Amy woke up miserable. She'd spent another evening, raw with loneliness, marooned on her desert island of a bed. She ate a slice of takeaway pizza she'd bought from a bar round the corner, watched a DVD of a bad thriller starring Harrison Ford that she'd got room service to send up and tried not to worry about Gaby.

It was no good. She had to get home. She thought about the hotel booked in Capri for Saturday. Forget it. She'd had enough of this honeymooning solo lark. She would call British Airways right now and get them to put her on the first flight to London.

They kept her on hold for twenty-five minutes and when an operator finally came on, the news was not good.

"So sorry, Mrs Fraser. All the flights out of Rome today and tomorrow and even the next day are booked solid. It's the holiday season. The earliest I can get you on a flight is Saturday morning."

"But there must be something you can do," Amy pleaded, her voice like an old-fashioned kettle reaching the boil.

"You can come to the airport and we can put you on the waiting list for a cancellation. But many people are

212

doing this and there are no guarantees. You can try another airline, of course, but looking at my computer I can see no spaces."

Amy hung up, miserable and defeated. Her bedside phone rang.

"Hello?" she said, determined not to get her hopes up.

"Amy? It's Lisa."

"Lisa! How are you?" She tried to sound as chipper as possible.

"I'm fine. How's hubby?"

For a second, Amy had no idea what she was talking about. Then she remembered. "Oh, still not well, I'm afraid."

"Poor sod." Lisa giggled conspiratorially. "Well, listen. I expect you're gonna say no. But Simon's busy with Christine all day, doing a more in-depth investigation into Justina Maguire's dramatic weight loss. I mean, like she's not anorexic! And the boys from yesterday have invited us to spend a day at the beach. I know it's not very nice leaving your sick husband in the lurch, but if you fancy some sand dunes and salty air and whatever else the song says, they're going to pick us up from here at eleven."

Amy considered briefly. She could mope around scorching Rome all day, or she could go to the sea and finally have that swim.

"No, that's cool," she said. "I'll come."

"Are you sure?" Lisa was surprised. "Aren't you going to check with hubby first?"

"No, he's asleep. I'll leave him a note. He won't mind. He knows he can trust me."

"Wish I could say the same for Si." Lisa guffawed. "All right then, doll. I'll see you down in the lobby at eleven."

Twenty minutes later, Amy and Lisa were sitting on a beige sofa, clutching beach bags. Amy was in a purple shirt dress, which in the shop she'd decided had a certain sexy secretary chic. Why did she always fall for such clichés? She didn't look remotely as if she was about to remove her glasses and shake down her bun like Wonder Woman. She looked like the PA of the chairman of a small widget factory outside Devizes. It had been the same with boho chic, the aim was to metamorphose into Kate Moss, but in her long skirt and waistcoat she'd looked as if she was missing her dog on a string and pile of *Big Issues*. Lisa, on the other hand, was in cut-off denims that were seared to her perfect bottom and a sleeveless gingham shirt. She looked like a fifties starlet.

"To the sea, to the sea, to the bee-yoo-ti-ful sea," she sang softly, under her breath. "Oooh. I can't bloody wait."

Yet despite her words, she seemed oddly subdued.

"Are you all right?" Amy asked.

"Me? Oh, yeah, I'm fine. Just . . . you know, missing Emily." She sighed. "Had a bit of a . . . discussion . . . with Simon last night. About Sabrina, our dog. Lovely old thing. But Simon doesn't want her. Says she'll have to go to my sister's. But my sister doesn't want a dog, she's got three kids and a tiny house. But Emily loves that dog and . . ."

"What kind of dog is it?"

"Springer spaniel. Wouldn't hurt a fly. I mean, sometimes she does wee on the floor but that's not her fault, she's just old. But Simon hates animals. He did say at the outset it wasn't a goer, but I thought I'd be able to talk him round." She sighed. "Emily was asking me about it this morning and I had to tell her it would all be fine, but it won't be."

"Maybe you should ask your sister again."

"She'll go mental. She's already not happy having Emily for these few days. I mean, she loves her, but she's so busy with her job and the children."

"And your mum?"

"She lives in a one-bedroom flat on the seventeenth floor. Not a goer." She looked down at her hands. Amy noticed she'd removed her engagement ring. Then she looked up and smiled as Massimo strode into the lobby. "Hey, hey, over here!" she shouted and he bounded towards her, kissing her very enthusiastically on both cheeks. "Lisa, *ciao, come stai?*" Then his expression changed as he noticed Amy. "Why are you here? Lisa said she didn't think you could make it."

"Well, I can." Amy smiled.

"A shame. Luigi had to cancel at the last minute." He shrugged. "Never mind."

Outside the hotel a BMW convertible was waiting for them. It was obvious Amy would have to squeeze into what passed for a back seat. Massimo took the wheel. As they drove to the coast, he and Lisa flirted noisily, while Amy bitterly regretted her decision to come. The situation reminded her a bit of the time seven years ago when she and Pinny had decided to go to Paris for the weekend.

As they were checking in at the airport, they had been joined by an intense-looking man called Harry, who turned out to have once worked with Pinny in a bar. Pinny, it transpired, had bumped into him a few days earlier and had invited him to accompany her, not mentioning Amy would be coming too. Amy was furious not to have been consulted and Harry — who clearly thought he'd been asked on a dirty weekend — was equally peeved. Amy was still a student then and Pinny was in some dead-end job, so the three of them had to share a cramped room in a fleapit off the Boulevard Saint Michel. The first night, Amy was kept awake by loud snoring. Seething, she lay for hours, wishing she had the guts to prod Harry and tell him to shut up. The following morning, as they sat in a café, Amy volunteered that she was quite tired.

"Me too," said Harry. "Your snoring kept me awake all bloody night."

"*My* snoring? What do you mean? It was *your* snoring." They both turned to look at Pinny who, innocently, was shredding a croissant.

"There is no way *Pinny* would snore," Harry said. "She's too beautiful."

It had been a miserable weekend. Every time Amy emerged from the stinky bathroom, she found Harry on his knees in front of Pinny, begging her to slip away with him, while Pinny simply didn't see why everyone

216

couldn't get on. But that was then, this was now. As the car sped along the same motorway Amy remembered from the airport, she determined to be positive.

"So where are we going?" she asked brightly.

"Lido di Ostia," Massimo yelled from the front. "The Roman beach. Perhaps not the most beautiful, but very good fun."

Ostia was a very built-up town that, as far as Amy could see, sat directly next door to the airport. As Massimo drove round the narrow streets past a huge Cineland complex and a bowling alley, cursing at the lack of parking spaces, aeroplanes flew so low overhead she could see the undercarriages and easily spot the airline logo. Why wasn't she on one of them now?

Eventually, having parked in a space meant for a tortoise, they got out and walked down towards the sea. Amy saw it twinkle on the horizon. Despite a sewagey smell in the air alarmingly reminiscent of Glastonbury, her heart leapt. At least, she was going to get her swim. But the beach, when they reached it, was nothing like she'd imagined. Instead of randomly scattered towels, there were rows and rows of neat, uniformly coloured umbrellas and bronzed bodies, basking on loungers, whose owners had clearly never heard the expression "minimum of factor 15".

"Lovely," said Amy, raising her voice to be heard over the roar of an incoming 747. "Shall we have a swim here?"

Massimo looked at her and laughed. "No one goes to Ostia to swim."

"But it's the beach, isn't it?" Amy was confused.

"Yes, but the sea is very, very *inquinato*. How you say? Pollutioned. Full of rats. So only crazy people swim in the sea." And indeed, Amy now saw the greyish waters were virtually empty. "They swim in private pools. They are all along the beach, but you must be a member to use them and I am not. I swim in Sardinia."

Amy couldn't believe it.

"So what are we doing here?"

Massimo looked as if she'd spilt balsamic vinegar on his silk shirt.

"We are here to have lunch," he explained patiently. "And then to sunbathe."

Lisa squeezed her arm.

"Hey, sweetie. I'm sorry. I thought we were going to have a dip, too. But lunch by the sea doesn't sound too bad, does it, eh?"

The restaurant was in a breeze-block structure that rose out of the dirty waters. Their table was in the middle of the room with a view of a faded photo of a mountain. Massimo ordered green salad and steaks for everyone. It was a long time coming, during which they drank their way through a carafe of rough red wine. Lisa seemed completely unbothered, laughing and joking, but Amy could feel herself growing more and more morose. What a waste of a day. She should have gone back to the Vatican or to the Forum, instead here she was with a man who wanted her far, far away and a woman behaving very, very badly. Of all the low points in Amy's honeymoon, this was the nadir.

"So, Amy, how long do you and Lisa know each other?" said Massimo when the food finally arrived.

"Oh, two days," Amy said without thinking.

"Two days?" He looked understandably surprised. "I think you are old, old friends."

"No, we've only just met. We're staying in the same hotel."

Massimo looked at her very strangely. "So you come to Rome to stay on your own?"

"OK, we'd better 'fess up," cried Lisa. Her nose was tinted a becoming pink from the alcohol. "Amy's not here with me, we just met. I'm here alone, but Amy is on honeymoon."

For the first time, Massimo looked at her with interest.

"On honeymoon? But where is your husband?"

"He's ill," Amy said, wondering what on earth she was doing, "so he told me to go out and enjoy myself."

There was a moment's confused silence, then Massimo asked, "And where is your wedding ring?"

Amy was amazed no one had asked her this yet. Her excuse, however, was pathetic. "In the safe at the hotel. I didn't like to wear it on the streets."

Massimo looked rightly insulted. "Hey, this is Rome, not Baghdad, you know. We Italians are not thieves. Our standard of living is higher than you English. The first time I go to England, there is no bidet in the bathroom. I mean, how can you live without a bidet? It's disgusting."

"A bidet?" crowed Lisa. "That's what you wash your socks in, isn't it?" She stood up a little unsteadily. "I'm going for a wee. Want to come with me, Amy?"

"Sorry," she hissed, as they washed their hands at the rather grubby basins. "I shouldn't have spilt the beans. I just got carried away. But do me a favour. Keep mum about my situation. Because I really, really fancy Massimo and I don't want anything getting in our way."

"Perhaps I should just beat a retreat," Amy said, drying her hands on a paper towel.

"No! Stay!" Lisa said unconvincingly, then, "Amy, are you pissed off? Please don't be pissed off. Only he *is* gorgeous and Simon's not and . . . I just think I deserve a little treat before I get married."

"You don't have to marry Simon," Amy pointed out. She wasn't annoyed with Lisa, nor was she judging her. She felt strangely detached, as if another person was having this conversation.

"I do have to. I do. Who else will pay off my debts? I've got ten grand on store cards, Amy. Who else will look after me? But don't begrudge me a day of fun."

"I don't begrudge you," Amy said. "You enjoy yourself." And they returned to the table.

CHAPTER
TWENTY-SIX

It was five before Hal fell asleep. The Bazotti script was so good he couldn't stop reading it. And the part! The part was quite different from anything he had come across before, meaty, emotional, provocative and without a laugh to be had from it anywhere.

After he'd finished the manuscript, he lay in bed, his mind buzzing, imagining the potential reviews. "Hal Blackstock — a revelation." "Beautifully played. Mines new depths of emotion."

He could see himself up on that stage, clutching the gold statue, though annoyingly the face he could see applauding madly in the audience was not Flora's but Marina's. He almost picked up the phone to call Callum — it wouldn't be the first time he'd woken him in the middle of the night — but he managed to restrain himself. He'd get on to him in the morning; Callum would get in touch with LA and the ball would start rolling. This was going to be the turning point in Hal's life, the moment screen historians would look back on and marvel at how an acting legend was formed.

Yet when he woke some time around noon (he'd called downstairs when dawn started breaking over the gardens and left strict instructions nobody was to disturb him), his mood had changed. Perhaps the script wasn't as great as he'd first thought. Perhaps it was a bit crass and obvious. OK, so Bazotti was hot at the moment but his last film hadn't been quite as good as the one before, so maybe he was on the turn. He'd have to read it again before coming to any firm decision. Most of all, though, was the worry which had pervaded Hal's dreams that he just wouldn't be up to it. Either he'd fly to Hollywood and audition (which he hadn't done for years) and he'd be rejected in favour of bloody Jude Law, or else he'd get the part and let the whole thing down. "Could have been a masterpiece were it not for the woeful performance of Hal Blackstock, painfully miscast . . ."

The thought made him quite nauseous. He imagined Marina reading that review and laughing. Talking of Marina, why hadn't she phoned? He'd made the effort of paying her the courtesy, she could bloody well be polite enough to return his call.

He picked up the phone.

"Nessie, it's me. I'd like some breakfast please. And the English papers."

"Certainly, Hal," she said, then paused. "You're in all of them, you know. And your interview with Christine Miller's already in the *Post*. She must have worked like a banshee to get it done so quickly. I suppose the Marina news gave it an extra dimension."

"Oh, that's not why I want to see them," Hal lied. "I want to know the cricket score."

Half an hour later, he was on his terrace sipping his pomegranate juice and looking balefully at the pile of papers in front of him. Nessie hadn't been kidding. He was in the *Sun*, the *Mirror*, the *Express* and the *Mail*, not to mention the gossip column of the *Telegraph*. In the *Daily Post*, he distinguished himself by featuring on the front page and over two pages in the middle. Just as he'd feared. WHO'S THE HAPPIEST GIRL IN THE WORLD? ran a headline over that picture of Flora on the boat and another one of Marina and that plonker Fabrizio gurning ecstatically at the camera on some red carpet. And "Who's Being Taken for a Ride?" read a second, smaller headline over a picture of Hal on the Vespa, which some vermin pap must have snapped yesterday.

The interview was in the middle of the paper, accompanied by a picture which made Hal look tired, haggard and irascible. He'd known that tosser from the *Daily Post* had had an agenda to make him look as bad as possible. It was long, far longer than the article on the current crisis in the Middle East and entitled:

HOW HAL LET ANOTHER ONE GET AWAY.

Losing one beautiful girlfriend might be unfortunate, but two is definitely careless.

It's been quite a day for Hal Blackstock. His ex-girlfriend, Marina Dawson, has just announced her engagement to Italian tycoon Fabrizio de Michelis. It can't be the easiest of moments, yet when I met him

223

in Rome yesterday Blackstock was swearing he was fine with the situation. "I'm delighted for Marina," he told me between gritted teeth. "I wish her and Fabrizio all the best. I don't really know him, we've only met a couple of times, but I hear he's a great guy."

There was a bit of waffle about how Hal and Marina had been together for ten years and split eighteen months ago, amid rumours of infidelity on both sides.

"Our separation was just one of those things," Hal says. "Relationships come to an end."

Well, that's his story anyway . . .

The article then launched into a long and detailed analysis of Hal's defects, how he was a vain, snobbish, fading star who, "friends said", had driven Marina away with his inveterate womanizing and refusal to commit. Things had now reached a crisis point with Flora. His quotes about *The Apple Cart*, how he'd loved working with Ben again and what fun it had been, had all been ignored, instead there were merely some snide references to the film's pathetic performance at the US box office.

With his love life in tatters and his career on the skids, Blackstock is clearly in the throes of a midlife crisis. Whether the fading star can turn things around will be his biggest test to date.

"Bollocks," Hal said aloud, as he always did when he read anything about himself which wasn't a five-star review. Though the problem was, it wasn't bollocks at all. In fact, Christine Miller seemed to have an almost eerie insight into his mind, though "fading star" was a bit unfair. After all, Andreas Bazotti wanted him. He toyed with the idea of having Nessie call a few show business diaries to let this be known, but then recoiled — that was the kind of behaviour which he and Marina had always laughed at in other so-called stars.

Why hadn't she called him back?

Stop thinking about her! Surely the most important question now was Flora. Was she getting tired of his womanizing and refusal to commit too? Hal knew it was crunch time. If he didn't propose when — if — he finally saw her, he would probably be all alone again and that bitch Christine Miller would probably get some huge pay rise off the back of her prediction. But you couldn't marry someone just to piss off Christine Miller.

The phone rang and he jumped. Marina at last? But no, Nessie.

"Hair and make-up will be with you in an hour, Hal, and then we'll take you over to the Spanish Steps. There's a photocall for you and Justina at six forty-five and the premiere starts at seven thirty. All right?"

"All right," Hal said gloomily. To his surprise he found himself thinking about the doctor who had cured his spot. Her life was about more than parties and photo-shoots. He suddenly wished he could talk to her. Where was the meaning to it all? He'd always mocked them, but he was beginning to see how Guy and Madonna had fallen for all that Kabbalah stuff. And maybe Tom had the right idea when it came to Scientology?

CHAPTER
TWENTY-SEVEN

Amy, however, wasn't thinking of Hal at all. Her concern was how to get away from Lisa and Massimo. After a disappointing lunch — the steaks had been overcooked, the chips soggy and the salad drowned in vinegar — they walked along the seafront. It was jammed with honking scooters driven by lissom teenagers and lined with amusement arcades, like Blackpool for beautiful people. Lisa and Massimo were ahead of her, hands occasionally brushing, shrieking with laughter, pushing each other playfully.

"*Gelato*," Massimo called over his shoulder. "We will go for a *gelato*."

He led them up a side road. The pavement was narrow and Amy, her sandals rubbing, fell even further behind. To her left she saw the station. She looked ahead at the others, locked in conversation. With a sudden flash of determination, she ran across the road and into the marble ticket hall.

"Rome," she said to the bored clerk behind the glass. "I want to go to Rome." He sold her a ticket for what seemed like very little money and pointed her in the direction of the right platform. A train was sitting there and five minutes later, Amy found herself chugging back in the direction of the city. She pulled Lisa's number out of her bag and sent her a text, saying she'd lost them and decided she ought to get back to her husband. Then she leaned her forehead against the window and watched the uninspiring landscape pass by. Already, she was filled with regrets. She'd ruined the day. Why hadn't she tried to make more of an effort? All right, so she was the ugly friend nobody wanted but she could have tried to be better company. She was so boring, no wonder nobody liked her. Doug was right, she didn't know how to have fun any more.

She stopped herself. All this self-pity, when Gaby was in a far, far worse situation. She called her. She was bedbound and sounded very, very anxious.

"You'll be OK. Just rest. No getting out of bed, except for going to the loo. See it as a treat. Get as many DVDs and magazines as you can. After all, you won't have time for any of that once the new baby comes."

Gaby asked what she'd been doing. Amy gave an abridged account of her day and confessed she'd been invited to a premiere that night, but didn't think she'd go.

"But you *must*, you absolutely must. What's the worst that can happen? You see a free film. Do it for me, Amy."

She was right, Amy decided. So back in Rome, she caught a bus to the hotel (which wasn't nearly as difficult as she had feared) and, once in her suite, applied her make-up just like the woman at the Bobbi Brown counter had taught her to do for her wedding day. She thought she'd end up looking like a member of a drag Abba tribute band, but to her amazement she looked like herself only prettier. She put on her new dress and looked again. She felt like Marilyn Monroe about to sing "Happy Birthday" to President Kennedy. She briefly considered taking her picture with her phone and sending it to Doug, but stopped herself because a) she didn't know how to send photo texts and b) it would have been insane.

She strapped on her Emma Hope shoes, meant to be her wedding ones, and at half past seven set off again, down the Via del Babuino towards the Piazza di Spagna. The square was packed with camera-popping tourists gazing up at the Spanish Steps. As Amy tried to squeeze through them, to get to the red carpet flanked with heavies, she heard a sudden roar. She looked up. At the top of the steps stood Hal Blackstock, in a tuxedo, waving and smiling at the crowd. His arm was round the waist of Justina Maguire, who was both much tinier and much bigger than Amy had imagined, with breasts like torpedoes and a body like a clothes line. Amy smiled. Just think, here was the man who'd been fretting about a zit on a chest and only she — and Signor Ducelli — knew.

As Justina and Hal began their descent, a thousand flashes exploded, a thousand more state-of-the-art mobiles were held in the air so everyone could capture this moment. The screaming was deafening. Amy squeezed through the crowd until she found herself at the end of the red carpet. She showed her invitation to a guard who nodded her through. Legs wobbling, she walked as fast as she could towards the marquee, sure every spectator was questioning her presence. Another guard waved her invitation under a fluorescent light and, satisfied by the glow it gave off, gestured her through. Inside, the first person she saw was Vanessa, impeccable as usual in a tight-fitting dove-grey shift.

"Oh hi," she sneered, "so you decided to take up our invitation?"

"Yes," Amy snapped back. "*Hal* invited me."

"Husband still poorly?"

"Unfortunately, yes. He made the mistake of drinking the tap water."

"I hope you come to the party. There's quite a buffet laid on, you should enjoy it." And with a condescending smile she turned to the lackey next to her and muttered something in her ear. Both tittered.

Amy had no idea how to reply so she moved into the cinema area, with its rows of padded seats, occupied by two hundred or so of the most dressed-up people she had ever seen. She almost choked on the cocktail of Fendi, Gucci, Angel and Dolce & Gabbana. Not a thread was out of place, not a cuticle loose. All the women were so brown they looked like saddles with eyes. Never before had Amy so acutely felt her lack of gold jewellery. Thank God, Lisa had persuaded her to buy this dress. The lights started to go down. Quickly, Amy slipped into a seat four rows from the back.

"*Io sono sempre stato celibatorio . . .*" said a fruity male voice over a montage of Hal waking up startled, grabbing the alarm clock, gasping in horror, jumping out of bed and getting dressed in record time. "*Ma fino a quella mattina in aprile, non avevo mai conosciuto . . .*"

The movie was dubbed. Why hadn't anyone warned her? Amy had to sit through an hour and a half listening to Hal Blackstock declaiming in Italian, like a foghorn on Valium. Justina, on the other hand, had a phone-sex purr. Not that you exactly needed a degree in Italian to work out what was going on. Someone had been stealing apples from the orchard and Hal and his dog had to set about finding the thief.

In any case, the Italian audience seemed just as bored as she was: the man on Amy's right spent the second half of the film reading texts on his mobile, while the woman in front of her fiddled incessantly with her bracelets. It made Amy remember her own, never-worn wedding ring, in a box in the wardrobe at home. No engagement ring, of course, there never had been. Amy thought back to that night she'd asked Doug to marry her. It was January last year. She'd been on her way to see Ambrosial play for the nine hundred and eleventh time in the back room of a pub in Notting Hill when Gaby rang.

"I've got news for you," she breathed.

"Oh yeah?" Probably the chairs for the marquee didn't come in yellow, but orange, or some such disaster.

"I'm up the duff!"

Amy stopped still in the street, assailed by a mixture of delight and envy. "Gaby, that's great!"

"Isn't it? Three months now. Amazed you, the doctor, didn't notice."

"You said you were on a pre-wedding detox and you've been so obsessed I'd have believed anything."

"I ain't going to be a size zero bride now. I'll be Mamma Cass."

"When's it due, then?" Amy asked.

"July. So I'll be eight months gone at the wedding. Not ideal, but what can you do?"

After an hour more of such discussion, Amy arrived at the gig just as the band ran on stage. To her surprise they had been magical. Pinny was electrifying, her delicate mouth bawling out raucous choruses. They had a whole new set of songs and the audience went wild. At the end, an A&R man from Virgin asked Doug for a tape.

"For real?" asked Nico, checking his mascara in the tiny dressing room mirror.

"For sure."

They all cheered and then descended on the bar. Within an hour everyone was very drunk. Amy, keyed up with Gaby's news, was in the worst state she'd been in for ages. A DJ took the stage and they danced and danced and danced. Amy had forgotten how good it felt to be covered in sweat, heart pumping with adrenalin, high on the beat, though everyone else was high on quite a few other things.

"This is a perfect night," she shouted to Doug.

"It is, isn't it?" He pulled her to him and they started kissing like they hadn't kissed for months. As it grew more urgent, Doug held her at arm's length.

"Shall we go outside?" he asked.

Amy grinned. "Why not?"

They found themselves in an alleyway, round the back of the club. Amy was up against the wall, her legs wrapped around Doug's waist. He was in such a hurry he didn't even unzip his trousers properly.

"Wow!" he said afterwards.

"Wow!" Amy replied, heart thundering. This was it, unadulterated, filthy, of the moment passion. It was what love was all about.

"You're great, Amy," he said, belching faintly.

"Lessgetmarried," she heard herself saying.

"What?"

Amy's heart drumrolled. But they were both so drunk. If he said no, she could always say she'd been joking.

"Let's get married?"

"OK," Doug replied. "Yeah, why not?"

Without further discussion, they went back inside and danced a lot more. They didn't mention their decision to anyone. At five, they took a mini cab home. Doug was asleep within a couple of minutes of walking through the door, but Amy lay awake as dawn broke over London, the momentousness of it all sinking in. She slept for perhaps three hours before she jerked awake, her mind buzzing. She knew exactly the kind of wedding she wanted: a room filled with lilies and dark red roses, a soloist singing "Ave Maria". Her in a Bianca Jagger trouser suit and Doug in a Nehru collar. Gaby reading that bit from *Captain Corelli* about love is a temporary madness. A Thai meal afterwards, dancing — perhaps Ambrosial doing a sort of thrash-metal version of "The Way You Look Tonight" for her and Doug's first dance. She pulled herself up on her elbow and looked at Doug sleeping peacefully. There was so much to organize. How could he not share her sense of urgency?

While she waited for him to wake up, she decided to call a few people and break the news. First on the list was Gaby.

"Have you set a date?" she asked immediately.

"No, of course not. We only got engaged in the early hours of the morning."

"Because you can't have it on the second of June."

"Gaby, of course we're not going to have it on the second of June. That has been in my diary for a year as your wedding date. I'm not going to forget and double book, am I?"

"Sorry. Sorry. Just getting a bit stressed what with the baby and everything. Well, congratulations. It's about bloody time. And hurry up and get pregnant too, please, so I have someone to go through all this with."

Amy's parents shrieked. "Oh, darling," her mother said. "We've been waiting for this moment all our lives. I can die happy now."

"I just hope Douglas bucks up and gets a proper job," her father chipped in.

Doug didn't call anyone.

"What's the rush?" he said, yawning, when he finally stirred around noon and Amy offered him the phone. "We'll tell my parents when we see them. And ditto with the band."

At least he hadn't forgotten, which Amy had feared. Nor, in the cold light of day, did he change his mind.

234

"It's cool. Why not? A wedding could be a laugh."

"Gaby's pregnant," she told him.

"Is she?" Doug blinked. "Why?"

"Why? Well, I guess she and PJ wanted a baby."

"Did they? More fool them. Goodbye sleep, hello stinking nappies, farewell freedom. You know what Cyril Connolly called the enemy of literature? The pram in the hall." He shuddered theatrically. "Yuk."

Amy stared at him for a second. Perhaps they should have the conversation she'd been putting off now? But no. They were hungover and newly engaged; hardly the right moment.

On the way to work on Monday morning, she took a different route which just happened to involve her passing the Emma Hope Sale Shop on Amwell Street. She stared in the window, transfixed by one particular pair of shoes. They were gorgeous: cream satin kitten heels, classic, pretty, perfect for dancing and a snip at only eighty pounds. If the shop had been open she would have bought a pair, but luckily it was still only half past eight, so she got a latte from the café instead. It was just as well, she reflected, pushing open the doors of the surgery. How Gaby you get buying wedding shoes when you'd been engaged less than forty-eight hours?

She couldn't resist telling Andrea and Rosa on reception. They shrieked.

"You did it!" Andrea cried. "You're marrying Jude."

"Jude?" Amy hoped she knew what Andrea was getting at. She'd never thought of Doug like that before, but now she mentioned it there was a passing resemblance.

"Jude Law!" Andrea confirmed. "That's what me and Rosa call him, don't we?"

Rosa looked a little troubled. "No, Ands," she said anxiously, "Jude's not Amy's boyfriend, he's Madhura's. Amy's boyfriend is Simon."

"Simon?" This time Amy had a premonition of doom.

"Simon Cowell. You have to admit he does look a bit like him. Anyway," Andrea added hastily, "Simon's a very handsome man. Yummy, I think."

"Never mind that," Rosa interrupted. "Where's the ring? C'mon, make us jaded old ladies jealous."

"Actually," Amy said, "there isn't a ring. Yet. It was a spontaneous proposal."

"Well, make sure he bloody gets you one. And soon."

Amy thought about that as she opened the door to her surgery. Obviously she needed a ring, but there was no way Doug could afford the kind she'd like. She couldn't pay for her own engagement ring, could she?

As Sophia Franklin told Amy about how her second IVF cycle had failed, her mind was far away focussing on the planning that had to be done. She couldn't see why people made so much fuss about weddings. All you needed was a good list and Amy was a list genius. OK, so Doug did sometimes take the piss out of her when he found pieces of paper around the flat saying things like "brush teeth" and "write list", but Amy found it very reassuring to know all her problems could be contained on a scrap of A4. If the Israelis and Arabs just got some Post-its they could have all their problems sorted out in no time. The date and the venue and the dress could be chosen in under fifteen minutes. It wasn't as if she and Doug wanted some ostentatious affair like the one Gaby was planning. Amy loathed those impersonal numbers which were so huge you weren't even quite sure whose wedding you were at . . .

"So what do you think I should do?" Sophia was saying.

"Huh?" (Remember to put on list "listen to patients", even Sophia F.)

"Do you think it's a good idea?"

"Oh, yes, yes, I do."

"Good. I thought you might think an all-pomegranate diet was a bit cranky, but I'm convinced it's going to work."

When Sophia had gone, Amy told Andrea and Rosa she had to make an urgent work-related call before they sent in the next patient. She got on Google and within seconds had found a bridal check list. It ran to one hundred and seventy eight items and, as well as the obvious things like bridal gown, bridal shoes, included things she had never even heard of such as plume pen, sixpence coin for your shoe, gown preservation and aisle runner. Amy's limbs felt weak. Oh bloody hell. This was like cramming for finals all over again. How was she ever going to get to grips with this?

Breathe, breathe. If you can qualify as a doctor you can arrange a bloody wedding.

Her phone rang. Seeing Pinny on the caller ID, Amy braced herself, preparing for snide congratulations.

"Hello," she said serenely.

"Hiya. How's it going? Just had a moment out of rehearsals, so I thought I'd call. Saturday night was a laugh, wasn't it? Though in the cold light of day it looks like the Virgin deal's another no-goer."

"Uh," said Amy.

"I was wondering. Do you think you could get me some Valium? Help me come down after the big nights."

Amy was poleaxed. "You know I can't prescribe drugs to friends, especially for recreational use."

"I know, just trying it on. I live in hope. We should get together some time for a curry. Catch up without your boyfriend on the scene. Thanks to him, I never see you alone any more."

"Is he there?" Amy asked, her throat dry.

"Yeah, he's around somewhere. Why? Do you want to speak to him?"

"He didn't have any news for you this morning?"

"News? What kind of news?"

"Oh, nothing," Amy said. "Listen, my next patient's coming. I've got to go." She found it hard to concentrate on Mr Iqbal and his sore throat. At the end of their session, she had a cancellation, so she got up, put on her coat and went straight out to the newsagent's. She wasn't going to think about why Doug hadn't told his band mates. He would just be waiting for the right moment. Amy had a lot to do and distractions were not to be tolerated.

CHAPTER
TWENTY-EIGHT

At the premiere party on the hotel terrace, Hal was beyond bored. Having skipped the actual film, he'd retreated to his suite, but had then been summoned to stand in a corner, holding a champagne cocktail and trying to make conversation with George Williamson, one of the studio executives. As usual, George was boasting about how much money he'd made this year and how much he expected to make next year, while his wife, whose much altered face looked as if it had only been partially downloaded, nodded beside him.

"So how do you find Rome, Hal?" she asked.

"Oh, it's marvellous, marvellous. Beautiful city. Yeah, great. I used to live here, you know. So it's been fun rediscovering my roots." He plucked another cocktail from a passing tray, carried by a waitress with pointy Scooby Doo ears on her head. They made her look rather cute. Hal's eyes followed her bottom with its little doggy tail pinned to it as it wiggled through the crowd. In the old days he would have definitely waylaid her, though the terrace presented a smorgasbord of talent, so perhaps he'd have gone for that cute blonde in the silver dress in the corner or maybe the black girl with the amazing legs. She was looking at him over one shoulder and was she . . . yes, she was definitely smiling at him.

With just the faintest nod of the head he indicated she could approach.

"Hello," she said.

"Well, hello," he said, dimly aware he sounded a little bit like Leslie Phillips. "I'm Hal Blackstock." Of course she knew that already, but saying it never hurt, it imbued him with a bumbling air of modesty which the chicks loved.

"I know. I'm *such* a fan." American. "I *loved* the movie. *God* it was funny! And you were fantastic."

OK. Either she was a liar or she was very, very stupid. Hal suspected the latter.

"Gosh, thanks." He fluttered his eyelashes. "So what's your name, sweetheart?"

"I'm Kaylisha."

"Wow. What a name. And you're obviously a model, Kaylisha?"

"Gaad. How did you guess?" She did have amazing tits, although Hal was pretty sure they were fake. He was an expert on the subject, having known Marina before and after the implants. To be honest, he'd quite liked the feel of silicon. Flora's breasts were definitely real, and very small, although everyone said it was marvellous how well clothes hung on her. He tuned back in to Kaylisha.

"So I think I'd like to retrain. Maybe as a psychotherapist. My own personal journey has been so full of peaks and troughs."

"Oh, really?" He looked around for a waiter to refill his glass. Was it worth the risk? How likely was she to kiss and tell?

"Yeah," Kaylisha continued. "I learned how to nurture my inner child, you see, and that really made a difference. Now I go on regular workshops to nourish that part of me. I've just done an amazing one in France. I met a guy there called Antoine, who's a breatharian."

"A breatharian?"

"Yes. He doesn't eat. He exists by light alone."

"He doesn't eat?" Hal knew such behaviour was common in the fashion industry so he qualified his question. "At all?"

"Not a morsel. Doesn't drink anything either."

"Not even Diet Coke?"

Kaylisha looked shocked. "Oh no! His spirituality fuels him."

"Is he a bag of bones?"

"He's slim," Kaylisha admitted, "but not dangerously so. I mean, no worse than Justina. He's a wonderful person, Hal. You'd love him."

"I'm sure. So living without eating? That's pretty cool. Maybe he should go to Africa and teach the starving masses how to do it."

Kaylisha looked impressed. "Wow. That's a *really* good idea. You are a wise, wise man, Hal."

Hal looked around in desperation. There was always a catch. Why did he never learn?

"You should meet him."

"Yes, I'd love to." Where the fuck was Nessie? It was her job to save him from situations like this. And then to his relief, he saw the doctor, looking ten-thousand times hotter than he remembered her, standing alone under one of the torches that illuminated the garden. She was wearing a pink dress, which gave her the kind of figure you saw on those girls they painted on B52 bombers.

"Hey!" he yelled. "Doctor. Over here."

Relief was on her face as she moved towards him. "Excuse me," he said to Kaylisha and turned his back on her.

"Hi."

"Hi," she said.

"I'm sorry," he said, "I don't know your name."

She smiled. "It's Amy."

Pretty. "So, Amy, what did you think of the film?"

"It was hilarious," she said quickly.

"No, it wasn't," he rebuked her. "It was diabolical. Tell me. I can take the truth."

"Well, actually I can't tell you anything about it because it was in Italian and I didn't understand a word."

Hal threw back his head and laughed. "Was it? Oh, sorry, darling, I didn't know they were going to dub it. Shit, I'm sorry. And now here you are at this shitty party. You really must be a glutton for punishment."

"I thought it would be fun."

"Fun?" Hal looked around the terrace, full of beautiful people, laughing much more than they would have been at the movie. "It may look like it. But for me

242

this is work. I'd rather be back in my suite watching the cricket on the sports channel."

"You wouldn't really," Amy protested.

"I would, I promise you."

"Why are you here then?"

"It was in my contract. Had to attend the UK and US premieres and one European. Usually the studio doesn't bother with Europe but the film was such an unmitigated flop it's desperate to claw some cash back somewhere, so they're putting on a show here, hoping to con the Eyeties into parting with their cash." He sensed every eye in the room upon him. "Anyway, married woman. Where's your husband?"

"Still ill unfortunately."

"What?" Hal felt outraged on her behalf. "What is it with all these sickly people? What's wrong with him? Did he stub his toe?"

He felt rather proud of being able to mock his own hypochondria, but instead of laughing, she looked into her glass, embarrassed.

"Well, nice to see you," she said, stepping away.

Hal didn't want her to go. "Hang on a second. There's something I need to ask you."

"Oh, yes?"

"Is chickenpox serious?"

"Chickenpox?"

"Yes. I know some children who have it." He was strangely unwilling to mention his girlfriend.

"Oh, the poor little things. But don't worry, it's not terribly serious. Just like a bad cold really with some

243

itchy spots thrown in. They'll be as right as rain in a few days."

"Oh, right. Good. Good." He fumbled for something else to keep her there. "Your husband must be loaded if you're staying in that suite. What does he do?"

"Oh, he didn't pay for it. I did."

Hal raised his eyebrow. "So *you're* loaded? You don't look it."

"Thanks very much!" She laughed.

"No, no, it's a compliment." And it was. Because it wasn't as if she wasn't pretty or — in this new pink dress rather unexpectedly glamorous — but she lacked the polish of the super-rich, like Flora. Marina had been a bit like that in the early days, although now she always looked as if she was professionally wrapped in cling film. "So how come you're in the suite?" he persisted.

"I emptied my savings account. As a special, surprise treat for . . . my husband because he'd always wanted to take me to Rome. Not that I've seen much of it so far," she added. She looked as sad as an unwanted kitten on Boxing Day.

"Not seen Rome. That's terrible. It's the most beautiful city on earth. I used to be a tour guide here, you know."

"You?"

"Yeah, I lived here for a year. Way, way back when. Before all this happened to me." Hal looked at Amy and a mischievous idea formed in his mind. "Why don't I take you for a tour now?"

"Now?"

"No time like the present."

"What about the party?" she asked, looking round.

"The party can look after itself. I'll get my Vespa. We'll go and explore."

Smiling at the thought of the furore he would cause by leaving so suddenly, Hal grabbed Amy by the hand and dragged her through the hordes of gaping guests down the steps that led to the lower terrace.

"Hey, Hal," shouted an Irish voice behind him.

"Callum," he said, turning round.

"Where are you off to? The party's just started."

"My friend Amy and I were just going to go on a little tour."

"All right," said Callum, his face indicating it clearly wasn't. "But just before you go, tell me, did you read it? Because they're on at me for an answer."

With the doctor at his side, Hal suddenly felt emboldened. All the doubts he'd had were — he now realized — ridiculous.

"I did and I loved it. Tell them I'd love to see them."

Callum raised two thumbs in delight. "Nice one, Hal. I'll call them straight away. We'll talk in the morning. Now be a good boy."

"When was I ever not?" Hal shouted, as he pulled Amy across the lower terrace and into the lobby.

CHAPTER
TWENTY-NINE

At the front desk, Signor Ducelli was telling off the receptionist for falling asleep on duty yesterday. But at the sight of Hal Blackstock approaching, he whirled round, all smiles.

"Mr Blackstock. How are you this evening? What can we do for you?"

"I'm fine, Signor Ducelli. Just a favour to ask."

"Anything," said Signor Ducelli, his mind doing yoga contortions at the unexpected sight of Hal Blackstock and the woman from the Popolo suite whose husband still had to check in. "You just have to ask."

"Can you get my Vespa out for me?"

"No problem," said Signor Ducelli, eminently relieved not to have been asked for a posse of East European hookers or a cache of best Colombian marching powder. "Just let me have a word with the garage." He picked up a phone and gabbled hastily. "It will be ready in five minutes. I take it you prefer to leave from the back entrance? There are a lot of paparazzi at the front."

"Good idea," Hal said with a little wink. He wanted to have fun tonight as well as pissing off a few people, but he didn't want to drive through the barrage of paparazzi, who would then inevitably tail him, leading to some sort of Princess Diana situation.

"Please follow me," said Signor Ducelli. He passed through the lobby, then pushed open a discreet door and suddenly they were in a long corridor. Amy could see pipes and bins full of laundry, all the machinery that kept the wheels of a smart hotel in motion. Signor Ducelli opened another door, leading into a huge, underground garage. In the middle stood Hal's Vespa. A porter handed over two helmets. Hal buckled his on, then turned to Amy.

"Are you ready, baby?" he said in an Austin Powers voice as he climbed on it. "For the ride of your life?" He over-revved the bike and it roared like a lion in pain.

Amy wasn't sure. Hal had had a couple of drinks, after all. But then again, he *was* Hal Blackstock, how could she turn the opportunity down? So she climbed on behind him and the bike juddered off up a ramp and through a gate into a street she had never seen before. Amy was in slight shock. It was so intimate, her bare knees nudging Hal's thighs, her cheek against his warm back. At least she was used to being on the back of Doug's Vespa and didn't feel the need to wrap her hands round his waist; she knew they were better off dangling at her sides. Niftily Hal turned right, then left. Amy's skirt fluttered high over her knees as they twisted and turned through a maze of back streets, high slumbering buildings on either side. But just as she was getting into the rhythm, the bike slowed down, then halted.

"Are you ready for the first great sight of Rome?" Hal asked.

As Amy climbed off the bike, she could hear pounding water. Carrying her helmet like an astronaut in evening dress, she followed Hal — still with his helmet on — down the street, round the corner and into a tiny square, dominated by a huge, marble fountain. A colossal Neptune stood in the middle steering his chariot through stone waves, while two writhing, muscular men tried to restrain his horses. Around the edges, Americans wrestled with their camcorders, Bangladeshi men pressed roses on couples and two men dressed up as centurions tried to persuade them to part with five euros for a photo. A blonde teenager in hot pants climbed over the edge to dip her toes in the water and was immediately reprimanded by a tired-looking policeman.

"The Trevi fountain," Hal announced, as if he had designed and built it himself.

"It's beautiful," Amy said politely and it was, though a bit smaller than she had imagined.

"Not bad, huh? But actually I brought you here to show you something else. Follow me."

He led her up another side street full of bars and souvenir shops then turned and gestured at a small, brightly lit café with people spilling out of the doors. Gelateria di San Crispino, read the sign above the entrance. She followed him into a tiny room consisting of a long marble floor and an equally long glass counter, displaying an array of silver lids.

248

"The best ice cream in the world," Hal said smugly, pretending to be oblivious of the German couple nudging each other and staring. Amy tried to ignore them too. "What are you going to have?"

Amy looked at the array of neat labels on the lids, slightly dizzied. She wasn't very good with choices, she'd wasted hours of her life in front of the Tesco's Finest section wondering what Doug would like. The man behind the counter, who'd been looking at her expectantly, sighed.

"The zabaglione's good," Hal told her. "It's like custard and wine. Or the *lampone*, that's raspberry, if you like them fruitier." He giggled like a schoolboy at the innuendo. "Or have both."

"OK," Amy said. "Um . . . zaba . . . zaba . . . That one. And the raspberry."

"What size?" asked the man, gesturing at an array of paper cups.

"Oh. Sort of medium, I guess. Can't I have it in a cone?"

"Afraid not," Hal said. "It interferes with the purity of the ice cream."

"Oh. OK." The cone was the best bit: all sweet and crunchy.

Hal gabbled something to the man. As their cups were prepared, he slammed his fist to his forehead.

"Oh, shit. One thing."

"What?"

"You're going to have to pay."

"You don't have any money?"

"Sorry. I never carry any. I almost never get let out alone, you see. And there's always someone to pick up the tab."

Just like Doug, Amy thought, as she settled up. They walked out into the warm night, headed back to the fountain and sat on the low surrounding wall. Amy took a mouthful and felt the creamy mixture slide luxuriantly down her throat, like liquid nectar.

"It's delicious."

"Told you," Hal said. He spooned a mouthful through the gap in his helmet visor. "I love this. It's like *Roman Holiday* in reverse."

"You mean the film? I've never seen it."

"Never seen *Roman Holiday*? God, how can that be possible? Well, it's the story of Gregory Peck, who's an American living in Rome, in fact on the street we drove down right next to the hotel. He takes Audrey Hepburn, who's a sheltered princess, on a tour by night on a Vespa."

"So you're the princess?"

He laughed. "That's me. Spoiled, petulant, cossetted. But for one day with Gregory she gets to live life to the full."

"Do they fall in love?" Amy asked. Only after the words were out, did she realize how presumptuous that sounded.

"Of course they do. But it can't be. She's a princess and he's a commoner." For a moment some thought seemed to distract him, then he grinned and lowered his voice. "But he does show her the time of her life."

250

Amy felt a tightening in her stomach. Hal Blackstock was flirting with her. What would Gaby say? Not to mention Doug? Of course she couldn't help fancying Hal a tiny bit, even though he was smaller than her. So why not have some fun?

"My mum thinks you're gorgeous," she found herself blurting out.

"Your *mum*?" For a moment, Hal looked displeased, then he rallied. "How sweet of her. A lot of mums are keen. They seem to think I'm actually the character I play in my films — the boy next door, not some ageing, screwed-up has-been." Before Amy could formulate a tactful reply, he gestured to the fountain. "Anyway, listen. You have to throw in a coin. That way you'll come back to Rome. I should too. Always have before."

"OK," said Amy. There was a pause as Hal smiled at her winsomely from under his helmet.

"Uh. No cash, remember?"

"Oh yes," Amy said, wondering if she should just get it over with and have the words ATM tattooed on her forehead. She opened her purse and emptied a few coins into Hal's hand.

"Sorry, darling. Like I say, I will pay you back."

"Oh, don't worry," she muttered, just as she always had to Doug.

"Shall we?" said Hal, turning his back on the fountain like all the other coin throwers. Amy stood with him. "One. Two. Three." She chucked in her coin backwards over her shoulder. Hal, however, threw in a whole handful.

"Congratulations," said a man standing near them. He was in his thirties, wearing a cowboy hat and leopardskin trousers. "You are going to have an exciting visit."

"We're both going to come back several times," Amy said.

"Not just that. If you throw in two coins you will fall in love in Rome. If you throw in three you will get married here."

"She can't do that, she's married already," said Hal.

"And you, Hal?"

"Oh, you've recognized me," Hal said, with what was obvious false modesty.

"A true fan can see behind a helmet." The man held out his hand. "Vincenzo. But you can call me Vinny. It's my pleasure to have you in my city. I am your number-one fan."

"Thanks, darling," said Hal. He'd always got on well with his fag fans. Rumours had floated around for years that he was gay, or at least bisexual, and had never troubled him at all. The more admirers the better.

Amy was puzzled. "Have we met before?" she asked.

"I think the same thing." Vinny slapped his thigh. "I know. You are the woman I pick up from the airport. On honeymoon."

"Oh my God." She looked him up and down, now taking in the low-cut slashed T-shirt, the jewellery, the carefully applied make-up. "I didn't recognize you out of the chauffeur uniform."

Vinny shrugged. "I'm glad to hear it. So where is your husband? Still not arrived?"

252

"He's sick," Amy said hastily, as Hal gave her a puzzled look. But he had a question for Vinny.

"What are you doing in Rome? Shouldn't you be at the beach?"

"Ah, no!" Vinny cried. "Summer is the best time in Rome. The families are gone, the workers are gone. Only the true *Romani* remain and the city is our playground."

"Oh yeah?" Hal asked. "Can you show us where the swings and the slides are?"

Hal knew he was behaving badly. He was quite aware that tomorrow or the next day, pictures of him in Rome with a mystery woman and a semi-transvestite would almost certainly be all over the tabloids. But he didn't care. The dissatisfaction that had been bubbling inside him for weeks was coming to a head. Being at that party, surrounded by all those doggy-eared waitresses, he had felt more worthless than ever. What was he doing with his life? What was the point of standing in clothes that weren't your own, wearing make-up and often a wig, repeating other people's idiotic lines? At the same time he knew that any pictures would annoy Flora. For some reason that thought amused him. Marina might not like them much either.

"But you?" Vinny was saying. "What are you doing? Why are you not surrounded by bodyguards?"

"I'm having the night off," Hal explained. "It's our very own *Roman Holiday*."

"Ah, I looove that movie. You know it is based on the adventures of Princess Margaret." He clutched his heart theatrically. "My idol. She sacrificed so much for duty. And Audrey Hepburn." He kissed his fingers. "She is the personification of elegance. In fact, I name my cat after her." Vinny's eyes lit up with an idea. "Hey. You would like me to give you the *Roman Holiday* tour? Show you where it all happened?"

"Why not?" Hal said, just as Amy exclaimed, "That'd be fantastic."

"You have your Vespa," he said, nodding at their helmets. "And I have my *motorino*. So you follow me."

CHAPTER
THIRTY

They climbed back on the Vespa and set off again behind Vinny, through the narrow streets then on to a wide square dominated by the wedding cake and along a main road past the pillars and stones of the Forum and the huge Colosseum. They circled it, then sped off down a main road. A rat scuttled across their path as they stopped at a traffic light, a pair of lovers walked home in the moonlight. The only sound was their engines vroom vrooming. Somewhere a clock chimed the half hour. Amy had no idea what the time was, no idea what was happening to her, zooming through Rome with her breasts pressed against Hal Blackstock's back.

They drove into what was clearly a happening area full of hip restaurants and bars pumping trance music into the steamy streets. Vinny's bike stopped opposite a large warehouse with forbidding iron doors, guarded by a burly man.

"Audrey went dancing at the Castel Sant'Angelo," he said, locking his bike with a thick chain. "But these days she would have gone to this club. We are in Testaccio." He smiled at Amy. "Once this was the centre of the meat trade. Full of abattoirs. But today, it is a different kind of meat market."

While Amy and Hal were stowing their helmets in the Vespa's coffer, Vincenzo had a quick, excited word with the doorman, who ushered them in with a nod and a wave. As they walked through the heavy doors, Amy's body was hit by a wave of sound; she felt the floor sagging beneath her under the weight of dancing feet. Following Vinny, they pushed through the crowd of dancing bodies to a padded corner booth.

"*Stupendo!*" said Hal, approvingly, sitting down. A waiter in jeans and a Hawaiian shirt appeared. "*Champagne, per favore. Una grande bottigilia. Grazie.*"

"You like it?" asked Vinny a little anxiously. "I mean, it is not London or Los Angeles. Rome is still a very provincial city."

"It's perfect," Hal reassured him, just as the music turned from Doctor Dre into MC Solaar. "'Bouge de là'! My favourite song of all time." He smiled at Amy, his teeth eerily white in the fluorescent lighting. "Come on, Amy. Let's dance."

He grabbed her hand and pulled her onto the dance floor and began gyrating against her. Vinny followed. At first, Amy felt embarrassed, then the rhythm took over and she began gyrating back. The floors and walls rattled, everything in the room pumped to the lazy beat — the glasses behind the bar, Hal's turned-up shirt collar, her slinky skirt against her legs, Vinny's cowboy hat as he twisted with a pretty, young boy. Amy was transformed into a vial of golden energy, just like she used to be in the early days watching Ambrosial. But as soon as she thought it her legs jerked and stuttered, the tempo was lost and she felt like a robot with a run-down battery.

"Can we sit down?" she mouthed, nodding towards the table. Reluctantly, Hal nodded agreement. The champagne was waiting for them in a bucket, with three flutes.

"Cheers," Hal yelled. "Chin, chin!" They clinked. Amy was dimly aware of clubbers' eyes sliding sideways towards them, then, having noted the celebrity in their midst, sliding away.

Hal downed his drink in one.

"Perhaps you should take it easy," Amy cautioned.

"Why?"

"Well, you *are* driving. And everyone's looking."

"Let them look," Hal yelled. "Fuck it. I never wanted to be a movie star anyway. It isn't a proper job. That's what Dad always says. I've made enough money never to have to work again, so why should I? Why shouldn't I just enjoy myself?"

Amy shrugged. "No reason why not. Though you might get bored."

"How can you get bored having fun? Having fun means you are happy and therefore aren't bored."

She could have been wrong but did she sniff someone who was protesting too much?

"God, I'd kill for a cigarette," he moaned. "Gave up five years ago."

"Then it'd be stupid to start again." Amy knew she was sounding super-doctorly, but the memory of

Ambrosial had made her thoughts all vinegary. "Anyway, smoking's banned in public places in Italy." Five years ago the thought of a smoking ban anywhere would have appalled her, but since she'd referred twenty or so patients to hospital for incurable lung cancer, she'd changed her mind on the issue. She and Doug had had quite a few arguments about it, with him saying people should enjoy themselves as they chose, and her saying why should children be left motherless because of a stupid addiction?

Clearly Hal was on Doug's side. "Smoking banned? In Italy? For Christ's sake. God, no one has any fun any more. With Flora it's all vegetarian this and no alcohol that." He sighed. "Marina loved her booze and fags. In both senses of the word. She was always screaming and mincing around with them. Them telling her how gorgeous she was looking. Shrieking and bitching. It used to really get on my nerves. But then again, she could be such a laugh. She and I would have gone dancing and it wouldn't have mattered if everyone saw us because we were the It Couple. A picture of us in a club together could be worth a big movie deal — or that was how she always saw it."

"Do you miss her?" Amy asked.

There was a long pause. Hal looked at his hands. "I miss some things about her. The way she was always game for a laugh. Her sense of humour; she was very witty. But I don't miss the ambition, the sense that I was part of the game-plan, that one of the reasons she loved me first was because I was going places. Once I'd helped her on the ladder everything had to be about a photo-op and there was no such thing as a quiet night in in front of the telly any more. It was all dinner with Elton and weekends with George Michael and holidays with Guy and Madonna. Flora's not like that. She keeps her inner self to herself and I respect that." Finally he made eye contact. "Yes, Flora's a wonderful woman." He sat up straighter. "Fuck, Christine Miller would have killed to have been a part of this conversation. I'm bored talking about me. What about you? What about your poor sick husband? Won't he be wondering where you've got to?"

"No, I sent him a text. And anyway," Amy felt another splurt of sadness, "it's not as if he's known for his early nights in with a cup of Horlicks."

"So what does he do?"

"He's a guitarist in a band," Amy said reluctantly and sure enough . . .

"Oh, yes? Anyone I've heard of?"

"No. They're called Ambrosial, been doing the rounds for years now with absolutely no sign of a record deal."

"Your husband's a rock star." Hal looked impressed.

"No, he's *not* a rock star. He'd like to be one. There's a difference."

Luckily, Hal's mind had moved on. He refilled his glass. "You know, I've never married."

"I do know. I've read all about you. You're a classic commitment-phobe." Amy couldn't quite believe she was talking to Hal Blackstock so bluntly. But then what did she have to lose?

He laughed. "So the gossip mags say." He shrugged. "Well, I guess it's true. Everyone thought it was bloody odd when I didn't marry Marina. We'd been together for ten years after all. But you know, I did almost marry her after two years. Neither of us had hit superstardom and she was keen, so I bought a ring and took it on holiday to France and I was going to ask her one evening after dinner but then while we were there reviews started coming out for *Evening Class*, which was my first big movie, and Hollywood started a-calling. We were invited for an all-expenses meet 'n' greet with all the studios, first-class flight, two weeks at the Beverly Hills Hotel, so we flew out the next morning, and the moment to propose never came up again."

"Never? But the whole world was talking about it." Amy and Gaby could probably have solved global warming in the time they'd devoted to discussing Hal and Marina's relationship.

"We never talked about it. But you know, it was easy for us to avoid reality. I became huge and then she became even huger. It was all holidays with Mick in Mustique or Richard on Necker; we were both filming most of the year so we were apart for months at a time. It was the perfect excuse for not confronting reality. The years just flew by and when we saw each other the last thing I felt like was discussing dreary things like weddings and kids. It would have been like admitting we were . . . mortal. The thought of being without each other was weird, but the idea of growing old together seemed even more absurd."

"But you're going to marry Flora, aren't you?" Amy was sure she'd read that in the last *Closer* she'd nicked from the waiting room at work, when she could take no more of *Brides* magazine.

He shrugged.

"We'll see."

The way he said it reminded Amy of Doug, always procrastinating, never committing. It made her angry.

"You'd be mad not to," she said with some feeling. "I mean she's beyond gorgeous. And she seems so . . . classy."

"She *is* classy, isn't she?"

"So why wouldn't you marry *her*?"

For a moment he didn't reply. "It's such a big decision. I don't want to mess up. My parents have been together for forty years, you know. That's a lot to live up to."

"I know," said Amy sadly. "Mine have too."

"It's so tricky to get the timing right," Hal continued. "You have to have your heart go boom-boom-boom if you're going to get married, so you have to be in the first flush of love. It's no good once you know that she leaves toenail clippings in the loo or picks her nose."

"Flora doesn't pick her nose!"

"No, but Marina used to. And she'd sometimes reuse knickers from the dirty clothes bin. Until she got a house-keeper." He seemed lost in a memory, then, "So yeah, about marrying Flora. I don't know. But having said that, I don't want us to break up. I mean, I don't desperately want to be with anyone else. And being single when you're forty-three is not exactly the same as

261

being single when you're twenty-five. All my mates are paired off. I feel like a freak. They're having families, their lives are evolving. I'm still stuck in a mindset where the most important thing in my life is who I bumped into at the Ivy on Saturday night."

Amy felt a knife twisting under her heart. This was going to be her. Alone and unevolved, left behind in the race of life. And she wasn't going to be bumping into people at the Ivy, more like Nando's on the High Street.

Vinny was leaning over them, shiny with sweat. "So have you seen enough of the dancing? Shall we continue with our tour? There's one more thing you must see. La Bocca della Verità."

"The what?" Amy asked.

Hal smiled. "The mouth of truth. Come. You'll see."

Outside, the fresh air was like a cool flannel on a feverish forehead. Hal wobbled a little as he moved towards his bike.

"Are you sure you should be driving?" Amy asked.

"Oh, Doctor! Give me a break."

Vinny looked anxious. "No, she is right. Forgive me for saying so, but you are a little drunk."

"Then what can we do?"

"I can drive," Amy said.

The men looked at each other. "You?" asked Vinny. "You can drive a Vespa?"

"Yes. My boyf — my husband has one."

Amy climbed on the bike and Hal sat behind her. She squirmed uneasily as he wrapped his arms around her waist. She'd bet Flora didn't have love handles. As

262

for Marina everyone knew she existed on two bowls of courgette soup a day. Amy had even tried to copy her once and lasted precisely three hours and seven minutes before caving in and eating a whole loaf. But she forgot this as she put her foot on the accelerator. The bike jolted over the cobbles and she followed Vinny into the Roman night. The sky was pearl grey now, the sun's rays beginning to warm the city's yellow stone. One by one the street lights were snapping off. They overtook a lorry, crawling along the streets sluicing the gutters and spraying the pavements clean. They pulled into a little square dominated by a medieval church. As Amy turned off the motor they could hear the birds singing madly. She glanced at her watch — 4.30. She didn't feel remotely tired.

They followed Vinny across what would in daylight be a busy main road, to another, smaller church.

"Here we are," said Vinny, pointing through the bars that shielded the portico to a wall where a huge marble disc portrayed the face of a bearded man with a wide open mouth. "Put your hand in the mouth and if you tell a lie, it will bite you."

"But we can't get close to it," Hal said.

"I can fix that." He pulled a phone out of his pocket, dialled a number and had a quick, excited conversation. "My friend, Gianni," he said hanging up, "is watchman here. He will open up for us."

"That's very kind," said Hal, not sounding particularly grateful. He obviously got this sort of treatment all the time.

Within minutes a yawning but excited Gianni had appeared from a flat round the corner, a leather jacket over his pyjama bottoms and a ring of keys in his hand. After some handshaking and Hal providing an autograph ("For my mother, she love you"), he opened the gates and they were let into the portico where the mouth gaped on the side wall.

Hal stuck his hand in its mouth. "Ask me a question," he cried.

"OK," Vinny asked. "Are you gay?"

"Yes! It had to come out sooner or later. Yes, I am." Hal let out a bloodcurdling scream. He pulled his arm out of the mouth. His hand had vanished. Amy shrieked in horror.

"Oh my God! What's happened?"

Hal laughed and shook his arm. His hand emerged from his sleeve.

Amy hit him. "You bastard."

"I can't believe you didn't know that trick from the film." He turned to Vinny. "Your turn, darling."

"Oh. No . . ."

"Come on!"

"OK." He slipped his hand in the mouth. Hal found he couldn't actually think of anything to ask.

"Do you fancy me?" he tried lamely.

"But of course." Vinny's hand emerged unscathed.

"So, now, Amy."

She knew it was just a silly old drain cover, a silly old superstition, but she felt suddenly, unaccountably nervous.

"Oh. No . . ."

264

"Come on!" Hal urged her.

Reluctantly, she approached the marble disc and put her hand in its mouth.

"What do you want to know?" she said with an attempt at a smile.

"Do you have any regrets about being married?"

From the expression on his face, she could see Hal was just fooling around, being facetious. But as surely as a heat-seeking missile the question hit a nerve. To Amy's horror, she started to cry, as the stress of the past few days unstoppered again.

"I . . . uh . . . Uh . . ."

She removed her hand from the open mouth and lifted off her helmet to wipe the tears away.

Hal looked appalled. "Hey, hey, I'm sorry! What did I say?"

She carried on crying, all the emotions suddenly released on the back of adrenalin and champagne.

"God, I feel terrible," Hal said. "Hey, hey, it's OK. It's not so bad." He slipped his arm over her shoulder. "It's all right. It's all right."

"I'm sorry," she sobbed. "Oh God, I'm so embarrassed."

"Oh no, don't be! We're in the land of emoting. It's compulsory to cry if you stub your toe."

She tried to smile, but the tears started again.

"Hey, calm down." His voice was as soft, as soothing as calamine. "Look, you're tired, I kept you out late and I obviously asked you a leading question, which was none of my business and —"

"I haven't got a husband," Amy gasped.

"I'm sorry?"

"The wedding was cancelled. I'm on honeymoon alone."

Hal stared at her for a moment and then laughed. "You *are* joking?" But then saw she wasn't. He stepped forward and leant his forehead against hers. For a moment, they stayed like that. She could feel the sweat on his brow, her eyelashes touching his cheek. A medley of confused emotions jingled inside her as his lips touched hers. They were warm and soft and firm and dry. Amy had forgotten how to kiss someone new. For a second she was frozen, then she began to respond, amazed how quickly it came back.

"Ahem," said an awkward Vinny. The moment was broken.

Amy stepped backwards. "We really have to go back now," she gulped.

"But . . ."

"I may not have a husband. But you've got a girlfriend."

Without another word, they climbed on the bikes and headed back towards the hotel. It was that hour of the day when a city still has a fresh, unused feel to it. Shopkeepers were pulling open their shutters and café owners were sweeping their mats for a new day. Unfeasibly well-groomed old men in boat shoes and pastel jumpers emerged from apartments to walk their little dogs. Amy's head span. Hal had kissed her and she hadn't wanted him to stop.

They pulled up behind the staff entrance with a squeal of brakes. A church clock struck six.

266

"Well, here we are," Amy said, removing the helmet and looking over her shoulder at Hal. "So sorry about that . . . performance." She turned to Vinny. "But thank you, Vinny, for the most wonderful night."

"Hey. Thank you. It was my pleasure." He kissed her hard on both cheeks.

"*Ciao*, Amy. Good luck." He turned to Hal and shook his hand. Then Hal followed Amy up the hotel steps into the lobby.

"Good morning, Mr Blackstock," said the receptionist.

"Good morning," Hal said haughtily, dropping the Vespa keys in front of him. He looked around for Amy, but she had already disappeared into the lift.

CHAPTER
THIRTY-ONE

For the second day running, Hal woke up around noon. He'd had the presence of mind before he fell into his dawn bed to cancel all calls and put the do not disturb sign on the door. Now, pulling back the curtains he could see it was another beautiful day. And here he was all alone in Rome, with no one to share it with.

Except that wasn't true. There was Amy from last night. He thought of how he'd crushed her against his chest, inhaling her sweetness and feeling her eyelashes brush against his cheek. What an amazing woman. So warm, so *real*. OK, so she was never going to make the cover of *Vogue*, but Hal was through with that way of thinking. As the details of their night returned, he realized this was where he'd been going wrong for so long. What had he been thinking of wasting all these years with airheads who cared about nothing more than how many pounds the camera put on or — and it was the first time he'd allowed himself to articulate this thought about Flora — how virtuous they appeared to the outside world.

Amy was properly virtuous. She helped people, old and young, rich and poor, but she didn't need to make a song and dance about it. Not like Flora who was followed by phalanxes of press whenever she cuddled another little black boy. No, Amy was genuine. Amy was real. Amy was clever and surprisingly sexy. In fact, Amy was perfect in every way.

This was it. At last. True love.

As he stood under the shower singing "All Things Bright and Beautiful", Hal pondered on what a relationship with someone like Amy could do for him. It would be so honest. She wasn't interested in all the bullshit that came with his job, the schmoozing, the vapid gossip, the stupid parties like last night's. She could make him a better person, a more sincere one. Together they could be dynamite. She'd remind Hal about what really mattered in life.

Think about the interviews he could give on the subject. Marina would be well and truly fucked off. He could have a wonderful time making sly digs at how superficial his past life had been and how important it was to look for a partner outside this shallow pond of the super-rich and famous. Someone with *values*.

Remembering how Amy had sobbed on him last night, Hal knew he would never make her cry. He bit his lip as he soaped himself vigorously. He'd get on the phone right now to Nessie and ask her to organize the perfect day for her. A day she would never, ever forget. He pulled on his bathrobe and turned on his mobile. It rang immediately. For a mad second, he thought it must be her — but then he remembered she didn't have his number.

"Hal?" barked an Irish accent.

"Hey, Callum. How are you?"

"Hungover. What about you? What was going on last night, sloping off early with that girl? Bit indiscreet, don't you think?"

"Nothing happened," Hal lied.

"I'm sure it didn't. But given how interested the media are in your private life right now, you could have possibly been a teensy bit more subtle. Or did you want it to get back to Flora?"

"No." Another fib, but whatever. Of course at the time he'd done it to annoy both Flora and Marina, but this morning that seemed irrelevant.

"Well, just be careful."

"Cal, you're my agent, not my mum. If that's all you have to say, then forget it." Hal was about to hang up in a huff, but Callum said, "No! Wait. Sorry, mate. Not lecturing. I'm calling with fantastic news. Bazotti wants to see you on Monday in LA. So you should fly out, say, Saturday?"

Hal's heart fluttered. "Oh. OK!"

"Good news, huh."

"Very good. Thanks, Cal."

"I'll get Susan to call Vanessa with the details. It'll cut into your holiday with Flora, but she'll understand. Though she'll probably be pretty damn jealous that it's you he wants, not her."

"That's OK," Hal said. "Not sure she was coming out anyway." *And not sure I give two hoots, now I'm in love with someone else.*

"You can have a very long holiday if you get the Bazotti. And I think the chances are good, Hal. I think they're very good. Now listen, I'm organizing a dinner tonight. Dominique and Vlad are in town and I thought I'd see who else is around and book somewhere fun for a little celebration. You up for it?"

"Definitely," said Hal happily. He hung up zinging. After the past couple of years of semi-stupor, all at once he was coming alive again. Work was back on track and he had found his future wife whom he would call in just a minute. But first he'd better deal with Flora. He could call her himself, but he didn't want to. Could be awkward. He'd delegate to Nessie: she could email Henrietta and say that owing to unforeseen work pressures, the holiday was off. He'd see Flora when he saw her. Hopefully she'd get the hint and bow out gracefully without the need for any unpleasant confrontations. Anyway, once all that was out the way, he'd get Nessie to go about organizing a perfect day in Rome.

As usual, Vanessa turned not a hair at the prospect.

"I'll get on to Henrietta and tell her to cancel Flora's flight. Then I'll arrange your trip to LA. And then I'll look into your perfect day. The concierge will be able to help me," she said. "We should have something ready within the hour."

"Great, Nessie. Thank you. You're a star."

He pulled on his favourite chocolate-brown T-shirt and jeans, then walked out of his door, along the corridor and rang the doorbell of the Popolo suite.

CHAPTER
THIRTY-TWO

On waking, Amy's first thought was: *I kissed Hal Blackstock. I can't believe it. I kissed a movie star. I kissed Flora DBC's boyfriend. Marina Dawson's ex.* What will Gaby say? And Mum — not that Amy would ever tell her. And Pinny? Madhura and Andrea and Rosa? And Doug?

It had been very chaste. No tongues. But still, incredibly exciting. Amy realized she hadn't had a full-blown passionate snog for years now. If she and Doug did kiss like that it was always as a brusque prelude to sex. Why was it that in every relationship the kissing for the sake of it stage passed, that a bed sooner or later became the place you slept in rather than shagging passionately. She imagined herself as Carrie Bradshaw in vest and knickers, tapping her laptop. *Can you ever hold on to that early passion?*

The usual wave of sadness washed over her, but then her bedside phone rang.

"Hello?"

"Hiiiii. Is that Amy?"

An Englishwoman's voice. "Yes?"

"Amy, hi. How are you doing this morning? This is Christine Miller, I work for the *Daily Post*. I believe you've been hanging out with Lisa, our Simon's fiancée, a bit. I also believe you went to *The Apple Cart* premiere and the party last night and I was just wondering if there was anything you could tell me about it?"

She had a lovely voice: warm and bubbly, like a Badedas bath. Amy blinked.

"Um, not really."

"Oh, come on. You must be able to tell me something. What the canapés were like, that kind of thing." There was a tiny pause and then she added a little more firmly. "We'll pay you, naturally."

"There's nothing to tell," Amy said, feeling panicky. "The canapés were nice. Just sushi and some olives with chilli. And chicken satay sticks with —"

"OK," Christine said abruptly. "*Interesting.* And you didn't happen to see who Hal Blackstock left with? Apparently it was some mystery girl. Just wondered if you might be able to give us a description."

"Oh, sorry, I didn't see that."

"Really? You didn't see anything? Really, we *will* pay you."

"Not a sausage," Amy said, wondering why she always used her granny's expressions in times of stress. "There were so many people around Hal Blackstock, I hardly saw him."

"Apparently she was tall and dark and wearing a pink dress."

"I'm so sorry, I just can't help you."

"OK," said Christine Miller, sounding as if it were anything but. "But if you do remember anything, I'm in room five two five. I'll give you my mobile number too."

Amy wrote the number down feeling faintly sick. She and Hal had cavorted round Rome all night. They had kissed in public, albeit at five in the morning. How could they possibly not have been seen together? But before she could worry more, there was a ringing at her door.

"Hello?" she shouted, sure it would be scary Christine.

"Amy. It's Hal."

She opened the door, remembering too late her bare face and wild hair.

"How are you this morning?" Hal's eyes were glowing, his voice excited. It was almost as if he were on drugs.

"Fine," she said startled. "I've just woken up."

"Me too. And listen. I was wondering . . . would you like to spend the day with me?"

"With *you*?"

"No, with the Pope," Hal said exasperatedly. "Yes, with me. I thought we could go for a picnic. And I could show you more of Rome."

Hal Blackstock wants to spend the day with me. "OK," Amy said, trying not to sound too excited. "When do I have to be ready?"

"Say, half an hour? Come down to the garage like last night. And bring your bikini."

And so it was that a frantic half an hour later, having made herself look as pretty as possible in a red sun dress and a floppy black sun hat she thought was rather

274

glamorous, Amy found herself sitting in the back seat of a Bentley, next to Hal. He'd been waiting for her, a big smile on his face. As she climbed in, he leaned forward and gently kissed her on both cheeks. "Hello, beautiful," he muttered and handed her a red rose.

"Thank you," she said, wondering where to put it. Her hands shook a little. This handsome, charming and — OK — famous man had just given her a rose and called her beautiful. She gulped and then asked, "Where are we going?"

Hal smiled. "To my favourite sight in Rome. We couldn't go last night because it was closed. And actually," he added glancing at his Rolex, "it's officially closed now for lunch. But I've arranged for us to have a special tour, so we have it all to ourselves with no hoi polloi."

They were already drawing up outside a church at the foot of a wide, sweeping boulevard. A pretty undistinguished church by Roman standards.

"What is it?" Amy asked, as they climbed out.

Hal grinned, gesturing her to climb the steps that led to the entrance. "You'll see."

On the threshold, a monk in floor-length brown robes and a shaved head was waiting for them.

"Very *Da Vinci Code*," Hal muttered in her ear.

"Meester Blackstock," he cried, throwing his hands in the air, "this is such an honour. Welcome to Santa Maria della Concezione. It is our pleasure to have you here." He nodded a little brusquely at Amy. "And you too, signora."

Being with Hal was just like being with Doug, Amy thought. She'd always be second best. The afterthought that people tolerated because they had to. She buried the idea as she followed the monk and Hal into a long, dark corridor.

"Wow."

She couldn't quite believe it. In gloomy chambers all along the side of the church there were bones nailed to the wall, arranged in patterns: crosses, flowers, arches, triangles, circles. There was a lampshade and a large clock. An altar was made up of ribcages, a shrine had been constructed from skulls and leg bones, the ceiling tastefully trimmed with forearms.

"I don't believe it." She giggled, looking above her. "Even the chandelier is made from metacarpals and phalanges."

"Come again?"

"Hand and foot bones. What is this place?"

"It's the crypt of the Capuchin monks. All these bones belong to dead monks. More than four thousand of them. The idea was to make spectators aware of their own mortality."

They walked down the corridor to the last chamber, where Hal pointed at a sign. " 'We Were Like You. You Will Be Like Us'," he read in his best Hammer House of Horror baritone. "In several languages. Just so everyone gets the message."

Amy grinned. "It's amazing." She nodded at a child's skeleton attached to the ceiling, holding a scythe. "I wonder if Ikea do them?"

"It doesn't freak you out?"

276

"I'm a doctor, remember? I'm used to this. Do they have a gift shop? Imagine the presents. Vertebrae napkin rings. Backscratchers from a real hand and arm. They'd love it back at the surgery."

Hal smiled at her. "It's the best sight in Rome. Far more fun than the silly old *Pietà* or all those paintings of glum-looking Madonnas."

Amy was enchanted and impressed. This was a genuinely original idea and Hal had thought it up specially for her. He *must* like her. But how could he?

"I'm getting hungry," Hal said, after a few more minutes. "It's nearly two. So I think we'll move on if you don't mind."

They climbed back into the waiting car, which this time carried them out of Rome.

"Are we going to the sea?" Amy asked, thinking of yesterday's adventure.

"Nope."

"Then why did I bring my bikini?"

"You'll see."

They drove along a stretch of motorway which, Amy was relieved to see, led away from the airport and after about forty minutes turned off into what quickly became a country road and even sooner became a dirt track, surrounded by dense and ever denser forest. Thick blackberry hedges lined the track. A deer ran across their path.

"This is a bit *Blair Witch*," Amy said.

Hal laughed. "Don't worry. The spooky part of the day is over, I promise."

They stopped in a tiny clearing. From the boot of the car, the unsmiling driver took out a huge picnic rug and a wicker hamper. He had a quick word with Hal, then climbed back in the car and started reversing.

"Where are we?" Amy asked again.

Hal smiled. "You'll see in a minute. But before that, we have to eat. Because I'm bloody starving."

He laid out the rug and they picnicked on salty focaccia, which they dipped in pools of olive oil, tiny crunchy biscuits of dough, fennel seeds and chilli, slices of toast piled with sweet tomatoes and blessed with a silver crucifix of fresh anchovy, ripe, juicy figs, slices of Parma ham, bland balls of mozzarella and stinking slices of Gorgonzola. There were bunches of sweet red grapes and slices of fresh melon. All accompanied by a bottle of Prosecco. The only sound was their munching and birds singing in the trees. The hot sun seared Amy's bare thighs and she was glad she'd worn her hat otherwise, with the heat, her tiredness and the alcohol, she really would have been quite woozy.

"It's all delicious," she gasped, unable to resist popping another fig in her mouth.

Hal grinned. "You've got fig juice running down your chin."

"Have I?" Amy wiped it away, horrified.

He laughed. "It's sweet. After Flora, it's great to see a woman enjoy her food."

Was he being sarcastic? Amy wasn't sure. She put down the slice of Parma ham she'd been intending to stuff in her mouth.

"Where is Flora?"

278

"In Jamaica." Hal shrugged. "With her sick kids."

"Oh, are *they* the ones who have chickenpox?"

"Yeah. Didn't I say?"

"No. You just said some children you knew." A tiny pause, then, "How are they now?"

Hal shrugged almost rudely. "Haven't a clue."

There were so many questions Amy wanted to ask, like what is going on with you and Flora? What are you doing here with me? Are you trying to seduce me? Because that's certainly what it looks like. But she knew that to probe too deeply would shatter the moment and whatever happened, she wanted to preserve this memory for ever and ever of her and Hal Blackstock in a shady clearing.

"You still haven't told me why you brought me here," she said brightly. "Apart from to murder me and take my skeleton back to that church."

Hal stood up.

"I'll show you now."

She followed him down a narrow footpath, until they heard running water. Turning the corner, she saw a stream bubbling gently down the hill. Amy didn't get it.

"Very pretty," she said politely.

Hal smiled smugly.

"Feel the water."

Amy bent down, dipped her fingers in and shrieked in shock.

"But it's hot!"

Hal smiled indulgently. "It's a natural hot spring. There are loads of them in the hills around Rome."

"Are we going in?"

"Of course we bloody are. Why else did I tell you to bring your bikini? Run back and change." He fluttered his eyelashes and lowered his voice. "Unless you want to go in in your birthday suit."

Amy's stomach somersaulted. "I'll get changed," she stuttered.

Back in the clearing, surrounded by the remains of the picnic, she pulled on her bikini. It didn't matter if she was nineteen times the size of Marina Dawson, she told herself. Those women were paid to look perfect. No real woman could exist on the raisin diet. That was what she always told her teenage patients whose anxious mums had dragged them in because they'd started to refuse family meals. As usual, Amy found it easier to preach than practise. She slapped her thighs despairingly. She should have applied some fake tan to make them look a bit smaller. And, shit, there was definite regrowth in the bikini area. Why hadn't she been plucking every day?

With a towel wrapped defiantly round herself, she reappeared at the stream. Hal was already sitting in the water, submerged to his waist. Amy had no idea if he was naked or not.

"Come in; water's lovely," he shouted.

Amy climbed in. The water was as warm as a bath, in fact if they hadn't been in the shade it would have been uncomfortably hot. She sat on a boulder, a few yards from Hal, her spare tyre reassuringly concealed, and exhaled.

"It's divine."

"When I lived here we used to come out at weekends, bring a few bottles of wine. Get the whole spa experience before the phrase 'me time' was invented. Flora pays six thousand bucks a night for this kind of thing."

Amy wiggled uncomfortably. She knew her face must be beetroot red, her mascara was probably running. But Hal was continuing unchecked.

"It's so great to be free of the city, of the crowds, of the fans, of people wanting things from me. At last I feel like I'm on holiday."

"But you're always on holiday, aren't you?" Amy asked, recalling everything she'd read. Then she saw Hal's face and regretted it.

"Not as often as people believe," he said tartly. "A lot of the time people think I'm on holiday it's actually work-related. Anyway, there isn't going to be much holiday from now on because I'm off to LA in the next couple of days." He paused to give what he was about to say maximum impact. "Going to meet Andreas Bazotti."

"Who's Andreas Bazotti?" Even as Amy opened her mouth, she realized it had been a bad move. Hal looked even more put out than before, though he quickly hid it.

"I love the way you know nothing of my world," he said with a laugh. "Andreas Bazotti is *the* hottest director of the moment. Everyone wants to work with him. George would give enemas to rhinoceroses every day for a year for the chance just to be in the same room as him."

Amy thought of asking George who, but decided she'd better not. "That sounds like an amazing opportunity," she said soothingly, struck by how remarkably similar a conversation with Hal was to a conversation with Doug.

"It will be," Hal said. He turned and smiled at Amy. "You know, until today, I was feeling seriously lost. But now the way seems clear again."

"I'm so glad."

"But tell me about your fiancé," Hal said, leaning forward. "What happened. How could anyone hurt someone as gorgeous as you?"

Amy flushed. "Oh, well . . ." But before she could say anything, Hal's phone rang inside his trousers on the grass.

"Jesus Christ," he sighed, "is there anywhere on this planet you can't get reception?"

He stood up. To Amy's relief he was wearing Vilebrequin trunks. She wasn't quite sure she was ready for Hal Blackstock in his birthday suit.

"Shall I leave it?" He was already climbing out. "Shit. I'd better get it. It might be important. Hello? Bugger. Is it that late already? OK, OK, we'll start heading back."

He flipped it shut. "The ever faithful Vanessa reminding me that my presence is required at a dinner in Rome tonight and if I want a little nap before it we should head back now."

"Oh, OK," Amy said, suddenly dejected.

Hal stood on the bank, dripping. "Would you like to come too?"

282

"To the dinner?" Amy shook her head. "No, no. I couldn't. Thank you anyway, but . . ."

"You could," Hal said firmly, leaning forward and offering her his hand to pull her out of the water. "I'd love it if you did." He whispered, even though no one but the birds were listening, "Please say yes." And pulling Amy towards him, he kissed her again on the lips. Her heart tom-tommed but before she could kiss him back properly they heard the sound of a motor revving in the clearing.

"Shit. Bloody driver. Must be the only punctual Italian since Mussolini." Hal chucked Amy a towel. "Come on, darling. We'd better get dressed."

CHAPTER
THIRTY-THREE

Two hours later Amy was standing under the shower in the Popolo suite, washing her hair and reflecting on her extraordinary day. Finding herself in a Bentley with Hal Blackstock. Going to see the monks' bones. The picnic. The hot springs. And that second kiss, so warm and promising. She shut her eyes, recapturing the moment. It couldn't be true, but it was. Hal Blackstock was after her. He wanted to be her boyfriend.

As she did the final rinse, Amy had a brief, mad moment fantasizing about their future life together. Premieres, parties, glamorous holidays, all the fun that once had been there with Doug but had then disappeared. Of course she had no intention of giving up her job or anything silly, but at the end of the day she would climb into a Bentley Hal had sent over to the surgery and be carried back to his house in Chelsea. Briefly, she questioned how much she was attracted to Hal just for himself. She couldn't honestly claim to be overwhelmed with lust, but these things took time, or should take time. She'd been overwhelmed with lust for Doug and look how that had ended up.

Towelling her hair dry, Amy compared her situation now to this time last year. She and Doug had been engaged for five months but she still had no engagement ring because — as he pointed out — he could only afford Argos's cheapest. Although he had eventually told the band their plans, trying to get him to focus on actual details was about as easy as an oil tanker doing a three-point turn in a paddling pool. It took several attempts before she eventually pinned him down to a date in August the following year.

"August?" Gaby had asked, nine months pregnant and still radiant from her own successful wedding (even Doug had been impressed, although he thought she'd invited far too many guests and the choice of fish or chicken had been very unimaginative; Amy meanwhile had been thrown into a tailspin when Gaby chose the "love is a temporary madness" bit from *Captain Corelli* as her reading). "But everyone'll be on holiday."

"It's the only time he can guarantee the band won't be touring."

Gaby shrugged, her face neutral as it so often was where Doug was concerned. "Fair enough."

Thanks to Gaby and an ever-growing stack of wedding magazines, that she hid under her bed like porn, Amy was getting panicked. Her original plan of a wedding for under a couple of grand was looking about as unlikely as a cure for male hair loss. Every day, despite her better judgement, she increased the budget. She had three thousand pounds in savings but that was nothing like enough; her parents had offered another three, which was more than generous, given their badly paid occupations.

She decided to tackle the subject on a breezy weekend at the end of August, when she and Doug flew up to Inverness for a long-overdue visit to his parents. It was a two-hour drive from the airport to their house and Doug, stuck behind the wheel of a hire car, would have no choice but to listen to her. Which he did, his expression growing increasingly hunted.

"I still don't see why this thing has to be so extravagant," he said. "We don't need to give people a three-course sit-down meal."

"No, definitely not," Amy agreed. "Though we *will* have to feed people. I mean, if they're coming all the way from Scotland, they won't be happy with a bowl of crisps."

"Do a buffet, then."

"But buffets are a bit naff, don't you think?" Amy scribbled a note to that effect on the Post-it pad on her lap. "Anyway, what we really need to get a move on with is venues."

"But the wedding's still nearly a year away."

Amy tried to keep the rising note of hysteria out of her voice.

"Gaby says everywhere gets booked up."

Doug raised an eyebrow. "Gaby, Gaby, Gaby," he said wearily. "Sometimes I wonder if you're turning into her. So materialistic. I don't want a wedding like hers where you get sent a forty-page instruction book a year in advance, telling you what to wear and how expensive the hotel is and where to buy her presents that she doesn't actually need. Why do we have to have a wedding like hers? Can't we just sneak off to Vegas and then have a bit of a party when we get back?"

For a moment, the idea was very tempting. Not eloping, because it would break Dad's heart not to give her away, but the rest of it. Amy wondered why she was getting so carried away ensuring every detail of the wedding was perfect. Did it really matter if they had the reception in some grungy church hall with a few vol au vents from Tesco's (no, Waitrose, she couldn't bear to go more down-market than that) and a short set from the band? But it was no good. Her wedding to Doug had to be the most stylish of all time. She knew it was silly, but Amy couldn't help hoping that by making such a public statement, he would be inextricably bound to her, that the slippery grasp she always felt she had on him would finally tighten.

Her phone rang. She looked at the caller ID. "Speak of the devil." She could hear month-old Archie bleating in the background. "Hi, is everything OK?"

"Everything's fine," Gaby said airily. "Guess what? I'm reading *Grazia* while feeding and I think I have just seen your wedding shoes."

Most people would have had enough on their plates right now. Not Gaby. "Oh. Right."

"Are you OK? You sound stressed."

Well, my boyfriend's just told me I'm turning into you. "No, we're in the car. In Scotland."

"Oh, bloody hell, of course. Visiting the in-laws." She giggled. "Good luck then. Buy *Grazia*, page forty-one and let me know what you think."

By the time she hung up, Doug was pulling off the main road and turning onto the long private drive that led to his parents' house. It was only the second time Amy had visited them and the first since they'd got engaged, so she felt more than a little nervous. They were definitely several notches posher than Amy's family. She'd noticed how Doug's mum flinched when she'd said "toilet" and "pardon."

The car crunched over the gravel and, as Doug pulled up the handbrake, they were greeted by the noise of yowling dogs.

"Hey, hey, guys." Doug laughed, climbing out of the car to be leaped upon by what looked like three wolves. "Calm down." He grinned at Amy, terrified in the car. "Get out, babe. They're just excited; they won't hurt you."

Gingerly, Amy climbed out. Immediately a smelly mutt flung itself upon her.

"Awagh!" she shrieked, as she heard Doug's mother shouting, "Trotter, get down! Down, I say!" Looking over the dog's slavering head, Amy could see her standing in the lit doorway, small and stout in tweed trousers and an apron emblazoned with a picture of Edinburgh Castle.

She wiped her hands before striding out. "Good journey?" she asked, giving Amy a diffident pat on the arm. Doug's family thought kissing was a suspect, metropolitan practice. "Hello, dear, nice to see you. Congratulations on your engagement." The tone she used was the same one Amy reserved for telling patients they had severe angina.

288

"Thanks," Amy said, as Doug asked, "Have you been baking, Mum?"

"Och, nothing much. A couple of cakes. Alan, Jessica and Poppy got here an hour ago." Alan was Doug's high-flying lawyer brother, Jessica was his uptight wife who worked in IT and always looked exhausted and Poppy their cute baby daughter. "So now you're here we can all have tea."

"Is it chocolatey?" Doug asked, pulling the bags out of the boot.

"Possibly," his mother replied coyly. They followed her into the kitchen, full of dog baskets and with the inevitable Aga as the focal point. On the table were enough baked goods to feed a Sumo convention.

"Wicked," Doug said, grabbing a biscuit and cramming it in his mouth.

"Douglas! Anyone would think Amy didn't feed you. Mind you," she added, giving Amy a reproachful look, "you career girls are often too busy to cook."

"Amy's the queen of the microwave," Doug said cheerily, plonking himself down in a chair. "And nothing wrong with that."

"Do you need any help, Mrs Fraser?" Amy said, wondering if garrotting Doug would be more enjoyable than disembowelling him. As a doctor, of course, she was perfectly capable of both.

"No, dear, I'm sure you've been working very hard in your job, so you should just relax. Eat something. You're looking very skinny, you know. I hope you're not dieting for the wedding."

"Oh, heavens no," Amy lied, delighted at this news, but she was drowned out by the noise of little Poppy bursting into the kitchen, yelling, "Gaddy, gaddy, gaddy!", followed by her parents. There were greetings all round, then Alan slumped at the table, shovelling an enormous slice of cake into his tiny mouth.

"Christ, it's been a nightmare of an afternoon," he said. "To get a mobile signal up here you have to drive about fifteen miles. I don't know how Mum and Dad survive without Broadband."

He pulled his BlackBerry out of his pocket and stroked it anxiously, like parents at the clinic with a feverish child. God, he was unattractive with his lardy body and face like a baboon's behind. Thinking this, Amy suddenly realized that that face was part of the Fraser gene pool. Oh my God, suppose she and Doug had a baby girl, who looked not — as she'd always imagined — like her but like Alan? For the first time it dawned chillingly on Amy that Doug's family were no longer simply a collection of assorted freaks that she occasionally had to humour, but her future family for ever and ever, amen.

"Cake, cake," baby Poppy was yelling. As she dashed past him, Doug patted her head ineffectually, his nose wrinkled as if he'd detected some vile odour. As with all small children, Amy longed to pick her up and cuddle her, but she didn't dare. To show affection to infants and toddlers might give Doug a clue to her secret, growing obsession. So she merely smiled as she dashed by, shouting, "Caaaake!"

"No, darling, no cake," Jessica said. "How about a lovely apple?"

"Noooowagh! Cake!"

"Can't you keep the volume down?" said Doug, wrinkling his nose. He wasn't joking.

"Oh, tsssk," said Mrs Fraser, scooping Poppy up. "Let the little mite have some cake. Cake's good for children."

"Well, actually, Fenella, research shows . . . oh, darling, oh no!" For Poppy had snatched a mansize slice from the table and was cramming it in her mouth with loud mmms.

"See, they love it. My boys did too. We didn't go in for all this neurotic parenting stuff when they were growing up and they've turned out totally fine." Everyone's eyes fell on Alan's love handles, but Mrs Fraser continued unruffled. "All this Jamie Oliver nonsense about humus and bulgar wheat. Everything in moderation, that's how it should be. What do you think, Amy? You're the doctor."

"Em, I . . ." Amy felt Jessica's eyes upon her. "I think a little bit of cake never did any harm," she continued cravenly, deciding it was more important to keep in with the mother-in-law.

"I thought so!" Mrs Fraser smiled. Alan smirked as he stuffed a piece of cake into his mouth.

"So how's the life of a rock 'n' roller?" he asked Doug in sarcastic tones. "When are we going to see you on *Top of the Pops*?"

"Actually, Alan, *Top of the Pops* doesn't exist any more." Doug yawned. It was the most asked question after "So have you written something I might actually . . . know?"

"And the wedding plans?" Jessica said, turning to Amy. Amy could see from her body language she would never forgive her betrayal.

"Oh, coming along," she said lightly. "It's always much more of a palaver than you think it's going to be, isn't it?"

"It's certainly hard work," Jessica said, with a meaningful look at Alan. "No, darling, no, no, *not* more cake. Oh, all right then, just a sliver."

"Hello, hello," said a loud voice in the doorway. Mr Fraser in green cords and a check shirt, back from his daily walk across the hills. He had only recently retired and was finding long hours of relaxation very stressful. "Doug, my boy, good to see you." He pumped his son's hand. "Hair a bit long, is it not? Amy, good to see you too. Comfortable journey, I hope?"

"Yes, thanks."

"Good, good. Well, so, gins and tonics all round then."

"Not for me," said Jessica.

"What? Oh, come now, Jessica, don't be a lightweight. Everyone needs a gin and tonic to start the evening."

"No, honestly, I'm fine. I'm on antibiotics." She caught Amy's eye and Amy, with a thud of envy, guessed she must be pregnant again.

"If she's on antibiotics, she really shouldn't drink," she said hastily. She couldn't believe how upset this realization had made her. But she was getting like that

292

at the surgery. Every time she had to refer a pregnant woman to hospital, she found her voice getting papery. When bloody Sophia Franklin had turned up the other day joyfully announcing that the fourth IVF cycle had worked, she'd felt nothing but pity for herself. What was *wrong* with her? The hormones she'd never really believed in must be kicking in.

"So, Mick Jagger," said Mr Fraser, from the dresser where the gin was kept. "How's life on the stage? Found stardom yet?"

"Working towards it," Doug said.

"Making any money?"

"Not a lot."

"So how are you paying the bills?"

"Amy's being very understanding," he said, smiling at her. She smiled uneasily back.

"Hmmm." Mr Fraser sliced through a lemon. "And when's the wedding?"

"This time next year," said Amy.

Muttering, "Bathtime," Jessica picked up Poppy and carried her yelling "Cakecakecakecakecake," out of the room.

"So how are you funding that?"

"Well," Amy demurred, "we don't want it to be a lavish affair."

Mr Fraser plonked a quadruple gin in front of his future daughter-in-law. "You may be heartened to know that — since we made a contribution to young Alan's nuptials — we will of course be making one to yours."

Amy's heart flooded with relief. Secretly, she'd hoped this trip might pay this sort of dividend. "You don't have to, Mr Fraser, really that is very kind."

"Call me Mungo. And that's quite all right, dear. Alan got five hundred pounds, then you shall have it too."

"Five hundred pounds?" Out of the corner of her eye, Amy could see Alan trying not to laugh.

"That's very generous — er — Mungo. Thank you."

"Yes, thanks, Dad," Doug said.

"That's all right. I know these modern affairs can be costly. Heaven knows, I'm sure our wedding cost about a fiver. But times change." He sat up in his chair. "Now, there's a more serious matter to discuss. As you may or may not know, we also gave Alan and Jessica a rather more significant sum of money after their wedding, to help them buy a family house." Amy's heart banged in her ribcage. "I'd like to do the same for you two, but there has to be a caveat. I need to see you're earning a decent wage yourself, Douglas. I didn't bring you up to be a layabout and a sponger. I'm not having you leaching off your wife. So the deal is this: find a proper job again and you can have the money because you will have proved you deserve it."

For a second, all you could hear was one of the dogs munching a biscuit Poppy had dropped on the floor.

"Dad, I do have a proper job," Doug said calmly.

"A proper job is not driving a van around the country containing a bunch of pot-smoking hippies. A proper job is what Alan does."

Alan nodded complacently and picked up a scone.

294

Doug took a deep breath. "Alan has a proper job, but I do too. Music is a serious industry. It makes billions of pounds every year."

"Not for you."

"Not for me, no. Not yet. But it will make me some money. In the end. In any case, money isn't important. What's important is happiness. And I wasn't happy being a solicitor."

"Do something else then." Mr Fraser's face turned slightly purple, as he tried to think of a job that didn't involve law. "Be a . . . be a . . . banker! My old friend Ranulph works for Coutts. I'm sure he could find you something."

"I don't want to be a banker. I don't want to be like Alan always checking my e-mails and on the perpetual verge of a heart attack. I've always wanted to play music and you wouldn't bloody let me. I wasted four years of my life on that stupid law degree, plus all that time doing articles. I'm not wasting any more. And using some stupid bribe about a house is not going to sway me, is it, Amy?"

All eyes turned to her. She realized she was going to have to respond.

"But you said if the music thing didn't work out, you'd jack it in after a year, so . . ."

"Christ!" yelled Doug. It was so unusual to see him angry, they all jumped. "I can't believe this. I thought I was going to get support from my own fiancée."

This was hideous. "I am supporting you, it's just . . ."

"It's just nothing. God, Amy, I thought you understood. This is my dream."

"But what about poor Amy?" Mrs Fraser said. "She's having to pay all the bills. Working her fingers to the bone, I shouldn't wonder."

"Amy loves her job." Doug said, as Amy reeled at this unexpected backing. "She doesn't mind."

"What about when she has a baby? A mother's place is in the home, whatever these so-called feminists like Jessica may think."

"Now don't criticize Jessica," Alan broke in. "There's nothing wrong with the way we live our life."

"Well, yes. It's just a bit heartbreaking, though, isn't it, when you see how excited the wee one gets at the sight of a slice of home-made cake."

"Look," said Doug, "forget all this." He turned to his father. "Dad, thank you for the kind offer but given the small print, as a former solicitor, I can't accept it. And I know Amy will back me on that."

"I . . ." All Amy could see ahead of her was a lifetime of early mornings and late surgeries, of slog and grind and Sophia Franklinses and a baby she never saw. She'd always promised herself a long break from work to devote to her family. Mum had always been at home for her and she was determined to do the same.

"Won't you, Amy?"

"Of course," she said quietly, looking at the flagstones. "Of course."

And of course, Doug was right. He couldn't abandon his dream for a cash bribe. She wouldn't want him to be like horrible Alan. But at the same time that money

296

would have been so incredibly useful. They couldn't have a baby without it. Well, they could, lots of people with no money had babies, but it would be so bloody hard in that minuscule flat and the poor nipper would have to go to nursery when it was tiny, which was against everything Amy believed in.

She ought to talk to Doug, but just as with dumping Danny, she couldn't summon the nerve.

Back in London, on a night out with the band, she had to listen, with gritted teeth, as Doug recounted his version of the story.

"Well, I think what you did was quite right," Pinny said, as only someone in possession of a large trust fund could. "You're an artist, not a wage slave. What do you think, Amy?"

"Well . . ."

"Well, what? If Doug was a businessman in a suit, he wouldn't be Doug. And you wouldn't love him. *We* wouldn't love him."

That "We" sent a shiver down Amy's spine. She resolved to be far less uptight and far more forgiving of Doug in future; to accept him for what he was, not what she wanted him to be. But the next morning, on the way to work, she found herself looking up Danny's name on her contacts list. For a mad second, she considered calling him. Danny hadn't really been that bad, had he? He'd always made her breakfast in bed at weekends and he adored children. OK, so that animal passion she and Doug had, had never been there but you couldn't build a life on animal passion. Amy shook her head to free herself from this madness. Doug was her man and money or no money, they would manage. So circumstances weren't always ideal, but then whose were?

CHAPTER
THIRTY-FOUR

Amy was just applying a final coat of lipstick when her phone rang. She expected it to be the front desk, saying the Bentley was waiting in the garage.

"Hello?"

"Amy?"

"Lisa!" Amy cringed as she thought of how she'd rudely run off. "How are you?"

"I'm fine, thanks." Amy braced herself for an upbraiding, but instead Lisa said, "Listen, just calling because Simon's pissed off you kept me out so late yesterday and I said you could explain in person."

Her voice was theatrical, slow, laden with warnings. Amy got the message. "OK," she said, but Simon was already on the line.

"Hello?"

"Hello, Simon. I'm . . . sorry I kept Lisa out so late yesterday. We went to the beach and . . . I fell asleep and she found it hard to wake me up and we missed the last train back to Rome." Shit! Amy had no idea what Lisa had told him. But she heard a semi-appeased grunt.

"Didn't help that her bloody mobile battery failed again," he offered.

"No, that was a nightmare! And I'd lost mine and we didn't know how to use an Italian payphone, so . . ."

"All right, Amy. I accept your apology. Bye now." And he was gone. Amy waited a few minutes to see if Lisa would call back, but she didn't. Obviously the day out in Ostia had turned into a night out as well. She still couldn't find it in her heart to blame Lisa, Massimo was so much more attractive than Simon. But why was she with Simon in the first place? Surely the promise of a jacuzzi couldn't be enough.

Pondering this she took the lift downstairs. Hal was waiting for her in the Bentley. He wore a green shirt and a pressed pair of trousers. As Amy climbed in, he looked her up and down.

"Um. What are you wearing?"

Amy glanced down. "My Prada dress."

"But didn't you wear that last night?"

Amy's heart donkey-kicked in anxiety. "Well, yes, but it's the only smart dress I have."

"Shit." Hal looked at his watch. "Is there time for a detour? Are the shops still open? I can buy you another dress."

"Oh no, no, no," cried Amy, half tempted but mainly horrified. "I couldn't let you."

"In any case, the shops are just closing, signor," the driver informed him.

"Oh, right. Well, never mind. You look very nice, anyway."

"Thanks," Amy said uneasily. She swallowed and tried to change the subject. "So who are we having dinner with?"

Hal settled back in his seat. "Callum, who's my agent. Old friend. Remember, he tried to stop us leaving the party together? Thank God, he failed. Anyway, he's a good bloke. I'd like you two to get to know each other. Possibly his girlfriend, Robyn. She often joins him on these jollies, though she wasn't there yesterday. I meant to ask if she was coming but I forgot. Apart from that I'm not sure. Dominique, I think he said. She's a model, you'll recognize her. She's bound to be designered up to the eyebrows. You'll be a refreshing contrast." As Amy reeled from this unintended insult, he added, "And her boyfriend, Vlad."

"He's not a model too?" she said anxiously. This sounded hideous. Her earlier fantasy of life as Hal's girlfriend was replaced by an ominous hint of a future where everyone was taller, thinner, prettier and richer than she was.

Hal hooted. "God no. Unless you're talking for the uglies agency. No, Vlad is a Russian tycoon. Owns the whole of Siberia. I've heard he's thinking of buying a football club. Thought I might try and persuade him to make an offer for Didcot Town."

Amy wasn't really listening. *I'd like you two to get to know each other.* Serious boyfriend talk. She didn't know how to respond, so she looked out of the window at the Roman evening. Armies of tourists bustled along the Via Nazionale, a Hari Krishna band wove through them like an orange snake. The restaurant they were going to was in a lemon grove, in a hilly suburb, where, according to the Bentley's driver, all the government ministers had houses. Hal and Amy walked across a large terrace covered in vines and were escorted to a table in the far-left corner where a crowd of glossy people were talking and laughing loudly.

"Hal!" yelled one of the women, standing up so everyone could admire her pin-thin body and shock of white-blonde hair. "Hey, over here. Guys, look, here's Hal."

"Fuck," said Hal. "It's fucking Justina. I'll kill Callum." But before he could elaborate, he was surrounded. While he shook hands and air kissed, Amy stood there meekly, like a toddler on its first day at nursery. Only as silence fell did Hal clear his throat.

"So, guys, this is Amy."

"Hi, Amy," chorused the table. Amy raised a timid hand in greeting.

"Amy, this is Dominique. Justina. Vlad and, sorry, was it Trader?"

"Trailer," snarled Justina's escort, who was young and had a baseball cap obscuring most of his rather spotty face.

"Do you think his surname's Trash?" Hal muttered in Amy's ear and she stifled a giggle.

"Where's Flora, Hal?" asked Dominique. She had a face you could teach geometry with. As Hal had predicted, Amy definitely recognized it.

Hal blinked rapidly. "Flora? She's stuck out in Jamaica. The girls have got chickenpox."

"Chickenpox! Oh my God, poor babies. We must send them a get-well present. Darling Flora. Send her

302

my love when you next speak. What an amazing woman she is."

"Hey, Amy," said a voice behind her. She turned round. It was Callum. The relief at seeing a genuinely friendly face was enormous. "Let's get you a drink. Some Krug?"

"Oh no, thanks," Amy said. She felt sick enough without adding alcohol to the mix.

"Are you sure? Would you prefer Cristal? Dom Perignom? Or maybe a cocktail? Sit down, anyway." He patted the chair beside him.

Amy was touched by his eagerness to please.

"I'm fine," she said, sitting down. "Just a glass of water, thank you."

As the others gabbled, Amy studied the menu. Not that she was particularly hungry, far too stuffed after the picnic, but at least it kept her occupied. On her left Callum was deep in conversation with Justina, while on her right, Vlad, who looked like a potato which had mated with a Shar Pei, was gabbling in Russian into a platinum phone. Hal was roaring with laughter with Dominique and seemed to have forgotten Amy ever existed, while Trailer, between Vlad and Dominique, was jabbing at his BlackBerry.

"And what do you do, Annie?" Dominique asked eventually, looking up from her soup spoon where she'd been admiring her reflection.

"Amy. I'm a doctor."

"Really? Cool." But Dominique's attention was on the embossed menu. "Oh good, they have gazpacho! That's practically calorie free. Though they do tend to pour oil all over it if you don't watch them." She smiled condescendingly at Amy. "You are so lucky having a job where you don't have to watch your figure. I'm getting so much shit at the moment about all this size-zero stuff. I mean, like it's my fault I'm naturally skinny."

"And what do you do?" Amy asked, although she knew.

Dominique raised a perfect eyebrow. "Oh, sorry, didn't I say? I'm a model."

"Dom's the face of Jodanne all-day pantyliners," Vlad interjected gruffly, before returning to his arms deal.

"Oh, so that's where I know you from," Amy said before she could stop herself.

Dom looked annoyed. "I only did that because the money was so great. And you can't really tell it's me the way they've shot it."

"That's why I got out of modelling," Justina said from the other end of the table. "I hated my face being attached to all those tacky products. Being an actress is so much more satisfying."

The evening was a misery. Dominique monopolized Hal, Justina and Trailer spent virtually all of it with their tongues deep in each other's throats. Amy tried to talk to Vlad on her right, but at every attempt at conversation, he just grunted, before returning to his phone. Callum kept smiling at her kindly, but every time he tried to ask her a question one of the other women interrupted.

She shouldn't have come. She could never be part of this world. *Pretend you're not here, pretend you're watching this on television*, she chanted mentally. In a month's time this'll be a funny story to share with Gaby. Gaby whom she hadn't called all day! Amy was consumed with guilt. What a terrible person she was forgetting her best friend because of Hal Blackstock. She'd sneak out and ring her in a minute. The thought was comforting. She looked round the terrace, packed with jolly groups, talking loudly and clinking glasses. Only one old man sat alone, immaculate in a button-down shirt and pressed flannel trousers, a finished plate of pasta in front of him. He kept dipping a long spoon in a jar, then licking it slowly. With a jolt, Amy realized it was the communal pot of Parmesan.

"So any news of Sukey?" Justina asked Dominique.

Dominique looked the happiest she had all evening. "Apparently, she got sacked from the Eres campaign."

"I'm not surprised. Though you'd have thought all that coke would keep her thin enough."

"Too many nights in Chinawhite."

"Miaow," said Callum in Amy's ear. She giggled, mainly out of relief that she hadn't vanished. "Shit, it's a nightmare that Justina's here. She and Hal loathe each other. But she heard I was in town and got wind of my plans and for whatever reason insisted on joining us."

"Oh. Right." Amy had no advice to give on when your dinner is gatecrashed by an A-list star.

"So did I hear right, Amy, are you really a doctor?"

"That's right, a GP." Callum had a nice face, not handsome, but cheerful and friendly.

"Bloody hell. You mean you actually have a serious job? I don't think anyone who gets paid a monthly salary has ever been allowed in Hal's presence before."

Amy smiled politely.

"Not to mention into Hal's life." His tone was meaningful.

"Oh, I'm not part of Hal's life," Amy said hurriedly. "We're just friends. We happened to be staying at the same hotel and we . . . got talking and . . ."

"Just friends, huh? Well, just be careful for your sake to keep it that way. The man's not used to having women resisting him. You'll do terrible damage to his ego. Does your doctor's training teach you how to soothe a star's frazzled self-esteem?"

"Of course it does." She smiled, as the main courses were put in front of them. Vlad looked down at his bowl of pasta.

"Cheese," he bellowed. "I need cheese."

"Certainly sir," said the waiter. He returned with the communal bowl. Amy watched in horrified delight as Vlad picked up the spoon covered in geriatric spittle and dolloped Parmesan all over his linguine.

"What are you smiling at?" Callum asked, with genuine curiosity.

"Oh, nothing. So, Callum. Hal said your girlfriend might be here."

Callum shook his head cheerfully. "Shows how much interest Hal pays to my personal life. Robyn and I split up two months ago. If Hal had asked after her I'd have told him."

"I'm sorry," Amy said abashed.

"Don't be." Callum shrugged. "It had run its course. Came to a natural end. No feelings hurt. It's very rare to have such an amicable break up. I treasure it. And as for Hal — well, he's the talent. No reason why he should be interested in my little life. None of my other clients are." He spoke entirely without bitterness.

"Still, he should have asked . . ." Amy said with feeling, but before Callum could say any more, Dominique was pulling at his arm, wanting to know the latest gossip on Kate Moss.

Amy squeezed out of her chair and went to the loo. As she washed her hands, she stared in the mirror. By some mystical power of osmosis, the models appeared to have sucked off all her make-up. Her face was pale as lard, all the blemishes beaming like lighthouses on a winter's night, her eyelashes were like an albino's. She realized her lipstick and hairbrush were sitting in her bag under the dining table.

"What am I doing here?" she said aloud to her reflection. "I don't belong in this world. I want to go home. Home where I belong."

Wanting to delay her return to the table she stepped out onto the back terrace. Beneath her, Rome took on a spectacular aspect, red, blue, green and white lights sparkled as if a giant hand had scattered gems across the city. The moon loitered palely in the sky above. Amy gazed up at it, wondering if Doug was looking at it too. Unlikely. He was almost certainly snuggled under a sheet with Pinny.

"Amy?" said Hal from behind her.

She jumped. "Oh, hi."

"Are you OK?"

"Yes. Fine."

He came over to her and put his arm round her shoulder. "I'm sorry. I know you were bored. Dom is so boring and Justina is a bitch."

Amy giggled. "You said it, not me."

"But please don't be put off. It's not like these people are my friends. Apart from Callum and he's OK, isn't he?"

"Callum's lovely. But anyway, it doesn't matter to me. I'm only here for the evening."

"Actually," he said softly, "I'd like you to be in my life for a lot longer than that."

She turned round and looked at him. He put his arms round her, bent over and, for the third time in twenty-four hours, kissed her softly on the lips. Then he pushed her back and, holding both her arms, looked into her eyes. Amy's head spun with the weirdness of it all.

"You're so lovely. I think I'm falling in love with you. Will you come back to my suite later?" he asked.

"I don't know," said Amy, flattered but confused. "I'll have to see."

"I'd like you to," he said. "But now we'd better go back, before that cow Dominique gets on to the *News of the World*."

As they walked back onto the front terrace everyone fell silent. Amy looked around nervously, unsure if her skirt was tucked in her knickers. Then she realized nobody was watching her, all eyes were on the far-left

308

corner where a beautiful dark woman stood in a long, orange dress.

Amy looked at Hal. It was as if he'd seen a ghost.

"Hello, Hal," said Marina. "Surprise, surprise."

CHAPTER
THIRTY-FIVE

It was dawn and Hal was sitting on his terrace, wrapped in a bathrobe, watching the sun come up over the gardens. For the second night running, he had hardly slept but whereas last night it had been out of excitement, tonight it was from shock. The sight of Marina in the restaurant had hit him like a missile. He'd hardly been able to breathe. Thank God, he was an actor and had just about been able to pull himself together enough to step forward, kiss her on her cheeks, inhale that familiar ambery Prada scent she wore and mumble something about "How lovely" and "What a surprise", while she'd smiled at him and said yes, wasn't it, adding that she and Fabrizio had just arrived on their yacht and were spending a couple of days in Rome before heading south to the Aeolian islands.

"Congratulations on *The Apple Tree*," she added with a completely straight face. "Fabby and I caught it when we were in the States last month."

"Yeah," boomed a voice behind her, that was a curious mixture of Cape Cod, Belgravia and Aiglon College, Switzerland. "It's a hoot. Well done, Hal."

And there was Fabrizio, so tanned he looked as if he had been carved out of a lump of polished oak,

310

stepping forward and holding out his hairy, beringed hand.

"Thanks," Hal muttered. "Um. Ah. Congratulations, Fabrizio."

"Is Flora here?" Marina asked, in her piercing voice, glancing round the table. Hal noticed a rock the size of an eyeball glinting on her left hand. "Oh, hi, Dominique. I saw you in the Jodanne ad! Callum, darling, great to see you. Justina. Tray. Vlad." Her blue eyes, which had they been set any further apart would have made her look inbred, turned on Amy. "Hello," she said, holding out her right hand, no easy feat given the amount of bling it bore. "I'm Marina."

"I'm Amy."

"Flora's daughters have chickenpox," Hal said loudly and, with only the faintest of quizzical expressions (the Botox prevented more), Marina said, "Oh what a shame. Well, listen, we'd better not keep the rest of our table waiting. Good to see you, Hal. So long."

And with a whisper of silk and a clatter of Gucci heels, she was gone.

Hal had struggled to keep things going after that, but he knew he'd done a feeble job. He couldn't understand how the girl from the sticks who presented a stupid modelling contest could still have such a visceral impact on him.

He'd been so hypnotized by the sight of her, he'd plain forgotten all about Amy. It was only when Callum asked her a very direct question about modern medicine and she'd replied in a soft, almost frightened voice, that he'd remembered her presence. Jesus. Half an hour earlier, he'd been telling her he was in love with her, believing she was his salvation, his key to a better life.

He'd smiled at her across the table, but she didn't see him. In the car on the way home, he'd tried to be nice to her, saying how pretty she looked, how he was sorry he was suddenly really tired. He thought all the sun today had been a bit much for him, knocked him out, but he'd had a lovely evening and she was very sweet and did she mind going into the hotel first and he'd follow a bit later?

He kissed her platonically on the forehead and watched her walk alone into the hotel. He felt bad, naturally. But not bad enough to jump out and follow her. He had his own problems to deal with first.

Now, he tried to analyse what was really going on with his life. He'd had this vision of a new start with Amy. Someone he could live in the country with, laughing and swimming like they had done yesterday, far away from all the parties and photoshoots and photocalls with Justina and dinners like last night's.

But the problem Hal now realized with sudden startling clarity was that he was in love with the idea of Amy, not with Amy herself. Just like when in a film, he screwed up his eyes and whispered, "I love you" to the actress in his arms, he meant what he said at the time. But he couldn't really be in love with Amy, delightful as she was because he barely knew her, just as he barely knew the various co-stars he'd held in his arms. It was exactly the same with Flora: he'd fallen in love with the idea of this talented, intense actress before he'd even

312

spoken to her and he had never made a real effort to get to know the real woman, whoever she might be.

He *had* been in love with Marina, toenail clippings in the loo and all, but because bits of her didn't live up to Hal's ideal he'd let her go. It had been a terrible mistake. He needed to get her back. Marina was the only woman for him. Always had been and always would be.

His phone rang.

"Hello?"

"Hal?"

"Marina!" Telepathy. They'd always had this connection. She'd read his thoughts and she was calling to say it was all OK.

"Good to see you last night. Funny."

Did she mean weird or hilarious? "Yes," Hal said.

"I was wondering. Fabby's got a bit of business to do this morning. I thought perhaps you and I could have breakfast together. That is," she added, "if you're not otherwise engaged."

"That would be great," he said, sitting up and running his hands through his hair.

"Shall I come over to your place as it were? We could have breakfast in your suite. It'd be more private than in a restaurant, don't you think?"

"Absolutely." Hal's heart was hammering so hard he could hardly hear himself speak.

"I'll be there in half an hour."

Hal got into the shower, his heart singing the Hallelujah chorus. He'd been granted a reprieve. Marina was on her way. She was going to tell him she loved him, she'd just got it together with that idiot Fabrizio to wind him up, and now everything was going to be OK. They'd spend the whole day in bed and at the end of it, he'd ask her to marry him. They'd go and live in the country and have the zillions of babies she'd wanted.

"Thank you, God, thank you."

He ordered her favourite, toast and Marmite, a big pot of coffee, a vat of freshly squeezed blood oranges and a bottle of champagne. Then he got dressed, cursing that his favourite green shirt was dirty from yesterday. He went to his safe, keyed in his birthdate and removed the ring box, placing it on the table by the window. Then he sat back and waited.

She was only half an hour late, not bad for Marina. When he opened the door, she was standing there alone in dark denim cut-off jeans and a chiffon, polka-dot blouse, her bosom busting out of it.

"Hello," he said, as overcome as a teenage girl at a boy-band concert.

"Hi." She walked into the living room and straight past him to the terrace. "Is this the best suite in the hotel? I'm sure Fabby and I stayed in a better one."

"You're right. There are a couple of better ones. But Justina's in one and honeymooners are in the other."

"Why would you go on honeymoon to Rome in August? Fabrizio and I are going to the Maldives." She smiled at him triumphantly. "Our own private island."

"You always wanted to go there."

"But you said you'd be bored, stuck on a piece of sand with nothing to do but look at fish." She was still smiling, but her tone was accusatory. Women. They never forgot a thing.

"I was being an idiot. I'm sure it'd be amazing." He followed her onto the terrace, a little bit paranoid about the fact anyone in the gardens could see them if they looked up. "I've ordered some breakfast."

"Oh, that was sweet, Hal," she said absently, leaning on the parapet. "But I don't think I'll be staying. I just wanted to say hello in a little bit more of a personal way than last night. That was a bit awkward, wasn't it? Everyone looking at us. It didn't give me a chance to say what I've been planning to tell you for ages, were I to bump into you."

Hal's heart stopped.

"Which was?"

"That I wish you all the best with Flora. *If* she's lucky enough to hook you: because, basically, I was hung up on you for a very, very long time, Hal Blackstock. I never thought I'd get over you. I used to howl myself to sleep every night, literally howl. Like an animal. But then I met Fabby and he's so sweet and kind, and gradually I started to heal and in the end I realized he was so much better for me than you ever could be. He's a grown-up, not a child. He knows what he wants and he can give me what I want."

"But . . ." She held up her hand to silence him.

"It's not your fault, Hal. You're a very sweet person. Funny, good-looking. Not a bad actor, though you probably shouldn't have done *The Apple Tree*. You just don't know what you want out of life. Or maybe the papers are wrong and you do want Flora. And if you do I'm sure you'll be very happy together."

"I . . ."

"Though, of course, maybe Flora's history. Dominique texted me about your date last night. A doctor, apparently. Very highbrow, Hal. I'm impressed. Well, if she's the one now, then again, good luck."

Marina had always been a lousy actress. Looking at the way her eyes glittered, how tightly her lips were pressed together, the way she was twisting her jewel-laden fingers, Hal was sure she was saying all this merely to hurt him, to extract a revenge which he deserved. So now was the time to do it, to grab the ring and shout, "Marina, I adore you, I always have. I was a snob and an imbecile and I got it all wrong."

But he couldn't. The words stuck in his throat. That old Hal fear of making a fool of himself, of being seen to try, held him back.

"Well, I'm very happy for *you*, Marina," he said instead. "Fabrizio is a great guy and I think you'll be perfect for each other. I hope you're going to invite me to your wedding."

"Hope you're going to invite me to yours." She smiled, but her dark eyes were sad.

"Nothing's on the cards for now, but I'll keep you posted." He nodded at the breakfast table, his heart like a stone. "Sure you're not going to stay?"

"No, thank you." She paused for a moment, then added, "By the way, I know everyone thought I was the sad little victim eating her heart out over her dashing man. But I was having affairs too. Andre. Robbie.

316

Daniel." She smirked slightly. "Just wanted you to know it wasn't all as one-sided as you seemed to think."

"I don't believe you."

"Well, you'll never know now, will you?" She leaned forward and kissed him on the cheek and Hal inhaled that intoxicating Prada scent. He wanted to grab her, kiss her hard, push her onto the bed, but all he said was, "Enjoy the yacht."

"Oh, we will," she said at the door. "We're off tonight at ten. Some time you and Flora, or whoever, will have to join us on it."

"I'd like that," he croaked and the door shut and Marina Dawson walked out of Hal's life.

CHAPTER
THIRTY-SIX

Amy too had a tormented night. At six, she was wide awake staring at the ceiling. Last night all the illusions had been stripped away. For a few hours she'd been able to kid herself that there was something between her and Hal, that he was going to whisk her away to be a film star's girlfriend, but the dinner had changed everything. She could never be part of some Hollywood set and she'd been kidding herself to think so. She wasn't pretty or glamorous enough to be accepted into that circle, nor did she want to be part of it.

In any case, that was beside the point. The point was that Hal wasn't in love with her, whatever he claimed. He was in love with Marina. That had been blindingly obvious. After her appearance it was as if all the life had been sucked out of him.

Hot tears splashed down her cheek at the memory of the humiliation. It wasn't really about losing Hal, because, in all honesty, she wasn't remotely in love with him either. She was far more taken with the idea of such a glamorous replacement for Doug. No, her tears were for the fact she was alone again.

She'd never meet anyone else. She couldn't do this relationship thing.

Once again, she was transported to the build up to the wedding. With only six months to go, she still hadn't found a venue, chosen a dress and no decisions had been made about the menu. Partly this was because Doug was completely uninterested, saying he was happy to "go with the flow", mainly it was because he was so often away touring. Amy felt ambiguous about his absences. She was haunted by what he might be getting up to, unfettered and surrounded by groupies. At the same time, it was lovely to come home and find the flat just as she had left it that morning, to be able to get into bed wearing a pore strip, with a pile of wedding magazines and *Catwalk* with Marina Dawson on the TV.

On the nights Doug was there, he was often knackered and just wanted to slump and she had to chivvy him to go out. She remembered that horrible February night they went to a dinner party at Gaby and PJ's new house which they'd just moved into.

"Do we have to?" Doug moaned, as they sat side by side on the Northern Line, clutching a bunch of flowers and a bottle of cava. "PJ's so fucking dull. And Christ knows who else they'll have found to bore us with."

"It'll be fun," Amy said, although she knew what Doug meant. A lot of PJ's friends were bone-achingly tedious, with jobs in the City and an obsession with six-figure bonuses that Amy found faintly obscene.

The train pulled into Waterloo and a couple got on. A tall, kind-looking man in a blue coat and a pretty girl in a grey mac. He bent over and kissed the girl on the nose, and she laughed. With a sickening jolt, she realized it was Danny. Amy buried herself in her copy of *London Lite*. She did not want them to see her, tired, strung-out, with this sulky man behaving like a teenager beside her. Danny pointed at an advert on the wall and the girl laughed again. They looked so pleasant and normal. Why had she rejected such an existence for a world that more and more seemed to her to be about nothing more than skinny limbs, tight clothes, Jack Daniels and top-quality Jamaican skunk.

Fortunately, as Amy hoped, they got off at the next stop. But all the way to Gaby's she was edgy. Her mood wasn't improved when the door of 49 Sylvester Road was opened not by a red-faced PJ, carrying Archie, but by Pinny.

"Hello? What are you doing here?" Amy's question sounded ruder than she'd intended.

"I bumped into Gaby on Oxford Street and she invited me," Pinny explained, radiant as usual in, of all things, a tracksuit which made her look like Kate Hudson jogging on the beach in Malibu. Amy would have resembled Vicky Pollard popping to the corner shop for twenty Rothmans.

Doug looked like he'd just heard he'd won the Lottery. "Nice one, Pins," he said, kissing her. Gaby appeared in a Cath Kidston apron.

"Hey, guys. A surprise guest for you. Come into the living room and have a drink. I'm just putting the finishing touches to the cassoulet. Oh, lovely flowers. And cava. How *interesting*."

"Is Archie still up?" Amy asked hopefully, longing to stroke that soft, downy head.

Gaby looked shocked. "Of course not, bedtime is seven sharp."

"Can't I go in and see him?"

"I don't want his routine thrown out."

"I'll be as quiet as a mouse," she begged. "Please!"

Archie was breathing heavily. Amy stood marvelling at his perfect, smooth, chubby, baby flesh. *She wanted one of those.* She gazed covetously for about fifteen minutes, before descending to the living room; Macy Gray was playing. PJ was sitting on an embroidered Moroccan foot-stool, while a couple — he in a suit, she in jeans and a cashmere jumper — were on one sofa. Pinny and Doug sat a bit too close for comfort on the other.

"Amy! Have a drink. Thought you'd got lost up there. And let me introduce you. This is Nickey and this is Paul."

Hands were shaken. Paul, she discovered, was a merchant banker, Nickey was in PR. They lived down the road and had two small children, "little horrors".

"And Doug, I gather you're in a band with Pinny here," said Paul. "When are we going to see you on *Top of the Pops*?"

Pinny and Doug just looked at each other and giggled. It was left to Amy to explain *TOTP* had died a couple of years ago.

"I don't believe it." Paul looked quite distraught. "I used to love *Top of the Pops* when I was a boy. Thursday evenings. Christ. Times have changed."

"So how's the band going?" PJ asked, waving a bowl of cashews under Doug's nose.

"All right. A gig here, a gig there."

"It took Pulp twelve years to make it, you know," Amy said, as ever compelled to defend her boyfriend's wayward choice.

"Pulp? Oh yes, Jarvis Cocker. Where is he now?"

Gaby ushered them into the dining room. "I actually had an idea about the band, Doug," she said serving him his portion of Nigel Slater roasted butternut squash.

"Oh, yeah. What?"

"Why don't you audition for the *X Factor*?"

There was a mini pause and then Doug and Pinny started laughing.

"The *X Factor*? Can you imagine? Ooh, Sharon, what's your verdict?"

"I don't see why not," Nickey said. "It'd give you an amazing platform. I think the prize is a million-pound recording contract." She looked at Doug closely. "Actually, do you know what? Has anyone ever told you, you're the spitting image of Simon Cowell."

"Simon Cowell?" Pinny fell about laughing. "You know she's right, Doug. I never noticed it before. You could be twins."

With Doug looking as happy as a constipated buffalo, Gaby persisted. "But *why* don't you?"

"I'd rather shave off my eyebrows. Are you asking me to lose all my credibility?"

"But not all the people who win those shows are losers," said Gaby. "Look at Kelly Clarkson. Or Will Young."

"Will Young? Not a loser?" Doug and Pinny snorted. Once Amy would have agreed, but looking at him she thought, *Yes, Will Young's a multi-platinum artist and you are . . .?*

"Who's that paint colour by?" she tried instead.

"Farrow & Ball," Gaby said, delighted. "A bit of a cliché, but they really are so lovely."

"It's beautiful, Gaby," Nickey said. "You've done so well getting a place here and I can't believe you're in the catchment for the Belmarsh. You couldn't have done better."

"So how are the wedding plans going, Amy?" PJ enquired. "Amy and Doug are getting married in August."

"Amy and Doug?" Nickey looked puzzled, as her head swung from them to Doug and Pinny. "Oh. Right. I thought . . ."

"Doug and Pinny are just in the band together," Gaby said firmly.

"We still can't find a venue," Amy said, delighted for an opportunity to air her worries, to which Doug remained stonily indifferent. "I went to see a church hall in Stoke Newington last night that I'd heard good things about, but I had to step over a junkie to get in and there's a Chinese takeaway next door. It'd be fine if you were talking about a girls' night out in Soho but it definitely ain't OK for grannies. Anyway, I think we'll have to rule out all church halls. I'd feel like we were at an Ambrosial gig."

Doug failed to disguise a yawn. PJ tried to look interested.

"Running out of time, aren't you?" PJ said. "I mean, you've got what . . . less than six months to go?"

"I know. I've looked at every hotel, every restaurant, every bar in London and basically there is nowhere we can afford for a wedding reception unless we get married on a Wednesday morning."

"Wednesday morning?"

"You get cheaper rates if you do it in the week."

For the first time in ages, Doug looked interested. "Oh, right. Well, maybe that's what we should do."

"Doug! People are coming down from Scotland, up from Devon, we can't ask them to take two days off work just so we can save a few hundred quid."

"Then we'll have to pay a bit extra. We'll cut down on something else. Like the food. Anyway," Doug continued, smirking, "the wine'll be all right." Oddly enough, he had been quite happy to accompany his fiancée to a wine tasting.

"You sound a teeny bit behind," said Gaby. "What about your wedding list? You've got to register for presents."

"Presents?" Doug looked blank, as well he might. On the rare occasions they went to one of his friend's weddings, it was always Amy who found the wedding list on johnlewis.com and whose credit card paid for a bath mat or coffee grinder for a couple she barely even knew.

"Yes. Presents. People like to give a marrying couple a little something, usually for the house, to set them up for married life."

324

"But we don't need anything for the house," he said. Which wasn't true. Amy was sick of pans handed down from her parents, which had been on *their* wedding list back before the invention of electricity.

"But you're putting on a fabulous show," Gaby said. "Spending a fortune on all your friends. The least people can do is give you some kind of present."

"Christ, that was hideous." Pinny giggled, as a couple of hours later the three of them sat in a mini cab, heading north. "So bloody bourgeois. 'How much do you pay your cleaner?' 'Do you think Verbier's better than Meribel?' " Her impression of Gaby and Nickey was spookily spot on.

Amy agreed with her, to a point, but she still felt pissed off. "Why did you go then?"

"Gaby invited me. It'd've been rude to turn her down. And I knew you and Doug would be there, so it would be a laugh." She wiggled in her seat. "Shit, I hope you two aren't going to be like that when you're married. All property values and architects' fees."

"Course we're not," Amy said quickly.

"Though I still think you should chill out on the wedding plans, Amy," Doug said from the front seat.

"I still can't believe you two are getting married," Pinny said. "It's just too freaky and grown-up."

The cab pulled up outside their flat. "Fancy a nightcap, Pins?" Doug said, as Amy looked at her watch. It was after bloody midnight and she had to be in the surgery at 7.30.

"Yeah, don't mind if I do." Pinny looked in her purse. "Shit. Do you mind if I borrow a tenner for my contribution."

"Don't be silly. Amy will pick it up."

So Amy paid the thirty-pound bill and they climbed the stairs to the flat where Pinny immediately headed for the stereo and put on Nellee at industrial-drill-level volume.

"Shhh." Amy tried to smile. "You'll wake Nirpal downstairs."

"Oh sod Nirpal," said Doug who was drunker than she'd thought. "Let's dance."

"You two dance. I'm going to bed."

"God, Amy. Live a little," Pinny said.

"You're no fun any more," Doug added as was his wont.

"I am fun," she said with a lightness she didn't remotely feel. "But I have to be up very early. Pinny, if you want to stay on the sofa, Doug can find you some sheets and towels. And please keep it down a bit."

Of course, she couldn't sleep at all. For a start, her heart felt as if it was hammering away right against her skull. She lay there listening to the bump of the music, giggling, the occasional crash as if some furniture had been knocked over, then hammering at the door, when Nirpal, who was a mild-mannered accountant, inevitably complained.

She thought about the evening, trying to work out why she felt so torn. Part of her definitely found the world of Gaby and PJ smug and limiting and a little

326

scary, but an equal part of her envied how content they were with their pretty house, their garden, their nine to five jobs and their child. Why did Doug have to want more than that? Her thoughts spun like a roulette wheel then rested on chunky, serious, rugby-playing Danny. By now, if she'd stuck with him, she could have had all that. And she would have probably been going out of her mind with boredom. Or would she? Now the bloody clock had begun to echo in her ears, she could see how you could make any sacrifice, any compromise, to fulfil your biological destiny.

She had to stop thinking like this. Doug thought she was no fun any more. She would lose him, she knew it, he would slip through her fingers and there was nothing she could do to stop it. She'd have to do without sleep in order to be, once more, the sparkly girlfriend he loved. She'd look perfect, cook delicious meals and fling him onto the bed as soon as he walked through the door in order to keep him.

"Ooh, get you!" Pinny yelled next door.

Whatever Doug said, she'd go on arranging an amazing wedding, a wedding that was the ultimate in cool and good taste. And afterwards, she'd surprise him with the perfect honeymoon at his dream destination. She'd blow all her savings on it, to show him how wonderful she was.

He came to bed some time after three.

"Pin's gone home," he whispered beerily in her ear. "Said she didn't fancy being woken by you crashing round the flat at the crack of dawn."

327

"I'm sorry I might have inconvenienced her," Amy said, then immediately felt a bitch. But Doug didn't hear.

"I'm sorry I said you were no fun. Pinny told me off. Said someone had to have a respectable job."

"That's OK," Amy said. She felt Doug pulling at her pyjama bottoms. Even though she was shattered she felt a surge of triumph. He wanted her after all. She was being paranoid and mad. Afterwards, she lay snuggled on his chest, listening to his breathing.

"Could you move a bit?" he said. "You're squashing me."

She moved. And in the morning, she called Gaby and asked her to arrange the most fabulous Roman honeymoon of all time.

"Doug and Pinny are very close, aren't they?" Gaby said, having written down all her friend's requirements.

"Of course they are, they work together," Amy snapped. Perhaps she'd have been better off going through some online travel agent who wouldn't ask such rude questions.

CHAPTER
THIRTY-SEVEN

Amy didn't feel like breakfast. Instead, she took the lift down to the leisure centre, where she changed into her bikini. It was still damp from yesterday. How could it be that less than twenty-four hours ago, she'd been splashing about in warm water with Hal and now life seemed utterly bleak again. She climbed into the hydrotherapy pool. The bubbles pulsated against her skin, but they felt an artificial replica of yesterday's simple pleasures. When she returned upstairs she'd call the airlines again and beg for a seat out on the next plane.

"Hiya!" said a voice behind her. She looked round. It was Lisa, resplendent in a tiny red bikini. There was a little dolphin tattoo just below her belly button.

"Hey, how are you? I hope I didn't land you in it yesterday. You caught me a bit on the hop, you know."

"I'm sorry," Lisa said, sliding into the water beside her. "Simon had me right on the spot. I didn't get back until one. I mean, I reckoned he'd be busy covering the premiere and he wouldn't notice where I'd got to. But he was hopping. So I had to blame you. But I appreciate you taking the slack. It just means . . . well, it just means I've had to make some more concessions."

"Oh yes?"

"Yes. We've agreed about the boarding school. I've signed the papers. Emily starts in three weeks. She wasn't too chuffed when I told her."

"I bet she wasn't."

Lisa sighed. "Simon swears it's for the best. Says she'll have all the opportunities I never did. I told her, there are horses and a swimming pool and I'll come and see her every three weeks and it'll be just like Hogwarts, but she was still ever so upset, Amy."

"Mmm." Amy didn't know what to say, except, "You shouldn't have done it," and her medical experience had taught her people never wanted to hear those words.

"And then there's the dog."

"Oh, yes?"

"He insisted I told Emily this morning that she'll have to be put down."

"Put down!"

"Well, my sister won't have her. And she's old. Probably only got another six months to a year left anyway, so it's pointless finding a new home for her. But Emily cried and cried. It was awful. I was so upset."

But not as much as Emily. Amy was going to have to say something. "Do you really love Simon?" she tried.

"What do you mean?"

"Is he really the right man for you? Because I get the impression Emily is the love of your life, not him — which is how it should be. So maybe you should be marrying someone who'll put Emily first."

330

"But he *will* put Emily first. He'll pay for her to go to a good school and to university. She'll have all the advantages I've dreamed of for her. Simon's saved us, Amy. Of course I love him."

"What about Massimo?"

"Massimo's cute. But he was just a fling." She raised a perfect eyebrow. "Darling, I'm just doing what guys do. You have fun with a bit of fluff, but you marry someone serious."

Amy tried a different tack. "But Emily would be happier with her mum, not far away at some horrible, posh school."

Lisa's mouth hardened. "With respect, Amy, you don't know what you're talking about. Emily will not be happier with a mum who's always struggling to pay the bills, a mum who can't even give her a week's holiday when all the other kids are going to Spain and Florida."

"But those things don't matter," Amy said, appalled.

"I think they do." Lisa contemplated her huge ring. "I've always wanted pretty things, Amy."

"But you've got a job. You can afford the odd holiday, can't you?"

"Not the kind of holiday I deserve. I've got so many debts, it'd take me a lifetime to pay them back. But after I marry Simon they'll be gone in one fell swoop. All over. Finito. I can't do it any more, Amy. I'm so bloody tired. I need a fresh page."

"Fresh page with someone you don't love."

"I just told you, I do love him. But anyway, love isn't that important. What's important is security." She stood up, her magnificent body dripping wet. "Better be off.

Got a hair appointment." She looked back over her shoulder. "It's all right for you. You've got a *good* job. You haven't made the mistakes I have. You can still believe love's the most important thing."

She clicked across the mosaic tiles in her gold flip flops, not looking round. And Amy lay back in the water and wondered if she should judge Lisa harshly. Because, in the end, wasn't security what she wanted too? Didn't she want to know that she and Doug could pay their mortgage, buy nice furniture, relax a little, rather than it always being her slog, slog, slogging her guts out to keep the show on the road, while he invested all his time and energy in the band? Hadn't she even reached that mad point where she'd considered texting Danny to see if he'd have her back.

She had loved Doug, she really had. But she hadn't been sure love was enough either. Maybe she'd been too greedy. Perhaps her standards had been too high. Possibly she'd wanted the stars, when actually the moon had been more than enough.

But thinking about it, Amy knew her problems with Doug had run deeper than that. They hadn't just been about money and status and a big house. It had been about something more fundamental. It had been about growing up. It had been about the dawning realization that a future of gigs and late nights and spliffs and DVDs and meals out simply didn't satisfy her any more. Amy had been so crazy about Doug, she'd tried and tried to convince herself it didn't really matter, but all along she'd known it did.

"Excuse me," said a gentle female voice behind her, "are you Amy?"

Once again, Amy twisted round. A pretty blonde woman, with bobbed hair, in jeans and a flowery shirt was smiling down at her.

"Yes?"

"Amy, hiya. So nice to finally put a face to a name. I'm Christine. From the *Daily Post*."

"Oh, hi," Amy said, confused.

"Now I was just wondering if we could have a little chat about your relationship with Hal Blackstock?"

"Sorry? There is no relationship." For a day she'd been lying about that, but now it was the inescapable truth once more.

"Oh, but I think there is," said Christine, as she squatted down and in one deft movement revealed both a tiny tape recorder and a copy of a newspaper.

HAL'S ROMAN HOLIDAY shouted the headline. And underneath it was a rather grainy picture of Hal and Amy, lips locking in the dawn light, in front of the Mouth of Truth.

"Taken by an onlooker," Christine said. "It seems like a very close relationship to me, Amy. So perhaps you'd like to tell me all about it."

"I . . ." Amy had a vague idea that in these situations you were meant to say "no comment". But the words just wouldn't come out.

"Shall I read you what it says?" Christine asked kindly. "Then you can tell me which bits are true or false?"

"I . . ." Amy wished she wasn't soaking wet and vulnerable.

"Hal-lo, hal-lo, hal-lo. Film star Hal Blackstock is seen kissing a married woman in Rome, early yesterday morning. The forty-three-year-old boyfriend of fellow star Flora de Belleville Crécy enjoyed his embrace after a night out in the Holy City with honeymooner, Amy Fraser, thirty-six."

"I'm thirty-four," Amy objected.

"Oh, right." Christine nodded. "Hot on the heels of his ex-girlfriend Marina Dawson's announcing her engagement to tycoon Fabrizio de Michelis, Blackstock seems to have wasted no time in wooing Mrs Fraser, a guest in the exclusive five-star Hotel de Russie, where suites cost up to four thousand pounds a night."

"Mine wasn't nearly as much as that!" Amy exclaimed. "I mean, it was bloody expensive, but . . ."

"It's quoting the rack rate." Christine smiled. "While Oscar-winning Flora, Hal's girlfriend of more than a year, has been busy working with female prisoners in Jamaica, Hal has been living up to his nickname, Holiday Hal. He and Mrs Fraser, a social worker from North London, spent an evening touring Rome on Hal's Vespa, then danced in a nightclub, before enjoying this embrace in front of the Mouth of Truth, a Roman landmark, made famous from the Audrey Hepburn film *Roman Holiday*."

"Vinny told you all this!" Amy exclaimed. "He sold you that picture." The bastard.

Christine merely smiled. "We never reveal our sources. 'There was a definite chemistry between them,' said one onlooker. 'They just couldn't keep their hands off each other.' Bizarrely, Mrs Fraser is on her honeymoon with her husband of less than three days. She is also believed to be around three months pregnant with their first child.

"'Amy's husband's a very nice young man and they seemed completely devoted to each other,' said fellow hotel guest, Marian Otterley, sixty-four, of Marlborough, Wiltshire. 'But these past few days he's been confined to his room with a headache and I guess Amy just fell into temptation. I have to say, I am rather shocked at her behaviour. She was so proud and happy to be having a baby and it seems very strange for her to go gallivanting off like this.' "

"Marian's never met my husband! Anyway, he's not my husband."

"Oh, yes?" Eagerly, Christine leaned forward. "So you're not on your honeymoon."

"Well, yes, I am. But . . ." There was something you were supposed to say in these situations. Oh yes. "No comment!" She put on her robe, and went towards the changing rooms. Christine followed her.

"Hey, Amy love. It's all right. Calm down. That's why I'm here. So you can tell *your* side of the story and not be misrepresented. I tell you what, howsabout we go and have a quiet breakfast somewhere and you tell me what's what and then we can make sure what's printed in the paper is all true."

"No thanks," Amy said, pulling the robe around her.

Christine shook her head mournfully. "Honestly, Amy. It is all for the best. You can't stop people printing things about you, so wouldn't you rather have some control over it?"

What Christine was saying made sense. This report was so full of lies, she had to correct them. She thought of her parents, reading their *Daily Post* over breakfast and freaking out. But would the true version of events make them feel any better? The whole thing was a mess. She'd been so naive. How could she have thought it was possible to spend time with someone like Hal Blackstock and it go unnoticed?

"We'll make it worth your while, Amy," Christine said. She was very pretty and she seemed nice. "We'll pay you a substantial sum for you to put the record straight."

Amy was just about to say, "All right, then," when another female voice barked, "Amy!"

They both looked round. Vanessa. Looking even more tetchy than usual.

"Amy, stop talking to this . . . person immediately. You're to come with me."

"Why?"

"There's no why about it, Amy. You're to come with me. Immediately."

Amy stood between the two women — nice, rosy-cheeked Christine and vile Vanessa. She disliked being spoken to in this tone. Was Vanessa offering her money? What did she owe her or Hal, anyway?

She looked at both of them.

"I think you're better off coming with me, Amy," Christine said softly.

336

Vanessa screwed up her eyes. With a huge effort of will, she breathed, "*Please.*"

That settled it. "Sorry," Amy said to Christine. She felt genuinely apologetic. "But I think I have to go with Vanessa."

CHAPTER
THIRTY-EIGHT

After Marina had gone, Hal sat on his terrace for a very long time, staring out at the gardens. Inside the suite, the phone rang incessantly. A tiny part of him wanted to pick up, just in case it was Marina apologizing, but he knew that was just another mad dream. So he let it ring and ring. He got up and unplugged all the phones in the suite and turned off his mobile. Everyone could get lost. He needed to be alone, to think.

Then the knocking started. At first Hal ignored it, but it persisted and Nessie cried, "Hal! Hal! Terribly sorry to disturb you, but I need to talk to you."

"Go away, Nessie," he shouted. "I'm sleeping."

"I'm sorry. I wouldn't if it wasn't urgent."

"Nothing's ever that urgent. Tell me later. I'm not in the mood."

"I really think you should know about this."

Hal got up, marched over to the door, and opened it a smidgen to see Vanessa, looking unusually agitated, carrying a newspaper. Oh bollocks, more crap in the press, no doubt. That was hardly urgent, they printed lies about him every day.

"Darling, I said go away."

"But Hal . . ."

And then a voice from behind her in the corridor, said, "Hal?"

And over Vanessa's shoulder, Hal saw the willowy blonde woman whom the world believed to be his girlfriend.

"Flora! What the fuck are you doing here?"

"Oh, charming," said Flora with a little humourless laugh. She was wearing jeans that showed off her non-existent bottom, and an embroidered peasant top, which Hal knew had cost about the same as the annual GDP of Guatemala. Her blonde hair hung poker straight down the side of her face and her no-make-up make-up was immaculate. She put her arms round him. "I've come all this way to surprise you and this is the welcome I receive."

"I'm sorry, Hal," Vanessa said, looking terrified for the first time since Hal had known her. "I couldn't get hold of Henrietta yesterday before they'd left for the airport."

Hal's mind turned cartwheels. "Sorry, sorry, darling," he muttered, giving her a quick peck on the cheek. "You just gave me a shock. Why didn't you say you were coming out? How are the girls?"

"They're fine now, thank you. It's not a serious illness. And as for coming out, forgive me, but I thought it would be romantic." Flora turned to her assistant Henrietta, who looked pale and dishevelled, and the porter, who stood next to a loaded baggage trolley. "Guys, leave us alone for now. Hal and I want to catch up. I'll call you later, Henrietta, when it's time for us to plan our day."

"OK, Flora," said Henrietta, looking mightily relieved as the prospect of bed after an overnight flight loomed.

"When we next talk I'd like you to have organized the planting of at least a hundred acres of Brazilian forest. We flew here in a private plane," she explained to Hal as Henrietta's face fell. "Only way to get from Jamaica to Rome with minimum stopovers. But you know how bad that makes me feel about the environment." She swept past him into the suite. "See you guys later," she called as the door shut.

Like Marina, she made straight for the terrace.

"Hmm. Pretty gardens," she said, over her shoulder, "but you're a bit on display. I don't think this is the best suite in the hotel. I'm sure when I stayed here with Pierre —"

"Yes, there are better suites," Hal confirmed miserably. "Honeymooners are in one and Justina's in the other. This suite does have two Picasso lithographs."

"How insane to have your honeymoon in Rome in August." Flora shrugged, then looked with disapproval at the untouched breakfast things on the terrace. "Hmmm. I need a shower. Should have had one on the jet but I was going through my notes for the trip to Madagascar. And then I'd like some lunch. Nothing fancy, maybe a salad. Get them to fix one for me, while I get myself ready. Remember no tomatoes or eggplant!"

"Sure, Flora," Hal said, grateful for the opportunity of losing her for a few minutes.

While she was in the shower, Hal found himself consumed with panic. Bloody Flora ambushing him like this. Just one look at her high cheekbones, her thin, unamused mouth had convinced Hal of something he'd secretly known for months. He didn't love her. He never had. He never would. She was a good actress and a well-connected woman who raised squillions for charity, but it wasn't enough. How had he ever been able to think otherwise?

He supposed it was a good thing really. He was going to have to dump her sooner or later, so it might as well be sooner. He couldn't help feeling a little sorry for her, having flown all this way just to get the boot. Poor Flora, so in control on the surface, but she had terrible luck with men. He wondered if the reason she'd broken up with Pierre was because he too found her a crashing, conceited bore. One day they'd have to have a drink and compare notes. By the time Hal had called room service and asked them to bring up two vegetarian salads and some wheatgrass juice, he was feeling quite sorry for Flora. But not as sorry as he felt for himself — about to be single for virtually the first time in his adult life. Of course, plenty of candidates for his next girlfriend would soon be queuing round the block but Hal was no longer in the mood for another casual relationship. Next time would be true love, no substitutes accepted.

Mentally, he prepared his little speech. "Flora, you're an amazing woman but . . . it's not you, it's me . . . I just need some me-time right now . . . You deserve someone who can give you all the things I can't."

"Hal!"

Flora was standing in the doorway in a bathrobe, a strange smile on her face. She held her hands out towards him. Her bony fingers were cradling a little black box.

"Hal, I'm so sorry. I wasn't snooping, I swear. I was just looking for some mouthwash in the bedroom. And look what I found! Sorry, sorry, I know you'd have been planning an amazing, romantic proposal, like on the terrace with the sun setting over the gardens, but pretending I knew nothing is one role even I couldn't take on." She laughed delightedly. "The ring's beautiful, Hal. Really beautiful. Though it might be a little loose for my finger."

Hal swallowed. "That was naughty of you, Flora. You shouldn't snoop."

"I know, I know. I've already said sorry." She ran across the room to him. Hal recognized the look in her eyes as the same one she'd used in *Bracken* where she'd played the sweet, innocent daughter of a serial killer. Batting her eyelashes demurely, she handed him the box.

"So?" she lisped.

"So?"

Flora looked a little less sweet and innocent. "So are you going to ask me? Properly?"

"Oh, that. Right. Well." Hal wiped sweat from his brow, even though the air-conditioning was running full blast. "I was going to do it later."

"But let's be spontaneous! Do it *now*!"

"OK," he said wearily, but just then came banging on the door.

"Hey, it must be lunch arriving," he said gratefully, hurrying to open it. But on the other side stood Callum.

"Cal!" he cried. "Hey, mate, good to see you. Come in, come in. Shit, you'll never guess who's decided to pay us a visit."

"Who?" said Cal, blinking at this unexpected bonhomie. Like Nessie, Hal noticed, he was holding a copy of the *Daily Post*.

"Sorry to disturb you like this, but your phone's unplugged and your mobile's off and I really think you and I need to look at this and work out some damage limitation." He stopped short as he reached the terrace. "Flora! Shit! I mean, hi! What are you doing here?"

"Why does everyone keep asking me this?" Flora said. "I've come to see my boyfriend. Is that a crime?"

"Oh no, no, no, far from it," Callum said, although his normally smooth facade seemed oddly ruffled. "Would you mind if Hal and I had a quick word in private? Boring business stuff. And then you two can relax together."

"Why can't I be there when you talk to Hal?" Flora said. "There are no secrets between us, you know. Not when we're about to be . . ." she caught Hal's eye and then continued momentously, "man and wife."

"I'm sorry?" Callum said.

"You should be the first to know. We're getting married."

"You are?"

"Well, Hal hasn't officially asked me yet. But I discovered the ring and that accelerated things and so . . ."

"Congratulations then, to both of you." Callum stepped forward and kissed Flora, then shook Hal's hand. "Fantastic news. But listen, Flora. What Hal and I need to talk about really isn't romantic, so why don't you just sit out here for a moment and enjoy the sun and Hal and I will have a quick word indoors and then he's all yours."

"Just gimme a clue what this is all about," Flora whined. Despite himself, Hal grinned. She was so competitive, she simply couldn't bear to be left out of the loop. Briefly, he caught Cal's eye and nodded. He knew all this had to be about the Bazotti film, that Callum was nervous because Flora would be furious Hal had to fly to LA tomorrow for the audition. Bless him. After all, how was he to know that by tomorrow he and Flora would be history? And sure enough, Callum said, "Well, strictly between the three of us, Hal's up for a part in the next Andreas Bazotti. We just need to talk a few logistics."

"The new Bazotti." Flora eyed Hal with unaccustomed respect. "Well, well. I can't wait to hear more about this." Then she yawned. "Sorry. Jet lag catching up on me. OK, but you boys be quick. I want my Hal to myself." She nodded at the newspaper under Callum's arm. "Why don't you leave me that to look at?"

"That?" Callum looked down at the paper as if it were radioactive. "Oh you don't want to be reading this, Flora. It's one of our British tabloids. Full of mucky froth. I'm sure I could get them to bring you up a copy of the *New Yorker* or . . ."

"No, I like your British rags," Flora said. "They make me laugh. We don't get anything so frivolous in the States. C'mon, Callum, hand it over."

"Actually, there's something in it I need to show Hal."

Flora's face darkened. "Hand it over, Callum," she repeated, as if she was a cop confronting a gun-toting bank robber. When he said nothing, she stepped towards him and snatched the paper away. She put it down on a side table and studied the front page in silence.

"Oh," she said.

Hal looked over her shoulder, bewildered.

"Oh fuck," he said.

CHAPTER
THIRTY-NINE

Vanessa bundled Amy down to the garage and into a limo with blacked-out windows. As the driver pulled out into the Via del Babuino, Amy's phone began ringing.

"Don't answer it!" Vanessa yelled.

"But it's my mum."

"Oh. Right. OK, then. But you must tell her not to talk to *anybody*."

"Hi, Mum."

"Amy, sweet pea, what on earth is going on? You're in the papers today, you know. Apparently you're having an affair with Hal Blackstock. And you and Doug got married after all. And you're *pregnant*."

"We're not married. And I'm not pregnant. That was a misunderstanding." Vanessa's head whipped round so sharply, Amy thought it might fly off. "And I'm not having an affair with Hal Blackstock."

"Oooh," Mum made a noise like air coming out of a pair of bellows. "Are you sure?"

"About which bit?"

"Well, Hal Blackstock," her mother said, making the order of her priorities quite clear.

"Totally. I know him. But nothing is going on."

"And you're not pregnant?" Smash. Another shattered dream. But then she rallied. "You know Hal Blackstock! Oh, goodness, Amy. You must tell him how much I loved him in that film about the American civil war. And do you think you could get an autograph? Not for me, but for Pat next door."

"I'm not sure I'll get a chance now."

"Well, see what you can do. If you could get him to write 'To Pat with love from Hal', that would be so exciting. Anyway, I'm glad you're having fun, darling. I mean, Daddy and I were a bit embarrassed by the pictures but . . . Oh! There's someone at the door. Hang on, I'll just have a peek through the curtains. It's two men. I wonder who they could be."

"I think they might be journalists."

"What?" trilled Vanessa.

"Journalists? But however could they have found us?"

Vanessa snatched the phone. "Hello? This is Vanessa Trimingham, Mr Blackstock's assistant. Now, if there are men knocking on your door, you mustn't answer it. I don't want you to pick up the phone either. Everyone is going to be agog to know about your daughter's relationship with Mr Blackstock. You must make no comment. If anyone does penetrate your defences, you must say 'no comment'. Have you got that? No co-mment." There was a tiny pause and then, "No. I'm not being patronizing. I'm sorry you've taken it that way . . . well, you may just not be able to go swimming today. I think we need to get our priorities in order. It's more important we kill this story at birth . . ." The yabbering at the end of the line grew louder. "All right, I'll put you back on to your daughter."

"Amy!" Her mother sounded very upset. "That woman says I can't leave the house. But I always go swimming with Pat on Fridays. Tell her."

"It might not be a good idea today." Amy heard the doorbell ring. At the same time, her phone began bleeping insistently, as caller upon caller tried to get through.

"Oh crumbs. More people at the door. Whatever shall I do?"

"I think Vanessa's right," said Amy, "you're just going to have to stay in."

Having finally persuaded her mother of this, she began scrolling through her texts. Just as with the wedding, everyone wanted to know what was going on. She bashed one out to Gaby, assuring her it wasn't what she thought and she was hoping to be home soon and give her a full report. Then, scrolling on, her heart stopped for a second as she saw the name *Pinny*.

Good girl. You've given that useless man of yours a right shock.
Congrats, P xx

Amy stared, puzzled. She'd been sure Pinny would have made her move on Doug as soon as she'd left the country. How odd. But rather than think about it, she turned to her voicemail messages. All the usual suspects plus calls from the *Sun, Daily Mail, Daily Express* and

News of the World. How had they got her number? Then a wheedling Christine. She deleted it. The next was a man.

"Amy. This is Vincenzo. From the other night. The hotel gave me your number, when I picked you up at the airport. Amy, I am so sorry. So sorry. It wasn't me, you must believe me. It was Gianni. I am so angry with him. Please. If this is difficult for you, call me. You can come and stay with me, if you want, away from the newspaper men."

Amy looked at Vanessa then at her phone.

"Wherever you're taking me, there's a change of plan."

"What do you mean?"

"I want to go to my friend's house, not to wherever you want to hide me." As Vanessa opened her mouth to argue, Amy delivered the clincher. "If not, I tell my mum to tell the newspaper she thinks Hal and I are engaged."

Back at the hotel, the fallout was inevitable. Understandably, Flora was very angry. She shouted at Hal a lot, threw the ring in his face, told him the whole thing was off and stormed from the room yelling for Henrietta to pack up and leave immediately.

As the door slammed shut Hal and Callum looked at each other. Both of them started to laugh. They laughed until they were weakly clutching their sides, tears running down their faces.

"Sorry," Callum managed eventually. "I don't think I should be finding the end of your relationship so funny. But I do. Sack me if you want to, sack me now."

"It's all right," said Hal. "She'd have found out soon enough, I guess. Just a shame she had to fly over here to do so." He giggled. "You're right, it's not funny. She's very hurt." The last two words came out in a little scream.

They both started laughing again. "I didn't realize you felt *so* little about her," Callum said, as he eventually calmed down.

"Nor did I, until the last couple of days."

There was a tiny pause. "Have you and Marina got back together?"

Hal shook his head, lips tight. "Nope. Nope. That was never on the cards. She's marrying Fabrizio. You know that."

"But last night the chemistry between you was so strong —"

Hal cut him off. "Marina and me are over. Now let me look at this paper properly. And then I think I'd better call Amy and apologize for buggering about with her life."

"Actually," Callum said, clearing his throat, "we've taken care of Amy."

Hal looked aghast. "Taken care of her? This isn't a fascist state any more, you know."

Callum grinned. "It's not that bad. But the hotel's surrounded by press and paps, so Vanessa took her away to a secret place they found for us in the country.

350

We thought she could stay there until the fuss dies down and we put her on a flight home."

"Poor girl." Hal thought about Amy. It hadn't been love, but he had liked her a lot. "Can I go and see her? I think I owe her a personal apology."

CHAPTER
FORTY

A couple of hours later, Hal and Amy were sitting in Vincenzo's tiny flat, which he shared with his mother, in the suburb of EUR, a hideous collection of modern tower blocks.

An apologetic Vincenzo had been thrilled to welcome them, while his mother — who wore a leopardskin bustier and tight leather pants and was, in all, nothing like Amy's image of the black-clad Italian mamma, made them coffee and plied Hal with cakes. None for Amy, however, as a *donna*, apparently, she needed to consider her figure.

Hal asked if he could have a word with Amy alone. Vincenzo ushered them on to the balcony, with a view of some grotesque stone monolith.

"That's ugly," said Amy.

"Mussolini built it. I mean, not personally, but it was his neo-fascist style of architecture. Never caught on." Hal wondered how long he could hide in such small talk, but his guilt suddenly got the better of him. "I'm sorry," he blurted out, "I flirted with you, made you think there was something going on between us, when actually I was just playing, and I knew at some subconscious level we wouldn't be able to get away with it. The paps are always lurking."

"Or some dodgy friend of Vincenzo's."

"Or some dodgy friend of Vincenzo's."

"Apology accepted," Amy said, deeply touched. "I forgive you."

Hal smiled. "Thank you. This'll all blow over, you know. Fish and chip paper."

"I guess. Only I didn't really want the whole world to know about me and my imaginary husband. Kind of humiliating."

"I understand." Hal paused a moment and then asked, "You're not really pregnant, are you?"

She shook her head a little sadly. "Nor ever likely to be at this rate."

"I *am* sorry, Amy. I thought I meant what I said. But I was confused. I didn't mean you to get caught up in the disaster that is my private life."

"It's OK," she said. "I had great fun with you. And I realized fun's been missing a bit in my life recently."

She looked so pretty, sitting in the sun, Hal wondered for a second if he hadn't made yet another horrible mistake. "Why did you split up with your husband?" he asked. "Only you never told me."

Amy smiled ruefully.

"I made an awful lot of allowances. Compromises. But one thing was a deal-breaker."

"Really?" Hal turned to her, fascinated.

"Mmm." But from the look on her face, he saw she wasn't going to elaborate. "It's so hard," she continued. "Everyone tells you that relationships are difficult, that you have to persevere and stick out the rocky patches. But suppose you suspect it's just never going to work out? When do you throw in the towel?"

"I wish I knew," Hal said softly. "That was the mistake I made with Flora, tolerating something that was only adequate for an easy life." He paused, then said, "Marina wouldn't do that. She saw us ambling along but not moving forward. It was like we were on a treadmill. She wanted us to take the next step. She wanted me to grow up. She gave me an ultimatum."

"What, last night?"

"No, no. When we split up. I had a month to propose or it was all over."

"And so?" Amy said, although she knew what the outcome must have been. What was it with men and deadlines? It was as if they wanted to believe they were immortal, that time constraints didn't apply to them, that they had as long as they wanted to set their houses in order, reverse their mistakes and put their lives on the right track. Why was it only women who understood how short life was?

"I didn't propose. And it was the worst mistake I ever made in my life. I lost my great love because I was being pathetic, having stupid doubts about things that didn't really matter. And now it's too late. I goofed. I goofed big time."

"There'll be someone else," Amy said. It was what she'd been telling herself, but she didn't really believe it. But then Hal was a movie star. Of course there would be someone else for him.

"Someone like you?" Hal said in his usual teasing voice, so if she knocked him back he could say he was only joking.

"Not me." Amy smiled. "It wouldn't work. We're from different planets you and me. And I don't mean Mars and Venus. You're on planet celebrity, you're surrounded by beautiful women, you jet around all over the world. There's no way we could be together."

"I could change. Jack it all in. We could go and live in the country. You'd tend to a better class of sick and I'd tend to our garden." But he was only being gallant, he didn't mean it really.

"No way, you'd die of boredom. You need to be working more. Not less. Fly to America. Get the part in the Bavotti movie, or whatever it's called. And tell Marina what you've told me — that you categorically goofed."

"I had my chance this morning," Hal said. "She came to see me. I'm pretty sure she was hinting that it wasn't too late. But I bloody blew it."

"Why?"

He sighed. "Pride. Fear. Mainly pride, though."

"It's still not too late. Call her. Tell her it was pride and fear. Grovel. Tell her you're an unmitigated idiot and you'll die without her."

"I can't do that."

"Yes, you can," Amy said passionately.

"If your man did it, would that work for you?"

Amy thought for a second. No. It was over with Doug. Maybe Lisa, maybe Hal, someone over the past few days had made it clear to her what she knew anyway, that the way she loved Doug wasn't enough. He needed to love her the same way back and that would never happen. It wasn't his fault, it was just the way Doug was.

But Hal was different. Hal really loved Marina and he was ready to change for her. She'd seen it in his eyes, the previous night.

"Just go for it," she begged.

"I can't." But as Hal said this, he looked at his watch. Marina had told him she was sailing at ten; still plenty of time.

"Please." Amy couldn't bear it.

"Will you come with me?" Hal asked.

"I don't think my presence is going to help."

"She needn't see you. But I'd love to have you with me in the car. I need the moral support."

"All right, then," Amy said.

"Great," said Hal, picking up his phone. "Hi, Nessie? It's me. Listen, tonight I . . . Sorry?" Amy could hear her yab-yab-yabbering down the earpiece, while Hal's face changed from irritation, to amazement, to amusement. "So you're going to work for Justina?" He listened again. "Well good luck to you, Nessie. It's a blow to lose you. But you're right. She has a long future ahead of her. And it must be a drag sorting out my sordid little messes. All right, darling, *ciao*. My new assistant will be in touch in a few days to sort out all the paperwork."

CHAPTER
FORTY-ONE

For various reasons, involving Amy's girlfriends' flakiness and the unavailability of a white stretch limo on any other date, both the hen and the stag night ended up taking place not a sensible four months prior to the wedding, but the night before.

"This is a terrible idea," Amy said. "Everyone knows you'll wake up tomorrow a thousand miles away, chained to a lamp post, tarred and feathered."

"I will not," Doug said. "I'll just have a few drinks, like any Friday night. Frankly, what else am I supposed to do on my last night of freedom? Sit at home wetting my pants?"

Amy had hoped for a quiet dinner involving the Gubbinses and the Frasers, but she knew a lost battle when she saw one. She couldn't control Doug, but she determined she'd only have one cocktail, then stick to water and be home by midnight. In the end, of course, accompanied by giggling, L-plates and chocolate willies in an Italian restaurant in Soho, she had three cocktails and half a bottle of wine. At 11.45p.m. she found herself in a club a few streets down, where in seconds Madhura was dancing on a table. Amy watched indulgently.

"I'm only staying another fifteen minutes," she shouted in Gaby's ear.

"Fair enough. Me too. This bloody baby is knackering me."

"I'll just pop to the loo, then shall we see if we can find cabs?"

She pushed through the fire doors into the hallway slam into a tall, serious-looking man in cords and a blue shirt unbuttoned to his waist.

"Amy!"

"Danny! What are you doing here?"

The last time they'd been face to face had been the day he cried and begged her not to go. Now he was red in the face and glowing with cheeriness.

"It's my stag night."

"No! It's my hen night."

They looked at each other. Amy, who had chewed over her decision so much in the past few months, now knew without any doubt she'd done the right thing. Danny held about as much interest for her as the long-term weather forecast for Calgary, Canada. Though she still hoped her mascara hadn't run and he noticed how much weight she'd lost.

"So, yeah," Danny was saying in his slow, deep voice that used to grate on Amy's soul. "Getting married in three weeks. But we thought it would be sensible to have the stag and hen a bit early. Not that Alison's having much of a hen. She's five months pregnant, you see."

"Oh," Amy said, shocked at the feelings this engendered. Taking a deep breath, she said, "Congratulations."

"And congratulations to you too, Amy. So when's your big day?"

"Tomorrow. Five p.m."

"Bloody hell! Cutting it fine, aren't you? But that's typical, isn't it? Well, good luck. I hope it all goes with a swing."

"And you too." She'd been considering staying another hour and relying on Guerlain's Midnight Secret to get her through tomorrow, but now she decided she would get that taxi after all.

She was in bed by one and fast asleep, dreaming of canapés and speeches, when the door slammed. Doug crawled into bed beside her, reeking of booze, spliff and cigarettes. His cheek bore a big red mark in Pinny's unmistakable pillarbox-red Chanel lipstick. Pinny, naturally, had opted for the stag over the hen.

"Hey."

"Hey." She yawned. "Was it fun?"

"It was a laugh." Doug sighed, burping faintly. "I'm quite getting into this getting married malarkey. I wish you'd tell me where the honeymoon's gonna be."

"It's a surprise."

"Can't you just give me a clue?"

"No." Amy rolled over. "Goodnight, Doug. See you in the morning."

"We will be back by the fifth of September, won't we?"

Amy was amazed to hear such a specific question from Doug's lips. "Yes. Just. Why?"

"Because we're going on tour on the sixth."

Suddenly Amy was wide awake. "On *tour*?"

"Yeah."

"But you never told me. Where are you going? For how long?"

Doug gave a huge yawn. "I'm sure I did. Belgium, Holland and France for three weeks."

"Three weeks?"

"Yeah. It's not far, doll. I could pop back to see you for the odd weekend."

Sun was starting to peek through the blinds. Amy's throat felt as if it had been blocked by a stone. "But that isn't the point. You never told me you were going. And I thought we agreed that after the wedding, if the band wasn't going anywhere, you were going to wind it up."

Silence.

"Doug? That's what we agreed."

Doug sat up. "Ames, what else am I going to do? I can't go back to working in an office. You're going to have to give us a little bit more time."

"But I *keep* giving you time. And what about time for *me*? What happens when I have a baby, Doug? I'll want to go part time then. Unless you want to stay at home and bring it up."

There. They'd been together three years and they'd never addressed the subject. But all of a sudden, here it was, as exposed as a hiker in the middle of moorland. And the look on Doug's face said it all.

"Doug, you do want babies, don't you?"

He lay very still.

"I don't know," he said eventually, in a small voice.

She felt eerily calm. "You don't know? Or no?"

"No," he said, his voice even fainter. "I don't want children. They're noisy and smelly and messy; they interfere with your life too much. The band'll never make it if I'm distracted by kids. And I want to travel round Australia. You can't do that with children."

What could be noisier and smellier and messier than the band? Amy thought, but she said. "You'd rather travel round Australia than create a new life?"

"Yes, I would," Doug said. "Sorry, Amy, but any moron can create new life. Not anyone can be in a band. Anyway, there are far too many kids in the world already."

It was like the lid of a grand piano crashing shut. Amy felt numb. Deep down, she'd always known it just as she'd always known Doug would never give up the band. He didn't want children. He was far too much of a baby himself. Of course there were things she could do. She could wait for years in the hope she could change his mind. Or she could "accidentally" forget her diaphragm. But such dishonesty repulsed her. She'd seen far too many unhappy children at the clinic — not just from the surrounding estates but from the big Islington houses that cost more than a million pounds — whose mothers or fathers hated them, or each other. And she'd also seen far too many single mothers struggling to make a go of things whatever their income bracket, to contemplate that idea.

It was one thing to go into a marriage knowing that not everything would be perfect. That there would be rocky moments along the way that could not be predicted but that would be dealt with as and when. It was quite another to stand in front of your family and friends making vows, when you disagreed about the most fundamental thing of all, knowing that the only way to fulfil your deepest yearning would be by a deception that would probably lead to disaster.

They should have had this conversation a long, long time ago. They had, sort of, the morning after they got engaged. But Amy had hoped, ridiculously, that if she just shut her eyes and ignored it, Doug's lack of interest in children would somehow disappear, a bit like the scratching from the cupboard under the sink, which — realistically — she knew had to be mice.

"Doug," she said, "if you really don't want kids then we can't get married."

He looked at her in astonishment.

"But you've always known I felt this way."

"I kind of did, but you never spelt it out so clearly. It's my fault. I should have asked you straight. Years ago." She was amazed how clear-headed she felt, and how strong. "But it does mean the wedding's off."

"But the wedding's tomorrow. Today. You don't mean this, Amy."

"I think I do."

"It's just nerves. You'll change your mind."

"I don't think I will."

Doug got out of bed and stood there in his boxer shorts. He was a very handsome man. Amy had adored him.

"Fine," he shouted, in his petulant way. "In that case, I'm off."

362

"Where to?" Amy said, panicking as the enormity of what she'd just done hit home.

"To Pinny's, of course. She'll understand." He was throwing things in his tatty black overnight bag. Amy watched paralysed with shock, as the man she'd invested everything in for the past three years was ready to leave in three minutes.

"Can't we talk about this?" she tried.

He shook his head. "No, Amy. I'm sick of you trying to turn me into something I don't want to be. A PJ clone. I thought you were different from other girls but you're not. You all want the same bloody boring thing."

"Maybe I don't. I don't know . . ."

Doug softened. "You do, Amy. That's been obvious for ages." He reached for the door handle, then stopped. "We need some time apart, Amy. Time to cool off."

Amy started to sob.

"Is it all over?"

"Maybe," Doug said and the door shut behind him.

CHAPTER
FORTY-TWO

As the Bentley, driven by Vincenzo, sped back down the airport road, which then forked off towards the coast, Hal's heart swung like a pendulum up into his throat then down into his boots. Amy was right: he had to try to win back Marina. For the first time in his life he was going to have to make a real effort. If he didn't give it a go, he would always regret it, always beat himself up, brooding on what might have been if he'd just gone that extra mile.

"What time is it?" Amy asked. In all the kerfuffle of being hauled out of the health club that morning, she'd forgotten to put a watch on.

"Almost nine," said Callum, whom Hal had roped in after Vanessa's defection. "They'll be leaving in an hour."

There'd been some debate about the best tactic to take. Hal had favoured calling Marina, but Amy and Callum had been dead against it.

"Her phone might be off," Callum said.

"Or Fabrizio might be standing right next to her." Amy fixed him with the look she gave patients when they were whingeing about taking their antibiotics. "You've got to make a grand gesture, Hal. You've got to go to her and fall on your knees and beg her to marry you. Women love all that. And it's the least she deserves."

"OK," Hal had said. But now he was getting cold feet. Marina had given him chance after chance after chance. Why should she change her mind now? And why risk rejection?

He would just have to get used to being on his own. He realized he'd been in a relationship more or less nonstop for more than twelve years. Maybe it would be good for him to have some time on his own. He could read more, some philosophy maybe. Get his French and Italian back up to scratch. Perhaps start doing some painting. He'd always liked art at school, but he'd ditched it in favour of an O level in Latin. Perhaps he'd follow Madonna and Guy's lead and adopt a little African baby, he thought as the car took the road to Civitavecchia, Rome's port. He could bring it up as a single father, he could . . .

The car was turning into the dock crammed with yachts, dominated by one mega-number, the size of an iceberg.

"That's Fabrizio's," said Hal. "Thinks having a big boat equates with having a big willy." He stared at it and sighed. "This is ridiculous. What am I going to do now? Stand and wait at the foot of the gangplank like a stalker? She might be on board already. Do you suggest I smuggle myself on like James Bond?"

Amy and Callum frowned. They'd both been enjoying the romance of the situation and not really considered the practicalities.

"Call her," Amy suggested. "Find out what she's doing."

"But you just said not to call her!"

"Mmm. So I did." Amy thought. "There's someone I could try."

She rummaged in her bag and took out a fraying napkin. On it was Lisa's number. Amy dialled.

"Hello?" said a suspicious voice.

"Lisa?"

"Yes?"

"It's Amy."

"Amy! How are you? Bloody hell, Christine and Si are looking for you everywhere. Are you going to give them your story? They'd pay you loads."

"I'm sorry. I can't. But I want you to do me a favour. Remember, you owe me."

"What is it?"

"Find out where Marina Dawson and Fabrizio de Michelis are right now."

"Why?"

"Never mind why. Just tell me."

"I'll have to ask Si. I'll call you back. But I warn you he'll be bloody suspicious."

"OK."

"This is your number on my phone?"

"Yes," Amy said, "please don't tell Christine I called you. Thanks, Lisa."

It was a tense ten minutes. Hal was chewing his nails and kept threatening to walk out on the whole shebang.

"I'm going to make a fool of myself," he moaned.

"You've been making a fool of yourself your whole life," Callum retorted.

"Why not do it for a worthy cause for once?"

Finally, the call came.

"They are at a pizzeria just down the coast road heading south," Lisa hissed, clearly adoring the intrigue. "La Donna Nera. You'll know it because there'll be a crowd of paps outside."

"Thank you, Lisa, thank you."

"It's OK. I owed you one." There was a pause and then she said, "Good luck, Amy, whatever happens to you."

"And to you too, Lisa."

"You'd like me to say I've seen the light and I'm going to dump him."

"Mmm."

"Well, I'm not. I'm sorry, Amy, but I'm just too scared."

"You're much braver than you think," Amy said. Hanging up, she knew she would never see Lisa again. But there was no time to dwell on that as she told the others what she'd learned.

"All right, so we go for it," Callum said excitedly. He was very attractive when he smiled.

"I don't know." Hal wiggled reluctantly in his seat.

"Hal!" They both turned on him. "Come on!"

Vincenzo knew the restaurant. The car sped along the coast road, pulling up in a car park outside a white stucco building. Sure enough, a small crowd of photographers were waiting outside the door.

"You can't seriously expect me to go in there and ask her in front of all those people," Hal groaned.

"What else are you going to do?" Amy asked.

He opened the door, climbed out, then turned round.

"After this, Callum, I'm going to sack you."

"Fair dos," Callum replied cheerily. "I'm sure Justina will have me." But his retort was drowned out by a sudden bellow and a fusillade of flash guns.

"They're coming out," cried Amy. "Quick! Quick!"

On the restaurant steps stood Marina and Fabrizio. She was wearing white flared trousers and a flimsy green halterneck top. Amy wondered what kind of bra she was wearing. Almost certainly from her own lingerie range. She'd have to check it out.

The couple stood for a moment, smiling and waving at the photographers. Then, they started walking down the steps towards a waiting car.

"Hal, you have to do it. Do it now."

Hal started to walk towards them.

"Faster," Amy shouted. "Go on."

Fabrizio and Marina were standing at the door of their limo, posing for a final set of pictures. Hal still seemed to be wading slowly through sand.

"Hurry!" Callum yelled, as a heavy opened the limo door and Fabrizio gestured Marina to get in. She obeyed him and Fabrizio walked round to the other side. Suddenly, finally, something snapped in Hal's brain. He started to run across the car park and, as the limo motor revved up, began banging on the window.

"Marina!" he yelled. "Marina, wait! Please! Wait for me!"

The paparazzi, sensing a sensational scoop, surrounded him. Scores of flashes exploded as Hal banged and banged, his heart still swinging wildly. Marina stared at him through the tinted glass, then turned away. She was ignoring him, Hal thought in despair. But then, having said something to Fabrizio, she put her hand to the door, opened it and climbed out.

"Marina!"

"What is it, Hal?" she asked, her expression, illuminated by the flashes, a blend of scepticism and ill-concealed excitement.

"Marina, you mustn't go on the yacht. I love you. I love you with all my heart. I made a terrible mistake ever letting you go and all I want is for you to come back to me and marry me and I promise I will be the best husband ever and we will live happily ever after."

Marina's face was showing something very much like wonder.

"Are you proposing to me, Hal Blackstock?"

"Yes, I bloody am."

It was the longest moment of Hal's life as Marina sized him up. Then she said, "You'd better get down on your knees."

The flash volume tripled as Hal obeyed her and Marina, now grinning like a maniac, held out her left hand and removed Fabrizio's rock. Hal, who had been fumbling in his pocket, got out the little black box and took out the ring. He put it on her finger, then stood up and pulled her into his arms and kissed her. The excitement and noise was deafening, but all Hal could hear was his heart rate finally slowing down and Marina whispering in his ear.

"I'd given up, I'd bloody given up."

"I'm sorry, darling," he whispered. "So sorry. I'm an arse. An idiot. But I'll never let you down again."

Only Amy, delightedly clutching Callum's arm by the Bentley, saw the look on Fabrizio's face as he climbed out of his door. It was the look of a man whose heart had fallen from a great height and could never be repaired.

CHAPTER
FORTY-THREE

The drive back to Rome was a bit embarrassing: Hal and Marina were snuggled up together clearly longing to be alone. Callum made jovial small talk. Amy had no idea what to say, until Marina decided to make her the subject of conversation.

"So aren't you the married woman Hal is having an affair with? What are you doing here?"

Amy stuttered but Hal said smoothly, "We weren't having an affair, darling. We were just hanging out together. You know how the papers lie about everything. As a matter of fact, it was Amy who persuaded me to run after you, to make the grand gesture. So I think we both owe her big time."

Marina looked at them both dubiously, but then she looked at the ring on her finger and smiled. "Well then, thanks, Amy. I'm for ever in your debt. I'll make sure my assistant sends you a complete set of my lingerie and bath range." She turned to Hal. "You do realize we're going to be on every front page in the world tomorrow morning? So if you change your mind it's gonna be very embarrassing."

"I won't change my mind," Hal promised, nuzzling against her. "Cal, do you think we could get married here in Rome? Tomorrow."

A flicker of anxiety passed over Callum's face. "Tomorrow you're flying to LA, Hal. Bazotti?"

Hal's hands flew to his head. "Oh. Fuck. I'd completely forgotten."

"Bazotti?" Marina said.

"I'm up for a part in his next film." Hal couldn't stop the pride from entering his voice.

"You're never!" Marina clapped her hands in delight. "Wow, Hal. Well done."

"Would you mind if we flew out tomorrow?" Hal asked her. "I'll do the audition and then we'll plan the wedding. Wherever you like, darling. LA, Paris, New York."

"Swindon," Marina said decisively.

Hal swallowed. "Swindon?"

"Yeah." Marina grinned. "I want us to get married in the church round the corner from Mum and Dad's house and have the reception in a hotel in town. I want my sisters to be bridesmaids and I want to wear Mum's old wedding dress, even though it's the most unflattering garment on God's earth."

"Are you sure? Didn't you and Fabrizio have some fancy thing planned for the Cipriani? I can give you a better wedding than he could."

"No, you couldn't. Poor Fabby's a zillion times richer than you'll ever be, but that's not the point." She giggled and nudged him playfully. "I mean, you're probably rich enough. The point is the wedding with

Fabby was all a big show to make me feel better. The wedding with you's the one I really want."

Not for the first time that evening, Amy felt a pinching in her nostrils and a prickling in her eyes.

"But you'll go to LA first?" Callum asked anxiously.

"Too bloody right we will! Shit, Hal, a Bazotti film! That's major."

"I know," Hal said, with false modesty, "but let's not count our chickens. I feel I've had enough luck for one lifetime getting you back."

"Aaah," Marina said and they started kissing and cuddling. Amy and Callum smiled at each other awkwardly. They'd both got quite emotional watching the proposal. Callum had confessed he was a sucker for things like that and his favourite scene in movie history was when Patrick Swayze announced that nobody put "Baby in a corner", which made Amy wonder if he was gay and realize, to her surprise, that she really disliked that idea.

The car pulled up in the Hotel de Russie's garage.

"Well, this is us for tonight, I guess," Hal said, almost dragging Marina out of the door, such was his desire for her. "And then we'll be flying off in the morning. So it may be goodbye, Amy. But not adieu. Because I hope we'll keep in touch."

"Yeah," Marina said. "You must come to the wedding." She sounded as if she genuinely meant it.

"Would you like my suite for the night?" Amy said with a smile. "It is the honeymoon suite, after all?"

She could see that Hal was actually tempted, but then he said, "No, no, don't bother. We'll survive." He leaned forward and kissed Amy on both cheeks. "Thank you," he whispered in her ear. "I'll never forget you, Amy."

"I'll never forget you, Hal," she said. And meant it. With Hal, she'd discovered what it meant to be frivolous and silly again, to have fun without worrying about the consequences.

The couple disappeared laughing and hugging into the hotel.

Amy and Callum sat back in the leather seats. Both sighed.

"Well," Callum said, "I don't know about you, but I'm starving after all that excitement. Fancy some dinner?"

CHAPTER
FORTY-FOUR

It was eleven o'clock the following morning and Amy was packing. Goodbye to her two bikinis, the Emma Hope wedding shoes, the Prada dress, the various sundresses and strappy tops and strapless bras, most of which had never been worn and which she doubted she would ever wear now, such were the memories they would bring back.

Callum had kicked arse, got one of his assistants on the case and managed to find her a seat on a flight that left at four that afternoon. Just time for a last leisurely breakfast and maybe a last wander round the cobbled streets that she'd finally grown to feel affection for. Vincenzo was going to take her to the airport at one thirty, which he assured her would give her more than enough time, though Amy still wasn't 100 per cent convinced, what with all the security checks these days. Perhaps she'd move it forward by half an hour. If she'd been with Doug they'd have turned up fifteen minutes before take off, had a row with the check-in staff but would somehow have made it onto the plane, although at what cost to Amy's blood pressure she couldn't say.

But all that had changed now.

She walked out onto the terrace and for the last time looked out at the Roman rooftops.

"*Arriverderci Roma*," she said. "I don't think I'll be coming back."

She went inside and put on some make-up in the bathroom. She thought about dinner last night. Callum had taken her to a quiet little restaurant called Da Emilia in the Ghetto. They'd had huge plates of gnochetti alla matriciana, potato dumplings covered in a spicy, tomatoey sauce, followed by coda all vaccinara, which was an oxtail stew. By the end, she felt as if a brick had lodged in her stomach. Then Callum walked her back to the hotel through the warm streets and by the Trevi fountain she was hungry again, so they stopped off at Hal's gelateria and had ice cream. In cups.

At first their conversation had been about Amy's mugging by the press, how shocking it had been and how humiliating, but then they had moved on to more general subjects like other holidays they'd been on and movies they liked. Callum obviously led a far more glamorous life than she did, he was out virtually every night of the week at the theatre or cinema, but he was genuinely interested in her job and the future of the NHS.

"I'd like it if we had dinner in London some time, Amy," he'd said as they arrived back at the de Russie.

Amy swallowed. She'd sort of been hoping for this. He'd made enough appreciative, although not lechy, remarks over dinner about beautiful women that she was pretty certain he wasn't gay: just a little camp.

"That would be lovely," she'd said. They'd exchanged numbers and he'd kissed her on both cheeks and promised he'd be in touch soon. Thinking about it now, Amy felt a warmish glow in her stomach, a promise of more hopeful days to come. Not that she was jumping into anything too quickly.

She thought about Hal and Marina. She was pretty sure things would work out for them. She felt a bit of a fool, having kidded herself for that day or so that there could ever be anything proper between her and a movie star, but their encounter had been far from a waste of time. It had made her honeymoon unforgettable.

She picked up her phone and called Gaby.

"Amy! What the hell has been going on with you? You're famous."

"Nothing's been happening. Well, a few things happened. I'll tell you this evening if you like. I'm on my way home. But how are *you*?"

"Bored. A bit worried. But generally fine. Watching lots of cheesy chick flicks. But don't worry about me. I can't wait to hear your story. Did you have a good time?"

"You know what? I really did."

"Did you hear from Doug?"

"No, but I thought about him a lot. And I know now. I still sort of love him, but I've moved on. He's in one place and I'm in another. We want different things out of life. If I'd had the nerve I'd have faced that fact ages ago. Like I should have faced it with Danny. With my next boyfriend, if things aren't right, I have to tackle it early instead of looking the other way." Even with Hal, she'd started falling into that trap. But she'd never do it again.

As soon as she hung up, the phone rang again. Vincenzo? she wondered looking at the handset but the number that came up took her quite by surprise.

"Pinny?"

"Amy! We've found you!"

"Sorry?"

"We had no idea where you were. And then the papers said you were in Rome."

"Right." Amy wasn't quite sure what to make of this.

"Amy, can I just say something. I'm sorry our friendship hasn't quite been the same these past few years. Well, since you met Doug."

Amy swallowed, unexpected tears stinging her eyes. "I'm sorry too."

"I know I was a bit funny when you two got together. But Doug is such a flake. I was worried for you."

Once Amy would have dodged the issue, but the new, more courageous Amy decided to have it out. "Doug said you had the hots for him."

"Did he?" Pinny snorted. "In his dreams! Oh sorry, that sounds awful. I mean, Doug's great and everything, but no I never had the hots for him. He was probably just trying to make you jealous."

Amy knew she'd never truly get to the bottom of this one. But she'd forgive Pinny. She'd missed having her properly in her life.

"Anyway, forget all that. That's not why I'm calling." Pinny giggled. "I'm calling because I want you to go out onto your terrace and look down."

"What?"

"Just do it."

Amy's stomach did a fairground flutter. But she obeyed, putting down the phone and going outside. She looked down at the Piazza del Popolo. Directly below her window stood Ambrosial. There was Pinny in shorts, vest and flip flops, Gregor fiddling with his guitar, Baz sitting behind the drums. And there was Doug, in drainpipes and a baggy blue shirt, his guitar round his neck.

"Amy!" Pinny yelled, waving up at her. And then Doug looked up and waved, a little shyly.

Pinny grabbed her microphone. "Are we ready, guys?" she asked. "C'mon then. A-one, a-two, a-three, a-four."

They started to play. Pinny bounded round the square like the big show off she was, singing breathily into the microphone. Baz battered the drums. Gregor strummed, blinking in the bright sunlight. And Doug strutted and pouted and plucked at his strings.

"Vooolare," Pinny was singing. "Ooh. Ooh. Cantaaare. Doo-bi-di-doo. Di blu, dipinto di blu." It was their thrash take on that old Italian classic. Amy couldn't help smiling. After a few bars, it merged into "One True Love", which was Ambrosial's most romantic song. A small crowd of tourists gathered to watch as, on the last verse, Doug took the microphone from Pinny.

"So I gotta say," he squeaked in his David Beckham treble. "A-a-a-a-a-my, You're my one true love, Be with me today. Hey, hey, hey, hey."

With a squeal of feedback, he laid down his guitar. The crowd clapped enthusiastically. Baz started walking round, holding out his baseball cap. With a jolt, Amy noticed Christine Miller, followed by Simon holding a camera, push through the crowds and start talking to him rapidly.

"Amy!" Pinny yelled up at her through the microphone. "We came to find you. We've got amazing news, babe. We've got a deal. A proper record deal."

Beside her, Doug nodded proudly.

"Are you going to come down and see us?" Pinny yelled.

Amy shook her head, transfixed by the sight of Christine Miller, gathering information from Baz and Gregor.

"You come up to me," she shouted.

"What?"

She beckoned to Doug. "You come up to me."

Doug looked at Pinny for guidance. "Go on then," her amplified voice told him and he started walking in the direction of the hotel entrance.

In the suite, Amy's legs were jelly. She hurried into the bathroom and, with shaking hands, hastily checked her make-up. She brushed her hair, wishing she'd blow-dried it that morning, rather than leaving it to dry naturally. She took off her trainers and sensible flight socks and replaced them with the Emma Hope shoes. Doug was outside, making a big, romantic, Hal-like gesture, and even though she'd declared herself over him, now he was coming up, Amy no longer knew how she felt.

She sat on the sofa and waited. And waited. And waited some more. After about ten minutes waiting, she could bear it no longer. She went back out on the terrace. Far below the band minus Doug were surrounding Christine Miller, gabbling away, eager for any publicity they could get. She went back inside and waited some more, then went to the door and flung it open. Doug was standing outside, his arm raised as if just about to knock.

"Oh!" they both cried.

"You scared me," Doug said.

"I'd come looking for you. You'd vanished."

"I couldn't find your room. First I had to persuade the guy on the door I knew you. Then I had to persuade them to give me your room number. Then I got out on the fifth floor instead of the sixth." He leaned forward and kissed her on the cheek. "Anyway. You look nice. Got a bit of a tan." He looked slowly round the suite and whistled. "Hey. This is all right, isn't it?"

"Yes, it is," Amy said. "It's where we were supposed to have our honeymoon."

Nervously, Doug approached her.

"I'm sorry, babe. But you were putting me under so much pressure. I didn't know what to do. I've felt so bad. I've had a terrible week."

"Mine hasn't been a lot of fun either."

"Oh yeah?" He raised his right eyebrow, like Roger Moore. "Didn't sound like it from my end. All this cavorting with Hal Blackstock. Kissing in the Roman moonlight. Sounded like you were having a bloody amazing time."

"Nothing was going on."

"Really?"

"Really. If you read the papers this morning, you'll find out he's marrying Marina Dawson. We were just hanging out."

Doug smiled. "You? Hanging out with a film star?"

"Well, I *was* engaged to a rock star," she said, stung.

"Sorry, babe, sorry." He put his arm round her. As ever, he smelt of dope. Amy hoped fervently he hadn't tried smuggling anything illegal into Italy. "Babe. I don't know exactly what happened. But you know what? It's just as well the wedding was cancelled because it meant we were able to do this dynamite gig at the Notting Hill Arts Club last week and off the back of it we've got a contract. Not a big one. But still a contract. So it's all sorted. And we can get married after all."

He grinned at her, that familiar slightly cocky Doug grin that used to make her heart do backflips. But now it was beating calmly. Despite her momentary wobble, Doug in the flesh was a complete letdown. She didn't hate him, he wasn't evil, but he was stuck at one stage in his life, while Amy had moved on. She was no longer interested in him, just as she was no longer interested in Simon Le Bon or any of her teenage heroes.

"And whatever went on with you and Hal Blackstock, I forgive you," he continued munificently. "I mean, it's actually kind of cool my girlfriend having a fling with him."

382

"I won't say it again. I never got it on with Hal."

Doug ignored this. "So I said to Pins: 'What can I do to win Amy back?' and she said, 'Well, why don't we go to Rome and surprise her?' And I said, 'Cool, Rome's my favourite city.' It was an excellent idea of yours, Amy, to organize a honeymoon here. Maybe now I've arrived this is where we should have the wedding. Though before we get down to that, we do just have to clear up this business about you being pregnant. I mean, you're not really, are you?"

"I'm not."

He made an exaggerated gesture of wiping sweat from his brow. "Well, thank Christ for that."

Even up to this point, Amy had left the door open just a tiny chink for him. But with that it slammed shut for ever.

He smiled at her. "So what do you say we do it here?"

"There won't be a wedding," Amy said.

"Sorry?" Doug, who had flopped down in an armchair, sat up a tiny bit straighter.

"There won't be a wedding. We called it off, remember?"

"We said we'd have a little break. Think things over. And that's what I have done. And I want to marry you, Amy." He sang, "You're the girl for me."

"But you're not the man for me. We discussed it. You don't want children. And I do."

Doug looked uncomfortable. "Does that have to be an issue?"

"Of course it does," Amy said firmly. "It doesn't get more issuier than this. I've given you a lot of space, Doug. I've backed a lot of your decisions. If you want to stick with the band, I'd support you. But if you don't want children then we have to go our separate ways."

Doug looked at her aghast.

"But I've come all this way for you, babe. I've made a big gesture. Don't girls love big gestures? Pinny told me they did." He ran his hands through his hair. "Children are horrible. We'd be like Alan and Jessica, never having any time for each other."

The phone rang. Amy was glad of an excuse not to talk to Doug for a second. There was simply nothing left to say.

"Hello?"

"Amy? It's Callum. I'm getting a flight out this afternoon as well. Just wondering if my car passed by to pick you up, perhaps we could go to the airport together?"

"I'd like that," Amy said. "Though I was going to go with Vincenzo."

"No problem. I'll call him and get him to pick us both up. You know, Hal's been on at me, asking if he should make Vincenzo his new assistant. Probably not the greatest idea, but who am I to interfere?"

Amy laughed. "Let me know when you're outside. I'm all packed and ready to go."

She hung up.

"I've got to check out now, Doug," she said calmly. "So thanks for taking the time to talk things through, but it's over. I've enjoyed my honeymoon — without you."

She picked up her suitcase and wheeled it down the corridor towards the lift. She pressed the button, the doors pinged open and Amy stepped forward into her future.

Also available in ISIS Large Print:

Handbags and Halos

Bernadette Strachan

Nell Fitzgerald suspects there must be more to life than pampering celebrity egos at the theatrical agency where she works, especially when she's blackmailed into playing girlfriend to a closet gay, perma-tanned TV presenter.

Vowing to inject a little depth into her existence she volunteers at a local charity. But when her red carpet appearances spark tabloid headlines that raise eyebrows at the volunteer centre, Nell realises that doing good isn't easy.

Chaos reigns as she tries to juggle these two very different worlds as well as her eccentric family. And there's an added complication: Nell's growing feelings for her boss at the volunteer centre — a very grown up, frighteningly sexy single dad . . .

ISBN 978-0-7531-7900-0 (hb)
ISBN 978-0-7531-7901-7 (pb)

Kissing Toads

Jemma Harvey

Delphi, garden programme presenter, and Roo, TV producer, have been best friends since childhood. As different as night and day, they've been there for each other's every merciless heart-break, every evil critic and knotty wardrobe choices.

But now, Delphi's career seems slightly stuck and the spectre of the has-been garden presenter looms large on the horizon, while Roo's long-time boyfriend has secretly gone and married his long-time Romanian girlfriend. They decide to ditch their life of urban glamour (Delphi) and overworked late nights (Roo) and sign on for a garden make-over programme in Scotland. Draughty castle, craggy rock star with ambitions to be the laird and a cast of very strange characters included — the two are in for a big surprise.

ISBN 978-0-7531-7868-3 (hb)
ISBN 978-0-7531-7869-0 (pb)

Marrying for Money

Chris Manby

When the glamorous Grosvenor sisters arrive in the exclusive Hamptons beach town of Little Elbow, they can't help but cause a stir. Gorgeous Grace and Charming Charity are soon hot favourites on everybody's guest list. Except that of their neighbour, Marcella Hunter.

Heiress Marcella doesn't want the competition, and when Grace starts dating Marcella's "Plan B" man — dull but extraordinarily rich Choate Fitzgerald — the gloves are off. Marcella determines to find out where the sisters really came from, and exactly how they can afford to rent a six-bedroom beach house in this millionaires' playground. In the process, however, it's discovered that quite a few of the people spending that summer in Little Elbow are not exactly what they seem . . .

ISBN 978-0-7531-7810-2 (hb)
ISBN 978-0-7531-7811-9 (pb)

A Question of Love

Isabel Wolff

Sometimes the questions you ask yourself are the hardest ones to answer . . .

Laura Quick is an unlikely candidate to present a quirky new quiz show. But her boss, Tom, sees that her quick-wittedness and knack for general knowledge make her the ideal choice and offers her the chance of a lifetime.

When old flame Luke turns up out of the blue, Laura's sisters think it's time for her to move on and lay to rest the memory of her husband, Nick. But dating Luke again is a step back in time — and may spell trouble. Luke is every bit as charismatic as when he broke her heart. But this time around he's got a 6-year-old daughter in tow — as well as an ex-wife whose behaviour is a little extreme.

As Laura questions whether to gamble everything on a past love, she must also face up to the unexpected truth about Nick and the life she thought she once knew . . .

ISBN 978-0-7531-7652-8 (hb)
ISBN 978-0-7531-7653-5 (pb)

The Love Trainer

Julia Llewellyn

Katie can solve any relationship problem. Except her own.

Katie Wallace had her heart broken once and she's not going to let it happen again. What's more, she doesn't want it to happen to anyone else if she can help it. After discovering a talent for advice, Katie becomes a unique service provider, a Love Trainer, capable of coaching men to act as women want. But can you really teach a man like you would a dog? Or is Katie about to learn that when it comes to training, the work needs to start much closer to home . . .

ISBN 978-0-7531-7247-6 (hb)
ISBN 978-0-7531-7248-3 (pb)

ISIS publish a wide range of books in large print, from fiction to biography. Any suggestions for books you would like to see in large print or audio are always welcome. Please send to the Editorial Department at:

ISIS Publishing Limited
7 Centremead
Osney Mead
Oxford OX2 0ES

A full list of titles is available free of charge from:

Ulverscroft Large Print Books Limited

(UK)
The Green
Bradgate Road, Anstey
Leicester LE7 7FU
Tel: (0116) 236 4325

(Australia)
P.O. Box 314
St Leonards
NSW 1590
Tel: (02) 9436 2622

(USA)
P.O. Box 1230
West Seneca
N.Y. 14224-1230
Tel: (716) 674 4270

(Canada)
P.O. Box 80038
Burlington
Ontario L7L 6B1
Tel: (905) 637 8734

(New Zealand)
P.O. Box 456
Feilding
Tel: (06) 323 6828

Details of **ISIS** complete and unabridged audio books are also available from these offices. Alternatively, contact your local library for details of their collection of **ISIS** large print and unabridged audio books.